A R E N A
A *Just Cause Universe* Novel

Ian Thomas Healy

Local Hero Press Edition

Arena: A Just Cause Universe Novel
Published by Local Hero Press, LLC
http://localheropress.com

1st Printing
Local Hero Press: trade paperback, April 1, 2018
Printed in the United States of America

ISBN-13: 9781971445113

Cover art by Scott Story
Book design by Local Hero Press, LLC

Books by Local Hero Press

The *Just Cause Universe*

Just Cause
The Archmage
Day of the Destroyer
Deep Six
Jackrabbit
Champion
Castles
The Lion and the Five Deadly Serpents
Tusks
The Neighborhood Watch
Jackrabbit: Big In Japan
Arena
Hero Academy
The Path
Cinco de Mayo
Search and Rescue
Rooftops
Plague
Soldiers of Fortune
Just Cause Universe Compendium
Destroyer of Earth
Flint and Steel
The Club
Jackrabbit: Rinse and Repeat
Posse
Extinction Event
Rain Must Fall

Pariah of Verigo

Pariah's Moon
Pariah's War

Three Flavors of Tacos

The Guitarist
Making the Cut
The Scene Stealers

Collections

Airship Lies
High Contrast
The Good Fight
The Good Fight 3: Sidekicks
The Good Fight 4: Homefront
The Good Fight 5: The Golden Age
Muddy Creek Tales
Caped

Other Novels

Assassin
Blood on the Ice
Funeral Games
Hope and Undead Elvis
Horde
The Murder Squad (2026)
Roast Wyvern (and Other Recipes)
Starf*cker
Strings
The Oilman's Daughter
Troubleshooters

Nonfiction

Action! Writing Better Action Using Cinematic Techniques

For Jerry Pournelle, who cowrote what I believe is the greatest alien invasion story ever told.

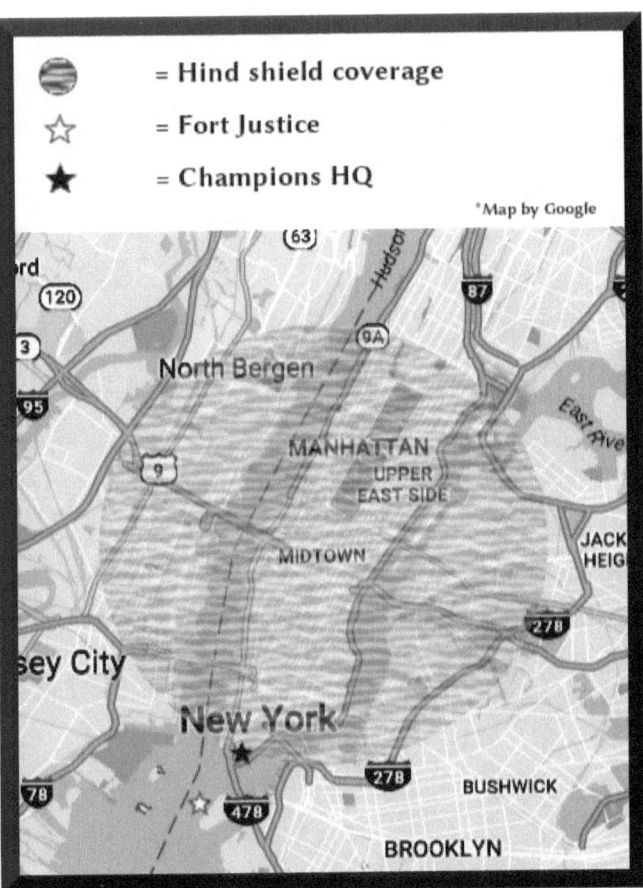

CHAPTER ONE

♘

May, 2013
Fort Justice
New York Bay

Sometimes, it seemed like all of Sally's old friends were leaving her.

First had been Juice, announcing his appointment to direct the Parahuman Resources Agency at the same Christmas party where Jason had proposed marriage, and Sally had accepted. Then only a month after they moved into Fort Justice, the repurposed oil rig in the middle of New York Bay, Jack had announced his own retirement. It might have been because a small but noisy part of the fringe media still thought he'd been the one who shot Senator Goodwin, even after his innocence had been proven. She was the high priestess of the anti-parahuman movement, and some days it felt like her acolytes were Legion.

Doublecharge retired from her command role in Just Cause Denver after a great many years of her humorless leadership. That she would be carrying on her humorless leadership as the Assistant Director of the Parahuman Resources Administration was a joke not lost on Sally. Even MetalBlade and his wife Icebreaker, co-commanders of Just Cause Richmond had finally succumbed to the call of a life of relative quiet as the principal and Dean of Students at the Hero Academy.

The upheaval in command structures was matched by the rapidly expanding population of American parahumans, and it felt to Sally like Just Cause New York had become the Management Training Program for future Just Cause Team Commanders. It was, as Jason liked to say, a heavy trip for someone who wasn't yet thirty years old.

The other thing Jason tended to point out about her age was the risks of pregnancy complications after age thirty increased. It was no secret to her he wanted children. His mother hounded him far more than she thought was appropriate about wanting a grandchild to spoil rotten. Neither of his younger brothers seemed the least bit interested either in settling down or making an effort to pass along their genes, so Jason's mom had settled upon him as her last chance to achieve some form of immortality.

Sally loved Mrs. Tibbets dearly—almost as much as she loved her own mom—but she wished the woman would just *stop*.

It had become a topic of frustration in their marriage. Sally didn't mind being around children so much. Jason had taught her that much over the ten years they'd been together. He loved to visit youth centers and shoot hoops with the kids who didn't have as much good fortune in their lives, or toss around a football, or teach them to play the guitar. He was always patient and cheerful with the kids, even when they were crawling all over him. Of course, being strong enough to toss a car half a block meant he had to be extra careful.

In Sally's mind, the best thing about other people's kids was they didn't have to come home with you. If she wanted to spend an off night binge-watching a season of a show, she could without the interruptions that kids always seemed to bring. Or she could walk around naked. Or have a quickie with Jason up against the wall without worrying about prying eyes.

There hadn't been much of anything with Jason recently, quick or otherwise, and Sally had the sinking feeling it was her fault. There had been arguments—she hesitated to call them *fights*—some of which had resulted in them sleeping in separate parts of their suite. She'd rearranged duty schedules to limit the amount of time off they had together in the hope that perhaps absence might make their hearts grow fonder, but instead it meant she had more time on her own to brood.

She was getting pretty good at brooding.

"You need to knock it off," Sondra told her. Her dear friend had accepted the Team Commander position for the new Just Cause Dallas team and had Skyped in to chat. "You're going to give yourself scowl lines."

"Better than stretch marks," Sally retorted, and then wished she hadn't.

Sondra didn't seem to mind. She just smiled and patted her expanding belly. In direct opposition to the wishes of her doctor, she'd gone ahead and gotten pregnant at the age of forty. Not only that, she'd decided not to retire like so many other superheroines had when getting themselves knocked up. Conventional wisdom was being a superhero was too much of a high risk occupation for a pregnant woman, but then, Sondra had never taken much stock in conventional wisdom. "Stretch marks don't bother me," said the raven-haired woman. "I just wish my damn feathers would make up their minds about molting." She flapped her magnificent brown and white wings for emphasis, sending a shower of tiny pinfeathers scattering in the breeze.

"How long is that going to go on?" Sally asked.

"I have no idea. I've never been pregnant before."

"Do you guys know what it is yet?"

"No, not yet. It's still a little early to determine that." She chuckled. "Jack's hoping it's an egg."

Sally's eyes widened. "Could it be?" After all, she reasoned, her friend was part bird.

Sondra broke into real laughter. "No, of course not. He just wants to take my picture sitting on one." She winked. "I think it's a fetish."

"We're failing the Bechdel Test right now, you know." Sally's scowl returned. "We're supposed to be talking about when I'm going to come visit Fort Kennedy."

"Soon, I hope. Maribel is planning my baby shower and you better clear your schedule, because it's going to be epic." Maribel was one of Sondra's teammates, a savvy young superstar called It Girl, whose power of self-duplication was only secondary to her social media skills. The Just Cause organization had been without a broad media-appeal personality since Jack retired a few years earlier, but It Girl appeared to be the real thing. She wasn't just a trending topic, she was the one setting the trends. She could change platforms as effortlessly and quickly as turning pages in a book.

"It sounds terrifying," said Sally. "I can't wait."

"Look, things with Jason will settle down. He's got to respect your wishes. After all, it isn't him who'll be blimping up for the full forty."

Sally snickered. "He might anyway. He's getting love handles."

"For all you know, your own baby clock might go off tomorrow. Or next year. Or ten years from now. Girl, you're twenty-eight and at the top of your game. Enjoy it. Gray hairs will come soon enough."

"True. My grandma and mom both waited into their late thirties. Maybe I will, too. Maybe by then I'll feel like growing a parasite of my own."

Sondra snorted. "Nice. That's not going to give me nightmares tonight."

Davey appeared at Sally's office door. Her hyper-competent assistant had her mass of hair pinned up into artful disarray around her face as she chewed on the end of a pen. "Hey, I've got to go. Duty calls. Tell Jack hello and call him a punk ass for me."

"I will. Hugs and kisses to Jason." Sondra broke the connection, leaving Sally facing a blank chat window.

"Sorry to interrupt, Boss," said Davey. "I was going to let you finish."

"It's all right, Davey. We were finished for the time being. What's up?"

Davey held up a stack of folders. "Personnel reviews. They're due tomorrow, and I know how you like to wait until the last minute for this sort of thing."

Sally felt like melting into her desk. Paperwork. She'd never realized just how much paperwork was involved in the daily operation of a government superhero team. There were reports. Reviews. Forms. More reports. Reviews of reports. Reports on the reviews of the reports. "How many forests did we decimate this week?"

Davey smiled. "Maybe you'd like to know that I've managed to eliminate about forty percent of our paper usage in the past year, and I'm a good eight percent ahead of my annual goal already."

"You're amazing. Are you sure you're not a superhero?"

"Nope. Just damn good at what I do. I've pre-filled out the reviews and added a page of comments for each one with my recommendations." She set the stack of folders on Sally's desk. "Use or ignore them as you wish. You're the boss. But if you use them, you should probably put them into your own words." She winked. "Juice will know it was me."

Juice was Sally's boss. He'd been in charge of the Parahuman Resources Agency since 2006, and had quietly managed to become one of the most powerful politicians in the country. He would argue the point, of course, and he'd likely win because he was the best lawyer Sally had ever seen. Still, he had at his fingertips the ability to summon and direct the total power of America's strategic parahuman resources. Unlike the United States Armed Forces, the PRA could act solely on the orders of the President. Juice took his authority seriously, though, and Sally knew he'd never buck the President without a very good reason. On the other hand, as Jack had once told her, it's much easier to ask for forgiveness than for permission. Knowing she had that kind of support system behind her made it a little easier to be the team commander of the most important branch of Just Cause in the country.

She spread the folders out on her desk and looked at the names, feeling like more than half of them were strangers to her. JCNY had acquired a few recent graduates from the Hero Academy, and they all seemed so ridiculously *young* to her. Had she ever been such a gawky teen herself? She liked to tell herself of course she hadn't.

She liked to tell herself lots of things that she didn't always believe. Her eyes fell upon Jason's folder, simply entitled *Mastiff*, and a wave of guilt washed over her. He wasn't even in headquarters. He'd been spending a lot of time in a studio in Manhattan, working as a producer for an up-and-coming group of young rockers with hipster beards and man buns. She'd granted him the extra time off. He didn't seem very interested in being a superhero anymore, and she suspected he might be the next one to retire from the life while he still had much of his left. Maybe if he did choose that path, he'd get back into music full time. Maybe he'd get too busy to think about becoming a parent for awhile. Maybe he and Sally would get through their rocky stage.

And if not, well, perhaps she'd look into Plan B, or more accurately, Plan March.

She'd met March a couple of years back when she'd returned an owed favor to Harlan Washington, the Destroyer. March was his nephew, conceived in an act of violence, raised by a sociopath, and still somehow turned out to be a pretty nice young man. Sally hadn't meant to be attracted to him. She certainly hadn't meant to get . . . *involved* with him. And yet, the attraction was undeniable, and even though they'd barely acted upon it since, it was always there in the back of her mind like a familiar song. She hated to think she might turn out like her mother, but perhaps the apple truly didn't fall far from the tree. Sally had thought for most of her life that her long-dead father was Audio, her mother's husband and a member of Just Cause back in the '70s and '80s. The truth was her father was the equally long-dead Lionheart, another Just Cause member and her mother's side thing. The more difficult things became between her and Jason, the more she considered reaching out and making that call to March, just to let off a little steam.

God, maybe she *was* turning into her mother.

Fort Justice
New York Bay

Minerva floated high above the floor of the The Tank and watched a man made of metal put the newest Just Cause members through their paces. The Tank was the unofficial name for Just Cause New York's Combat Simulation Chamber, a heavily armored and reinforced room inside one of the legs that supported the repurposed oil rig. What it lacked in square footage, it more than made up for in sheer volume. Nearly a hundred feet separated the chamber's floor from the roof, and the CSC technicians spent a lot of time configuring it to resemble skyscrapers, that being one of the most common terrains in the Greater New York area. Stockpiles of raw materials filled tanks in the platform's other legs, which became building blocks for the tiny nanotech robots that built the various settings molecule by molecule. The technicians likened it to working with LEGO elements, or *Minecraft*.

The metal man's name was Hector, and he was a former Champion, a former convict, but still an asshole even after years of working with Just Cause. Sally had

7

befriended him when she went undercover with the Champions and Minerva knew she had covered for the murder he had committed. She never said anything about her knowledge, because it wasn't her story to share. The man Hector had killed intended grievous harm to the world, and in Minerva's opinion, the world was a better place thanks to him. Thus, she tolerated the near abuses of the young heroes as they tried to translate the directions mixed into his unending stream of profanity.

"Come on, you sorry-ass bitches. That's the best you got? When you out in the field, ain't nobody gonna do ballet dancing with you. They gonna try to kill your asses. You got to know what it is to get fuckin' hit. *Really* fuckin' hit. You got to know you can take that shit and still come back fightin'."

"That's easy for you to say, metal man," said the young man called Spray. He stood in a puddle and water coalesced out of the air upon his skin, giving him a perpetual damp sheen. "Nothing can hurt you."

It was a brave statement, but Minerva could smell the stink of fear rising off Spray like a cloud of steam. Her senses were her greatest gift, and she could learn more about someone from their scent than a detective could in a half hour of conversation. She drifted a little lower, still watching, waiting to see how Hector would react to the challenge.

She wasn't disappointed. The silvery color of his skin darkened to a more natural skin tone, tattoos on his arms and torso and face becoming visible as the nickel from which he took his name vanished. "You think so, huh?" He took a threatening step toward Spray. Then another.

"What are you doing?" Spray took a step back. Water started to run down his skin, dripping off him like he was standing in a shower. It was a fascinating ability, and Minerva had never seen anything like it before.

Hector got right into Spray's face and pushed him. "Stop me, fucker."

"Q-quit it!" Spray backed off. Clouds of water vapor swirled around him and his skin seemed to be swelling, absorbing the ambient humidity. The entire CSC transformed from a sweaty, humid metal tank to an oven. The simple act of removing the water from the air raised the temperature several degrees.

"Make me." Hector pushed him again.

"Hey, cut it out, dude. This isn't how we're supposed to train." Chinook flew over to him, gossamer gold and white silks swirling around her like clouds in her winds.

"Make me," Hector repeated. He shoved Spray hard enough to make the young man trip over his own feet. He fell backwards with a splash as if he'd landed in a wading pool. "Come on. You gonna let me do that to you? You're a fucking *superhero*. Don't take that shit. I ain't nobody, understand? I ain't a fucking supervillain. I'm just some piece of shit asshole on the street who ain't gonna take a knee because you got a badge." He made as if to kick Spray while he was down.

"That's it, you're done," shouted Chinook, and she fired an invisible blast of high-pressure air at Hector.

"No, wait!" cried Jackdaw, who was flying around in ineffectual circles.

Hector sprang clear of Chinook's blast, letting it catch Amber full force. The young elementalist shrieked as the wind sent her flying. She barely managed to create a ramp of pure amber to turn what would have been a nasty impact into a sliding deceleration.

Chinook gaped in astonishment at the effect of her wind blast, allowing Hector to grab onto one of her ankles. He swung her around like an Olympic hammer thrower and sent her careening toward one of the walls.

"Dammit!" yelled Spray, and a jet of water erupted from him like someone had broken open a fire hose.

The stream caught Hector in the chest, but instead of letting it fling him back, he crouched down, leaning into the stream, and fought through it toward Spray.

Jackdaw hovered in midair, flapping his wings like a bird of prey ready to dive onto a small rodent, and emitted a sonic cry powerful enough to give Minerva an instant headache.

Blood streamed from Hector's ears as he took the full brunt of Jackdaw's shriek, but he still managed to angle his arms to deflect Spray's water jet right into the diminutive winged parahuman. Jackdaw's cry became a choking cough and he crashed to the floor, wings too sodden to fly.

Hector dove beneath the water cannon and swept Spray's legs out from under him. Spray went down hard, and would have hit his head on the floor had Hector not slipped one sly hand beneath it to deflect what would likely have caused a concussion. Minerva noted the move and nodded in silent approval. Despite his rough training methods, Hector's willingness to hurt the trainees didn't extend to permanent damage, and he was an expert at preventing it. Trainees would have bumps and bruises, aches and pains, and in the end, they would learn some real fighting skills instead of the phony ritualized parahuman combat taught at the Hero Academy.

Minerva had seen Hector train four years' worth of Academy graduates in the Tank, and every one of them had become a fearsome Warrior in his or her own right, understanding their powers and how to use them to maximum effect in combat situations. Hector rightly pointed out time and time again that *honor was fuckin' stupid and graveyards were full of honorable assholes. If you can take your opponent down with a cheap shot,* he said, *you're a dumbshit if you don't. You'll be alive and maybe the next asshole will think twice about engaging you.*

It had all the tact of a beer mug to the back of the head, but Sally trusted Hector completely, and Minerva respected her team leader's judgment.

Still, Hector's stream of invective was enough to make her ears burn as he dressed down what he called *failures of the Zero Academy* for not having the slightest bit of goddamn sense, letting a single man best four parahumans without using a single ability of his own.

"They really hate him," said the familiar voice of her love, Ment. She turned to see him watching from one of the observation galleries high up on the wall of the Tank. He had dispensed with his long black overcoat but still wore black jeans and a t-shirt as he looked down upon the trainees.

Minerva flew across the chamber to perch on the railing of the gallery beside him. "It's a good thing. It will help them to work as a team if they see a common enemy."

"Sounds like Academy-level bullshit to me." Ment had little respect for the Hero Academy, feeling it had as much in common with real superhero work as watching a video about nuclear power prepared one to take charge of a reactor. "Seems like every year the graduates get less prepared for the real world." He rested his elbows on the railing. "Is the Academy getting soft or is it the kids themselves?"

"Neither," said Minerva. "The world is getting harder."

"Well, they better toughen up before something *really* hard happens."

NYPD Explorers Seminar
Manhattan

The first part of the seminar was the easy one. They'd set up outside the old Arsenal in Central Park and bused in a load of NYPD Explorers, kids who were still in high school and thought they might like to become police officers. Penny Lane donned her Just Cause gear for the occasion of trying to sell law enforcement as a career to the cynical children of the Big Apple, who'd already seen everything by the time they were three. Her tactical outfit for Just Cause was almost identical to the one she'd worn for three years as a Special Weapons and Tactics officer for the NYPD and then later as a Champion once her parahuman ability—such as it was—had become apparent. The only difference was it fit better, as Just Cause had its own tailors who were well-versed in fitting unusual outfits to people with unusual proportions.

Penny, being short and stocky, was less of a challenge than some of the mesomorphs with the overactive pituitary glands on the team, like Mastiff or Detroit Steel. The first time she'd tried on a pair of combat boots that had been designed based upon 3-D scans of her feet, she'd almost broken out in tears because they were so comfortable. Her years in the NYPD had been plagued by athlete's foot thanks to always needing three pairs of socks to get her tiny feet into the smallest boots available for the department.

Unlike the NYPD, Just Cause didn't require her to wear a helmet on duty, which made it a lot easier for her to use her powers. The heavy armored helmets favored by SWAT officers threw off her sense of balance and distance, and made her much less accurate in her shots. Even so, she'd still achieved top marks and become one of the very few elite women to achieve the sniper rating in the NYPD. Her inspiration was the WWII Soviet sniper Lyudmila Pavlichenko. Nobody knew whether or not Pavlichenko had a parahuman ability, but Penny's was well-documented, and the first part of the seminar involved a lot of her demonstrating that ability.

It really wasn't much of a power, as far as parahuman abilities went. On the Devereaux Distribution, which ranked parahumans on a 9-point scale, she was barely a 1. In all honesty, she shouldn't rightly have been called anything better than a really good shot, but her genes spoke otherwise. The higher-ups in the Just Cause organization liked to point to her as a success story, showing that a minor league Champion could eventually earn a call-up to the Big Time if they worked hard enough. She knew the truth, though, and it galled her.

She was perhaps the world's first superhero who got her position thanks to parahuman affirmative action.

She had her gear with her, of course, including the rifle she'd named Mila after the Russian legend. The Explorers got to look at all her gear up close, and even got to take turns holding some of the lesser weapons. Nobody laid a finger on Mila, though. After showing off the equipment of a NYPD SWAT officer came the demonstrations. Since it was Central Park in late Spring, they couldn't let Penny go around popping off shots left and right, even though with her abilities a miss was as unlikely as a misfire. It only took one mistake, one moment of distraction, and someone could get hurt or killed.

So instead, Penny had two fifty-cent rolls of pennies, and she proceeded to flip them through the air at various targets. Nobody had been able to come up with a glib name for her ability. *Super-sniping* came close, but sounded stupid. The scientists at the Musashi Institute for Parahuman Research confirmed her power was a form of telekinesis, but she preferred the phrase her firearms instructor had coined after she'd made ten improbable or impossible shots in a row.

She made her targets want to get hit.

She launched pennies through the air, dropping them neatly into Explorers' breast pockets, or igniting a match one held. She ricocheted them off rocks and trees to strike targets she couldn't see directly. Five pennies in a row lodged themselves in a crack in the Arsenal's mortar, each one touching the edge of the previous one. The Explorers went from polite applause to cheers and shouts of approval as she successfully completed trick shot after trick shot. She saved the last ten cents for special requests and managed to fulfill all ten of those suggested by the Explorers, including popping open one's hair barrette and intersecting the intermittent spray of a sprinkler to deflect the water at another Explorer.

Penny could have gone on for the rest of the scheduled time of the seminar just throwing pennies, but the second half of the hour was reserved for a question and answer session. She dreaded those because she would inevitably say something impolitic. Her lack of a filter was one of the main reasons she hadn't started out right in Just Cause, but instead went to a Champions team first. Just Cause management didn't think she had the right mindset to represent the world's premiere superhero team and could use some tempering in the Champions.

The eventual promotion came after longtime hero Crackerjack retired and Just Cause New York found itself without a tactical specialist. Somebody suggested *that lady sniper in the Champions* and the next thing Penny knew, she'd received her call-up to The Show.

Unfortunately, that call became the final straw in her failing marriage. Her husband, tired of her unavailability, her short temper when she was around, and with his eyes wandering to someone more suited to trophy status than Penny, filed for divorce. That wasn't as devastating a blow as it could have been. Penny hadn't felt the marriage was particularly successful, although she'd done her best to abide by the vows she'd spoken seven years earlier. It hadn't taken long for her to realize that maybe marriage wasn't for her.

If it wasn't for Avery, she'd have signed the papers and walked away without a look back.

Avery was her son and the single bright spot from her marriage with Edward. He was a bright-eyed, inquisitive four-year-old boy with perpetually tousled blonde hair and a face like an angel. She lavished what love she could upon him even while harboring the secret guilt that she'd let herself get pregnant in the hope it would bring her and Edward closer together. Her intent had backfired and Edward was suing for full custody. It was bad enough for her to have been a NYPD officer, but once she'd become a Champion and then part of Just Cause, he felt it was inappropriate for a young boy to be raised by surrogates in a dangerous environment.

They'd had some terrible fights about it, mostly along the lines of *how can you do this to Avery? What happens if he's at Fort Justice when someone attacks it?* Her attorney had said things didn't look good and she should prepare herself for limited visitation at best. "You're in a high-risk occupation, in an environment filled with dangerously powerful people," said the bespectacled young man who looked like he'd stepped out of a hundred-year-old book. "The current political climate is leaning anti-parahuman, thanks to people like Senator Goodwin. Your ex has a six-figure income, a house in a quiet neighborhood in Staten Island with good schools."

"But he's an asshole," Penny had argued.

The look on her attorney's face had been so clear he hadn't needed to say any words. *And so are you.*

The Explorers began asking questions and Penny did her best to answer them. *What was it like being on Just Cause?* Exciting, and interesting. *How had it been different for her as a woman going through SWAT training?* She didn't pay attention to it as she was more focused upon passing the tests with exceptional marks. *How had it affected her personal life?*

Boom, there it was. Every police officer was asked the same question or some variation of it. People assumed cops got divorced at a much higher rate than other people. The implicit explanation was cops didn't get along with others and it colored all their social interactions. Research had proved otherwise, but people were more interested in things that *sounded right* than actual boring facts. Penny could have discussed it at length with the Explorers, telling them how hard it was to find someone who understood the kind of things that cops had to deal with on a daily basis, someone who could accept the long hours, the sudden emergencies, the risks. Instead, she did what she always did, because in the end her attorney had been absolutely right about thinking she was an asshole.

She lied.

Axeship Blood Afire
Sharassar Battleclan

The announcement came over the ship's loudspeakers while Garragh was honing his spare axe. The warp bubble would decay in half a twelfth and the Battleclan would emerge into real space within striking distance of the target world. The news energized many of his fellow Warriors, but Garragh kept his attention tightly focused upon the blade of his axe, checking it with his claws for any minute imperfection along the tungsten edge. A passing companion would see nothing but a Warrior's patience and attention to the detail, which was right and honorable.

Nobody would see Garragh's fear.

In truth, he *was* afraid. In the basic schooling all Warriors received, he had learned how his people had tamed the steppes and hills of Hindraa, and how the roving bands of hunters had eventually become the powerful matriarchal Clans of the Hind. The Clanmistresses had warred with each other, battling first for resources, then for territory, and later for the honor of defeating one's opponents. Lesser Clans perished beneath the axe blades of the more powerful until only half a twelfth of Clans remained with the world divided between them. Each Clan was as the finger of a clenched fist, and Sharassar was the thumb that connected them all.

When the Hind took to space for the first time, it was with a Sharassar Submistress in command, even though all the Clans had pooled their resources to build the warp generators that hurled them across the reaches of space. They spread through the systems, first as explorers, then as conquerors.

Fighting between the Clans had become a waste of finite resources, of trained Warriors when there were hundreds of worlds waiting to be ground beneath the rear legs of the Hind. The Clanmistresses reached an arrangement, known as the Accord of the Fist. They would continue to battle and compete, but the battlegrounds would be against those lesser races. The power of the Clans would lie in those they had conquered, those who had prostrated themselves and sworn allegiance to the Clanmistresses.

Defeating an enemy was simple when one had warp technology. The activation of a warp field within the gravity well of a planet was sufficient to break that planet into pieces. Impressive? Certainly. Honorable? Not in the least. *Power* came from *control*. To destroy a world was a failure, and resulted in loss of face among the Clans. Lose too much face, and a Clan risked a coup by those Submistresses who couldn't stand the dishonor. It was better to die in a foolish attempt to gain control of a failing clan than to live under the darkness of dishonor.

Conquering an opponent was infinitely preferable. If said opponent surrendered without battle when confronted by the obvious superiority of the Hind, it was a great victory, and the Clan of record would rise in the hierarchy of the Accord of the Fist. However, if the opponent fought tooth and claw and the Hind prevailed, it was the sweetest win of all, and all the Clans would heap accolades upon the victor.

Clan Sharassar had conquered three worlds, two of which they had beaten in open war. It was the most of any of the Clans, and made Sharassar the most powerful of all. The Clanmistress was unwilling to sit back on her haunches and enjoy the fruits of her power, so she ordered her Axeships out to seek new worlds to conquer.

That was why Garragh was crammed onto the barracks deck with twelve twelfths of other Hind Warriors. They were the chosen weapons of Clan Sharassar, ordered to bring war upon the talking primates of the blue-white planet that was their goal.

And he was afraid.

Fear was a response of lesser beings. Hind were supposed to be immune to such weakness. What else could it be that made him have to clench his hands tightly about the haft of his axe to keep them from shaking? That turned his insides to broth? That made all four of his feet as heavy as tungsten?

Warriors weren't bred for their intelligence as much as they were for size and strength. Garragh wasn't the smartest, but he knew enough to operate a databox, and he had researched fear among some of the lesser races. The Submistresses who collated data had studied the lesser races extensively. Reading their reports took time and effort, but Garragh could only spend so many twelfths honing his axes until the sheer mindlessness made him want to start a fight simply for the variety. If anyone had asked what he was doing at the databox, he'd have told them he was learning to recognize fear in lesser races so he would know when their morale was broken. It was a good lie, and he would have been proud of it had it not been so painfully false.

One fellow Warrior had actually asked him about it once and Garragh had delivered his lie with the careful practice of many twelfths of study. The other Warrior licked his chops and said that kind of initiative was bound to get Garragh noticed by the Deck Submistress, and perhaps he would get called into her quarters to perform congress with her. She had taken several other Warriors over the many cycles of their warp voyage, and to a man they had all returned to the barracks exhausted, bleeding from numerous gashes in their sides where she had raked them.

Garragh rather hoped he wouldn't be called for that reward.

At the announcement, the Warriors scurried about the barracks floor, stowing the accumulated pads and detritus of a long voyage. They checked the charges on their electrolasers, on their wrist shields, and most importantly, the edges on their axes. Two Warriors became so excited at the upcoming war that they set upon each other, bucking up onto their rear legs to rake with their forelegs as they punched and slashed with their muscular arms.

The other Warriors surrounded them, roaring approval as their orange blood splattered about the deck. The bloodlust ran high and even Garragh fell victim to its sway. He began to see his fellow soldiers as potential targets and gripped his axe even tighter as he yowled at the two combatants.

A piercing electronic whistle rent the air at a painful frequency and volume, making even the two battling Hind drop their axes to cover their ears. The Deck Submistress loped into the middle of the group and surveyed the result of her handiwork as she put away the calmer. "War is coming, and your time is nearly upon you, but this fighting your brethren is unbecoming of Sharassar. Let the lesser Clans gnaw upon each other for scraps even as we climb atop their broken corpses. We are the Thumb in the Accord of the Fist, and we will see the universe prostrate before us." She dropped her voice to a low purr. "And the talking Monkeys will be the next to kneel with our axes against their throats."

A hundred Hind Warriors shouted in joy, their axes held high over their heads. "Sharassar! Accord of the Fist!"

Garragh, too, raised his axe, but his hearts weren't in it.

The Preserve
Luna

Harlan sealed the chest plastron of his project and stood back from the workbench. He'd spent years building replicas of the two androids he'd encountered in his time on the Earth. At first, it had been in order to have something to do with his hands, to keep his engineering senses sharp while his self-replicating and self-repairing machines did the real work of building and maintaining his secret

Moon base. Then later, the project had almost become something else. It was a retreat to a simpler time, where he could envision a device and then create it from the parts he had available.

When he'd grown up in Harlem, he spent as many hours as he could in the junkyard at one end of the neighborhood, building fantastic devices and culminating in his first Destroyer suit, the one Just Cause had destroyed back in 1977. He debuted his second suit eight years later, when he took his revenge upon Just Cause in what the news media of the time called the single greatest parahuman tragedy.

His third suit was a brief foray into micro-electronics, and he tested it first against the Lucky Seven and later against Just Cause in Guatemala. Mustang Sally destroyed that suit with no regard for her own life. He had hated her for it, oh yes. He had dreamed of all the ways he would crush the life from that crimson and gold suit.

Time marched on, though, and his hatred lessened to a dull roar. Perhaps it was a side effect of getting older, or perhaps it was being entrusted with raising his nephew after the attack upon his sister left her in a coma for two decades. When Mustang Sally contacted him in 2007, she had needed his technical expertise, and he'd given it in trade for a favor. She fulfilled that favor two years later when she helped free his sister's mind from her comatose prison.

Harlan Washington, the Destroyer, had found himself without anyone left to hate. The Just Cause he'd detested was full of heroes he no longer recognized. Somehow, he had made his peace with Mustang Sally, and found a respect for her he didn't fully understand. He almost felt protective of her, and proud, like an estranged father watching his child succeed. She would never love him, certainly, and he would never ask for such a thing knowing he deserved nothing more than her contempt. And yet, her selfless effort to save his sister had awakened feelings he'd spent his whole life suppressing.

So he'd turned to tinkering, the way a suburban dad might escape to the garage to work on a project car that might take years to make operational. It was less about the completion of the project than it was about the meditation upon it, the way one sat and looked at the pieces, drinking a beer and nodding occasionally as if to say *someday, it'll all come together, but there's no hurry.*

If it came right down to it, he knew he could finish both his Steel Soldier and his Carousel creations with less than an hour of work between the two, but again, it was less about the completion of the project than it was the awareness of its existence that mattered most to Harlan.

An insistent buzzing in his forearm pulled him away from his thoughts. His body was suffused with millions of microscopic nanites of his own design, replacing his previous high-tech external armor with armor that was with him always. Additionally, it provided him a full suite of sensors that otherwise would have required an inconveniently large van to follow him around at all times.

He touched his fingertips together, then spread them out. A translucent membrane spread between them, framed by his forefingers and thumbs. Data streamed across the membrane, culminating in an impossible declaration. He concentrated for a moment and the membrane pulled itself back within his body. "March," he said aloud.

"Yes, Uncle?" the voice of his nephew sounded within his ears.

"Meet me in the Control Room. Now."

"On m-my way."

Harlan raced through the corridors of the Preserve, reaching the Control Room in less than a minute. At a single unspoken word of command, a stainless steel bowl filled with a signal-conducting gelatin extended to reach him on an articulated arm. He plunged one hand into the gel and at that moment became one with the Preserve. Its antennae and telescopes were his eyes and ears, its power couplings his lifeblood, its supercomputer his brain. The

Preserve's sensors repeated what his own body had told him only moments before.

Five objects had appeared in the space between the Earth and the Moon. One moment they were absent and the next they were present, their appearance heralded by a shimmering rainbow that ran across the entire electromagnetic spectrum. More data flooded in. They emitted far more energy than any natural object, and as sunlight glinted off them, they showed hard edges and angles that spoke of manufacture by hands that were not human.

March burst into the Control Room. "W-what is it?"

"Aliens." Harlan issued a series of commands via the gel that he'd never thought he would have to use.

"Aliens? You've g-g-got to be kidding."

Harlan brought the main screen to life and replayed the ships' arrival for his nephew. "It's an attack."

"Why an attack?"

"Those ships are massive. Each one is almost a kilometer long. That's three times as big as an aircraft carrier. You don't expend those kinds of resources for a peaceful first contact scenario. This is a show of strength."

"But, Uncle—"

Harlan whirled to face his nephew. "They have FTL technology. Faster than light. Do you realize what that means? It's like five fully armed modern battleships appearing off the coast of the Bahamas in 1492." Even as he spoke, he continued directing the resources of the Preserve, preparing for its defense. "You can't stay here. If they detect us, they will wipe us off the face of the Moon."

"N-no, I want to stay."

Harlan allowed one sad smile to cross his lips. "I'm sorry, March."

March had the same nanotech inside him that Harlan had. It was a precaution against the dangers of living in a fragile habitat surrounded by airless vacuum. Harlan gave it specific directions. March moved across the floor in a jerking, off-balance fashion as the nanotech overrode his musculature. "No! Stop! Uncle, p-please!"

"Go to Just Cause. To Minerva, or to Sally. They will keep you safe. I can't trust anyone else."

"Uncle!" March fought against his own body but to no avail. He left the Control Room. Harlan monitored his progress all the way to the emergency escape rocket. He'd already programmed the destination and if the rocket survived all the way to Earth, March would be safe.

Harlan intended to be enough of a distraction to keep the aliens busy until that point.

He stalked toward the airlock, his nanotech armor pushing itself out through his pores and forming into blue and red armor that could protect him from the worst that a conventional military or parahuman attack force could dish out. He didn't know what kind of weaponry the aliens would have brought with them, but he suspected he would be sorely tested against it.

The visor grew into place before his face and illuminated with data, targeting reticules, sensor information, power usage meters. Everything was nominal. The airlock door closed behind him and a moment later, Harlan stepped out onto the deck. The walls of the crater rose all around him, black as the sky above, illuminated briefly by the flash of the rocket engine as March's escape pod launched toward Earth.

Harlan ordered the Preserve to power down into standby mode in the hope that it might avoid detection by the aliens. He triggered his boot thrusters and broke away from the Moon's hold upon him. Without atmosphere to slow him down, the velocity of his super-efficient engines reached triple, then quadruple digits in seconds. He arced up and away from dark side, pouring on the speed as the great blue disc of Earth appeared over the horizon, and in between him and the world of his birth, five alien starships lurked.

He focused on them with his best magnification and confirmed his worst fear. Bays were opening all along the flanks of the warships and smaller ships were emerging from them and moving into a formation. "Just once I would have liked to be wrong," he muttered, and triggered a command to his suit.

His suit established a connection to an innocuous satellite purportedly of the GPS variety but actually a top secret United States military communications satellite. He overrode the onboard security like it wasn't even there and sent out a transmission that would break into all groundside communications.

"People of Earth, this is Harlan Washington, also known as Destroyer. An alien attack is imminent. Prepare to defend yourselves."

CHAPTER TWO

ʊ♞ʊ

Fort Justice
New York Bay

Sally was in the Command Center before the third cycle of the alert klaxon finished. It wasn't that she'd been hoping for something to go wrong, but after an unusually quiet winter and spring, punctuated by the uncommunicative silences between her and Jason, she was ready for a distraction. An emergency call-out would fit that need nicely, but the moment she stepped into the Center, she sensed something was different. Something was *really* wrong.

She recognized Harlan Washington's voice coming from multiple speakers, reciting a series of numbers that meant nothing to her, using terms like *right ascension* and *declination*. People in the Command Center were scrambling. The duty supervisor, a woman named Caitlin Leigh who had been with JCNY since the day it opened, was shouting something about why did they have all that technology and not a single goddamn telescope. Beyond all the hubbub, on the outside deck, Sally saw Minerva, standing stock still with her cape blowing in the breeze, her head craned back as she stared up into the sky. That more than anything gave her a sudden chill. "What's going on?"

Caitlin turned to her. "Boss, it's Harlan Washington. Destroyer. He's broken into the GPS network and is using it to transmit."

Sally shivered. She knew Harlan had his private little sanctum on the Moon, having visited it once. She also knew he didn't care to ever set foot on his homeworld again, so a worldwide broadcast made no sense to her.

" . . . I say again, people of Earth, prepare to defend yourselves. This is Harlan Washington, the Destroyer. I am engaging the enemy. Repeat, I am engag—" The transmission cut off in a burst of static and then nothing.

"What enemy?" Sally was a tremendous science fiction buff, and she knew she was leaping to conclusions, but it couldn't be *aliens*, could it?

"There!" a technician shouted. "I've got something, right where he said it was. Can't get clear enough resolution."

"It's daylight," said another. "You're not going to see anything, orbital or not."

"Media's going batshit," the social networking monitor called. "Half the people are saying it's a hoax, the others say it's the end of the world."

"Satellite is rotating now," said another tech. "Can't see anything yet. Seventy-five seconds."

Sally stepped outside next to Minerva. "What is it?"

"Spaceships. Big ones. I see a bright spark flying around them. I think it's Harlan."

"Spaceships? You mean aliens? *Real* aliens?"

"Yes. They've launched smaller ships. They're descending in formation." She didn't look at Sally. "I believe Harlan was right. This is an attack."

Sally squinted into the sky but didn't see anything. "Where are they coming down?"

"It depends on whether they change course or not."

"Dammit, Minerva, where are they heading *now?*"

Minerva looked away from the sky to gaze into Sally's eyes. "Manhattan, I think."

Sally's blood turned to ice water. "Jesus. How long do we have?"

"Minutes. They're in the atmosphere now. You can see them."

Sally turned her eyes upward and saw bright sparks trailing fiery contrails high up in the sky.

"What's going on?" Chinook floated over the railing to land upon the deck, a vision in gold and white silks, like she'd stepped right out of a Hollywood interpretation of a harem.

"Jason's in Manhattan," Sally whispered.

Minerva glanced at her. "Go. I've got this." She raised her voice. "Caitlin? On my authority, order the Emergency Alert System activated for the Tri-State Area."

Sally took a moment to squeeze her friend's arm in gratitude, and then she *ran*.

In all her years of super-speed, the one thing she'd never managed was to run across water. Maybe fear overcame the psychological barrier that had necessitated her becoming an excellent swimmer, because she didn't even stop to think it over as she raced down to the water-level exit and across the Bay. The water felt like concrete beneath her feet but exploded into a steaming rooster tail in her wake. She glanced up and saw the descending ships—bright, indistinct shapes that shimmered in the afternoon sunlight. They were so close already!

One ship dropped an object that erupted in a bright rainbow, launching a beam back up into the skies that began to spread out into an umbrella shape over the city. It arced over and down and Sally narrowly missed passing beneath it before it touched the water behind her, spitting like raw electricity from a tattered wire. Her comm chatter ceased instantly and she realized it was some kind of energy shield or field.

Then she was up the steps onto the ferry receiving platform and she realized she'd run all the way across New York Bay. She'd have been proud of herself if she wasn't so afraid for Jason. Civilians on the ferry platform who hadn't heeded the howling Emergency Alert sirens gaped at her, and at the shimmering rainbow energy that crackled across the water. "What are you doing?" Sally shouted at them. "Get off the streets, get to safety!"

"Yow!" called a familiar voice. "Don't touch this barrier. It burns!"

Sally looked and saw Chinook nursing her hand. "What are you doing here?"

"Supporting you," said Chinook. "Look, Boss, I'm the only one fast enough to keep up with you and you're going to need all the help you can get, right?"

Sally nodded. "Consider yourself written up for violation of orders. Now let's get these people to safety."

"I am very sorry for my actions." Chinook stuck her fingers in her mouth and let fly with a whistle that could have summoned a cab from three blocks away. "Everyone, you need to get off the streets right now."

People milled around, uncertain, edging in the general direction of buildings, but it took the arrival of an alien dropship to send them all fleeing for their lives.

The ship was cylindrical with a bulbous cabin at one end and four legs extending from the sides. It passed through the energy shield like it wasn't even there. The vessel's hull sparkled with rainbow energy, suggesting it, too, was shielded, and steam or smoke rose off it. It was bigger than Sally had first thought, looking like it was about the size of six city buses arranged in two rows, three abreast. She wondered how many creatures were inside it. Were they as hostile as Harlan feared or was this just some kind of elaborate visitation? Somehow, Sally didn't think an unannounced arrival followed by imprisoning an entire city was a good omen.

Whatever the vessel used for engines didn't create massive blasts of flame, but heat poured off it like a furnace. A subsonic thrum filled the air, making Sally's teeth rattle in her skull and causing windows in the vicinity to crack and shatter. It wasn't painted in a science-fiction gray or black, but instead was coated in a warm sienna brown with decorative whorls and triangles in red, orange, and white. It was quite beautiful in a way, but Sally would have enjoyed it more if it wasn't the vanguard to a potential invasion. "Over there," she said to Chinook. "Behind that bus."

The bus in question had been abandoned in the middle of the road by the terrified driver and its passengers, engine still idling. Sally and Chinook took cover behind it as the dropship settled down onto a clear spot in the street. The pads on its feet sunk inches deep in the asphalt. Wicked claws emerged from the sides and front of the pads to dig even harder into the ground below.

A hatch opened in the front of the vessel like a mouth yawning open, and Sally got her first look at the invaders as they poured forth.

Fort Justice
New York Bay

The first thing Minerva did was deputize Hector. He was against it, and told her in no uncertain terms exactly where she could shove her orders. "I ain't no team player," he said, after subjecting her to a full three minutes of nonstop invective.

When he finally wound down, Minerva turned away from the glowing hemispherical shield that had covered a large portion of Manhattan and fixed Hector with one of her patented soul-searing gazes. "Are you finished?"

Hector froze in mid posturing and lowered his hands. "Yeah. Yeah, I guess I am."

"Good." Minerva turned back to face the alien rainbow. "I can't use Ment as my second because I need him to use his telepathy to cut through the interference of the force field, and he's not psychologically suited for a command role."

"Thanks, love you too," Ment said from the corner of the deck where he was lurking like a shadowy, sarcastic scarecrow.

"My most experienced teammates are all inside that shield, which leaves me with you as my best option, Hector. Now are you going to knock off the *chollo* act or do I have to put you in your place?" She didn't bother to look at him. "You know I can do it."

"Yeah, okay. Fuck. What you need from me?"

Minerva squinted at the shield, trying to find any weakness, anything she could exploit in it. Her range of vision extended further across the spectrum than just visual light, but no apparent weakness was evident in either the ultraviolet or infrared frequencies. Likewise, sound gave her no clues. The field muffled sounds passing through it, but since she could hear the ships landing within, it told her there had to be some way to get through it. She would need time to analyze it, though, and time was something she didn't have much of to spare. The shield didn't just touch Manhattan; it also spread across a good portion of Brooklyn and across the Hudson into New Jersey.

"I need you to handle communication to the other teams and the military," Minerva said at last. "You already know the Champions. Just Cause Virginia is the next closest team and they need to be on standby. I haven't heard reports of additional dropship fleets striking anywhere else on the planet, but we can't assume that New York will be the sole target of the invaders. The governor is likely inside that shield and unable to reach us. Therefore, I'm taking responsibility under the Just Cause charter and ordering the deployment of the National Guard. Coordinate with their command structure and the other Armed Forces as they deploy in the area, and yes, I am requesting their immediate deployment. Contact the commanders at Indian Head and Carderock to get their best people up here to work on breaking through that shield."

"Goddamn, is that all? I thought you were gonna ask me to go kick ass. That's something I can do."

"You'll get your chance, Hector. Davey will keep you filled in with everything else."

"Davey?"

"Right here, Hector," said Davey. Minerva noted how serious she was taking everything by the number of pencils and pens stuck in the loose bun she'd cobbled up out of her mass of blonde hair. "Come inside the Command Center and I'll get you squared away. Minerva, Juice is on the shortwave for you." She handed Minerva a unit that resembled a thirty-year-old mobile telephone, complete with a spiral cord stretching to the base unit. It was one of the very few means of long distance communication available that didn't require satellites. Minerva understood the reason why—it would make intercepting and listening in to their conversation much more difficult. Unless the aliens were actively monitoring the high cycle frequencies Just Cause used, Minerva felt reasonably secure.

"Sir," she said into the radio.

It crackled and hummed with rhythmic interference that she suspected was tied to the alien shield, as it tended to pulsate at the same speed "Minerva, I can barely hear you. Is that the shield causing that interference?"

"Yes, sir. I'm sorry." Minerva concentrated on making tiny adjustments to the various adjustable settings on the radio, moving them fractions of their smallest measurable amounts in either direction until she managed to compensate for the worst of the shield interference. "Is that better?"

"Much. I assume that Sally is inside that thing?"

"Yes, sir, along with Mastiff, Detroit Steel, Penny Lane, and Chinook. I don't know if we have any other assets inside the shield right now. I've made Nickel my temporary second-in-command based upon his experience."

There was a pause, after which Juice said, "Isn't he the ex-con?"

"Yes, sir. We don't hold that against him."

"All right, I don't have time to judge. I need your take on this situation."

"It's not a full-scale invasion. All the data we have says they only brought a handful of starships with them, although they may have more where we can't detect them. They haven't attacked any other locations on the Earth as far as we know."

"Why New York? Why not Washington DC or London or Tokyo? If it's a big city they're after, why not Mexico City?"

"I have a theory on that, sir."

"I thought you might."

"I seriously doubt they came here by chance. I imagine interstellar travel is highly expensive in terms of resources, power, and financial means. You wouldn't just blindly wander from system to system, looking for a planet to attack. Surely they have either scouted our system before or they've received our signal transmissions. Based upon the number of television shows set in or around New York City, it's not unrealistic that an alien race might consider it the most important place on the planet."

"And in a lot of ways, I suppose it really is. If you had to pick a single city to represent the entire world, New York would be a strong candidate. What do you need from me?"

"Someone to help me coordinate Just Cause and the Champions with the Armed Forces, because I think we may need them."

"I know just the fellow. I'll call in a favor. Do you want me to pull in the other JC teams to back you up?"

"Not yet, sir. Keep Virginia on hot standby, but if we start calling in other teams, we're leaving a whole lot of the country unprotected. You should probably be coordinating with other national teams around the world if you're not already. We still don't know if this is an isolated event or a prelude to a larger attack."

"Minerva, I want you to take a team and see if you can break that shield. We can't see through it. We can't get radio signals through it. It's Manhattan. There are some very . . . important people trapped inside that field, people whom neither the United States nor the world can afford to lose."

32

"I understand, sir. I'll put together a strike force. Hold on, please." Minerva lowered the radio and muted the speaker. She shut her eyes for a full minute, concentrating on hearing through the hubbub of the Command Center behind her, across the open water of the Bay, and beyond the crackling shield over Manhattan.

What she heard did nothing to quell her concerns. She thumbed the radio on. "Sir? Do what you can to expedite our military and parahuman resources."

"What's going on?"

"War."

Central Park
Manhattan

"Go, get to the subways!" Penny shouted over the din of the alien invasion. "We'll hold them off here!"

The teenage police cadets had shouted in surprise at the approaching lights in the sky as the dropships came down. When the sparkling dome went up over Manhattan, all radio chatter had ceased, but after a minute, the civil defense sirens commenced howling.

Penny took charge, ordering the senior Explorers to guide the younger members and every civilian they could into the subways. She detailed two of the uniformed police officers to accompany them with curt orders to keep them safe until the sirens sounded an all-clear. "What is it?" one asked.

"Something bad," Penny said. "Get moving."

Ships burst through the rainbow dome, spreading out across the city in a pattern that Penny's practiced eye knew was one of tactical significance. Whatever the vessels were, they were bringing soldiers, not diplomats. She ordered the last two uniforms to gear up with whatever they had in their cars. She herself had her gear bag stowed in the back of the Just Cause van. She had only just started to rummage through it when a dropship roared down into

Central Park, landing hard enough to shake the ground and igniting the grass beneath it. The rainbow sparkling around it ceased and a bay opened in the front to let its occupants out into the afternoon sunlight.

They looked like centaurs, if centaurs were half man and half lion instead of man and horse. Four powerful legs carried them in great bounding leaps while they carried beam weapons or axes in their muscular arms. Penny couldn't see their faces beneath their helmets, but their exposed flesh was covered in thick brown and gray fur. Their armor seemed modular and reminded her of samurai armor. Every soldier's armor was painted and decorated in a unique way, but she had no time to appreciate the significance or beauty, as they began firing from their long rifles. They targeted moving vehicles but not fleeing civilians at first, but when one of the uniformed officers opened fire with her service weapon, the aliens' shots became more lethal and tracked toward her.

Penny and the other officer fired to try to defend their comrade, but a beam found her quickly and she fell with a smoking hole through her throat. The second officer went down a moment later, a beam having cut right through his forearm. He yelled, clutching at the stump. An alien charged at him, brandishing its axe, and Penny put a bullet just underneath the edge of its helmet. Bright orange blood splashed out from beneath the helmet and the alien went down in the grass chin first. Another beam caught the wounded officer in the chest and left a smoldering crater in its place.

A barrage of beams came at the Just Cause van where Penny was crouched. She crawled inside, snaking herself around the seats until she reached the front. The keys were in the ignition so she started it and pulled the shifter into gear. The van lurched forward. She didn't have anything to jam the accelerator down with, but the moving vehicle itself would be a reasonable distraction.

Something heavy thumped onto the roof. She rolled onto her back and fired up through the roof. A roar of dismay and pain came from above. She crawled back to her bag, found her submachine gun and a clip and slammed it home. The van jerked and bumped as it hit something unyielding and she knew its usefulness had about come to an end. She yanked the pins from two grenades and rolled them toward the front. Then in one smooth motion, she rolled herself over the bag, sliding through its strap, and ran into Central Park, the bag bouncing against her hips.

The van exploded a moment later. She didn't look back to check, instead pelting for the cover of the trees. She was dressed all wrong to hide among them—in SWAT black instead of camouflage—but her sniper's instincts told her to use any available cover. She dove into the underbrush and crawled until she had put some distance between her and the aliens. When she turned to survey her handiwork, she felt a smile crease her lips.

Several of the aliens had fallen near the smoking remains of the van. She couldn't tell if they were injured or dead. Six of them were still up and moving, ignoring their fallen comrades. They had slung their axes in favor of their rifles again and were spreading out in teams of two. They were being more cautious, using trees as cover. Penny knew they were hunting her, and she was out of her element. She needed altitude where she could see what was happening.

For a few seconds, nobody was shooting at her, and the image of her son's face swam before her eyes. Avery! Was he all right? Were there centaurian aliens hunting him like they were her?

She switched the submachine gun to single shot and fired two quick rounds. Her bullets struck one alien in the back of its rear legs, right where its leg armor straps were. The alien roared and yanked its helmet off, giving Penny her first glance at an invader's face. It had two perfectly round green eyes, set back in its skull beneath a heavy brow ridge. Its snout was extended, like a dog's, with a broad pink nose. Sharp white fangs lined its mouth with whiskers all around, but that was where its similarity to a terrestrial cat ended. Its ears lay flat against its skull, more like a human's than an animal's.

"Hello, ugly," Penny whispered. "Bleed some more." She fired again and the alien collapsed.

Beams tore into the underbrush, setting it aflame, but Penny was already on the move. She needed to get out of Central Park and into a building. Her skills were far more useful in the confines and dark spaces of stairwells and isolated rooftop corners than they were in the open. Even as she fled, she was gathering useful intelligence about the aliens.

They didn't go after their wounded. Human soldiers and police officers would try to protect the injured, try to get them to safety. The aliens were leaving their companions where they fell. She didn't know if that was because of orders or racial psychology or some other reason, but it was good to know.

Also, they weren't very good shots. They expended a lot of them trying to hit her and none came very close.

She reached the edge of the trees and ran onto the path toward the steps that led down toward street level. She heard roars of the aliens behind her as they spotted her. Beams hissed past her as she zigzagged across the path. As they thundered toward her, she saw them shoving their rifles into holsters on their backs and yanking their brutal axes free. They leaned their upper torsos forward when they ran, gaining on her with unbelievable speed, axes raised.

Penny jumped off the top step, twisting herself around in midair and firing off snap shots between her ankles. One of the aliens squealed as her bullets found seams in the armor and stumbled to its knees. She crashed onto the railing on her back, the case of her sniper rifle only slightly deflecting the impact as she slid downhill. The remaining four aliens reached the top of the steps. Two hesitated momentarily and Penny put bullets beneath their helmets. The other two sprang after her in clumsy fashion. Maybe they weren't used to

Earth's gravity. Regardless, she managed to get a shot off at one of them, catching the inside of the creature's elbow and forcing it to drop its axe. It struck the steps heavily with its feet splayed to keep it from tumbling head over heels.

The fourth alien brought its axe down in a blow that would have cleaved Penny in half, except she sacrificed her submachine gun to deflect the blow aside. The alien's heavy body crashed against hers, knocking her off the railing. It was dangerously fast in close quarter combat, and although Penny was no slouch when it came to martial arts, she'd never trained against a creature that weighed maybe three times what she did, with super-dense musculature and predatory instincts.

She slid on her back the rest of the way down the steps, trying to keep from bouncing her head off the concrete lips. As the alien brought its axe down, she rolled first to one side, then the other. Concrete splinters flew into the sky with each blow of the axe.

She hit something solid at the bottom of the steps and looked up to see an alien looking down at her through its helmet. Its fur had a distinctive muskiness about it, like a distant skunk over a field of cut corn in the fall. The alien emitted a gasping cough and she got the sense it was laughing at her as it raised its own axe. The alien that had pursued her down the steps bellowed and the one who'd stopped her hesitated.

That hesitation cost it dearly, for Penny shoved herself backward between the creature's legs, drew her service pistol, and emptied half a clip into the alien's unprotected underbelly. Orange blood and stuff she didn't dare think about splattered over her. She barely rolled free as the wounded alien collapsed under its own weight.

The pursuer swept its comrade aside and charged at Penny as she struggled to keep from vomiting at the feel and stench of the alien effluvia covering her torso and face. It swung its axe in a low arc intended to split her like a lumberjack splitting a tree trunk. She dove behind the torso of the wounded alien and the axe thudded into its side instead of hers. As the alien yanked its axe free, she finished it off with a shot to the throat.

Only then did she give herself permission to gag.

After some dry heaves, she decided she didn't have time for that kind of bullshit, and instead removed one of the aliens' rifles from its holster. It was a heavy weapon, more than her sniper rifle weighed, but it seemed sturdy and overbuilt. It would have to be when being fired by an overgrown pussycat. Its construction seemed logical enough: stock, trigger, barrel, and some kind of ammunition or power cell. She fired off an experimental shot and a beam blasted through the air to burn a hole in a building across the street. She had no idea *how* it worked, only *that* it worked.

And when another dropship approached, firing poorly aimed beams from its side-mounted turrets, it was the aliens' own rifle she raised and fired at what she figured was the cockpit.

Sharassar Battleclan Dropship
Monkeyworld

The descent to the aliens' homeworld was terrifying.

Of course, Warriors weren't supposed to show fear. They weren't even supposed to feel it. It should have been bred and trained out of Garragh when he was a cub. Any lingering doubts about bravery should have been dispelled after the many cycles of drills during the long voyage between Hindraa and this new world. The drills had been designed by the Submistresses to eliminate any need for the Warriors to think. Intelligence wasn't nearly as prized an attribute amongst the males as was strength, bravery, and obedience.

Nevertheless, no amount of drills could have prepared Garragh for the harrowing drop from the comfortable familiarity of the *Blood Afire* into the jaws of what the Warriors had taken to calling Monkeyworld. The dropship's pilot was a young Submistress, barely ranked above the highest officer of the assault squadron, and she snarled and spat at the controls as the winds of Monkeyworld buffeted the dropship.

From his vantage point near the ship's maw, Garragh could see all the way through the cockpit to the strange blue skies beyond. He'd grown so used to the cool indigo lighting aboard the *Blood Afire* that the brilliant azure of Monkeyworld made him want to shut his eyes. He clenched his fangs together so tightly they might crack, and held his axe in white-knuckled determination. It would be better once they were on the ground. They'd been training in low-oxygen conditions for many cycles to grow accustomed to the lower concentration of Monkeyworld. It would be like fighting atop a mountain, the Submistresses had explained, but the lower gravity would make them all feel like giants, able to leap tremendous distances and achieve seemingly impossible feats of strength.

Garragh could feel that gravity tugging at him as the dropship spun through swirling clouds, vibrating until he was certain it would shake itself to pieces. His hearts hammered a rapid fear roll between his forelegs, but he was even more afraid another Warrior might see a sign of his terror. A hand shaking, a gnashing of the teeth, the sharp tang of fear-musk—anything could betray him. Any Warrior who detected his fear would not only be permitted, but obligated to cleave Garragh's head in two. Fear was weakness, and only lesser creatures let it control them.

Still, no amount of drills could prepare Garragh for the sight of a vast expanse of water framing the Monkey cities as the dropship flew through the shield. It was poisonous, the Submistresses had warned, full of dissolved salts and minerals that would eventually kill a Hind who drank it. Why they would want to attack a city that was surrounded on all sides by the poisonous fluid was beyond Garragh's ability to comprehend. He only knew the drill that had been hammered into his skull more times than he could count. *Secure the perimeter. Conquer armed resistance. Capture unarmed natives. Await further orders.* Four simple tasks left wide open to interpretation by the troops upon the ground. Although they weren't generally up to creating new battle plans on the fly, the Submistresses encouraged their Warriors to employ a variety of strategies to achieve their goals. Occasionally a male slightly brighter than his companions would hit upon a uniquely successful tactic. He would be rewarded with breeding rights and his plan might be incorporated into future assaults.

As the ship passed through the shield, the Monkeys' tall buildings rose around them like great crystalline blocks. Hind didn't build *up*, they built *down*, hearkening back to the ancient times where their people sheltered from the heat of the days in deep caves, emerging at dusk and dawn to hunt prey and fight wars with other Clans. The ship's communicator hissed and Garragh barely heard another Submistress requesting assistance. The call for aid was cut off suddenly and Garragh wondered if something had gone terribly wrong. He hoped not. The death of a female, even a lowly Submistress pilot, harmed the greatness of the Hind. Where it was a Warrior's privilege to die for his Clan, it was also his duty to die in the service of his Clanmistress and by proxy her Submistresses.

Their pilot responded to the distress call and twisted her upper torso around to regard the Warriors lined up in their armor. "The Monkeys are fighting back," she said.

The Warriors cheered their approval.

"Get ready to disembark. We're coming down hot."

Restlessness filled the ship's cabin as the pheromones of aggression overwhelmed the air filters. Warriors fingered their axes, testing the edges, feeling the weight of the hafts. If they hadn't all been strapped to their couches like living saddles to avoid dishonorable injury due to turbulence or rough landings, a full-scale brawl might have erupted in the enclosed space. Even Garragh wasn't immune to its effects, and he struggled to keep from lunging at his seatmate. Instead, he turned his attention back to the cockpit windows.

The pilot disengaged the dropship's energy shield and slashed at the controls to activate the vessel's cheek-mounted heavy beam projectors. Packets of high-energy particles raced down a path of ionized air molecules like lightning, each one echoed by a blast of thunder. At first, Garragh wondered what the pilot was shooting at, but then saw a Monkey standing out in the open amid a field of odd-colored vegetation. It was doing the impossible—raising what had to be a Hind rifle.

Somehow, a thought bullied its way through his pheromone-soaked brain. "The shield—" he began, but it was too late.

The Monkey fired its weapon and a beam cut right through the cabin to expend itself in the ceiling, immolating the pilot's head as it passed. The Submistress's body jerked in its death throes, tearing out of reflex at the nearby controls.

The dropship was already coming in fast, as the pilot had warned, and it heeled over just as quickly without anyone to handle the controls. Garragh only had a moment to brace himself as his blood rushed into his head and the ground raced up to meet them.

The ship hit hard, sending anything loose spinning across the cabin. A deadly hail of shrapnel, axes, and loose armor pieces turned several Warriors into ground meat. The primary power coupling blew, followed by the twin backups, and two more Warriors flashed into ashes. The ship bounced off its roof, jarring some Warriors loose and dashing them against the bulkheads like insects inside a shaken jar.

With its second impact, the hapless dropship plowed its nose into the ground and it flipped up and over itself. Sudden showers of sparks illuminated the cabin for brief moments, showing the carnage of collision to those who hadn't yet perished. Something impaled Garragh's right hindleg as the ship slid on its side. Fire broke out in the cabin as toxic gas from the drive spilled from the system to begin dissolving the dead and those who couldn't get clear.

Garragh hung from his straps, his head still spinning from the crash. All the lights had gone out in the cabin but a cold gray light came from the direction of the ruined cockpit. The smoke made his eyes stream and he coughed, trying to draw enough breath in the thin atmosphere of Monkeyworld. The straps were slowly cutting off his circulation. He was going to die if he stayed where he was. He'd lost his axe in the crash, so he set to work sawing at the straps with his claws. They weren't as sharp as those of his ancestors, but the tough fabric began to fray under his assault until first one parted, then another.

When the last one tore, he fell across the cabin to land amid several dead troopers from his unit. He winced in pain as his wounded leg took the brunt of the impact. He fumbled around in the dark, gasping for air, and found an axe. It wasn't his, but any weapon would do in a war. That was a tenet of the Warrior's Way. He should have been reciting it to himself as a way to keep his intent focused and his hearts pure, but Garragh was afraid.

There, he'd admitted it to himself. Perhaps by allowing that one weakness, he could find strength enough to survive his current predicament. He crawled forward into the cockpit. The beam that caused the crash had carbonized much of the window, and it shattered after a couple of axe blows.

Garragh wouldn't fit through the hole he'd made in all his armor. He threw his helmet behind him, pulled his shoulder guards over his head, and yanked off the cuirass. The blanket skirt over his abdomen hips came off as well, leaving him clad like a barbarian, with only his arm, foreleg, and hindleg greaves. He threw the axe through the hole in the glass and wormed his way through after it, grimacing as sharp edges cut through his thick, furry hide.

He emerged, blinking, into the abnormally bright sunlight of Monkeyworld, blood leaking from several cuts on his thorax and abdomen. He discovered a long metal splinter sticking out of his hindleg, just inside the armor greave. Yanking it free proved to be unusually painful and he growled his discomfort. Blood ran freely from the wound. He wished there was something he could do about it, but Hind didn't concern themselves with injuries. Either a Warrior overcame his wounds or the wounds would overcome the Warrior. There was no in-between.

The Monkey who'd shot at the dropship was long gone, and Garragh realized he was all alone on a strange world without a Submistress to tell him what to do. A flash of heat came from within the dropship wreckage as the energy packs failed. All thoughts of his orders fled as his survival instincts took over.

Limping as fast as he could, he galloped for cover from the inevitable explosion.

Low Earth Orbit
Hind Fleet

Harlan Washington was in full-on Destroyer mode as he flew toward the invasion fleet. He'd put his nanotech suit through its paces over the years, constantly working at improving its abilities, but his tests were no match for the experience of sweeping in upon the five vessels, loaded for bear. His suit provided a heads-up display of data projected into the corner of his eyes. He had data available on his velocity, power levels, ammunition, and more. Everything was nominal as he armed his lasers and cannons.

Cannon was a misnomer, for he'd moved beyond such crude explosive-powered devices when making the switch to nanotech. They were more like railguns, using magnetism to accelerate projectiles the size of marbles to hypersonic speeds. Without the friction of an atmosphere to slow them, they would be devastating to unprotected targets.

Unfortunately, the enemy fleet was protected by some kind of energy shielding. His first laser blast splashed harmlessly across the bow of one vessel. Likewise, one of his cannon bullets flashed into particles. He started configuring his sensors to pull data on the fields. They extended out far enough beyond the ships' hulls that they had to stand well off from each other. It must have been a problem for them to intersect, he thought. Perhaps some kind of feedback might short them out? He wondered if he could duplicate the effect of an energy shield by adjusting the frequencies of his lasers.

At first, he wondered why he wasn't seeing any response from the enemy vessels. Surely they could detect his presence, especially when he'd tested his weapons against their defenses. His sensors reported a vessel behind him dropped its shields and he knew the answer as his suit automatically sent him into evasive maneuvers. A web of brilliant beams filled the black of space as the aliens fired an impressive barrage at him. Their fire was inaccurate, and Harlan smiled at their pathetic attempt and what he learned from it.

They couldn't fire through their own shields.

Knowing that gave him a huge tactical advantage. As he wheeled around, his suit squeezed him to keep his blood circulating in spite of the tremendous G-forces to which he subjected his body. Before the alien vessel could raise its shields again, he sliced into its hull with his right-hand laser while blasting a cannon round at it with his left. The laser left a long, glowing scorch mark on the ship's hull, leaking vapor and atmosphere through it into space.

The cannon round did far more interesting damage where it impacted. Since he didn't know what was a strategic target and what was merely cosmetic on the alien vessel, he'd selected a projection on the ship's dorsal side. When the cannon round struck it, it blew apart with a brilliant flash of discharged energy. He didn't know what he'd hit but it *seemed* important. The vessel rolled itself away, presenting its ventral side as its sparkling energy shield reformed.

He dove lower, skimming along the top of another ship's energy shield. By keeping himself aligned between ships, he was making it difficult for them to risk shooting at him without striking their comrades. With their apparent lack of aiming skills, he thought that might present more of a danger. "Go on, drop those shields. I dare you," he muttered.

His computer finished its analysis of the shields and suggested a modulated laser frequency. He adjusted his emitters and fired a test burst. His beam pierced the shield, albeit at a reduced intensity. It left a glowing streak on the vessel's hull but the damage was only superficial. Still, it was a start. He had plenty of power left, plenty of ammunition, and so long as they weren't going to commit to a full-scale attack upon him, he would keep harassing them until he found their Achilles heel.

Penetrating the shield must have galvanized the vessel's commander into panic, for it dropped its shields and the side seemed to explode outward as it fired particle beam after particle beam at him. He couldn't dodge beams at light speed, of course, but he could make himself impossible to hit. He cruised low, practically scraping himself along the ship's hull. None of its guns could track low enough to hit him as he ignited his own lasers and swept them back and forth, feeling like a hummingbird attacking a skyscraper.

He was doing a lot of damage to the ship beneath him. Explosions rose silently in his wake as leaking atmosphere gave fire its brief voice in the vacuum. He spotted the same construction he'd destroyed on the other vessel and switched from lasers to cannons. Fire and energy erupted everywhere the cannon rounds struck.

The superstructure blew apart like it had on the other ship, but he didn't stop firing. Cannon rounds penetrated deeper and deeper into the ship's interior, each striking with the force of a meteor. A flash brighter than the sun erupted from the massive hole he'd carved in the hull, overwhelming his own defenses.

Blinded, he stopped his assault and tried to blink away the spots in his vision. His nanotech, efficient though it was, couldn't repair everything instantaneously. In that moment, the aliens managed to catch hold of him.

One moment he was flying through space, trying to get clear of the vessel to which he'd done mortal harm, and the next his suit was screaming warning after warning at him as *something* had grabbed hold of him. It was some kind of tractor beam, strong enough to haul him back even with his own engines under full power. At first he feared they were holding him in place so their pathetic gunners would have a stationary target to shoot at, but the insistent tugging suggested they were pulling him aboard another ship. They wanted to talk, apparently.

Fine, he'd accept their surrender.

CHAPTER THREE

U 2 U

Lower Manhattan

Sally had battled against some terrible odds over the course of her career as a superhero—against the forces of Isotope's army of manufactured parahumans in Guatemala, against the magical minions of the Archmage, but never had she felt as overwhelmed as she did against the alien invaders. Without their parahuman abilities, she and Chinook would have been overrun as quickly and efficiently as the aliens had rounded up the civilians in the area.

Sally's ability to accelerate her perceptions gave her the best advantage: time to analyze and plan. The problem with the invaders wasn't so much their advanced technology—they had laser rifles and spaceships, but they also carried axes and wore armor that wouldn't have looked out of place in a movie set in ancient Japan. The real difficulty about them as opponents was their raw physical strength and their complete disregard for their own safety.

They were imposing creatures, with bodies the size of horses and legs like a lion's. Their torsos elongated above their forelegs and bent upright to support two powerful arms, giving them the appearance of a half lion—half humanoid centaur, and all Warrior. Sally was enough of a science fiction buff that she had already pegged them as coming from a world of heavier gravity, thanks to their massive legs and dense musculature. They were clearly apex predators and weren't above using their claws and teeth if they lost their axes.

The aliens weren't actively harming civilians who didn't fight back. If they ran, they were pursued, and the aliens were fast enough to catch any non-parahuman. When they grabbed the civilians, they wrestled them to the ground and bound their limbs using their version of a zip tie. As some Warriors secured the perimeter, others gathered up the imprisoned civilians and placed them inside of a portable shield, like a smaller version of the dome over Manhattan.

Sally and Chinook fought back, but it was difficult trying to actively protect civilians without getting taken themselves. The air was filled with dust as Chinook fired blast after blast of compressed air at the aliens. They lowered their heads against the wind gusts and continued to fan out, snagging captives when they could. Tears carved clean trails in the dirt on Chinook's face as she realized her powers were useless against the monstrous aliens.

On the other hand, Sally wasn't faring much better. She'd spent many years training against parahumans with super-strength and toughness. She'd even married one of them. Trying to engage one in direct combat was the quickest way to earn another concussion or worse, and no amount of training had prepared her for dealing with aliens who didn't fear to take a blow if it meant they could deliver one. She had to settle for harassment techniques. She ripped cables and wire from a nearby Con Edison truck and used it to trip up the aliens, binding their feet together or tying their arms across their bodies in a blur of super-speed. It seemed as fast as she took one down, another centaurian stepped up to do battle in its brightly colored armor.

Eventually, the aliens unlimbered their laser rifles and began firing at Sally and Chinook, and Sally was forced to call a retreat. Getting killed would do no good in the battle for Manhattan. At least the creatures were only firing with *Star Wars* Stormtrooper-level accuracy. Sally and Chinook dodged around the columns of a parking garage and then into the darkness of its depths as laser beams cracked against the cement around them.

Chinook's face was pale as she sank to the cool cement between two parked BMWs. Sally recognized combat shakes and zipped over to hold back Chinook's hair as the girl vomited. "It's okay," she said, recalling her own similar response to a brutal combat early in her career. "It gets better. You did good out there."

Chinook wiped her mouth with the back of a shaking hand. "I didn't do anything," she whimpered. "I couldn't do anything. They're too big, too strong."

"Hush, now. That's not a productive way to think." Sally led her young charge through the parking garage. "You and me aren't built to take on those kinds of opponents head-on. We have to be smarter than them. Use our brains."

"There are too many of them."

"Think back to your Academy combat training. What do they teach about fighting against large groups?"

"I don't remember!"

"Chinook, yes you do." Sally pulled her deeper into the garage. "Sunstorm has been teaching the same class for almost fifteen years. What are the Cardinal Combat Rules?"

Chinook sniffled. "Pr-protect civilians by drawing combat away from them. Use the terrain to your advantage." Her voice grew stronger as she recalled the terminology drilled into all Hero Academy graduates. "Observe the abilities of your opponents. Seek and exploit weaknesses. Retreating is not cowardice, because you can't win every fight."

Sally nodded. "Think about it. We weren't going to win up there. They were stronger and better armed than we were. There were civilians up there. Hostages. If we kept fighting, they were going to get hurt or killed. Yes, they've been captured, but *captured* isn't *slaughtered*. If the aliens are taking hostages, it means they're more valuable alive, and living hostages can be rescued. Dead ones can only be avenged."

"O-okay."

"That was one ship. Who knows how many came down here in Manhattan? There could be hundreds of those alien Warriors. The two of us can't fight a legion on our own. We'd die, and our deaths would be meaningless."

"Then what do we do?"

"We fight smart. We're not the only paras here in Manhattan. I know Jason and Penny are both here, and there might be others. We need to regroup. We need to figure out how to get through that shield, and then we bring together our own army. Parahumans. Police. The military. We will take back our city from these invaders." Sally smiled. "Humans may be bad at a lot of things, like getting along with each other, or taking care of the environment, or not being selfish assholes. But there's one thing that as a species, we excel."

Chinook turned to look at Sally, a question in her eyes.

"When we're done, I promise you these aliens will know they've been in a war."

Fort Justice
New York Bay

Minerva's respect for Sally and what she had to manage every day as leader of Just Cause New York had grown a thousandfold in the past hour. There were so many things of which she needed to keep track . . . even with her exceptional senses and highly organized nature, Minerva felt nearly overwhelmed. It was a new sensation for her when she was normally confident in her abilities and sure of herself, and her patience was wearing thin.

"No, man, what am I gonna do here? I'm wasted babysitting a bunch of stuffed shirts. Get me out where the action is, Minerva. Lemme hit something." Hector stalked after her as she floated down the stairwell inside one of Fort Justice's legs toward the boat dock.

"Hector, right now the only thing you could hit would be that energy shield, and it has already resisted all other physical attempts to breach it up to and including a five inch shell and Tomahawk cruise missile courtesy of the *James Scott*." The *Arleigh Burke*-class destroyer was named for one of the first American parahuman soldiers and had been steaming up the coast from Sandy Hook at flank speed at the first sign of the attack. It was the closest warship the Navy had available. Minerva had watched the impacts of both the cruise missile and the shell on the alien shield. She wished she had the ability to slow down her perceptions, the way Sally could, so she could better study the effect the human weapons had on the shield, which on the surface was nothing. But if she could have watched in extreme slow motion, she might have seen something they could use.

Instead, she was taking a crew out to investigate the shield in person.

"I'm tellin' you, I ain't no good to you up there."

Minerva sighed, turned around, and placed her index finger at a specific spot on Hector's metallic torso. He froze, his face stuck in the expression of a man who'd just had the wind knocked out of him. "Hector, I need someone up there I can trust to do the right thing. Someone who can see through the layers of political bullshit and keep those stuffed shirts in line. Can I count on you to do that for me?"

She removed her finger and he gasped like a fish out of water. "Aw, shit. That hurts like a motherfucker. Yeah, okay, I'll do it. Respect." He rubbed his chest, his fingers making a metal upon metal sound. "Wish I knew how you did that." He turned away and clanked back toward the elevator.

The rest of her team awaited Minerva at the boat dock. A speedboat idled beside the dock, giving the non-fliers a way to cross the bay. Spray, Amber, and

Ment were already aboard the boat, while Jackdaw circled around and around, eager to be underway. Spray would be at his most powerful with the water of the bay at his disposal. Jackdaw's sonic attack could have an effect upon the energy shield. Ment might be able to telepathically contact some of their assets inside the shield. Amber's magic was the wild card. She was the great-granddaughter of the one-time Archmage Stratocaster. She wore one of his guitar picks encased in amber as a bracelet. She channeled her innate magical ability through it, and although most of her power was based around the creation and shaping of magical amber, Minerva believed her abilities went far deeper and the girl had failed to explore them.

"Let's go," Minerva said.

Spray pushed the throttle forward to full and the speedboat roared away from the dock. Normally they would have had a Just Cause civilian employee operate the vehicle, but Minerva wasn't willing to risk anyone beyond her team. Across the bay at the southern tip of Manhattan, she knew the Champions were also attempting to breach the field. The field's edge passed right through their headquarters without seeming to harm the building at all. Some of the minor-league heroes were trapped on the other side of the field but all of them were working at trying to find a way to get through it.

Jackdaw paced alongside Minerva, making her feel like she was being shadowed by a particularly chatty sparrow. The young man kept up a steady stream of observations, some of which were so plainly obvious it made her grit her teeth to avoid letting a remark unsuited to a leader escape her lips. His size-changing ability was unusual in that his powers became more potent the smaller he became. He couldn't fly if he was larger than a dog, and his sonic attack was barely louder than the range of human vocalization at full size. He'd been prepared to accept his particularly useless wings as an unfortunate side effect of his Musashi gene.

His first shrinking had been accidental, but it had given him the ability to fly and to project his voice at tremendous volume. Once he learned to repeat the shrinking, he kept himself a height of twelve inches for all except the most important functions. He was large enough to interact with others and small enough to produce a shriek loud enough to crack stone.

It only took a few minutes for the speedboat to cross the bay. They came to the slips at Battery Park where the field crossed part of the water. Minerva ordered everyone to commence their investigation but not to test any direct attack on the shield without clearing it with her first. She found it fascinating the way the field seemed to pass right through solid matter without any harm to it. She manifested her spear, a weapon that was available to her when she needed it but kept *elsewhere* when she didn't. She didn't touch the field directly, but she pressed her spear into it. It felt spongy, like trying to penetrate a membrane that grew tougher and more taut the more pressure it received.

"Hey, boss, come look at this," Jackdaw called.

Minerva turned to look at the object of his interest where he knelt down right beside the field. As she zeroed her vision in upon it, she saw a spider bisected by the field. Its feet wiggled as it tried to move but the field held it firmly in place. "It's still alive."

"It's not going to be for long. It'll starve to death," said Jackdaw. "I wouldn't wish that on my worst enemy. Or a spider."

Minerva radioed Hector and told him to have the authorities perform as in-depth a perimeter check of the field as they could. People or animals trapped within it probably weren't injured, but they were frozen in place and that could be awkward or dangerous. "All right, everyone. Let's see what we can do to this thing. Everyone else back away to a safe distance and then one at a time, do your best."

As she feared, none of her team were able to mar the shield in the slightest. Jackdaw's sonic attack had the most success, if they could call it that. His sonic shout caused apparent ripples in the surface of the field but otherwise had no effect. Spray soaked the field with an impressive amount of water, drawing the seawater out of the basin and firing it like a high-pressure hose against the field. The water crackled like hitting a hot pan and ran down the side of the field in beads like a treated windshield. Amber's magical amber creations could neither force an opening in the field or even penetrate it with sharp needles.

"Ment, try to contact Sally," said Minerva. "Next to me, you're attuned to her the best. We need information about what's happening beyond the field." She could still hear the sounds of weapons firing and distant shouts and screams, but the densely packed buildings of Manhattan and the distortion effect of the field kept her from learning anything new.

Her phone buzzed and she raised it to her head. "Go."

"Yo, boss, it's Hector. Hey, we just got a call from the Coast Guard. They picked up a guy in the Hudson. He's askin' for Sally or you. Says his name's March. You want I should have them bring him in?"

Minerva didn't hesitate. "Yes." March was Harlan Washington's nephew. He might have come from Harlan's secret moon base, and if so, he might have some useful information.

"Hey, love, I got Sally," said Ment. His face looked drawn tighter than usual behind his dark glasses. "This field is causing psychic interference. It's like trying to have a conversation next to a busy freeway. I'm not getting everything but I'm getting through."

"Don't call me *love* in public. Yes, you may think it as often as you want, and I know you mean it." Nevertheless, Minerva smiled at the psychic's words. "Fill her in as quickly as you can and get a situation report from her."

She turned her attention to the shield arching up and over Manhattan. It had secrets. It had a way through. She just had to tease it out and find it. The disquieting memory of the spider struggling to move against it made her shiver.

Central Park
Manhattan

The alien laser rifle was a sniper's dream weapon. Unlike in the movies, it was nearly silent when it fired, except for a electrical crackling sound. The beam traveled instantaneously, like a flash of lightning. Penny didn't know how it worked, or how many shots it had before it went empty, but with one pull of the trigger she'd taken down one enemy dropship. In the grand scheme of defending the Earth from an invasion, that might not mean much, but a great victory was made up of many small ones, and they had to start somewhere.

Still, for all its power, the rifle was an ungainly weapon. It was too heavy, and balanced in such an odd way that Penny knew she'd be exhausted in minutes trying to use it. She wasn't willing to leave it behind, though, and managed to improvise a carrying strap for it from her tactical webbing. She slung it over her head and across her back as she crouched inside the grocery store she'd ducked into after shooting down the dropship.

She had watched the alien extricate itself from the wreckage and limp behind a concrete barricade just as the dropship exploded with a bang loud enough to shatter all the windows facing the street. She flinched as shrapnel and glass shards burst into the grocery store, peppering her face like tiny bee stings. The explosion made her ears ring and she hoped she hadn't suffered permanent damage.

The wounded alien staggered drunkenly, and she wondered how bad its injuries were. She raised her submachine gun and prepared to unload a barrage into the creature's unarmored flank. Then she hesitated, for a new idea had begun to gnaw at her.

She could capture it.

An alien prisoner would give humans some leverage. Maybe it wouldn't be much, considering she had yet to see any alien give another any sort of medical attention. On the other hand, prisoners could be interrogated. Cross-examined.

Dissected.

She didn't see any other aliens in the area. Either they'd died in the crash and explosion of the dropship, or they'd already moved on to other hunting grounds. She knew just because she couldn't see them didn't mean they weren't within shouting distance. What if they'd gone into the subway tunnels after her Explorers? She'd left them alone without anyone to protect them. Then she smiled. They were New York City police cadets. They'd grown up on the streets of Manhattan. They'd know how to keep themselves and their charges safe.

The alien was already favoring one of its rear legs. Penny had seen enough limping dogs and cats in her life to know that if it couldn't put weight on its leg at all, it would go a long way toward giving her the advantage despite being smaller and weaker. She didn't want to take the time to assemble her sniper rifle and risk losing her shot, so she raised the submachine gun.

When she took aim, time seemed to stop for her. It was as if her mind was calculating all the possible trajectories of the shot toward her intended target and discounting everything except the one perfect angle. All she had to do at that point was align the barrel of the weapon along that path and pull the trigger.

She found her angle quickly, a straight-line shot close enough not to be affected by gravity or wind speed more than a fraction of a degree, which was well within her error tolerance range. The gun barrel was still warm in her left hand as she lined up her shot and squeezed the trigger with the gentleness of a lover.

Time snapped back to full speed. Orange blood splattered across the cement as the bullet burst through the alien's already-wounded rear knee joint. It roared in pain and twisted its upper torso around and down to get a better look at the injury.

Penny ran out of the grocery, gun raised with her finger on the trigger, like she was back on the SWAT team again. She snapped off another shot, aimed to miss. It struck the concrete beside the alien and spattered chips against the creature's tough hide. It turned to stare at her and she got her first close look at the visage of the alien Warrior.

Its hazel-colored eyes were round and protected by a heavy brow ridge, but nearly three times the size of a human's in a head only half again as large. The short protruding snout ended in a triangular pink nose before splitting into whiskered jowls. A beard like a billy goat's curled beneath the creature's lower jaw. She could see its fur was far more colorful than just a simple beige. It was ticked in multiple layers with black and brown, gold and tan, even olive and forest green.

The alien raised its axe and Penny rang a bullet off the blade. It must have stung the creature's hand for the axe clattered to the cement, leaving the alien wringing its hands. "Don't move!" Penny shouted, although it might have been ridiculous for her to expect the alien to understand her. She gestured with the end of the gun. "You see this? I'll shoot you again if you do anything." She pointed with her free hand at the alien's arms and then raised her own. "Like this. Hands up. Do it!"

Something resembling comprehension dawned on the alien's face and he—she decided to arbitrarily call it a *he* until she found out different—raised his hands, showing off the stubby claws at the end of each of his twelve fingers.

"Now move. That way." Penny pointed across the street. There was a subway entrance. Her Explorers were down there, and she knew she was going to need some backup.

The alien bent to pick up his axe and Penny fired again, sending sparks ringing off the blade with her bullet. "No. Leave it. No weapons for you."

She began walking backwards, keeping the alien firmly in her sights while indicating to him he should follow her. He seemed to understand well enough and limped after her, leaving a trail of bloody orange footprints in his wake.

"Okay, Penny, you caught one of those bastards. Now what are you going to do?" she muttered.

Then she thought of Avery. He'd probably want to run up and pet the Warrior. Maybe ask for a ride. It made her smile, thinking of her son.

Whatever else it took, she would make sure she saw him again.

Monkeyworld

Garragh didn't understand the Monkey, or its weapon. It resembled the electrolasers Hind Warriors carried—at least at a superficial level—but instead of a beam, it seemed to shoot rocks. Garragh knew the Hind had used primitive projectile weapons many generations ago, but he didn't know any of the details about them or how they worked. The Submistresses didn't go into much detail in their schooling, because learning was not a strong suit for Hind males. Their strength was in their ability to fight, and to follow orders, and those were the traits for which they were bred.

Garragh wasn't a great fighter by the standards of his people, and his inquisitiveness had gotten him numerous demerits over the years as they trained for the invasion of Monkeyworld. He knew, deep down, that he would never get to breed with a Submistress, never see his cubs battling each other for the right to nurse.

But dying in battle? He'd always thought he would at least manage that. The Monkey had used its weapon to put a painful, bloody hole in one of his hind legs, and it hurt more than anything that Garragh had suffered during his training. All he wanted to do was lie down, whimper at the pain, and claw at the wound until it stopped hurting or he bled to death. Dying from a wound suffered in battle wouldn't be so bad, except he hadn't even had the chance to fight. The Monkey had shot him from a position of cover, like a coward, and Garragh never had the chance to retaliate. The Monkey had even shot his axe. His *axe!* It might have been one he claimed from the dropship wreck, but at the moment he picked it up, it became *his*, and he would have been charged to keep it and wield it until the moment of his death.

Hind Warriors were given their axes upon reaching the age of servitude. Before then, as cubs they would fight with sticks on their homeworld, or with simple plastic replicas aboard the *Blood Afire*. A Warrior's axe was his pride, his joy, the essence of what made him a Warrior. It had been that way forever, as far as Garragh was concerned, and the Monkey had shot his right out of his hands. Then it made him leave it behind. That was the worst of all.

He was a prisoner. There was no worse embarrassment for a Hind Warrior. He had been denied the right to die in battle. To flee would be to invite charges of cowardice. He couldn't have run even if he'd wanted to with the painful wound leaking blood with every step. The only acceptable response should have been for him to attack the Monkey, taking whatever damage it could inflict in his attempt to slay. The Stories spoke of Warriors who had joyously leapt upon the spears of their enemies in order to deliver killing blows. They were the heroes who shaped Warrior culture, and all Warriors hoped to have that same opportunity.

Almost all Warriors.

Garragh was afraid. He was lost, alone, wounded, and imprisoned. His entire unit had been decimated by a Monkey who had not only stolen a Hind electrolaser, but learned how to use it. He'd lost his axe. Monkeyworld's light gravity was the only reason he managed to stay on his feet. Its thin air wasn't helping him, and his breath came in wheezing gasps as he tried to draw in enough oxygen. He felt lightheaded and disoriented, and that was when he realized the Monkey was goading him down into one of their underground constructions, which at least brought a tiny bit of familiarity to him.

It stank of chemicals and smoke, and had small terraces instead of a sensible ramp leading downward. The terraces were sized for Monkey feet, but Garragh's large pads threatened to slip on the corners, and then he thought he would tumble all the way down to whatever torture awaited him.

The Monkey had a small handheld light to stave off the darkness, and it kept it trained upon Garragh. He could still see it even in the darkness, a warm red glow of body heat against the black of the surrounding construction. Then the Monkey chittered something and its comrades answered, and suddenly they were everywhere around him, a cloud of reddish demons with shrill voices taunting him in words he couldn't comprehend.

Garragh tried to draw a deep breath, to roar in defiance or challenge, but the smoke in the air flew into his lungs and he slipped on the terraces to fall painfully upon their corners. He coughed until he thought he would spray his lungs out across the surface below him. He lacked even the strength to lunge at the Monkeys in the hope they would end his pathetic life. His head spun and the infrared signatures of the Monkeys blurred around him.

He felt the Monkeys' awful, soft hands plucking at him, stealing away the remainder of his armor and survival supplies with their clever fingers. As if that wasn't bad enough, they clutched and pulled at him, dragging him over terrace after terrace until they stopped upon a larger plain. They lit more of their handheld lights and shone them all over Garragh, examining him from head to haunch. Their conversation increased in intensity and excitement as they looked at the wound in his leg.

They looked at his armor, testing its strength, its flexibility, even working its connectors with a dexterity that Hind could never match. Likewise, they went through the gear he'd carried clipped to his abdomen. His rations drew much chattering, His water bottle was remarkably intact and he hadn't realized how thirsty he was until a Monkey spilled some of it into its hand and sniffed at it. It drew a stern rebuke from the one who had captured him and he began to understand something about the Monkeys.

Even though they all looked the same in his eyes, the larger group was deferential to the one who had captured him. It was almost as if the Monkey was a Submistress and the others were Warriors, except the Monkey Submistress was *also* a Warrior, and that might have been the most terrifying thing Garragh could imagine.

Female Hind didn't fight. War was beneath them. They planned and plotted. They were the scientists, the engineers, the visionaries. They issued the orders to go to battle and the males carried out those orders. It was no wonder the Clanmistress had determined to take Monkeyworld, to educated the primates in the way society *ought* to be.

At last, after a lengthy argument between the Monkeys, some kind of conclusion was reached. The Monkey who'd captured him handed its large weapon and the stolen electrorifle to two other Monkeys, who pointed the weapons at him. Then it took his water bottle in one hand and a smaller device that could only have been another weapon in its other, and approached him, extending the water bottle.

He shouldn't have taken it. He should have slashed at the Monkey and died there on the terrace with Monkey blood drying beneath his claws, but he was so terribly thirsty. He reached for the water bottle with a hand that shook with surprising weakness. The Monkey chattered at him and then stepped back as he took the bottle. He didn't think it feared him. It didn't see him as a threat.

His embarrassment complete, Garragh drank his water and waited for a traitor's death.

Low Earth Orbit
Hind Fleet

Harlan made himself a model prisoner.

He'd never actually spent more than a couple of hours behind bars since the time when he'd been a guest of the New York Juvenile Corrections System when he was thirteen. Neither Just Cause nor any of the other hero teams had managed to catch and hold him. The longest he'd ever been behind bars during his time running a gang in Philadelphia was two hours, and that had ended with him sauntering out the front door of the station with several new officers in his pocket, figuratively speaking.

The tractor beam pulled him into an airlock. He kept his suit constructed around him as the lock cycled. The air pressure was higher than he would have liked, and he knew he would have to have his nanites monitor nitrogen levels in his bloodstream so he didn't get the bends. He also noted with interest that the aliens appeared to have some kind of artificial gravity technology, but its pull was similar to Earth's. He wondered if that was their native gravity or if they'd adjusted it to grow accustomed to Earth's. Before the inner lock hissed open, he disassembled his suit at its molecular level and pulled its parts inside his body. It would make him abnormally heavy for a human, but again, his nanites were up to the challenge. He stepped out into the corridor to face a phalanx of aliens with axes leveled at him.

Axes.

He couldn't help but smirk, knowing they wouldn't understand the significance of the expression. They'd crossed untold light years, managed to develop some form of faster-than-light travel, had advanced energy field and ray technology . . . and carried axes. Harlan was sure the odd retrograde technology would become clear to him in time, but for the moment, he was amused by the simplicity.

The aliens, on the other hand, were magnificent chimeras, as if some devious god had blended lions with men and then gotten bored halfway through the process. His embedded nanotech filled the edges of his vision with data about the creatures. They had thick-boned skeletons, with joints in expected locations. Their dense musculature and thick hides bore testament to a heavy gravity world with a harsh environment. From the size of their eyes, Harlan suspected they had excellent vision, but their poor tracking when firing at him suggested their depth perception may have been lacking.

Then, suddenly, he understood the axes. First of all, firing weapons inside a spaceship would never be a good idea. If the aliens truly were poor shots anyway, they would prefer to fight up close and in person. They had claws and fangs—he could see that much without any sensory subterfuge—but a razor-sharp axe driven by those powerful limbs would cleave almost anything in two.

Harlan raised his hands. "Here I am. Take me to your leader."

With grunts and threatening gestures with their axes, the aliens indicated which way he should move. He followed their demands, taking extra care to remain as nonthreatening as possible.

Information flowed into him from his nanotech. The metallurgy in the ship's construction was highly advanced, allowing for unbelievably lightweight yet strong materials. The aliens didn't appear to use much plastic. Perhaps they didn't have significant petrochemicals on their homeworld and had never developed the technology. It appeared that some sort of alternate organic material fulfilled the role where humans would use plastic. It almost seemed like wood of some kind, which could be incredibly practical if it were hardy enough.

One thing he found no indicators of either among his hosts or in the construction of their vessel was nanotechnology. Perhaps they had never developed it. He smiled again. Even Just Cause had managed make significant use of nanotech, and they were a bunch of morons. He was so busy noting the ways human technology exceeded that of the aliens that he nearly walked right into an axe blade barring his way.

The alien holding the axe before him grunted and growled. It made an unmistakable pointing gesture at a doorway. The room beyond was tiny by alien standards —one of the centaurian beasts would have been cramped within it—but to Harlan, it seemed like a large walk-in closet. It was unfurnished and he suspected it was a prison cell. That was fine with him, for he'd likely have time to dial up his sensors and *really* begin researching the weaknesses of his captors.

He stepped into the chamber and sure enough, a sparkling rainbow field crackled into place behind him. It was semitransparent, allowing him to see the aliens on the other side. One of them tapped the end of its axe against the force screen, which hissed and sparked. With what Harlan could only imagine was smug satisfaction, the alien turned its back on him and loped away.

Harlan sat upon the bare metal floor, resting himself against the high gravity for when he really needed to use his energy. He folded his legs and shut his eyes as if meditating. In a way, he supposed he was. He didn't need his vision to continue to analyze the technology surrounding him. Indeed, vision was far more limiting when the flow of information had to come through his eyes instead of going directly to multiple portions of his brain at the same time.

He would study the aliens' shield technology. He would learn its secrets. He would figure out how to duplicate it himself for his own purposes. And of course, he would learn how to breach it, and then no place in the entire fleet would be safe.

Harlan had grown up in Harlem, surrounded by bullies. Kids who were bigger, stronger, and meaner than him always managed to find the time to call him names, or beat him up. Eventually, though, he got his revenge upon them.

These aliens were bullies too, and when he took his revenge upon them, it would be as sweet as it had been before.

CHAPTER FOUR

U 2 U

Lower Manhattan

Sally and Chinook worked their way across lower Manhattan, heading toward Central Park, which was where Sally knew Penny had been conducting a workshop for New York City Police Explorers. She shivered as she thought of what the aliens might do to a bunch of teenagers with delusions of grandeur.

Power failed in their immediate area, if not everywhere within the shield, shortly after six o'clock. In the past, when power went out in Manhattan, people had rioted and looted. Now, with aliens roaming the city, most of them had abandoned their cars and tried to make it to safety on foot. The streets were littered with empty cars as people moved into buildings to hide in their darkened interiors. The Emergency Alert siren cut off mid-howl and the only sounds Sally could hear in the City that Never Sleeps were the energy weapons of the invaders.

Sally had managed a brief telepathic conversation with Ment but it appeared the energy shield had some sort of effect even upon psionics. Much of their dialogue had been garbled, like trying to have a cell phone conversation with only one signal bar during a hailstorm. The general gist she'd gotten from Ment was the team hadn't yet found a way through the shield, but they were trying. For her part, Sally passed along what she hoped was a fairly complete dossier on the aliens, but she had no idea how much of her speed-fractured thoughts had crossed through the barricade into some semblance of order in Ment's mind.

The dropships had stopped coming down but enough of them had landed in Manhattan that Sally figured there must have been at least a couple hundred of the large centaurians. They were rounding up civilians as they found them and forcing them into their pens, but otherwise leaving them unharmed. If anyone tried to fight back, they found themselves on the wrong end of a laser rifle or an axe. Sally and Chinook had found the bodies of numerous police officers, security guards, and even civilians who'd tried to fight against the might of the invaders.

Chinook was taking it hard. She floated through the air listlessly, almost carelessly. More than once Sally had to drag her out of harm's way when an alien spotted them and took a shot. At least the aliens were lousy at aiming. "It's like they all graduated *summa cum lousy* from the Imperial Stormtrooper School of Advanced Marksmanship," Sally said with a wry chuckle.

"Wh-what's that?"

"Star Wars reference."

"The movies?"

"Oh God, please, you're making me feel really old."

Sally said she wanted to get a bird's-eye view of the city, to get a better sense of where the aliens were clustering and what might be a safe route deeper into Manhattan. They went into an office high-rise and found workers cowering in the lobby, arguing in urgent whispers whether they should try to leave or not. A barrage of questions, some angrier than others, were directed toward them as they slipped in through the entrance.

Sally raised her hands. "Everyone needs to settle down right now. I don't have a lot of answers, but I can tell you a few things. Right now we're all trapped underneath an energy shield of some kind, and aliens have landed." She raised her voice to cut off a man who wanted to argue with her. "I said aliens, and that's what I meant. They're hostile, but they're not harming civilians so long as they don't fight back. I can't order you to stay here, but you're probably safer inside the building than you would be on the street. The aliens are large enough they'll have a difficult time getting through doorways. I bet they can't get into a typical stairwell."

"I need to get home to my family," said one woman.

"If you go out there, be careful. If an alien approaches you, don't run, don't fight back. You'll be captured and detained but not harmed." Sally sighed. "I really wish you'd stay here, though."

The man who wanted to argue stepped forward and raised a lecturing finger at them. "What are you superheroes doing about it? Isn't this your thing? Fix it. Or can't you?"

"Sir, I assure you, we're doing the best we can—" began Sally.

"Bullshit. You're hiding, the same as us. In fact, I think you're nothing more than a couple of—"

An invisible force blew the man off his feet and he skidded back across the floor until he hit a wall. "Shut up! Just shut up! Can't you see we're trying to *help*?!" Chinook screamed, her arms raised and directing a stream of air at the man strong enough to ruffle Sally's hair.

"Chinook, stop it," Sally said.

Chinook lowered her arms. Tears streamed unchecked down her cheeks. "We're trying to help," she whispered.

"I'll *sue*—" began the man as he scrambled back to his feet.

Sally zipped across the floor and stuck a business card in his hand. "Have your lawyer contact me. You might find someone here to testify that you're not being an asshole." She turned her back on him and faced the others. "People, the bottom line is that we are outgunned and outnumbered and we are doing everything we can to push back these invaders. It is going to take some time, and I promise you, I and my team will be doing everything possible in the meantime. We can't be everywhere at once, so if we don't have to look out for you all wandering the streets, that means we can devote more attention to the invaders. I'm not going to stop you from trying to get home, but I have an entire city—really, an entire planet to worry about right now. Be safe, be careful, and make smart decisions. Remember this: we all need to put aside our differences right now. We are *all* humans, and right now we have a common, inhuman foe."

A few people in the lobby nodded.

Sally smiled at them with a confidence she didn't feel. "You're safe here for the time being. Let's keep it that way. For now, though, can somebody point me to a stairwell to the roof?"

One quick spiraling trip up thirty flights of emergency-lit stairs later and Sally and Chinook exited the stairwell onto the building's roof. It was still warm but not as bright as it should have been. The rainbow energy shield over the city was diffusing the sunlight, making everything dim and hazy. The air was unnaturally still, suggesting the shield was also keeping back the typical afternoon sea breeze. Sally wondered if it was so airtight that they were in danger of suffocating.

No, she told herself. The shield wouldn't be up so long for that to become an issue. Just Cause would figure out a way to knock it down, and then they'd kick the aliens right back onto their ships and out of the solar system.

Chinook hovered near the edge of the building, looking out across the city. "It looks so peaceful from up here. There's no lights, no traffic moving. Not even any horns."

Sally nodded. "There are always horns. People are impatient." She spotted the familiar flicker of the aliens' laser rifles as a someone fought back a dozen blocks to the north. "I hope whoever it is gets away."

"We should go help them, shouldn't we?"

"We should, you're right." Sally sighed. "I just don't know where to start. I mean, here I am, the biggest science fiction buff on the team, and all I want is for Will Smith to come down, punch an alien in the face, and make it all better."

"So in all those movies and TV shows, nobody ever fought off an invasion before?"

"Well, sure. Right now, we're so outnumbered, though. We need to regroup so we can start forming a real plan instead of trying to attack this thing piecemeal." Sally pointed toward Central Park. "I know Penny had a thing going on today with young police recruits in the Park, and Jason was doing studio work over near Columbia. And Shawna's in East Harlem, standing in for Hector at his gym."

"I don't know New York geography very well." Chinook looked up at the shield. "I can't tell how far up it is. It makes me lose all my depth perception."

"It's like how the Moon looks bigger against the horizon," said Sally. "I don't want you flying up toward it to see how close it is. We don't know what will happen if you fly into it."

Chinook shrugged. "We're going to have to take it on sooner or later."

"We will, but for now, let's regroup with our allies. Penny's probably the closest."

"You sure you wouldn't rather go after your husband?"

"Of course that's what I'd rather do, but I'm looking at the big picture here, Chinook." Sally sighed. She hoped Jason was all right. They'd go after him soon.

"Okay, you're the boss."

Sally's phone buzzed into life. So did Chinook's. It was a single repeating word spoken by an odd, unfamiliar voice. "Attention . . . attention . . . attention . . ."

Sally stared at her phone, and then glanced up at Chinook. The girl looked terrified. "First contact," said Sally. "It's a real bitch. Come here, grab a seat. Let's listen to what they have to say." She sat on the gravel with her back against the parapet. Chinook dropped down beside her with a fluttering of silk streamers.

" ... Attention ... Attention." The message ended so abruptly, Sally wondered if her phone had lost power. Then her speaker came alive. "I am Clanmistress Rhaorhir of Clan Sharassar. Here are my terms. I demand your unconditional surrender to me or else I will destroy the city within my shield. Many of your people will perish. Then I will target another city, and the process will repeat until you surrender your world or it becomes an uninhabitable nightmare. Swear fealty to me and to Clan Sharassar and your cities, your citizens, and the prisoners my troops have taken will be unharmed. Under the protection of my Clan, you will survive, grow, and even thrive as a people. Perhaps someday, you shall even serve aboard Sharassar vessels as we continue our conquest of the cosmos. These are my terms. You have one full day to comply or else you lose New York."

The speech was in English, but Sally wasn't surprised. It didn't make sense to issue a threat in a language nobody could understand. The aliens had probably translated from Earth's ever-expanding wavefront of radio and television transmissions. She grimaced at the implications of the speech. "I know this story. It's a protection racket."

Chinook looked at her. "What's a protection racket?"

"Mighty nice planet youse guys got here," Sally said, affecting an old-fashioned Brooklyn gangster accent. "Be a real shame if somethin' were to ... *happen* to it."

Fort Justice
New York Bay

"I'm surprised to see you here," Minerva said to March. He was wearing a borrowed Just Cause jumpsuit. His own clothing had been soaked thanks to his capsule rupturing in the Bay. A typical rescued castaway should be shivering with his hands wrapped around a mug of hot chocolate with a generous dollop of bourbon in it, preferably in midwinter while a storm howled outside. Instead, he had politely refused anything except water and instead of huddling miserably in a corner, stood out on the Command Center deck with Minerva. He studied the energy shield through a pair of binoculars. "Was the Preserve compromised?"

"I d-don't know. Uncle Harlan figured the aliens w-were here for trouble. I guh . . . guh . . ." He paused, took a deep breath, and finished. "He was right."

Minerva felt bad for March. His stutter interfered with his need to communicate so much it was almost painful. She was empathic enough to feel his pain almost like it was her own. The worst part of it was she knew she could have fixed his stutter. She'd once healed an indestructible parahuman who'd been pierced by a magical spear by repairing and moving one cell at a time. Fixing March's stutter wouldn't have been nearly as complicated an operation, but she would never volunteer to do so. He would see it as an insult. She could tell that as clear as daytime about him. If he ever asked her if she could, she would tell him the truth, and if he asked for her help, he would have it. Until then, she would keep her quiet counsel, as she generally did in all things.

"Can you tell if the Preserve is still intact?"

"No. Uncle Harlan would have shut it d-down. Silent running. Only he or I can wake it again." He lowered the binoculars to look at her. "Why?"

"It may be a useful asset. Even if we break through this shield, and I believe we will sooner or later, given the number of brilliant minds working on it, we still have to deal with the four alien vessels in orbit, and I see no way of doing that without traveling into space ourselves to do battle."

"You said four? Uncle Harlan said there were five."

"One of them is adrift on a course that will cause it to fall into the Sun in approximately four months if it is not repaired. It appears to have suffered grievous damage at his hands. It may be permanently disabled."

"Can't we just launch muh . . . missiles at them?"

Minerva shook her head. "I am unfamiliar with this country—or any country's ability to wage a nuclear war in space. Somehow, though, I suspect these aliens would find it far less inconveniencing than would we. As strategic targets, their ships are small and mobile, with unknown energy shields and armors that might already be proof against nuclear explosions."

"Oh."

"We do possess the ability to reach space, and I've begun compiling a list of parahumans who might join such a venture. I hope you will consider yourself part of that contingent, March."

He nodded. "He's up there somewhere. F-fighting them. I know it."

"We believe he may have been captured."

March stamped his foot in a sudden flash of anger. "No! If he did, it was on pur . . . purpose."

Minerva touched his arm, using her power to send a healing, calming wave into him. "I believe you, March."

He sighed, coolly content after Minerva's subtlety. He didn't suspect she'd done it or she'd have known. The cast of his head, the way his hands moved, they all gave her far more information than if he'd shared a lengthy dissertation on himself. "I'll go with you into space. He may need my help."

"It's not just him, March. The world needs your help too."

"We need help from both of you," said a new voice.

Minerva turned to greet the newcomer, although she'd smelled his aftershave the moment he'd entered the Command Center. "General Gershwin. Thank you for coming."

"Minerva, it's nice to finally meet you." He gave her a firm handshake, not holding back because she was a woman, not trying to assert dominance over her. It was extremely professional, and she appreciated it more than he would ever know. "The President sent me here in the hopes that Just Cause can bring this to a speedier conclusion than the combined might of the United States Armed Forces. I'm not entirely convinced he's wrong, but then, I've had a bit of experience with heroes saving the world."

Minerva nodded. "I understand some of the Joint Chiefs are pushing to authorize a nuclear strike at the alien fleet."

Gershwin sighed. "The Joint Chiefs are a bunch of morons who miss the glory days of warfare that didn't involve drones and robots. There's absolutely no chance a missile launch would succeed. *If* we could successfully reprogram the targeting software to aim for a spaceborne target, and *if* the damn missile didn't malfunction, and *if* the Russians or Chinese didn't think we were making an opportunity strike against them anyway and retaliated, they're still goddamn spaceships. They can move out of the way."

"And they have lasers," said March.

"I'm sorry, we haven't met. General Gershwin." Gershwin offered March his hand, and March took it.

"March Washington."

"March has resources available to him that may help us tilt the conflict in our favor," said Minerva. "Nanotechnology developed by his uncle, Harlan Washington, known as Destroyer. Firsthand knowledge of the aliens' arrival. And he has spent more time in space than anyone not aboard the International Space Station."

Gershwin cleared his throat. "I, uh, doubt that's true. But again, that's why I'm here. The President has authorized me to make certain . . . *assets* available to you for a strike against the aliens."

Minerva fixed him with one of her unblinking gazes. "In space."

"Er, yes."

"You have a spaceship."

"In, uh, in a manner of speaking." He lowered his voice. "I know you have a security clearance, but I can't discuss this in front of a civilian. I'm going to have to ask Mr. Washington to leave before we continue."

"March," said Minerva. "Tell him about the Preserve."

"What's the Preserve?" asked Gershwin.

"Destroyer's moon base."

Gershwin blinked. "I'm sorry, I thought you said Destroyer had a moon base, which is clearly impossible."

"I've been there," said Minerva, and that settled the argument as effectively as any proof. Minerva wasn't given to flights of fancy or exaggeration.

"So these, uh, resources you spoke of. Would they be weapons that might be effective against the aliens, by any chance?"

March looked at Minerva for guidance.

"General, believe me when I say we're working on that. Now if you would be so kind as to tell me about Project *Daedalus* and how we can use it as the basis for our offensive."

"How do you know about that? It's classified!" Gershwin looked like he was afraid of lightning coming to strike him down out of a clear blue sky.

Minerva shrugged. "Do you really need to know that?"

Gershwin shook his head. "I thought I was done with all this after the rabbit fellow."

59ᵗʰ Street Subway Station
Manhattan

The alien hadn't wanted to go down the steps into the darkened subway station, but Penny wasn't going to put up with any pseudo-cowardly bullshit. After it drank some water, she'd used two sets of handcuffs to wrangle the alien's wrists behind its upper back, as it couldn't physically move them close enough together for one to suffice.

They'd gotten the alien down into the station proper where the MTA had cranked up the emergency lighting. Penny was as satisfied as she could be that they were secure for the time being, and the discussion turned to what they should do with their prisoner. More than a couple of the cops were for executing the creature on the spot and tearing it apart to find its weak points, but Penny put a stop to that line of thinking. "I don't care what you want to do," she said. "There are laws about that sort of thing. Geneva convention and the treatment of prisoners of war."

"Yeah, but that only applies to humans, don't it?" said the cop with the thick, black mustache. "Aliens don't got no human rights. Besides, they attacked us first."

"It's not for you or me to decide what legal rights these creatures have," said Penny. "But as far as I'm concerned, this thing is a prisoner of war and as such, we have to treat it that way. No torturing or tormenting it. It gets food, water, and medical care."

"Medical care? What're you, some kinda bleeding-heart—*ow!*" Mustache cop yelped for Penny had flipped one of her namesakes at him and it caught him right on the tip of his nose.

"Food. Water. Medical care. Look, how we treat this thing may make a big difference in how this whole invasion is resolved. Maybe if the aliens see we treated one of their own with kindness, they'll view us differently than if we murdered a prisoner in cold blood."

"Yeah? Or maybe they just won't give a shit about it."

Penny sighed. "All right, I'm pulling rank. You are personally responsible for this alien's safety, officer. Anything happens to him, I'm going to suspend your rights because it's fucking wartime, and I will put a bullet in between your eyes. Now are you going to stand down or do I have to get nasty with you?"

Mustache cop looked down at her. He had almost a foot of height on her but she didn't back down. She had the patience of a sniper. She could glare at him for hours until he broke. It only took a minute. "All right," he mumbled.

"I didn't quite hear that, officer."

"Yes, ma'am. The alien lives."

"That's what I thought you said." She flipped another penny right into his breast pocket. "Keep that as a reminder."

"What does it . . . eat?" asked one of the Explorers.

"Us, stupid. Aliens eat people," retorted another.

"You think maybe it does? It looks like a predator," said an MTA employee.

"I'm sure he's got food with him, but for now, let's get that wound on its leg treated. It's going to be bad enough escorting this thing halfway across Manhattan without him bleeding out on the way there." Penny glanced at the others. "Anyone want to volunteer to be a veterinarian? No?" She retrieved a first aid kit from the station wall. "Fine, I'll be Dr. Quinn, Medicine Woman." She looked over at Mustache Cop. "Don't get any funny ideas. Cover me."

He grumbled but kept his weapon firmly trained upon the alien.

Penny approached the beast, first aid kit clutched in one hand and a pistol in the other. She didn't expect it to understand her, but she held up the kit. "I'm going to bandage your leg. Any funny ideas and that guy over there will shoot you. He might do it anyway, so you better hold still."

The alien watched her with its large, hooded eyes, but otherwise made no sounds. She didn't think it would understand her, but the monstrous voice that had come over her radio suggested at least some of them spoke English. She moved around the creature toward its wounded hind leg where orange blood still leaked sluggishly from the bullet hole. She saw both an entry and exit wound and knew no bullet fragments remained behind, but she was pretty sure she'd done some damage to the bones or ligaments or whatever constructed the alien's knee joint. "Damn, I'll bet that hurts like a sonofabitch," she said.

She knelt beside the alien's wounded leg and opened the first aid kid one-handed, keeping the pistol leveled at the alien's head with her other hand. She removed items from the kit one at a time, moving slowly so the creature could see what she was doing. She knew antibiotic cream would be at best useless and at worst toxic to the alien, so she ignored it. Once she had bandages, tape, scissors, and a water bottle ready to use, she showed the alien her pistol and let it watch as she holstered it. It made a low growl in the back of its throat. "Don't get any ideas. This is for your own good. I could let you bleed to death."

She opened the water bottle, sniffed it, poured out a little into her hand, and sipped at it. Then, knowing it was a great risk, she held the bottle toward the alien's head. She decided his deep inhalation meant he was sniffing the water. He watched her as she poured the bottle over his wound, flushing thick orange blood away from the matted tawny fur. The alien hissed and his leg quivered but otherwise he didn't move. At first, Penny wondered if she should splint the wound as it was at the alien's knee joint, but she didn't know whether it would help or cause further harm. She decided a simple bandage job would be best. The alien's unwavering gaze made her skin crawl as she wrapped the fabric around the injured leg, keeping pressure against the bullet holes. Once she'd wrapped several layers around it, she used the tape to secure it.

The alien didn't move while she worked. She couldn't tell if he was curious, or afraid, or something else altogether. It would take some time to learn how to read the alien body language, if it was something humans could ever hope to understand at all. She finished her work and stepped back. "There, how's that?"

The alien twisted its upper torso around to look more closely at the bandage, then looked at Penny. She wondered if he was grateful or angry.

"What are you going to do with it now?" asked Mustache Cop.

"We can't just keep him here," said Penny. "We've got to get him to the authorities. Or at least to a more defensible location. This prisoner might be the key to resolving the entire invasion." She looked at the small group of transit cops and Explorers. "We're going to take him to Champions headquarters at the south end of Manhattan. The field edge is close to it and maybe the Champions are on the inside with us. If so, that's our best bet. If not, you can bet that's where we're most likely to find someone who can breach the shield. If we're lucky, there will be a telepath who can maybe read this alien's mind."

"That's a pretty long walk," said Mustache Cop. "I assume you want to go through subway tunnels to get there?"

"No, that will take us too long. Surface travel will be faster if we can commandeer a vehicle or two. Put this fellow in a truck."

Mustache Cop nodded. "I guess that's as good a plan as any. What do we do if we run across more of those soldiers?"

Penny smiled. "We already know they bleed."

Monkeyworld

The Monkeys were an endless source of mystery to Garragh, but he thought he was beginning to understand them. The Mistresses were also Warriors, which was hard to fathom, but it was the only explanation he could manage. The one who'd captured him was clearly more than just a leader of troops. Even though she fought like a Warrior, with an uncanny accuracy beyond the ability of any Hind, she also issued orders like a Submistress, and the other Monkeys scrambled to obey her. Even the ones who wore the same drab outfit as her, all one color without the barest hint of script detailing the heroism of one's ancestors, one's puissance in battle, or one's accomplishments of note.

Script your successes to stoke the fear of your enemies was part of the Warrior's Way. Every Warrior had the soul of an artist, and the personalization of their armor was far more than mere decoration. Even though Garragh had accomplished little in his life, he'd come from a great bloodline of great Warriors and cunning Submistresses, and could even trace his lineage back to one of the original Clanmistresses of old. He'd spent many cycles tracing out the scripts, patterns, and icons of power. Losing that armor had been like losing a part of himself forever. He hadn't studied it as much as he should have, and there were portions of the script he would never remember should he be called upon to do so. Only a trip to the Clan Archives would allow him to recreate what he'd lost, but he would sooner die of shame.

Being imprisoned by a bunch of Monkeys in a smelly hole wasn't doing much to improve his outlook. He hadn't understood why the Monkeymistress had sheathed her weapon and wrapped layers of cloth around his wounded leg. Indeed, she'd washed it first, diluting his blood with water. Perhaps it was a ritual to weaken him further. Surely the Monkeys must understand Hind did not treat their injuries, for it was a sign of weakness. *Blood is strength; to show one's strength in battle is to leave one's blood behind for all to see.*

The strangest thing of all was how the Monkeys didn't seem to be interested in torturing or mutilating him. Hind captives existed only long enough to die for their Clans, and yet the Monkeys hadn't done anything worse than point some of their noisy weapons at him. He should have been made into an example, a warning to other Hind that to approach meant a painful death, a death only worthy of a slave instead of a Warrior. Instead, the Monkeys had given him water to drink and treated him at least as well as he had been aboard the *Blood Afire.*

The Monkeys led him back up and out of their manufactured cave, and Garragh was only too happy to oblige them. The industrial and chemical fumes rising from the deeper caverns were making him light-headed. With the atmosphere on Monkeyworld already thinner than he was used to, he felt dopey and struggled to keep his focus. He knew he should be seeking a way to escape, to attack, to war for his honor and his Clan at the first opportunity, but all he wanted to do was lie down and sleep. His wounded leg throbbed with every step.

"*Kom*," the Monkeymistress kept saying, and he understood it meant he was to follow her. As a trained Warrior, at least he could do that much. The Monkeys pushed him into a vehicle that stank of wild animals. It had slitted windows he could peek through, but it was narrow enough that he couldn't turn around in it. Once inside, they shut the door behind him. He presumed they locked him inside. The walls of the vehicle seemed thin and weak. If he was fully rested and had his axe, he thought he might be able to peel open the sheet metal. Instead, he slumped against it and felt his eyes drift in and out of focus as the Monkeys climbed into and onto two additional vehicles. They moved across the streets of their city, slowly weaving back and forth between buildings, working their way around other abandoned vehicles.

The swaying of the transport made Garragh sleepy. He figured the Monkeys weren't simply taking him to his death; they could have killed him at any time if that had been their intent. They wanted to *use* him for some purpose. He couldn't imagine what that might be, but he would wait and see what lay in store for him in the future. Either way, he figured he would be alive for it, and that meant an opportunity for him to redeem his honor.

He folded his legs beneath him and lay upon the rocking floor. His wounded leg twinged with every jostle of the rolling cage. He wished it would stop hurting. His shoulders ached from the restraints holding his wrists together behind him at an unnatural angle. There wasn't enough air, and what there was stank of animals.

He *hated* Monkeyworld!

Why had the Clanmistress seen fit to claim such a place? There were so many other worlds in space, with civilizations ripe for the taking and exploiting by the Hind war machine. Why this one, with its dirt and stink and nightmare inhabitants that all looked like they'd been split in half?

Light flashed through the cage in which he rode, imprinting a green afterimage on his eyes. Thunder roared a moment later as matching smoldering holes had appeared in the thin metal above his head. In spite of his awkward discomfort and the risk of becoming a target himself, Garragh leaped to his feet. His people had come. He was going to be rescued!

If only such a thing was honorable.

Low Earth Orbit
Hind Fleet

Hind secrets were not going to be Hind secrets for very long. Ever so slowly, Harlan was unraveling them.

Despite their starships and advanced energy technology, the Hind were still a primitive race in many ways. From his vantage point in his prison cell, Harlan determined they didn't have ship-wide wi-fi, or at least if they did, it was inaccessible from inside a detention cell. That didn't deter him. They had never considered what someone with nanotech could achieve, and although he sat unmoving with his eyes shut, a slender thread ran from one of Harlan's fingertips into the seam between a light fixture and the wall. From there, he'd found the high-speed data cables, and he was learning everything he could about their systems.

Even without knowing their language, their file organization wasn't unfamiliar, and he soon found a database full of old human radio and television signals, suggesting it was how the Hind had learned of Humanity in the first place. The files were appended with what appeared to be translations, and Harlan set his system to work on decrypting and translating it.

The shield sealing him into the detention cell dissolved. He detached the thread of nanites from his finger and left it hanging out of the wall, innocuous enough it might not be seen. When he opened his eyes, he saw a new Hind standing before him. Unlike the Warriors who had first taken him captive, this one wore a vest-horse blanket combination that seemed more like clothing than protection. A harness bore various devices that Harlan didn't think were weapons. Perhaps this was a scientist? If so, it was about time he had a chance to speak with someone marginally intelligent. Then it occurred to him the alien's smock might be more practical to protect its fur from, say, blood splatters. Maybe he was about to be tortured, or dissected.

Anyone who tried to probe him was going to get blasted for their efforts.

The new alien took a step closer. Its hands were empty but it activated a device hanging from its throat. Two Warriors stood further back, laser rifles lowered and pointing past the newcomer at Harlan.

Harlan made no threatening moves, willing to let the aliens make the next move.

The alien spoke in its growling, hissing yowl, and a rough synthesized voice came from the device on the alien's throat in stilted but passable English, sounding rather like the personal assistant on an iPhone. It almost made him smile. He wondered what would happen if he asked it *Hey Siri, how do I stop an alien invasion?*

"I am Submistress Hsharra of Clan Sharassar. What is your name, Monkey?"

Harlan bristled at being called *Monkey*. He knew it was a racist term, not because of his black skin, but because to the Hind, all humans were no better than Monkeys. "I'm known as Destroyer." He didn't feel it necessary to share his birth name with these creatures from another world. It would mean even less to them than it did to him. *Destroyer* had been how he saw himself for many years, and he wasn't about to change that now.

Hsharra's translator growled at her. Harlan made sure his systems were recording the sounds. The additional data would help speed up his efforts to translate the Hind language. "Do you speak for your world?"

"What do you mean?"

"You are a great Warrior. You fight with technology unlike any we see Monkeys have. You fight alone. You must be highly favored in your Clans. Do you speak for your world?"

For a moment, Harlan felt like preening. It was about time *someone* recognized him for his greatness, even though it was a bunch of alien invaders. Still, he couldn't let his ego get ahead of him. "Hardly. I am a single man. There are hundreds of Warriors on the Earth more powerful than I. Most of the world below doesn't even know I exist."

"You speak of parahumans, yes?"

"Yes. You think I'm a great Warrior? There are those who make me look like a rank amateur. And I promise, they will come for you."

Hsharra's eyes narrowed. "They will come for me?"

"They will come for all of you."

"Explain yourself."

"They'll destroy your tiny fleet. They'll steal your secrets, your technology. Then, they'll go looking for the rest of your race. Your homeworld. And they'll find it."

Hsharra made a sound like a sneeze that didn't translate. Harlan suspected it was laughter. "You are only Monkeys."

"And I'm the Monkey who figured out how to shoot through your shields. You can't even do that, can you?" Harlan laughed.

Hsharra said nothing.

"I didn't think so. How much damage did I do to one of your ships by myself? Just one Monkey. There are *seven billion* of us on the world. You think you can frighten us with your axes and your five pitiful ships?

We've been practicing war for thousands of years. Now you've given us an opponent we don't have to feel bad about killing." He smiled. "It will be a slaughter."

Hsharra took a step backward, perhaps taken aback by the unexpected vitriol in the translation of Harlan's words. "You will submit to the Hind. You will submit to Clan Sharassar. If you do so, you will be spared the death of a coward."

Harlan snorted. Empty threats were the last ditch effort of all bullies. He knew this territory well, and he wasn't afraid of bullies. The Hind had asked him if spoke for the Earth, and in a way, he supposed he did. He didn't honestly know if Just Cause or the military would be able to fight the Hind in space, but he suspected they would manage it sooner rather than later. In the meantime, he represented the entire front line defense for the planet below. He may have turned his back upon the Earth, but he was still a human, and he was going to show these invaders what that meant. "Fuck you and your Clan."

He waited for the translation to take, and then grinned at Hsharra's reaction. "Kill him," she shouted, and the Warriors behind her stepped forward.

Harlan's armor burst through his skin to encapsulate him and he charged at the Warriors.

CHAPTER FIVE

♟

Central Park

Sally and Chinook continued to work their way north across Manhattan, but it was slow going for someone like Sally who was used to tearing across town in seconds. Chinook could fly at a pretty good pace, but she wasn't stealthy at all. In her gold and white silks, framed against the gunmetal grays of the skyscraper façades, she might as well have had a big glowing arrow pointing at her that said *shoot me.* She and Sally had found that out the hard way when they'd first left the rooftop after the Clanmistress delivered her ultimatum. A burn several inches long cut along Chinook's upper arm, and she was lucky the alien's shot hadn't pierced her chest.

Sally dispatched the alien Warrior quickly, delivering a rapid volley of punches to the creature's head and face, bolstered by the heavy iron horseshoes she carried for just such a purpose. The alien staggered under the vicious onslaught and finally collapsed, its face swelling and thick orange blood leaking from numerous contusions. A younger Sally might have been shocked at her own brutality, but she'd learned a lot from Hector and others like him. She'd learned it from Harlan Washington when he killed her father and her mother's husband before Sally had ever been born. When it came to war, there were no prizes for second place. It wasn't about the honor of dying for one's country; it was about making one's opponent die for his country first.

Sally was nothing if not a Warrior herself. Whenever she needed to bolster her emotional strength, she would remind herself the blood of lions ran through her veins.

The aliens were lousy shots, which was becoming more and more evident. They were dangerous up close, being far stronger than humans and made of much denser stuff. Even so, they could bleed. Sally had proved that. She couldn't run off and leave Chinook behind. To abandon her young rookie teammate, especially when she'd been wounded, well, Sally would have to court-martial herself for that kind of act. Instead, they'd gone into an abandoned clothing store, found a first aid kit in the back room, and Sally treated Chinook's wound as best she could.

Sally was worried about her. Chinook's eyes were glassy and she had the proverbial thousand-yard stare. Sally knew the girl was in shock—not the medical definition, but the kind of creeping, numbing fear that could turn into combat paralysis and indecision at a crucial moment. Chinook needed a place of safety, but they weren't likely to find something like that anytime soon. The best thing they could do was find the rest of their scattered teammates.

Penny's last known location was closest, on the east side of Central Park. Unfortunately, the park appeared to be crawling with alien soldiers. Sally knew she and Chinook couldn't have fought them all under the best of circumstances. The aliens were gathering their civilian prisoners together, collecting them inside smaller versions of the large shield encompassing so much of Manhattan. Their dropships were acting as central hubs for fortifications, and Sally could see that the invading forces had successfully established their first beachhead. She shuddered to think how much worse it might have been if Harlan

Washington hadn't broadcast his warning message. She wondered if he was still alive.

She hoped so.

Chinook had asked Sally if they should try traveling through the subway tunnels but Sally overruled that suggestion. The tunnels would be isolated and keep them better hidden from the aliens, but emergency lighting wouldn't keep them lit for very long, and eventually they would be plunged into darkness. If the aliens sent Warriors into those tunnels, Sally and Chinook could find themselves trapped between exits with nowhere to escape. At least on the surface they had a fighting chance. "We run into any kind of real trouble, the kind we can't deal with in a couple of seconds, you make for the nearest rooftop. Those bastards can't fly and they're too big to fit through a stairwell door. You'll be safe up there."

"Wh-what about you?"

"You're sweet. I could be six blocks away before any of these guys have unhooked their axe clasps."

They continued their slow trek across town, keeping to the shadows between the buildings and using parked or abandoned cars as cover. Sally didn't think they would run across many of the aliens. The invaders were digging in, preparing for a siege. In less than four hours, from her perspective, they had successfully controlled the streets of the most important city on Earth. Those citizens who weren't being held in force field pens were probably doing the sensible thing and hiding inside the buildings. She suspected they were watching from high up in the skyscrapers, watching the invasion unfold below.

She would do her best to keep them safe.

The sound of gunfire—*human* gunfire—interrupted her thoughts. The crackling of alien lasers in response galvanized her and Chinook into action. "Take them down!" shouted Sally, and she accelerated her perceptions as she raced out of the narrow alley she and Chinook had been traversing.

Four alien troopers stood at the top of a subway entrance, firing into the darkness below. One of them had been hit by gunfire and orange blood matted his fur. Sally's blood felt like it was boiling. She couldn't stop the entire invasion by herself, but she could make a difference in this battle. Someone else was fighting back and she would support them however she could.

She ran right up one of the trooper's backs and unclasped his axe. As she sprang over his head, she swept the heavy axe across the barrel. Although the alien was much stronger and heavier than her, the heft of the axe added enough force to her swing to deflect the barrel away from the subway entrance and point it right at another alien. Lightning flashed from the gun's mouth, still instantaneous even to Sally's accelerated perceptions. The beam caught the other alien right beneath its helmet, leaving its throat a smoking ruin.

Before she hit the ground, she twisted around in midair and threw the axe back at the alien from whom she'd stolen it. It flipped around to bury itself deep in the unprotected spot above its breastplate. Sally landed in a crouch and took a moment to take stock of the situation. She'd dispatched two of the aliens herself. An invisible blast of hurricane-force wind was carrying one of the aliens up and away from the ground, directed by a glaring Chinook. As Sally watched, Chinook shredded a small wooden shed and sent the splinters hurtling at the alien. Tornadoes and hurricanes could punch boards through tree trunks. Chinook did the same thing to the alien Warrior.

A hail of bullets burst from the subway stairwell. Although Sally couldn't see the bullets, she knew they were coming faster than she could move and threw herself to the ground. Bullets stippled the last alien's armor, bursting through and splattering his orange blood out in fan-shaped sprays. He staggered, tried to raise his axe, and fell.

Sally decelerated her perceptions to match the rest of the world. She saw a couple of uniformed police officers advancing slowly up the steps, inserting new clips into their pistols as they did so. "Good job, guys," she said.

"Hey, is it safe to come up yet? We've got close to two hundred civilians down below in the dark. Everyone's terrified."

"It's not safe." Chinook landed beside Sally, and the haunted expression had returned to her face. "They're everywhere."

"Except right here," Sally said. "Chinook is right. It's not safe. Not yet. Give us a chance to do our work."

"Are you gonna rescue all of us?" One of the cops shook her head. "By yourselves?"

Sally nodded. "If we have to. This is our town. Our world. We're not going to let a group of interstellar bullies come roaring in here thinking they own the place."

Cheers sounded from down the staircase.

"Listen, we're looking for Penny Lane of Just Cause. She was in the park over there doing a workshop for police Explorers. Do you know who she is? Have you seen her?"

One of the cops nodded. "She captured one of those bastards alive. Shot him in the leg, I think. She took a couple uniforms with her and they loaded the thing into a goddamn horse trailer."

"They're going to the Champions."

"Should we go after them?" asked Chinook.

Sally could see the hope in her young partner's face, and perhaps it would have been the right thing to do. But Jason was still unaccounted for, and so was Detroit Steel. Sally knew they could handle themselves well enough, as could Penny Lane, but she wasn't about to leave her teammates behind to die at the hands of the alien invaders. The centaurian beasts could be killed. She had proven that several times over. They weren't an impossible foe. The more weapons Sally had at her disposal, the sooner they'd be able to save New York. "No, we press onward."

"'Scuse me, ma'am," said of the transit cops. "But what should we do if more'a them things come after us?"

Sally picked up one of the fallen Warriors' laser rifles, zipped down the stairs in a flash, and placed it in the man's hands. "Convince them not to."

Fort Justice
New York Bay

"Welcome to The Tank," Minerva said to March. She'd brought him down into the Combat Simulation Chamber, which was currently filled with a gently swirling mass of gray goo several feet deep. The technicians had ordered the nanites within the chamber to fully disassemble all builds, leaving everything in a raw state. The idea had been Minerva's. She knew March's body carried much of the same nanotech that was inside Harlan Washington, and her hope was that tech had within it enough information to direct a rapid reprogamming of Just Cause's nanite resources.

Harlan Washington had become one of the world's foremost experts on nanotech, and Minerva had seen firsthand how he'd used it to construct devices, buildings, and even vessels. This last had piqued her interest. The Air Force had a secret project called *Daedalus*, which was a spaceship that flew using an experimental antigravity engine. Despite misgivings from General Gershwin, she'd asked for and obtained technical specifications for the *Daedalus*. Her hope was to use the pool of raw materials in the Combat Simulation Chamber in conjunction with the Air Force's plans and March's own nanotech to build an antigravity-powered spaceship that could carry her strike force to attack the invading force. Using the *Daedalus* wasn't an option, as the experimental vessel couldn't carry more than a couple passengers and she would need as many parahuman solders as she could muster in a short time frame.

"I hope it's enough," said March. He didn't have full control over his own nanotech, thanks to Harlan

Washington's infinite paranoia, but he had shown the ability to connect to the CSC computer systems and Minerva felt that would be sufficient for him to guide the construction process.

General Gershwin was against giving a civilian—especially one related to a wanted supervillain—access to classified technical systems, of course, but Minerva had expected nothing less. She'd spoken at length to Juice, director of the Parahuman Resources Agency, and they agreed this would be their best chance to take the fight back to the aliens. Juice gave her permission to plug March into the CSC systems, and began identifying and dispatching parahumans who would make up the strike force. All across the country, American parahumans were being pressed into service. It would take several hours, but Minerva hoped by the time they had a functional nanotech-built spaceship, she would have her parahuman Marines.

"What do you need from me to get started?" Minerva asked.

"Access t-to the systems for now. I might need help later." Minerva felt the palpable distrust from other Just Cause members and staffers and made a careful effort not to only show that she needed March's expertise, but that she trusted him. If they could see her willingness to trust the young man, it might put them more at ease, because lying to Minerva was generally considered an impossibility.

She brought March to the control room next to the Tank. The technicians looked apprehensive at the newcomer, whom they knew was a walking nanotech colony. "Everyone, this is March Washington. He is an outside consultant and has significant first-hand experience in nanotech-based construction of spacefaring vehicles and habitats."

"Huh?" asked one of the techs, who had ketchup stains on his shirt. With her advanced senses, Minerva could smell it from across the room, as well as the crumbs of the sandwich he'd eaten, and the cleanliness of the bakery that had produced the bread. It was a wonder she wasn't ill all the time, with her senses all jacked up many hundreds of times more sensitive than a normal human's. Luckily, she'd learned to filter out most of the massive data input and only really noticed when she was concentrating on something.

One of the other techs snorted. "It means he builds spaceships, Jerry."

"Oh. Cool."

"Mr. Washington is to be granted every courtesy while he's here, including full access to the CSC systems and the nanite bestiary. If he needs a raw material not within inventory, contact me immediately and I will obtain it. Does anyone not understand the gravity of our current situation?"

Nobody spoke up, and Minerva was pleased. "Very well. March, the CSC is yours. Build me a spaceship."

"Yes, m-ma'am." Minerva watched with fascination as a bulge appeared at the end of one of March's fingers, and then reshaped itself into a USB connector. He sat at a duty station and stuck his finger into the waiting USB slot.

Minerva left the CSC, knowing there was nothing else she could accomplish for the time being. Juice was sending her a list of every parahuman who could reasonably participate in an assault beyond the reaches of Earth's atmosphere and she would need to narrow that list down to her strike force. The task would be difficult enough to do if there wasn't a high probability that some or all of those troops would perish in the process.

For herself, Minerva didn't fear death. She didn't seek it out by any means, but when her time came and her end was inevitable, she would meet it head on with all the curiosity she could muster. She didn't want to place others in the line of fire, but knew she would have little choice when it came to saving the world.

Nobody ever wants to be in the position to pick who will live and who will die.

Minerva paused in her upward flight through the stairwell to the main deck. She usually kept a tight lid on her emotions, as they would cloud her judgment when it came to making difficult decisions. She didn't ignore them, because emotions often provided insight into things that logic and sensory perception could not. It was rare for her emotions to get loose and overwhelm her, and at that moment, she felt very small, alone, and unprepared for the hard decisions ahead. She slumped against the railing and took a deep, shuddering breath.

Babe, you all right? Ment's voice filled her head, originating from the spot behind her left ear that always tingled with his telepathic contact.

Michael. Are you stalking me?

Just keeping a few stray neurons on my girl. Your thoughts are tinged blue.

Ment often referred to emotions by color. At its simplest, it was a telepathic form of synaesthesia, but Minerva knew it was a shorthand method for explaining the shadings of emotion to non-telepaths. Michael had once told her an analogy that clarified it for her. Trying to help the telepathically blind to understand emotional coloration was like trying to explain hot air ballooning to a dolphin. *I am worried about Sally and the others, and I am afraid of the costs we will pay for our planned attack upon the aliens.* She took a deep breath and drove the fear and uncertainty from her mind, ascending through the empty core of the stairwell. *I am fine now.*

Babe, you might be fooling everyone else, but I can read your mind. Come up to our room. I'll make you some tea. Rub your shoulders.

Minerva smiled. For a globally talented psychic, Michael could be as transparent as freshly wiped glass. *I'm sure that's all you have in mind.*

Look, if we all gotta go tomorrow, I'd kind of like to celebrate tonight with a bang.

Crude. Crass.

You know you love it.

Minerva smiled. He was right, and he knew it. *Ten minutes. Not a second longer.*

Cool. That'll give us a good seven and a half minutes of cuddling time.

Minerva felt her own body preparing itself, like a naval vessel going from low watch to full alert. *More than I'll need.*

48th Street and 5th Avenue
Manhattan

The aliens got a lucky shot in their first volley, and the motorcycle cop who'd been riding escort got blasted right off his bike, the smoking hole in his chest a mute testament to the swiftness of his passing. Penny jammed down the accelerator in the Central Park Zoo truck she was driving, but with a trailer in tow, it wasn't going to win any races. She knew she should try to be careful about property damage. It was drilled into all their heads at every possible opportunity during training. The PRA would pay for any damage incurred due to parahuman combat in Just Cause's name, but that wouldn't come without a strict lecture and probably ass-chewing by everyone from Juice on down through Mustang Sally.

Penny didn't think *alien invasion* counted as avoidable circumstances, so she plowed the truck right through a pair of abandoned taxis. The cabs spun around with shrieking tires and the shattering of glass. The trailer behind her tilted, in danger of tipping onto its side. She had to slam on her brakes to keep it from bouncing right off the tow ball. She was furious; she'd put in far too much effort to capture her one alien prisoner, and wasn't about to let her captive get taken away from her.

"Follow me," she said to Mustache Cop, who'd told her his name which she'd promptly forgotten. "Keep low. We've got to draw the hostiles away from the trailer."

They spilled out from the driver's side door of the truck. Mustache Cop carried a standard police-issue shotgun while Penny clutched the alien laser rifle. It was long and unwieldy, but she was willing to bet she was far more accurate with it than the aliens were with theirs.

A half dozen of the centaurians approached east up 48th while a trio came at them from the west. They had their rifles slung, perhaps recognizing that they were as likely to shoot each other with their human prey trapped between them. With their axes out and roaring, it was like facing down a horde of barbarian lions. "Behind that truck." Penny raised the laser rifle. "Cover me."

Her first shot went high. Her second went wide right. It was no wonder the aliens were terrible shots; their rifles didn't fire in straight lines, or even along the same line every time. Some kind of failing in their technology, she figured. "This damn thing is useless!" She tossed it aside so it wouldn't encumber her further and drew her pistols.

Mustache Cop fired his shotgun and one of the charging Warriors stumbled and fell. Penny recognized the sound of a solid slug being fired and smiled in approval. Her pistol shots took down two more, one from bullets striking his unprotected throat and the other right in his open mouth. It cleared their path to the west, but the other six rushed in even faster. They didn't act like normal opponents should, taking cover and using it to advance upon the smaller, weaker force. Instead, they charged in upon Penny and Mustache Cop without fear or concern for their own safety. They had to know the humans were armed and dangerous; they just didn't care.

Penny needed to even the odds, and she saw just the thing. She emptied one clip into the fuel tank of a nearby box truck. Gasoline poured out onto the pavement, facilitated by the bullet holes in the top of the tank to allow it to drain more quickly. She didn't smoke, didn't have a lighter, but she did have one flashbang grenade. "Run!" she yelled at Mustache Cop, and threw the grenade toward the growing lake of gasoline.

The sudden, fiery explosion caught the Warriors unawares, and three of them staggered and fell, their furry coats smoldering. The other three continued onward. Penny didn't dare backpedal; if she tripped, she'd be done for. With one hand, she fired at one of the approaching Warriors, catching him in the throat, while with the other hand she threw the empty pistol in a calculated maneuver. The spinning pistol hit the ground right underneath another Warrior's foot and he stumbled. Her last bullet went up into the Warrior's chin, splattering his brains against the inside of his helmet.

The last Warrior reached her and swung his axe in a low sweep. With nowhere else to go, Penny flung herself backward, kicking up her legs so she wouldn't lose them. The whistling axe caught her empty pistol just as she let go of it, shattering it into useless pieces. Her holdout pistol, tucked into an ankle holster, might as well have been in the next borough for how far away it was from her empty hand. She crashed against a parked car, hitting her head hard enough to see stars. It stunned her and she felt trapped in slow motion as she looked up at her assailant. The alien Warrior yanked off his helmet and threw it away. His lips pulled back from his teeth in a fierce snarl or grin as he raised his axe to cleave her in two.

A taxicab slammed into the Warrior from the side, knocking him across the street and against a delivery van. The cab's engine roared as it sandwiched the Warrior between taxi and van. Mustache Cop fought his way past the deployed airbag, lowered his shotgun, and fired it at the alien's unprotected head. He checked his handiwork, then lowered the smoking barrel. "And that's why you don't jaywalk in New York City, you asshole."

Penny managed a shaky laugh. "I wish I'd said that." Her ears were ringing and she was pretty sure she'd suffered a mild concussion. No time for her to accept those symptoms, though. Not with a prisoner still in the trailer. At least, she hoped he was. "Come on, let's get out of here before any more of these guys show up."

They found their trailer still upright and in one piece, and their prisoner was still trapped in the back of it. "Still alive, I see." Mustache Cop peeked through the fresh hole in the trailer wall, still warm from the heat of the laser beam that had passed through it. "You still want to take this guy to Champions HQ?"

"Yeah. It's the best place to go. It's defensible, and if enough of the Champions are on this side of the field, it might be our best place to gather our forces."

"Gather for what?"

"To take back Manhattan." Penny pulled open the passenger side door, making no effort for the driver's seat. "My kid is on the other side of that dome thing. Sooner we knock it down, the sooner I'll get to see him again."

"How are we going to take it down? I figure they've been trying since the thing went up in the first place."

"I don't know, but I bet our passenger does, and we've got people who can get into his mind and find out what he knows."

"You think they'll even understand it?"

"I have no idea." Penny laughed bitterly. "It's my first alien invasion."

Monkeyworld

Garragh was strangely pleased to learn the Monkey Warrior who'd captured him was still alive following his fellows' ill-advised attempt at a rescue. Of course, they probably hadn't even known he was locked inside the wheeled box. They'd been out hunting easy prey, seeking the weak, the infirm, the alone. Based upon the number of dead Warriors he saw from his limited vantage point, Garragh knew that where they'd expected an easy victim, they had found instead a dangerous predator.

Under other circumstances, he'd be honored to be subordinate to one such as this Monkey, and at least in his mind, there was less shame in being captive of a powerful Warrior than a weak and fragile Monkey. At least, he kept telling himself that. He still lived, at least, which meant he still had an opportunity to die a proper Warrior's death and salvage his honor.

A death unearned is a life wasted. The phrase from the Warrior's Way had always seemed off to him in some way. One could live an amazing life, full of triumph and glorious victories, and it would all be for naught if one died from a simple accident or disease? How could a single event erase the magnitude of a life devoted to one's Clan? Garragh hadn't accomplished anything of note in his life. From his earliest days as a rough-and-tumble cub to the many years of Warrior schooling to becoming part of the group of Warriors chosen to open the throat of Monkeyworld, his life had been singularly uneventful. If he were to die here, now, on this alien world, he would be unremembered. Even if he were to manage to slay the great Monkey Warrior who had captured him, who would ever know of his success?

He would live. He had to. Death at the hands of the Monkeys would be weak. The greater Warriors of his Clan would expect nothing less of him. They already thought him a failure. He had more to accomplish in his life. Victories yet unearned taunted him. He didn't want to die a Warrior's Death. He'd take a long, accomplished life with a coward's death at the end. The thought was pure blasphemy, and his life was forfeit for even considering it.

The Warrior opened a door in the front of his cage and stepped into the sweltering hot box, pointing its weapon at him with one hand. It held a clear bottle in the other with clear liquid that he hoped was water. He licked his lips and opened his mouth, still unable to move his hands because of the clever binding the Monkeys had applied. The Warrior squirted water into his mouth and he swallowed as much as he could, trying to take strength from the life-giving liquid. The Monkeys were clever; in the space of only a few twelfths, they'd managed to capture him, find out what he needed, and implemented some kind of plan despite the presence of so many Warriors and the overarching shield. They weren't just clever, either. They were a force of might unto themselves.

It occurred to him that the Clanmistress might have underestimated the military prowess of the Monkeys. He began to see the purpose of his mission at last. He'd been captured not because of his own weakness, but because of a need for him to learn everything he could of the Monkeys in order to report back to the Submistresses.

The foolish Warrior charges blindly; the wise Warrior advances with eyes wide open.

Garragh kept his eyes open, studying the Warrior who had captured him, who had wrapped his wound, who gave him water. His head throbbed, either from blood loss, or from the heat inside the mobile box, or just from trying to understand the mysteries of the Monkey race. Just when he was beginning to think they were ready to leave, the other Monkey handed some items to his captor, and Garragh's nose wrinkled at the new scents.

The Warrior unwrapped some kind of food bar and took a bite. Garragh's stomach rumbled, reminding him it had been many twelfths since he'd last eaten. The Warrior chewed on its bar, gazing at Garragh. He wondered what thoughts were going through the Monkey's primitive mind.

When the Warrior tore a piece of its food bar loose and held it out toward Garragh, the move caught him completely by surprise. Was it offering him part of its food? That was tantamount to an insult, implying he couldn't provide for himself, except it was the truth. He'd lost all his rations when the dropship was destroyed, and had taken nothing but water since before first setting foot upon Monkeyworld. He decided perhaps it wasn't an insult any more than when the Warrior had wrapped his wound. It was some kind of primitive ritual. It had to be.

The bar didn't smell of anything but chemicals, and he turned his head away after sniffing at it. The idea of food sounded wonderful, but whatever the Warrior was eating was inedible as far as he was concerned. His rejection seemed to generate more interest from his captor, and shortly the Monkey brought him a selection of different offerings, unwrapping a clear covering from each.

He nosed with interest two things that he risked tasting. The first was some kind of smooth fat with an odd bacterial odor and a greasy texture. The other was recognizable as flesh, although it had none of the scents of fresh kill about it and in fact smelled preserved, like Hind did for long journeys when fresh meat wasn't available. It had a gamy, tangy flavor like nothing he'd eaten before. He didn't know if it would make him sick, but his stomach didn't reject it as he wolfed it down.

He knew the Monkeys were studying his every move, but he was studying theirs too. They were *kind* to their prisoners, in a way that bespoke of weakness. And yet, they were also ferocious Warriors. The dichotomy made no sense to him, and he wondered where it would all lead.

Low Earth Orbit
Hind Fleet

Harlan nearly died from his exuberance to attack the Submistress Hind. As fast as his nanotech armor fed itself out through his pores to become a second, impervious skin, the Warriors guarding Hsharra were almost faster. A flung axe creased the armor over Harlan's side where it hadn't fully solidified yet. The blade cut would have cut deep into his side and killed him where he stood if the armor had deployed the slightest bit slower. As it was, the blow staggered him and his monitoring tech warned him of the armor breach and wound. It hurt for a moment before nanotech nerve blockers shut off the local pain receptors and other began rebuilding his damaged flesh.

The Warrior who'd thrown his axe followed up with a flying tackle, bearing Harlan to the deck like a lion taking down a gazelle. The armor softened the blow but the impact still made his head spin. The heavy centaurian tried to crush him beneath his forefeet while reaching down to try to tear off his head. The fool creature thought him unarmed, but Harlan's blue and red armorsuit contained numerous surprises. He fired his wrist lasers into the Hind's belly. The Warrior collapsed with a groan as his charred organs failed.

Harlan activated the suit's buzzsaw feature, modeled after the parahuman ability of Just Cause Chicago hero Carver. Rapidly vibrating blades emerged from his knuckles. With a splattering whine, they carved through the fallen Hind like hot knives through butter, freeing Harlan from beneath the creature's bulk.

Hsharra was fleeing for the detention chamber's door, her instruments bouncing off her hide as she ran. Harlan targeted one of his shoulder-mounted micromissiles and fired. The missile struck the control panel by the door and shredded it in a small explosion. He'd already deduced what would happen based upon the knowledge he'd already gleaned from his subtle hacking into the Hind systems. The pressure door slammed shut, ostensibly to contain a fire from spreading to the rest of the ship, nearly cutting off Hsharra's toes as she skidded to a halt.

Harlan didn't have time to deal with her yet. He still had one more Warrior to deal with. That monster waded into him, swinging its axe hard enough to make it whistle. Harlan kept his buzzsaws activated. If the Warrior wanted to fight hand to hand, Harlan would oblige him. He could have just as easily used his lasers or another micromissile to finish off the creature, but Harlan had a reason for wanting to use a more brutal attack.

He caught the swinging blade against the armor of his forearm, thickened for just such a purpose. The armor held but warning indicators showed all over as the suit tried to compensate for the Hind's sheer strength. Before the Warrior could pull the axe back for another blow, Harlan used his buzzsaws to sever the Warrior's hand at the wrist. Orange blood splattered everywhere as the axe clattered to the deck. Undaunted by the grievous injury Harlan had just inflicted, the Warrior slashed at him with his claws. Harlan responded by slicing off its other hand. The Hind roared defiance at him and Harlan blew the creature's head apart with a missile.

He stepped over the smoldering body toward Submistress Hsharra. She had a pistol of some kind pointed at him. He targeted it with his lasers and melted it before she could pull the trigger. He smiled beneath his visor as he saw for the first time what fear looked like on a Hind. He paused in his approach, savoring her fear as he picked up the last warrior's fallen axe. "HSHARRA," he said, his suit modulating his voice to sound more resonant and threatening. "CALL ME *MONKEY* AGAIN AND IT'LL BE THE LAST WORD YOU EVER SPEAK."

"What will you do . . . human? Where will you go?"

Harlan pressed the tip of the axe against Hsharra's throat. Even though she was far larger and heavier than him, he knew she was no fool, and she had seen him tear apart two Warriors. If she so much as flicked an aggressive finger in his direction, he'd lay her open from skull to tail, and she knew it. "THAT IS NOT YOUR CONCERN. FOR NOW, THOUGH, TAKE ME TO THE NEAREST AIRLOCK AND I WILL LET YOU LIVE."

"My life is forfeit if I let you escape."

"PROBABLY SHOULD HAVE THOUGHT OF THAT BEFORE ATTACKING MY WORLD." Harlan used his lasers to cut a smoking hole in the pressure door. "NOW LEAD ON BEFORE I DECIDE TO MAKE MY OWN EXIT."

Despite her protest, Hsharra led Harlan through the ship's corridors. He kept the axe pressed against her throat. Every time his sensors notified him of other Hind approaching, he told her to warn them away. She did so, growling out orders that she probably thought he couldn't translate. His processor was learning more and more Hind with every phrase, and he already had a fair idea of what was happening. She was directing the Warriors to move parallel to them through the ship and to rush him at the upcoming intersection. As they approached the intersection, Harlan turned up the volume of his external speakers. "RETREAT OR I WILL KILL YOUR SUBMISTRESS." His suit broadcast his words in the Hind language.

"Do as he says," said Submistress Hsharra.

They crossed the corridor intersection. Harlan saw a dozen Hind Warriors waiting uncertainly down either direction, but none of them stepped forward to attack him. He was a little disappointed—he would have relished the idea of taking on so many at once. He'd never had the opportunity to cut loose in full combat in his nanotech suit. It seemed Hsharra was less interested in honor and more in her survival. He could respect that choice, at least. He spotted what he thought was an airlock. "THERE."

"You are going back into space? Do you not realize you will be destroyed? At least here, I can protect you. We can come to some kind of arrangement."

Harlan snorted. "I'VE SEEN HOW WELL YOUR PEOPLE SHOOT. I'M NOT WORRIED. YOU'RE NOT PROTECTING ANYTHING EXCEPT YOUR OWN PELT. I HAVE AN ARRANGEMENT IN MIND."

"What arrangement?" asked Hsharra.

Harlan stepped into the airlock. "I WANT YOU TO DELIVER A MESSAGE TO YOUR CLANMISTRESS. TELL HER TO LEAVE. ALL OF YOU. IMMEDIATELY. PICK UP YOUR TOYS AND GO HOME. DELETE ALL RECORDS OF THIS STAR SYSTEM FROM YOUR DATABASE. FORGET WE EXIST. DO THAT, AND MAYBE HUMANITY WILL FORGET ABOUT THE HIND. IF YOU STAY, WE WILL DESTROY EVERY LAST ONE OF YOU WHO CAME HERE HOPING TO CONQUER MONKEYS. THEN WE WILL TEAR APART YOUR SHIPS TO LEARN EVERY LAST SECRET ABOUT YOUR PEOPLE. THEN WE WILL COME FOR

THE REST OF YOU. THERE WILL BE NO MERCY. NO ARRANGEMENTS. THE HIND WILL BE EXTERMINATED, LIKE A HOUSEHOLD PEST."

Harlan blew open the exterior airlock door with a missile and let the sudden outburst of atmosphere carry him into space. He kept the Hind axe clutched in one hand as a trophy of his escape and flew along the hull of the vessel in which he'd been held. The vessel's guns tracked him, but as he'd seen his first time assaulting them, they were poor at aiming. He poured on the speed from his boot jets and for the first time in many years, began descending toward the planet of his birth.

CHAPTER SIX

U♞U

96th and Park

Darkness came early as the alien shield overhead blocked out enough of the evening sunlight for it officially to be too dark to see. The shield itself had a faint glow, coloring the sky a dull yellow-green, barely brighter than darkness but enough to obscure the stars beyond. It didn't cast any light upon the city beneath it, and with the power knocked out, it gave the late spring air a sense of oppressive foreboding. It reminded Sally of the supercell thunderstorms that occasionally roared across Denver in high summer, when the skies would turn greenish gray and hail would suddenly blanket the landscape. She'd been stuck in Just Cause Headquarters during a close call from a tornado, and it had been a solemn reminder that most superheroes were no more effective than ants when it came to the awesome power of Nature's fury.

The flat, featureless sky above gave Sally the peculiar impression that she was underground instead of outdoors. The giant shadowy faces of Manhattan's skyscrapers only added to that feeling. Occasional firelight flickered from high windows as civilians lit candles to stave off the unfamiliar darkness of an unlit New York. On one hand, Sally wished they would think things through and keep their lights hidden, for it made them targets. On the other, most of those she saw were well above ground level, and the aliens were clearly too large to pass through human-sized doors or stairwells. They were probably as safe as they could get, given the situation on the streets below.

Sally had been forming a theory on the nature of the alien invasion, and wished she had a real science fiction or history buff with whom to talk it out. She'd broached her idea to Chinook, but the younger hero had merely shrugged it off. Maybe she wasn't interested, or more likely, the stress of the situation was taking over her higher thought processes.

The aliens had strengthened their outposts. Bright blue-tinged lights shone outward from atop tall poles, fully illuminating the streets and buildings around their positions so approaching one unseen would be impossible without the benefit of parahuman stealth abilities. Guards paced outside the holding pens, carrying laser rifles and axes, yowling to each other occasionally while staring intently into the darkness beyond the edge of their lights. Atop the dropships, devices swept back and forth or rotated, suggesting radar or some similar kind of technology to Sally. The dropships also had turrets that swiveled around at regular intervals as if waiting for someone to come regain the controls.

Civilians cowered inside the holding pens, or slept. The aliens didn't allow them any privacy to relieve themselves, so most of the prisoners either managed a makeshift wall or else considerately turned away from their comrades. The aliens had raided stores and brought food and water to their captives, which gave Sally hope that they might yet end the conflict.

The blood on her own hands was bothering her. She'd killed before the aliens' arrival, and most likely would again in the future. Killing went with the territory for parapowered law enforcement, and sometimes it was unavoidable. Still, these creatures had crossed perhaps hundreds or thousands of light years to come to Earth. They'd evolved beneath a completely different star, with a completely different culture. Maybe this invasion they had staged was their own way of instigating a First Contact scenario. Maybe the idea of non-intervention that *Star Trek* had popularized didn't work in real life. She hoped once everything was resolved that future generations of humans or aliens wouldn't look at her and see only a monster.

"Hey, how you holding up, kiddo?" she asked Chinook to try to distract herself.

Chinook sighed. "I'm tired. Like, I could go to sleep right now."

"Me too. Believe me, I don't see sleeping as a necessity so much as it's my favorite recreational activity. Soon as it's safe to do so, we're taking a nap."

Chinook smiled in the near-darkness, or at least, Sally thought she did. She didn't want to pull out her phone and turn on the flashlight feature to check. She figured to conserve the battery was most important in case she really needed it later. "Hey, I see light reflecting off the windows over there. Like, firelight."

"Another candle?" Sally turned to look.

"No, a reflection. Something's on fire over there, a couple blocks away."

"We should go check it out in case someone needs help," said Sally.

They advanced cautiously, keeping close to the buildings to be less visible in the growing darkness. As they reached an intersection, Chinook gasped. A tremendous battle had been fought between the invaders and opposing forces. Sally counted what she thought was eight of the alien bodies—it was hard to tell, because a couple of them had been torn apart. Three dead humans lay amid the aliens, all wearing police uniforms. One of them had been shot by a laser while the other two must have fallen victim to the alien axes. Their bulletproof vests were gone, as were their weapons and radios.

Sally scanned the surrounding area, trying to piece together what had happened. Parked cars were dented and twisted. A couple of nearby buildings had windows or walls bashed inward. Sally's heart skipped a beat. Was this Jason's work? "Come on," she said to Chinook. "Pull yourself together. We might just have found the heart of the resistance."

Chinook's shoulders were shaking and although she could still hover, she seemed to have lost the will to fly. Sally took her hand and pulled her along like a child tugging a balloon. They rounded the corner and saw an honest-to-goodness human fort. Cars had been stacked like bricks, crushed together to form a solid wall. A row of trash barrels encircled the walls, fires blazing within them. Sally spotted people behind the wall of wrecks, watching as they approached. A van's engine turned over and it rolled back to reveal a gap in the wall. A figure stepped through that gap, with dreadlocks like steel springs and skin that blazed like chrome in the firelight.

"Shawna!" cried Sally. She ran forward to embrace her teammate, Detroit Steel.

"Damn, girl, am I glad to see you," Shawna said. "I was beginning to think I was on my own up here."

"Hey, what are we then, Steel? Chopped liver?" called a man from behind the barricade.

"Y'all can relax. The cavalry has arrived." Shawna smiled down at Sally. "Where's everyone else?"

Sally shook her head. "It's just us. We came looking for you, and Penny . . . and Jason. H-have you seen him?"

"Oh damn. No, I haven't. I been busy. When shit went down and those six-limbed assholes started coming after civilians, I rounded up what backup I could and started taking back the streets."

"On your own?" Chinook's eyes were wide, haunted with the things she'd seen over the past few hours.

"I grew up fighting in the streets of Detroit. Ain't no different than today, except these dudes can take a punch better than most." Shawna fingered a long scar in the metal of her left arm. "This will heal, eventually, but it hurts like a son of a bitch." She looked past Sally into the darkness beyond. "Listen, we best get behind the wall. Those guys have tried to hit us twice and we drove them back each time. It's safer behind some cover. I got some sentries holed up on the upper floors of these buildings around here, but radios ain't workin' so good."

Sally and Chinook followed Shawna inside the stockade where they found a makeshift combination refugee and army camp. Shawna's forces consisted of six NYPD officers, two private security men, an MTA officer, and four gangbangers, who'd banded together in the face of a common enemy. They'd raided the stock of a pawnshop and were all armed to the teeth. Shawna built the semicircular palisade of wrecked cars from the face of an eight story office building and about forty civilians were huddled inside, sharing food and water around. "You need something to eat?" Shawna asked. "There's a cafeteria inside this building here. We're keeping the cooler closed as much as we can to keep the food from going bad, but it'll take awhile for anyone to go hungry. I expect we'll have this situation wrapped up before it gets to that point."

"Is there any coffee?" Sally asked.

"'Fraid not, but they got energy drinks if you want one of them."

"Yeah, I do." Sally couldn't stand them, but she needed something to help her keep going. "You need to get all these civilians off of the ground. Hind can't fit through most doors or climb stairs. It's safer that way."

"Good idea," Shawna said, and ordered the civilians to get up to the third floor, high enough to be out of immediate danger but low enough that nobody should have difficulty getting there.

Sally and Shawna compared notes on the Hind. Besides what Sally already knew, Shawna had some important and useful information. "We already know they don't see so good, but we think they can see into the infrared. That's why we lit the fires. Since we did, they haven't come back. Either they got tired of gettin' beat or they decided we ain't worth the effort."

"Shawna, you've been in a lot more street-level fights than I have," Sally said. "What do you think? What are our chances?"

"Pretty damn good if you ask me. These Hind, I don't think they was expectin' resistance. They're like bullies. They assume folks are gonna just curl up and cower in fear around them. Bullies don't know what to do when people fight back against them. They make stupid choices in a fight, and they ain't afraid to die. That's a good combination to impress dumb folks, but anyone with half a brain can see they're mostly just frontin'." She scratched a steel finger across the curb on which she and Sally sat.

"That's a comforting thought," said Sally. "It sounded like there were only five ships that arrived. If that's all there are, and more haven't come while this damn shield is up, maybe we do have a pretty good chance."

"Listen, boss, one of the civvies in here is a surveyor. He went up to the roof with his gear and took some measurements before it got dark. He said this shield isn't really all that big. It stops about the middle of Harlem to the north and based on the arc, he thinks it might reach the southern tip of Manhattan. That means the Champions are on this side of it."

Sally wanted to say *Yeah, but they're only Champions*, because the Champions were like the triple-A minor leaguers compared to the major league Just Cause teams. She didn't follow through with the retort because she knew they might be the only other parahuman assets left to combat the Hind inside the shield. The GPS on her phone wasn't any help in telling her whether Jason's studio was on the inside or outside of the field. Either way, he had to have been very close to it when the cover came down over the city. Sally hated herself for what she was going to say, because it was the rational, unselfish route. "We need to get to Champions HQ. It's all well and good that the police and gangsters want to fight back, but if we're going to get this shield down, it's going to take the kind of help that we can only get from other parahumans."

Shawna slapped her knee, making a dull ringing sound. "Thought you'd never ask. When do we go?"

Sally sighed. "Soon as I can choke down this energy drink. Gack, it's like cherry-flavored ass."

"Eat a lot of that, do you?"

Fort Justice
New York Bay

Minerva composed herself after her brief interlude with Michael. Her psionic lover had successfully gotten her to relax and stay distracted for ten minutes, as promised. He lay back in the bed, covered modestly with a sheet. He looked satisfied, not bothering to speak to her with his voice when telepathy was far more intimate. *You okay, babe?*

She buckled her breastplate on over her burgundy shift. She didn't have to wear her costume in headquarters, but it made others feel more comfortable around her. *I am afraid*, she thought.

You're never afraid.

You are lying.

Michael rolled onto his side and watched as she wrapped her heavy cape around her shoulders. *Yes, I am, because I know it makes you feel better.*

To be lied to? She clasped her cape and slipped her helmet over her raven locks.

To be loved enough to be lied to about things like this.

Minerva smiled. "You're right," she said aloud. "I love you too."

"When this is over, we need to go away. Way away. Someplace exotic."

"I know just the place." Minerva flew across the room to plant a kiss upon his forehead, enjoying every molecule of his scent with her hyper-aware senses. "I've got to go to work. Keep trying to get a good connection through that shield."

"I am. It's weird. I've never encountered tech that could block psionics like this is."

"Perhaps it will give us some scientific insight into the process behind psionics."

Michael shrugged. "If you say so."

"I do. If you discover anything, report it to me." She knew she sounded cold and uncaring, but he would see through that. When Minerva was all set for business, she had no time for niceties like polite discourse. Her cape fluttered behind her as she flew from the room, not bothering to take the time to walk at a measured, calming pace.

They were at war.

She checked in on March's progress with the assault craft. She found him directly plugged into the CSC's control systems via bio-organic cables from his fingertips. His eyes were shut but she could see them twitching like he was in fast REM sleep. Behind him, General Gershwin was pacing a new groove in the floor. "I can't tell what he's doing," said the General to Minerva's inquiring gaze. "But he's definitely doing something." He gestured to the swirling nanotech storm below. "That pile there appears to be forming some kind of framework, while that group up there—" He pointed to the wall high up on the side of the CSC. "I'm pretty sure they're making a door."

Minerva smiled. "Makes sense. We don't want to be the folks building replica ships in their basements who then can't get them out into the water." Her smile vanished. "Do we have an estimated time of completion for a spaceworthy ship yet, General?"

Gershwin took his hat off and rubbed his hand across a head long devoid of hair. "He's the brains. I'm just here to flash the brass." He nodded at March.

"I th-think it's going okay," said the young man. "Uncle Harlan's nanites are d-doing the hard work. There should be room for a c-crew of eight plus the p-pilot." He paused, clearly gathering himself for a hard question. "Is there any n-news about S-Sally?"

Minerva shook her head. "The only way we've been able to communicate through this field at all has been via telepathy, and that has proven to be unreliable. She was alive as recently as two hours ago, and I believe she is resourceful enough to stay that way." She sighed. "Although she is well-considered for a speedster, she can be headstrong, as I'm sure you know."

March bowed his head and said nothing. He knew enough about Minerva's sensory abilities to shred any illusions that he and Sally had kept their feelings for each other secret.

"March . . . I'm not here to judge you," said Minerva. "I—"

Before she could finish her thought, Fort Justice alarms sounded. A moment later the public address system warned of an incoming object on a straight-line approach toward Fort Justice from an orbital vector. Minerva raced to the top of the Tank, through the exit, and flew down the hall to the Command Center. "Is it a missile?" she asked as she came to a halt, her cape flapping around her.

"Unknown, ma'am, but it's under power and descending on a collision course at supersonic speeds. ETA one hundred seconds."

"Arm all point defense weaponry. All active Just Cause members to the top deck. All civilians brace for impact. Do not fire without my direct order," said Minerva, and she flew outside.

She spotted the bright spark trailing a fiery contrail right away and zoomed her vision in upon it. She saw concentric shockwaves in the air around it from its supersonic descent. The object glowed white-hot from re-entry but despite that, she could make out its shape.

It was humanoid, with a blue-and-red-tinged metallic skin shining beneath its shielding. It wore shoulder-mounted turrets and control surfaces broke up its smooth edges. She raised her phone to her lips, still staring unblinking into the darkening sky. "All units stand by. Do not fire. I repeat. Do not fire."

"What is it?" Amber asked as she and the other team members hurried onto the deck. The raw, untested heroes practically radiated terror—Minerva could smell it even over the sea breeze—and having the clomping nickel-coated presence of Hector as their escort didn't help.

"It's Destroyer," Minerva said. "Or at least, it certainly appears to be."

"Ain't he the one who been hasslin' Just Cause forever?" Hector asked. "Why ain't you shootin' his ass down then?"

"It's . . . complicated. He did warn us about the attack. Past history is not always indicative of current attitudes." Minerva smiled at Hector. "I think you would understand that better than some, Hector."

"What do you want us to do?" asked Spray, already soaked from head to toe and standing in a puddle.

"Wait for him to arrive," Minerva said. "If he attacks, you may retaliate, but under no circumstances are you to attack first. I believe he may have important information about the alien fleet to share."

The glowing spark brightened as Destroyer approached, firing thrusters to shed velocity. Then all of a sudden he was hovering over the helipad on his boot jets, suit glowing a dull red. He had—of all things—an *axe* clutched in one hand, but he held it at his side instead of raising it in threat. "COOL ME," he ordered.

Minerva nodded at Spray. "Hose him down."

Spray cut loose with a jet of water, dousing the battlesuit. A great cloud of steam erupted, making everyone duck at the sudden blast of wet heat. Destroyer cut his jets and dropped to the platform. He stepped forward, keeping his hands open in a neutral position. As he moved, his armor seemed to fold in upon itself and absorbed right into his skin until he stood before them in a simple one-piece black bodysuit. He looked even older to Minerva than he had the last time she'd seen him. Fresh wrinkles marred his skin and his hair was more gray than black.

"Minerva," he said.

"Mr. Washington."

"I trust you received my warning."

"We did. We also received your nephew." Minerva glanced at the others. "Stand down, Just Cause, on my authority. I will assume full responsibility for Mr. Washington's behavior while he is here."

Hector didn't move, keeping his arms crossed. "I ain't part of Just Cause, and I ain't lettin' this dude out of my sight." He narrowed his eyes amid his shiny nickel skin.

"That's fine, Hector. Harlan, this is Hector. He will be acting as your liaison to Just Cause while you are in Fort Justice and make sure you don't travel unaccompanied to any sensitive areas." Minerva smiled at the Hispanic man.

"I'm gonna what?" he asked.

"You're guarding him."

"Oh, that's what I thought you said." Hector glanced downward. "You gonna lose the axe, *hombre*, or are we gonna have to have a discussion?"

Harlan snorted. "It's my prize. I claimed it from one of the Hind vessels. I'm not going to sully it with something so pedestrian as human blood. Or whatever you have."

"You stuck-up son of a—"

Minerva cleared her throat, a soft sound that made Hector shut his mouth like it was a mousetrap. She turned back to Harlan. "Now that's cleared up, we have some debriefing to attend to before we incorporate you into our plans." She gestured to the entrance to the Command Center. "Please."

Deep down, she dared to hope just a little. Harlan Washington was not a good man, but he was unquestionably a brilliant one, and with him on their side, their chances of success had gone up just a bit more.

Champions Headquarters—inside Hind shield
Battery Park, Manhattan

The closer Penny got to Battery Park, the more concerned she grew that the shield would cut them off. The sparkling wall drew closer and closer but when she reached the entrance to the Champions compound, she realized the field was literally bisecting the headquarters building.

Costumed Champions guarded the entrance. "Stop right there, please," said the unnaturally amplified voice of a chubby young man Penny had known for a long time as Shouty Ed.

She stepped out of the car. "Ed, it's me. Penny."

Ed came out from behind the cover of the guard shack. "Penny! Did Just Cause get through or are you stuck behind this field too?"

"No, I'm stuck here same as you. But I've got big news. We've captured an alien soldier. We have a prisoner. Tell me Dolittle is on this side of the field."

Ed looked amazed and relieved at the same time. "She is. You think she'll be able to communicate with it?" Dolittle was a veterinarian's dream: a telepath who could communicate with animals. Animals didn't speak in language so much as concepts, but she could translate them like a native.

"I hope so." Penny got out of the truck and turned to Mustache Cop. "Make sure our prisoner is still alive." He nodded.

"We haven't seen any of the aliens except at a distance," said Shouty Ed. "Surfboy's had us digging in to mount a defense if we need to. Most of the group is on the outside of the shield. There are only six of us on this side of it."

"Who's available?" asked Penny. She trained her weapon on the rear of the trailer as Mustache Cop prepared to open it.

"Me, Dolittle, Surfboy, E-Dog, Toxic, and Spotlight."

Penny tried not to grimace. Not a heavy hitter in the bunch. Toxic was closest to a high-powered hero with her ability to control man-made chemicals and pollutants. The rest were exactly the sort of parahumans that made up the bulk of the Champions: low-level powers that could be useful in limited, specific circumstances at best. "Get everyone out here. This guy is injured and I don't know how hard he's going to be to handle."

Shouty Ed nodded, turned, and called toward the headquarters building in the near distance, his voice booming with his parahuman amplification. "All Champions to the entrance. Repeat, all Champions to the entrance."

The other five Champions hurried out from the building up the short drive to the entrance, led by the low-flying team leader Surfboy. Toxic floated herself on a noxious cloud of pollutants she'd drawn out of the air. "Good to see you, Penny," Toxic said. "How's life in the big leagues?"

"Exciting," Penny said. "Especially when aliens are attacking. I brought you guys one. Let's get him inside and let Dolittle work her magic on him."

Dolittle was a reedy woman with glasses that made her face seem much smaller than it was. Her hair was pulled back in a sloppy ponytail and she wore some plain purple scrubs. "I don't know if I can talk to an alien," she said, watching as Penny and Mustache Cop worked at getting their captive out of the trailer. Penny couldn't tell if he was unconscious, asleep, or suffering from something else. He'd slumped to the trailer floor and they were having to drag him out.

Surfboy circled the area, keeping a watch out for any approaching enemies. His low-altitude flight power wouldn't be any help in moving the captive. "Nobody will have a better chance than you will," he said.

Penny struggled with the heavy alien. He seemed half asleep and not able to move his legs very well. "Come on, you bastard, get out." She struggled in the dark of the trailer, trying to pull on the soldier. "If you're faking it, I will put a bullet in the back of your skull." She stopped wrestling and turned to Dolittle. "Can you tell him that?"

"I'll try. Spot, can you give me some light please?"

Spotlight took off his sunglasses and light spilled forth from his eyes, illuminating the alien soldier inside the trailer. "Man, he's a big bastard, isn't he? Four legs and arms too. He's a whatchacallit, a centaur."

Dolittle stepped up to the ramp. Penny and Mustache Cop raised their rifles, prepared to unleash suppressing fire upon the alien soldier should he react aggressively. Sweat broke out on Dolittle's face as she concentrated, trying to reach into the alien mind to achieve effective communication.

After several tension-filled minutes, Penny began to think it was a lost cause, but then Dolittle moved clear of the ramp. "I got through to him. He's hurting and exhausted. I think he's used to a higher oxygen content than we have in our atmosphere, so it's hard for him to stay alert."

"So he's a him," said Penny. "Got that much right at least. Does he have a name?"

"Garragh."

"Sounds like a snarl. Can he understand us?"

"No. He thinks of us as monkeys."

"I'd be offended, but it's not really inaccurate," Penny said. "But can you make yourself understood? Can you talk to him?"

"Yes, I think so."

"Tell him we'll get him some oxygen and if he needs food or water or anything, we'll do our best to accommodate him, but we expect his cooperation. I gave him a piece of string cheese and some jerky, but I don't know if it's going to cause problems for him."

Dolittle looked at Garragh as he slowly backed out of the trailer on his wounded leg. "That's a pretty complex concept. I'm used to asking animals where it hurts and what they ate and stuff like that."

"You're a Champion. Stretch yourself." Surfboy landed beside her. "I can't see anything out there but I really don't like us being out in the open like this. At least the building is fortified. Let's go."

Shouty Ed stared in wonder at the alien Warrior. "I'm impressed you managed to capture him."

"I had help." Penny nodded at Mustache Cop, whose name she still couldn't remember.

"He'll never fit in through the door," said Toxic. "Take him into the garage, maybe?"

Dolittle wrinkled her nose. "It's gross in there."

Toxic shrugged. "I'll do what I can." She flew ahead of the others and shortly a cloud of noxious chemicals and sludge rolled out from the open garage door.

The very edge of the force field cut right into the side of Champions headquarters, bisecting it like a knife. Up close inside the garage it had a shimmering glow with rainbow swirls like oil floating on water. The field cut through one of the two Champions vans but appeared to have missed their motorboat, for it bobbed up and down on the dock, bumping gently against the shield and making traceries of energy skitter away with every impact.

Spotlight and E-Dog pulled some emergency blankets out of a supply closet and spread them on the floor so the alien would have a place to rest that wouldn't be on the floor, newly clean from oil stains after Toxic had pulled them out of the concrete. Under the watchful eyes of Penny and Mustache Cop, the alien Warrior limped into the garage and laid on the blankets, clearly weakened from his ordeal.

"E-Dog, go get him some water and food. Meat, raw or cooked," Dolittle said with all the presence of an emergency room doctor. "Toxic, are there any oxygen canisters in any of the maintenance cabinets or vehicles?"

"I'll check," Toxic said. She rummaged around the garage and eventually found an emergency oxygen bottle inside one of the vans. Between the roll of duct tape in Penny's bag and some hose from the vehicle maintenance locker, they managed to fashion a crude oxygen mask.

When they were finished, Penny held it up to show the alien. "Dolittle, tell him this is to help him breathe better."

"I'll try," said Dolittle. "I'm not sure I'm making myself understood. His mind isn't an animal mind."

"We're all animals," retorted Penny. "We have an opportunity here to try to understand the mindset of these invaders, and maybe we can figure out how to resolve this whole incident before they nuke New York." She held the oxygen mask up to the alien, who recoiled even though Dolittle tried to calm him. "Dammit, Garragh, we're trying to help you," she muttered.

"Garragh," said the alien, emphasizing the first part of the name and adding a rolling growl into the middle of it.

Penny's eyes widened. She glanced at Dolittle, who shrugged helplessly. She tried again. "*Garrr—*agh?"

"Garragh," the alien repeated.

Penny pointed at the alien and said his name, then pointed at herself and said "Penny."

"*Pern—rhee.*"

Dolittle jumped up and down in excitement. "That's it. That's the connection I was trying to find. I think I can understand his thoughts better now."

"Good. Find out why his people came here. What they really want." Penny cracked open the oxygen bottle and made a show of inhaling from the makeshift breath mask. When she held it up to Garragh a second time, he didn't back away. She watched his sides expand as he took in a lungful of oxygen. His eyes brightened beneath his brow ridge and he licked his nose like cats did.

E-Dog returned with a tray containing some slices of lunch meat and a bottle of water. "Sorry, it's just bologna. I didn't think I should go shopping and it's all we have."

Garragh's nose wrinkled and he lowered his head to sniff at the tray. "He's interested, and hungry,"

Dolittle reported. "I, uh, think maybe you should free his hands. It's hurting him to have them pulled back so tightly behind him."

"They're handcuffs. They're not supposed to be pleasant," said Penny. She looked into Garragh's eyes. "I'm going to release you. Behave yourself. You know I can kill you if I need to. Tell him that."

Dolittle frowned. "I'm not going to tell him that."

Penny glared at her. "This entire situation was precipitated by his people. They're the aggressors. We are defending our homeworld here. Tell him if he acts up, I'll put another bullet in him and he gets chained up again. He wants to live, he's going to have to earn his keep, starting by answering our questions. You got that, Garragh?"

"*Pernrhee*," said the alien.

Penny released his cuffs.

Monkeyworld

The Monkeys brought him better air, and slices of some kind of meat by-product, laden with salts and chemicals until they were nearly inedible, but Garragh made himself eat them. The Monkeys were treating him with suspicious kindness, which he didn't understand in the least. It must have been something unique to their species. Nevertheless, he thought he should do what he could to regain his strength and to learn about his captors, because what he learned might be useful to the Clanmistress.

The one with the lenses upon her eyes, whose name was an unpronounceable garble of howling and spitting, had some kind of way of communicating with him without speaking. It was as if she had a transmitter broadcasting right into his brain. She didn't use words, which would have been incomprehensible to him anyway, but with feelings and basic urges.

Throughout all of it, the Warrior who'd captured him, Pernrhee, kept issuing orders to the other Monkeys. It clarified her role. She wasn't a deviant, but a high-ranking Mistress. There were accounts in the Hindraa Histories of Mistresses who'd not only commanded their ranks of Warriors, but led them. A few of them had even contributed wisdom to the Warrior's Way. Perhaps the Monkeys had similar arrangements within their own primitive culture.

Pernrhee seemed very interested in Garragh's purpose, who he was, and why he had come. The one who spoke without speaking struggled to convey complicated concepts and, because she was a Mistress, he did his best to comply, all while doing his best to study the enemy.

Why did the Hind come to Monkeyworld? That was easy. To conquer it. He created the image of a Monkey rolling onto its back while a Warrior in full armor, axe planted in the ground, stood over it. The Mistress seemed to understand the idea of using mental pictures and changed her method of questioning. She created an image of the city around them in flames while a giant Hind used a weapon to start fires.

No, that wasn't right. That wasn't why the Hind came. He thought of the city, with its tall, gray buildings unharmed. Monkeys lined a street, prostrating themselves before a line of Warriors. How else was he to convey the idea that the Hind weren't there to destroy, but to conquer? True power and prestige came not in the destruction of a civilization, but in its conquest. To destroy a city, or to render a world uninhabitable, was not the mark of power, but of failure. It meant a Clan's reputation wasn't strong enough to secure a total victory. To destroy a city was a loss of prestige, but that could be overcome if the world capitulated. If a world never capitulated and had to be cleansed, it was the lowest kind of failure that could destroy a Clan's reputation for generations.

The Mistress sent Garragh's image of the city street lined with Monkeys back to him, but one Monkey at the end of the line was screaming and firing its tiny weapon.

That was another easy line of questioning. The Monkey would be appropriately culled, and the image Garragh returned made the Mistress sit back, her skin growing pale. She must have needed some bolstering from Pernrhee, for the Warrior-Mistress placed her tiny hand on the other's back as if to keep her from falling. Garragh watched the interaction, breathing in the oxygen and feeling his body grow stronger as he took in the life-giving gas.

After a short break during which Garragh finished the meat and water the Monkeys had provided, the Mistress brought him a new image to consider. It showed the Monkeys fighting back against the Warriors. The response image came to his mind before he could stop it, and he realized that the Mistress was using her ability in a sneaky way to get him to discuss things he shouldn't. He thought of the Bomb, and tried to squelch it immediately. Before he did, he flashed two clear image-thoughts. One was of the silvery-gray segmented sphere that was the ultimate culling tool and the other was of fire engulfing the city until nothing remained behind but ashes.

The Mistress inhaled sharply, and water began to leak out of her eyes. She pulled away from Garragh and Pernrhee. The Warrior-Mistress followed her and there was an animated discussion that attracted the attention of many of the other Monkeys.

Garragh knew he'd given away something important. The Bomb was the last resort of the Clans. If they couldn't convince an opponent to surrender over the threat of violence, the Hind had no choice but to follow through on their threat. The Bomb would be detonated. The target would be vaporized. The opponent would know the Hind were serious and would quietly surrender. It had happened before in the history of Hind conquests, but never with Clan Sharassar. No opponent had ever allowed more than one city-equivalent to be destroyed. Garragh made himself breathe the oxygen faster until his hearts raced and his legs quivered.

Warrior-Mistress Pernrhee stalked back toward him with the kind of fire in her eyes that Hind Warriors showed when battle was about to be joined. She drew her tiny weapon, like the one that had put the painful hole in his leg, and pointed it at his face. "Rherhssit!" she screamed at him. "Rherhsa pom!"

Her words meant nothing to him, but he could tell she was furious. With her weapon out but not firing at him, she was trying to get him to divulge information of some kind. He guessed she might be asking where the Hind had placed their city-destroying bomb. He couldn't tell her that and tried to calm his mind, keeping the mental picture of a city of Monkeys peacefully surrendering to the Hind locked in place.

Pernrhee glanced toward the mind-reading Mistress and said something, and in that brief moment where her attention was distracted, Garragh made his move. His super-oxygenated blood gave him strength and speed in the light gravity of Monkeyworld. He smashed aside Pernrhee's hand holding the weapon. It fired in his ear, nearly deafening him. Nevertheless, he shoved the Warrior-Mistress aside and in one bound, went over the edge of the dock and into the murky water below.

It was a move borne of desperation, for he remembered the water of Monkeyworld was supposed to be toxic to Hind. His people were poor swimmers. With their homeworld's higher gravity and their dense musculature, they were far more likely to sink than to swim, and it was an activity neither practiced nor endorsed. He heard the muted thunderclaps as the Monkey Warriors fired their weapons into the water after him, and twin beams of light diffused their way into the darkness as the Monkey with the spotlights for eyes tried to illuminate the Hind as he struggled through the unfamiliar surroundings. His powerful legs churned, kicking up silt and debris in the water as he bent forward at the waist to try to better streamline his ungainly body. He kept his jaw clenched tightly shut, for he'd been warned the water of Monkeyworld was toxic if ingested. He hoped it wouldn't kill him just from contacting his skin, but if it did, at least he would die where no other Hind would see.

A muffled splash and a glance behind him confirmed one of the Monkeys had dove in after him. It was the one who'd accompanied Pernrhee after she'd captured Garragh. He moved through the water with frightening speed, a short blade gleaming in the spotlights from overhead. As the Monkey closed with Garragh, he kicked backward with his powerful hindmost legs. Although the Monkey's blade scored a fresh slice across Garragh's haunch, he connected with the Monkey in the center of his chest, sending all the air from his lungs in a single burst. The Monkey swam back toward the surface and Garragh continued onward. Between his heritage of heavier gravity, larger lungs, twin hearts, and blood that had recently been super-oxygenated, Garragh managed to stay underwater for several minutes, moving further and further away from his captors.

Eventually when he could no longer stand to be beneath the surface, he pulled himself upward—a feat he couldn't have accomplished on Hindraa—until his nose broke the surface. Between the dark water and limited light coming through the Hind shield overhead, he didn't think anyone could see him. He couldn't tell how far away he'd moved from his captors, but he couldn't hear them any longer. He'd surfaced between some wooden pylons encrusted with the shells of sea life. Nearby, he saw a walkway over the water with dark shadows beneath it. That would do.

He crawled between the support pylons and scanned the area, looking for the telltale reddish heat-glow of nearby Monkeys. He didn't see any, and so he settled in as comfortably as he could in the shadow, waiting for full dark.

Fort Justice
New York Bay

"Minerva, I must protest most strongly at this course of action," said General Gershwin. "Harlan Washington is a fugitive from justice with dozens of municipalities and at least two countries seeking to extradite him for crimes he committed within their borders as well."

Harlan said nothing. The General wasn't exaggerating in the least about his actions. Harlan knew who he was and what he had done, and he didn't have a morsel of regret in his body. So when he'd asked for permission to connect his personal nanotech processor to the Just Cause mainframe for faster processing of the data he'd learned about the Hind, it was more a courtesy than anything else. He had enough respect for Minerva that simply connecting anyway would have felt like an imposition. Though if the General didn't back down and get off his high horse, Harlan thought he might just do it anyway.

"If I may remind you, General, he was also the only one to warn us. Without him, we might have been caught completely by surprise and be facing a far worse situation than we are," said Minerva.

"Worse? Worse than New York City being underneath a goddamned whatever-it-is while aliens are running around?"

Minerva said nothing until Gershwin wound himself down.

"General, I was on board one of those ships," Harlan said. "I attacked and nearly destroyed another. I have data—important data on the construction of those vessels. On their energy shields. Given some time and access to a more powerful processor, I can find a way to get through that shield over New York. If I can get inside it, I can destroy it."

"*You* can destroy it?" Gershwin asked in frank disbelief. "When the combined forces and might of Just Cause and the United States military hasn't made a dent in it?"

"Perhaps you've forgotten who I am," Harlan said.

A metallic finger flicked his ear painfully. "Hey," Hector said from beside him. "Be nice."

"He has a good point, General." Minerva turned away from Gershwin and with a subtle movement of her chin, indicated Harlan should follow her, which he did. "I've been ordered to fight a war, as, I'm sure, have you. Mr. Washington is an exceptional resource and I'm going to use every one I have at my disposal." They reached the elevator with Hector in tow.

Gershwin didn't push his way onto the elevator, understanding he was not to be part of what followed. "Fine, but it's on your head."

"It always has been," Minerva said as the doors closed.

The elevator descended in silence. Harlan appreciated the lack of Muzak. Nevertheless, he felt like he should say something. "Thanks," was as much as he managed, the unfamiliar word struggling to get free from his lips.

Minerva casually reached over and pushed the *Emergency Stop* button. The elevator ground to a halt. A warning bell sounded somewhere over their head. "Everything the General said was correct, Harlan. I am grateful for your assistance, but I cannot and will not forget your record of actions against Just Cause and its heroes. Sally believes you have changed your ways, and I trust her assessment of you. See that you do nothing here to change that."

"Yeah, *cabrón*, or it will be your last mistake," said Hector, who looked like he was itching to redecorate Harlan's face with his metallic knuckles.

"I'm . . . offended at these invaders," Harlan said at last. "Coming here like they already own the place when they barely have any power at all. They're no better than bullies." He glared at Hector, who said nothing. "And I know bullies."

Minerva restarted the elevator. "Your nephew is here. He arrived safely a little over an hour ago."

"Good."

"He is using his nanotechnology and knowledge of spaceflight to build a vessel in the Tank. We will use it in our assault upon the alien ships."

"His idea?"

"Mine."

Harlan smiled. The knowledge that March had survived his descent and landing improved his outlook considerably. He would have been upset had the young man been killed, because it would have been something he couldn't blame upon anyone else. "He's going to need my help. I can make the process faster and give you a better design than he could."

"Yes, I hope so." The elevator doors opened and Minerva escorted Harlan into the Tank's observation room. He had never been inside Fort Justice before, and he looked out through the large bay windows into the huge vertical cavern of the repurposed oil platform's hollow leg. Just Cause engineers had reinforced the interior of the walls with high-density, low-weight armor that could absorb a lot of energy. Bright lights sat behind clear panels set into the walls, but even with them all turned on, there was still a dingy dimness to the space that nothing short of bright sunlight could have eradicated.

Below, he could see the shell of a vessel starting to take shape amid a slow-flowing gray goo. March sat on a nanotech-built chair off to one side, a cable stretching from one hand to a port on a computer terminal. A group of white-coated technicians rushed to and fro, monitoring the slow development of the ship, recording designs for future projects, and generally being the sort of nosy, invasive busybodies that Harlan couldn't stand. "I'd like to speak to March."

"Of course. You can connect to the system from the same location as him." Minerva paused, as if listening to something only she could hear. "You're hungry and thirsty. What would you like?"

Harlan looked at her sharply. He'd forgotten how acute her senses were. She was correct. He was hungry. His nanotech had its own power sources but when he used a lot energy, it would convert some of his body fat to restore reserves. Between attacking the alien fleet and fighting his way out of Hind incarceration, he was running almost solely on the energy stored in his own body. It was a fancy way of saying he was really in the mood for some fatty carbs and caffeine.

Minerva went to the observation room workstation and touched a few keys. "Commissary, this is Minerva. Please bring down a selection of sandwiches and accompanying sides, along with pots of coffee, hot water, tea, and condiments." The replying voice said *right away, ma'am*. She turned to face Harlan. "We're well-stocked for sandwiches, but unfortunately our chef was in Manhattan to purchase fresh ingredients for the next few meals."

"Sandwiches are fine." Harlan's stomach gurgled with insistent agreement.

Minerva took him and Hector down to the Tank floor, where March was set up to work on the spaceship. "Hey, Uncle," said the young man.

"I'm pleased you made it here in one piece," said Harlan. "Fill me in." He extended nanite tendrils from his hand. March did the same from one of his and they interlinked, sending high-speed data flowing in both directions. It was much more efficient and complete a method of information-sharing than a conversation would have been, especially one exacerbated by March's stutter.

Harlan noted with great interest the engineering designs of the *Daedalus* and saw developments that would be a great boon to him for future projects. He also saw its limitations and sent March corrections to his design that would improve the vessel's performance and protection for its occupants.

"Thanks," March said. "This isn't my b-best skill."

"You're doing fine," said Harlan. He glanced at Minerva. "What are you going to call this ship?"

"I hadn't thought about it."

"All ships need a name."

Minerva considered for a moment. "*Boudica*," she said at last.

"What's that?"

"Boudica was a Celtic queen who led an uprising against the Roman occupying forces in ancient Britain."

Hector stared in disbelief. "How the hell do you know that?"

Minerva said nothing.

"It's because she reads, obviously," said Harlan.

"You wanna go? Because I ain't afraid of you." Hector stepped forward, only to be stopped by Minerva's spear that appeared out of nowhere. He and Harlan both looked to where she stood. Her eyes burned beneath her helmet with an intensity that made Harlan feel something he didn't often experience: fear.

"Now. Is. Not. The. Time." Minerva's voice was soft and controlled.

Hector shrugged and backed down. "I wasn't gonna hit him. He looks fragile."

Harlan thought about making a snarky remark, but it wouldn't get him any closer to his goal. Instead, he crossed his arms and turned to Minerva. "May I connect to your system now, please? Time is wasting."

Minerva put her spear back to wherever she kept it when she wasn't using it—some kind of pocket dimension or parallel universe that made Harlan itch with curiosity. She motioned to a couple of techs by the door. They brought over a chair for Harlan, a heavy-duty insulated data cable, and a folding table. The craft service was set up on the table and Harlan availed himself of a pair of sandwiches and the biggest container he could fill with black coffee. March took a sandwich himself and started to eat.

Harlan didn't have to actually go through the motions of eating. His nanotech could more efficiently pull food into his stomach and break it down there. When he was alone, he would refuel himself that way.

Eating had always felt inefficient to him, and his appetite evaded him until he was shaking from weakness. He had never seen food as anything but fuel, and he never understood the enjoyment others took from spending hours cooking, then sitting down and spending hours eating. Nobody was making more time, and Harlan felt like he needed to make the most of every hour available to him.

He plugged himself into the data cable and lost himself in the Just Cause mainframe for awhile, letting the huge processors in their refrigerated chambers crunch upon the data he'd recorded. He was dimly aware of March's craft continuing to develop before them, and overheard the occasional warning from technicians that the mainframe was running hot and calls for additional cooling units.

At last, with the computer's help, he consolidated his data down to some manageable chunks. Once he had the pieces in place, he began developing a plan. It was like building a molecule, atom by atom. He opened his eyes and disconnected from the computer. "I need to build something. With your nanotech resources, it'll take less than an hour. Then we need to go to the Hind shield. I need to speak to anyone we can on the other side."

Minerva nodded and gave orders to the technicians to release all nanotech assets to Harlan's control. "We'll go to Champions HQ," she said. "The field is bisecting the building. We have assets on both sides."

"Good."

General Gershwin was against the idea, of course. Harlan didn't care. He knew the General didn't trust him, and in all honesty, the man was right not to. Harlan was one of the most dangerous people on the entire planet.

The Hind were about to find that out.

CHAPTER SEVEN

♔ ♘ ♔

96th and Park

As full dark came upon New York City, the field over the sky took on a dull, uniform gray with occasional flickers of rainbow energy, like an oil slick across the water. Sally had grown used to a bland, colorless night sky in New York from all the light pollution, only punctuated by the occasional flicker of lightning from a spring storm or the constant stream of air traffic. The darkness from the Hind shield was different. It felt oppressive and weighty, like the air before a thunderstorm.

Sally led her ragtag militia down the darkened streets, helped by a flashlight and the headlights of the truck behind her. She focused on picking out a path for the truck around the abandoned and wrecked vehicles. Nearly every building was dark, but Sally did see some dim lights on upper floors, probably candles. People were laying low and staying off the streets, for which she was grateful. It was bad enough that so many civilians were being held in the Hind prison camps, but given the population of New York City, most people were probably still in safe locations. As long as they didn't get any foolish ideas about trying to travel during the crisis, it would make Sally's job easier.

Sally had a half dozen of Detroit Steel's militia accompanying her—hard-bitten men and women from all walks of life, armed to the teeth, and ready to unleash hell upon any Hind who had the discourtesy to interrupt their travel. There was an older truck driver who was an ex-Marine, his paunch no barrier to his skill with a rifle; an acerbic brunette in a power suit who'd said she went target-shooting on weekends with the young bulls in her firm; a pair of young black men wearing basketball shoes and were more comfortable using their own pistols; a Puerto Rican short-order cook who didn't flinch at anything; and a pleasant Somalian immigrant who'd said he hadn't fled the terrorists in his homeland just to see his new home overrun by more terrorists. A New York Department of Transportation inspector had offered her pickup truck to the heroes. Four of the militia members rode in the back along with Detroit Steel herself, and two in the cab.

Sally went ahead on foot, scouting the route to make sure no surprises or road blockages were waiting for them, while Chinook flew overhead, high enough to be hard for the Hind to hit with their generally poor aim but low enough for her to provide an effective overhead presence.

The rest of Shawna's militia remained behind in their makeshift fortress. The combination of police and gangbangers felt confident enough to resist anything up to and including a full-on assault, and should they get overwhelmed, they could flee into the buildings where the large Hind wouldn't be able to pursue easily. Sally had suggested that maybe they should pack it in and hide to wait it out, but one of the police pointed out that the Hind might have heavy weapons they hadn't used yet. What if they decided to start leveling buildings? He'd seen enough buildings fall in his lifetime, he said, and it made Sally's heart heavy. A great many superheroes had died when the Twin Towers fell.

Sally had been nervous about leaving them behind, but as Shawna said, it was wartime, and that meant tough decisions had to be made. The Woman of Steel believed in her army, and if anyone knew about mobilizing diverse people together into a cohesive unit, it was the native from Detroit.

They crawled through the streets, everyone on a hair trigger and wishing they could see better. Knowing the Hind could see into the infrared spectrum meant the humans would be shining like beacons—or targets—even in darkness. Sally wished the truck would move faster, and burned off her nervous energy by continually scouting forward then running back, like a dog escorting a party of hikers.

She tried to tell herself she was being diligent and making sure the civilians—because weapons or not, in her eyes they were the people she'd been charged with protecting, not fighting alongside of—were safe. Deep down, though, she knew she wanted them to hurry because she hoped Jason had found his way to Champions HQ. It only made sense, she told herself. Why would he go anywhere else when that would be the best place for him to reconnect with everyone? With Sally? She couldn't let herself imagine anything else.

Chinook let loose her cab-whistle from above. "Eyes right," she called. "Looks like a Scat patrol."

The ex-Marine with the rifle had started calling the Hind *scats*, and everyone else had picked up on it.

Weapons were cocked and raised. The Puerto Rican cook stopped the truck. With a heavy clanging sound, Shawna hopped down onto the pavement. "How far, Chinook?" she asked.

Sally squinted into the darkness. She couldn't see what Chinook had reported.

Chinook flew higher. "Close. Less than a block. I saw movement. It was . . ."

She stopped as a couple of dogs trotted through the pool of Sally's flashlight, tails wagging as they sniffed at the sidewalk.

The militia lowered their weapons. "False alarm, everyone," said the Marine. "But stay frosty."

Sally took a few steps toward the dogs, wondering if they were somebody's pets who had gotten out and were having themselves an adventure, or if they were strays. Either way, she hoped they had enough sense to stay away from the invaders. She'd been close enough to the Hind that there was no question in her mind they ate meat, and they might not be too picky about its origin. The dogs saw her and bolted. She could have caught them but she let them go.

"Chinook, are you all right?" Sally asked her young teammate.

The girl nodded. "Just tired. I need something to eat and a nap."

Sally chuckled. "I can't ever remember a time when I didn't need both of those things."

The group continued onward toward Champions Headquarters, picking up the pace a bit at Sally's order. They saw a few Hind camps at a distance, brightly lit beneath their portable shields. The Hind didn't seem to be venturing out from behind those shields and it relieved Sally to know she didn't have to fight her way through town. Whatever else the Hind were, they had rules, however alien they might have been, and the more she learned about those rules, the better chance she would have to defeat them.

They reached the Champions to less fanfare than Sally might have expected. Only the sonic-powered Shouty Ed guarded the entrance to the facility, which was neatly bisected by the Hind force field. "Mustang Sally!" he boomed as soon as he recognized her crimson and gold costume. "Am I ever glad to see you!"

She zipped over to him. "Ed, what's going on? Where is everyone? Are you the only Champion on this side of the field?"

"No, there's several of us, but they're all looking for the Hind who escaped." He pointed at his glasses. "I'm blind as a bat without these, and with them I'm still not great at searching for anything."

"Wait, you captured a Hind?"

"No, but Penny did. She brought him here so Dolittle could try to read his mind."

Sally blinked. "That was a brilliant idea. Did it work?"

"Yeah. She learned quite a bit about why they're here and their plans. We had to keep him in the garage, because he was too big to bring inside anywhere else. You know how we've also got a dock? He got free and went into the water and we lost him."

A dripping Penny Lane stalked up to Sally, a towel around her shoulders. "Either they can breathe underwater or they've got tremendous lung capacity. I bet it's the latter. Whatever the case, we had him and we lost him." She nodded a greeting at Detroit Steel and Chinook. "You guys look like you've had as rough a night as I have."

"Yeah, we could use a break. Unfortunately, I don't see that happening anytime soon." Sally sighed.

Surfboy flew over with a big bag of sandwiches. "They're just bologna and cheese," he said by way of apology. "We're low on groceries and traffic is murder out there."

Sally accepted one. "It's better than a sharp stick in the eye. Listen, the Hind are hunkered down behind their dropship shields. They've got human captives but they don't seem to be hurting them. They're not attacking unarmed civilians. They have rules of engagement. We can use those to our advantage."

"Basically, we ain't got to think like superheroes right now," said Shawna. "Right now, we're the resistance. The freedom fighters. We make our own rules and break 'em if we gotta."

Chinook swallowed a mouthful of sandwich. "You make it sound like we're terrorists."

"We are," said the Woman of Steel. "To them."

Sally nodded. "They came here to occupy and conquer Earth. We're not going to let that happen. If we have to use . . . questionable tactics, well, we'll let history judge us if we win." She wondered if she might be overstepping herself but reminded herself it was wartime, and they had think like soldiers. "What did you learn from the Hind you captured?"

Penny grimaced. "Step aside with me," she said. "You're not going to like what I'm about to tell you."

Fort Justice
New York Bay

While she waited for Harlan to finish his mysterious technical creation in the Tank, Minerva sat in her office and picked out the names of heroes she would lead to their deaths against the Hind fleet.

Accessing the Parahuman Resources Administration's database normally required a higher security clearance than was possessed by Minerva, or anyone on a Just Cause team for that matter. As Juice said, there was a time for protocol and a time for efficiency, and when a highly encrypted email arrived from an anonymous webmail account, Minerva was inclined to believe it had come from him. The first part of the hash was much less garbled than the rest—words with their letters rearranged. Minerva translated it quickly and recognized it as a quote from the speech Juice had given to her class at their Hero Academy graduation. A text came to her phone with a 128-character decryption code. She typed the meaningless hash into her computer and the email resolved itself into login and password access to the deepest levels of the PRA database.

The database was organized exceptionally well, with search functions that allowed for a wide variety of parameters. She wondered if the parahuman hacker Vanitha Bhat, also known as Kali, had been involved in setting up such an intuitive database or if the PRA just had an outstanding IT department.

It took her only a few minutes to comb through a haystack of data to find her needles. She'd sought heroes who could function effectively either in zero gravity, zero atmospheric pressure, or both, with an emphasis on combat abilities. All of them had to be able to reach Fort Justice within three hours or she didn't feel there would be enough time to prepare for the assault on the orbital fleet. The final parameter was one she had almost left off the search. A younger Minerva might well have neglected to include the number of immediate family members who would be affected should a strike team member die. She would have seen the relationships as irrelevant to solving her problem. Having spent so much time around her teammates and getting to know their families had changed her opinion.

She didn't want to think of her strike team as expendable, but she suspected some or all of them might not return from orbit, and she wanted to affect the fewest number of families possible. Her target was one or zero, with zeroes taking the top priority. It might have left some significant weapons off the results list, but it was a risk she was willing to take, and she was left with seven heroes she could call upon to save perhaps the entire world.

Black Ice was an independent hero working in Buffalo. She was a Hero Academy graduate who'd decided to return to her hometown instead of joining the growing ranks of Just Cause or Champions teams. She had the ability to coat herself in a thick layer of regenerating ice, which protected her like constantly renewing armor plate. While encased within it, she didn't require any form of life support. Her offensive abilities were limited to generating additional ice from her body, but it could freeze sensitive systems, make floors treacherous, and force apart sealed joints. Her only close family connection was an aging mother.

Blueshift was an experienced veteran hero, first part of the New Guard in Los Angeles and more recently a member of the Just Cause L.A. team. He was a nuclear physicist who had been instrumental in helping to shut down a dangerously overheating reactor and saving thousands of lives, including many of Minerva's friends. His abilities revolved around quantum energy, including a force field, particle beams, and the most useful ability of all: quantum teleporting.

Even though he was all the way across the country, he could come to New York in seconds, and he could bring another hero along with him.

Javelin would be the hero accompanying Blueshift, both as his teammate and his wife. They had no children and although between them they had three surviving parents, neither was close to their families. Javelin was the niece of the original Javelin, who had been with Just Cause for nearly three decades before dying in the attacks on the World Trade Center in 2001. She had inherited his backup battlesuit and all the notes on his tech. Over the years, she'd become a highly regarded engineer in her own right and upgraded her own suit until it was, outside of Destroyer, the most powerful single-occupant fighting vehicle in the world.

Gauss was another independent hero who hailed from the Rust Belt. Like Black Ice, he could encase his body, but he did so with iron he drew forth from the ground or surrounding materials. It became entrapped in the magnetic matrix that surrounded him, fusing together until he looked like he was made of grayish crystals. He would require additional life support to travel into space, but Minerva suspected he would come into his own if they could get him close enough to the Hind ships for him to draw iron out of their vessels. There was no theoretical limit to the amount of iron he could attract, according to the footnotes in his file. There was a scanned handwritten note attached to his file, warning that he should also be able to pull iron out of a living creature's blood, which would be instantly fatal as their blood cells would be torn apart and they could no longer process oxygen.

Failsafe had been a founding member of Just Cause New York, and was a success story in that he'd been an inmate in Deep Six and had assisted in quelling a breakout from the ultra-secure prison despite his status as a prisoner. His assistance had earned him parole, and he'd become a valued member of Just Cause New York before being transferred to work alongside Sondra in

Just Cause Dallas. His ability to generate fields of pure energy in varying shapes would be tremendously useful in transporting teammates and protecting them from vacuum and Hind weapons. Normally he would be too far away but the hero tracking software reported he was currently visiting the Richmond team.

Giant was a man who didn't want to be a hero, who detested his abilities, who lived in self-ordered isolation to protect others. Quite simply, he was the strongest person in the world. No parahuman had ever been able to match his physical strength pound for pound, even if using a different kind of power like telekinesis or force manipulation. He could tear apart a boulder as easily as if it were paper. He could punch the ground so hard that he could trigger a nearby fault line. Once, for a rare public appearance, he had pulled an aircraft carrier into dock by its anchor chain. His strength was literally impossible to measure by any current technology. If that weren't enough, he could also teleport himself. These two abilities would make him the most fearsome opponent in the world, except that he was a gentle man with a gentle soul who feared hurting others so much that he isolated himself to protect them. He would take some convincing, but Minerva thought she could do so with potentially the entire world at stake.

The last name on Minerva's list was troubling her like nothing else could. It was Amber, the youngest of Just Cause New York's new members and the only reason the search protocols flagged her was proximity. Her magically created amber gave her a powerful edge in surviving the hostile environment of space. It was resistant to physical attacks and numerous forms of energy, and she could create, dissolve, or move it around at will. Having her along would be like having a flexible battle tank. When she combined her powers with Failsafe's and Black Ice's, it should make an impenetrable defensive screen. True, between the three of them, their powers were essentially duplicating one another, but Minerva felt that kind of redundancy might mean the difference between death and survival. Could she ask that of Amber, who was a legacy superhero like herself?

But then, Amber knew the risks when she'd first joined the Hero Academy. Being a legacy hero didn't mean special privileges. She'd still had to prove herself over and over again to earn a spot not only with Just Cause, but with the top New York branch. If Minerva couldn't ask her to risk everything to take the fight to the Hind, how could she ask anyone else?

Sally would have agonized over the decision. Ordering any hero to head off to certain death was the kind of choice leaders dreaded to make, and it would have torn Sally apart emotionally. Minerva could distance herself from her emotions like few others in the world, but even she recognized how terrible it was to order someone to die. For a moment, she wondered what her grandmother, Lady Athena, the first leader of Just Cause, would have had to say about it. She could almost hear her voice, stately even in her last moments upon her deathbed. *Do what you know is right and leave it to the historians to judge whether you were correct.*

Minerva had to worry about the *now*, not the future. She would do her best to keep everyone on her strike team alive from the moment they left to the moment they returned home, or she herself would die trying.

She smelled Davey's approach and felt the change in air pressure from her presence before the woman knocked on the door frame. "Boss? Washington says he's ready."

Minerva nodded and pushed her chair back from the desk. "Davey, contact all the heroes in the open files on my desktop and order them to report to Fort Justice within the next three hours. Tell them the world needs them."

"Will do."

Champions Headquarters—inside of Hind shield
Battery Park, Manhattan

With no luck in finding their vanished Hind prisoner, Penny decided the best use of her skills would be to find the Hind bomb.

"What are you going to do?" Dolittle asked as Penny sorted through her gear, taking the time to set it up right for the most efficient access to her rifle, pistols, ammunition. "You don't actually think you can disarm an alien weapon, do you?"

"Of course not." Penny strapped holsters to her thighs. "But if I can find it, there are people who can. Or people who can destroy it without setting it off."

"You're going to get killed going out there."

Penny shook her head. "I don't think so. Sally said the Hind haven't been out and about since it got dark. Why do you think that is? You were in Garragh's head."

Dolittle bowed her head. She might have blushed but in the dim light from the candles they'd scrounged from the Champions' emergency supplies that were accessible on their side of the force field, Penny couldn't see it. "I don't know. Communicating with him was different than communicating with an animal, because he has higher thought processes animals don't possess. He could be secretive."

"I thought you couldn't keep a secret from a telepath."

"Maybe not, but I'm not a telepath. More like an empath." Dolittle shrugged.

Penny tightened the clasps on her tactical vest and hung a bandoleer of ammo clips over her shoulder. She knew she was weighing herself down, which could cause problems of exhaustion later, but she might have to fight her way through half an army, and she didn't want to be short on gear at a crucial moment. Her sniper rifle went over the same shoulder, its familiar weight comfortable against her back. She debated whether or not to bring the Hind rifle but ultimately decided to leave it behind. "He didn't give you any idea where it is, did he?"

"Somewhere around the center of the shield, I think. Maybe near wherever the thing generating the shield is." Dolittle watched Penny strap on her helmet. "Are you going by yourself?"

"Yes."

"No, you're not," sad another voice. A lighter sparked and Toxic's face shone in the light momentarily as she touched it to her cigarette. "I'm going with you."

"No, you're not," Penny retorted. "Did you know a sniper can peg you in the face from a mile away at night when you're smoking? That coal at the end of your cigarette might as well be a laser targeting system."

Toxic blew out a cloud of smoke. "Do you know how to disarm a bomb?"

"No, and neither do you."

"No, but if it's a bomb, it's going to have some kind of chemicals in it that I can affect. I have the lungs of a marathon runner. No tar buildup at all. All I have to do is this . . ." Toxic spat into the darkness. "I'm good at what I do, Penny. You can use me. Don't go thinking you're too good for us just because you're in the Big Show and we're still the Battery Park B-squad, asshole."

Penny sighed. Toxic was right and she knew it. Penny didn't have the slightest idea what she was going to do when she found the Hind bomb. She didn't doubt she could find it. She had a pretty fair idea where it was in town. After that, though, her plans went kind of fuzzy on the details.

Besides, Toxic was a unique parahuman with her ability to control man-made pollutants. Perhaps that ability would extend to Hind-made chemicals as well. Also, she could fly, which was always a useful ability, even if just for reconnaissance purposes.

"All right, you can come." Penny held out one of her backup pistols to Toxic, who looked at it as if Penny had just offered her a piece of roadkill pie.

"No thanks," said the Goth girl. "I'm more likely to blow off my own toes than I am to actually do something useful with it. You keep it."

"You're going to need a scout," said E-Dog. The tall, lanky man could transform himself into a dog. It wasn't the most dynamic or useful power, but he might be more likely to be left alone if spotted by the Hind. He could also approximate simple human speech in his dog form. It was muffled and rife with growls and squeaks because the dog's lips and tongue weren't designed for complex speech, but when fitted with a special earpiece and throat microphone, he could at least maintain communication.

Penny sighed. The two Champions were acting like they'd been assigned to her. With sudden insight, she realized they probably had. After telling Sally what she and Dolittle had learned about the Hind's explosive contingency plan if their invasion gambit failed, she'd offered to go locate the bomb herself as it would free up the other, higher-powered heroes for whatever their needs might be. Sally agreed it was a good idea. She must have asked Toxic and E-Dog to accompany Penny. It was a canny move on the Just Cause leader's part, bringing on two heroes who would ostensibly fit into Penny's mode of operation without putting her in a position where egos got in the way.

She showed Dolittle a flare gun. "If the shield isn't down by the time I find the bomb, I'll use to signal I have it. Three flares in a row. Get somebody in the sky watching Midtown."

"We'll figure something out. What are you going to do when you get it?"

"Bring it back here, I guess, unless I can figure out how to disarm it. Our best bet is to bring it to where the best and brightest superheroes are and hope we can disable it or contain it."

"That's the best idea you have?"

Penny looked up from her gear at Dolittle. "If you have a better idea, please don't keep it to yourself."

"No, I don't know anything about this. I'm just a veterinarian, Penny."

Penny squeezed her arm. "You're a Champion, Dolittle. Never forget that." She turned to Toxic and E-Dog. "I figure we need to get into Midtown. About five miles away, I think. It's in the center of this damn shield, and for the best explosive yield, you'd want to place your explosive in the middle. It's probably on top of a building, because an airburst is more effective than a ground-level blast. It'll probably be under guard, which means there will be activity we can see. We just need a quick, quiet way to get there."

"I can fly," said Toxic, supporting herself on a reasonably solid cloud of smog.

"I run," said E-Dog, who had already transformed himself into the Blue Heeler mix that was his alternate form.

Penny's eye fell on something in one corner of the garage. "Hey, think anybody will mind if I steal that bicycle?"

Monkeyworld

The sounds of Garragh's hunters faded away until the only noise was the gentle slapping of the tide against the pilings of the pier under which he hid. He couldn't see any of their heatsign either. The only warm spots he saw at all were some tiny squeaking creatures that crawled along a beam, chittering and spitting at him. He ignored them and waited. Being submerged as long as he had been meant his fur had been wet all the way down to his skin. Even waiting for many twelfths, it was still damp and matted, and his mane had taken on a fluffy, frilly appearance that was more appropriate for a court Submistress than a Warrior.

He wondered if he had poisoned himself with his desperate escape into the water. Were the dangerous minerals and chemicals leaching through his skin even as he sat, miserable, waiting until he felt safe enough to depart? He was afraid again, and his weakness galled him. Afraid to live. Afraid to die. Surely, he was the worst Warrior ever.

He could do nothing about his appearance. Without armor or weapon, he would be forced to run naked through the streets of Monkeyworld until he found his people. He was at a loss what he should do next. As a Warrior, he wasn't used to thinking for himself; that was why fighting units were organized the way they were, with Submistresses in command. His only hope was to find a Submistress who would listen to him tell what he'd learned in his time among the Monkeys.

He crawled out from among the timbers under the wooden overhang and scrambled up and onto the platform. He took a moment to shake himself, luxuriating in the water flying away from his fur for the first time in a half dozen twelfths.

Garragh knew from his training the Monkeys were generally more active during the daylight, but their electric lighting had allowed them to be more active at night as well. He would have to be careful as he sought out his own people. Their mission directives had been to secure their landing locations as darkness fell, not only to give themselves time to rest after their initial attacks, but to see how the Monkeys would respond to the landing. Would they fight back and risk the hostages the Hind had taken? Or would they hold back and consider acceding to Clanmistress Rhaorhir's order to surrender?

Study your enemy that you will learn his weakness, his habits, the best time to strike. The Warrior's Way spoke at great length about how important a trait observation was to successful conquests. Unfortunately. Most Warriors never developed the ability to focus upon what lay beyond the end of their axes. The studying of enemies fell to the Submistresses.

Garragh ran down the streets, grateful for Monkeyworld's lower gravity. On his homeworld, his wounded leg likely wouldn't have supported his weight. Instead, he was able to keep up a brisk trot through the darkness. Anytime he spotted the heatsign of Monkeys on the ground, he either put his head down and ran faster or changed his path onto a different street. He didn't know if they could see him well in the dark, but he wasn't anxious to get shot again.

He happened upon the remains of a battle many twelfths old, as the corpses had cooled to the same temperature as the streets. Two Hind Warriors lay dead, their flanks stitched with many wounds like the one in Garragh's leg. A half dozen Monkeys joined them, either split apart by axes or shot by rifles. The Hind rifles were gone but Garragh found an axe embedded in the side of one of the Monkey wheeled vehicles like the one that had taken him across the city. He wrenched it free and hefted it. It had different balance than the one he'd lost on the descent to Monkeyworld, but it was an axe, and it helped him to feel complete for the first time since he'd first crawled from the wreckage of his dropship.

Axe in hand, he gritted his teeth against the pain in his hind leg, and he ran.

The streets of Monkeyworld were filthy, he thought, now that he had a chance to really experience them firsthand. They covered their roads in some kind of stinking black paste, littered with debris, dirt, and garbage. Their loud wheeled vehicles were everywhere, in many cases abandoned in the middle of the road with their doors hanging open and their passengers nowhere to be seen. More than once, he had to climb over a pile of wrecked vehicles where they'd piled against one another, blocking the way through the streets. Twisted sheet metal and sharp glass threatened to slice open the pads of his feet, but he persisted. Somewhere, deeper in the Monkey city, he would find his people.

Soon, he spotted a distant island of cool, white light with a flickering rainbow dome over it and he knew he'd made it. He trotted toward the outpost, axe in one hand but with the blade down to indicate he was not charging in attack. It would have been a stupid way to die, getting killed by his own people because of their mistaken interpretation of his intentions.

Sentries raised the alarm as Garragh approached the outpost. He reached the edge of the shield and sat back on his haunches, his lungs struggling to keep him upright and conscious in the thin air of Monkeyworld. The outpost Submistress stepped up to the inside edge of the shield where she could get a good look at him. She noted his lack of armor, his frizzy mane from his recent swim in the ocean, and the bandage upon his leg. "Identify yourself," she said at last.

"Garragh, Warrior of Clan Sharassar, deployed upon *Blood Afire* and sent to conquer Monkeyworld." He said the words by rote, for they'd been trained into him during the journey from Hindraa. "I am the last of my twelfth with no Submistress to command me. I request immediate assignment to your command that I may once again follow orders."

"Lower the shield," ordered the Submistress. "Watch for renegade Monkeys."

A Warrior rushed to do her bidding, hurrying into the dropship to shut down the shield emanating from the projector that extended above the upper hull. The shield flickered out of existence and the Submistress wrinkled her nose as Garragh's odor reached her. "What is that? That stink?"

"Seawater, Submistress. I . . ." Garragh stopped as he realized what he'd been about to say. He had been going to say he was the prisoner of the Monkeys and had to swim to escape them. If he'd admitted he was a prisoner, that he'd been captured instead of killed while fighting to the very end, he'd essentially have admitted cowardice, and his life would have been forfeit. "A Monkey fired a weapon at my dropship, killing my pilot. It . . . . crashed into the water. Of those not killed in the crash, only I managed to escape my straps before drowning."

The Submistress narrowed her eyes at him. "I know the Monkeys managed to down at least two dropships. Perhaps you are being truthful."

"I swear upon the Warrior's Way, upon the Accord of the Fist," Garragh said.

"Very well. I am Submistress Laharsa. Garragh, I hereby place you under my command."

Garragh held his borrowed axe across his chest. "It is my honor to serve."

Laharsa turned away from him and ordered him to follow, which he did. The outpost shield went up behind him. "Warghar, I have placed Garragh under my command. See that he receives food and water and make the armor supply available to him."

A heavyset Warrior with dark stripes across his arms and torso bowed. "It is my honor to serve."

Garragh felt a little better, knowing he was in the familiarity of the Hind command structure, and getting some real food inside him and real armor over his fur would do wonders to improve his demeanor. Then he could consider how best to pass along what he'd learned about the Monkeys to Submistress Laharsa without giving away that he'd been a prisoner.

"Garragh, what is the wrapping on your leg?" Laharsa asked the question without turning to face him, which would have been a dire insult if it had been another Warrior.

"It's . . . It's . . ." Garragh stammered as he tried to think of a suitable falsehood quickly. He cursed himself for forgetting to remove the bandage before approaching the camp. He'd grown so used to the feel of it on his fur that he hadn't even noticed it any longer. "It must have gotten stuck there. The Monkeys leave trash lying around everywhere, in their water, on their streets. They are . . . they are filthy."

Laharsa stretched out on a pallet, twitching her tail, still speaking with her back to him, insulting him. "It has been many twelfths since the invasion began. Many twelfths, and yet it has taken you all these twelfths to find us. Far longer than it should have" She held up a portable screen so Garragh could see it. It showed an image of a Monkey—rather, *the* Monkey; the Warrior-mistress Monkey who'd captured him—with her gun pointed at a Hind Warrior. With a start, Garragh realized it was him.

"You allowed yourself to be captured by the Monkeys instead of earning a Warrior's death. Restrain him!" said Laharsa. Her Warriors leaped to obey, tearing the axe from Garragh's hands and locking his arms behind his upper back.

"But I escaped!" Garragh cried. "I learned about them!"

Laharsa yawned. "Take him to Submistress Rheayara for interrogation."

Garragh struggled but to no avail. Laharsa's Warriors had bound him efficiently and effectively. Submistress Rheayara was the commander of the companies ordered to gain a foothold on Monkeyworld. Her interrogation would be brutal.

Garragh fully expected it would kill him.

New York Bay
Champions HQ—outside of Hind shield

The axe Harlan had taken from the Hind vessel rode on his back in custom nanotech clips that emerged from the skin of his back. He rather enjoyed the idea of using the axe against the invaders and intended to swing it some once they got into real combat in the streets of Manhattan. He stood outside the Hind shield in Champions Headquarters—someplace he hadn't thought he would ever be—and allowed his nanite tendrils to brush gently against the energy field. Information about energy levels, frequencies, oscillations, and more traveled through his extended senses to flood his brain. Minerva, Ment, and Hector had accompanied him across the Bay to try out his machine.

He couldn't have easily explained it to the heroes. As with most of his creations, he knew what effect he wanted to create and his hands worked until they'd finished something which would do exactly that. He'd wanted to build something that could force an opening in the shield. He'd already learned how to fire an energy blast through a Hind energy shield. Even if the one stretched over Manhattan was a different sort than the ones that had protected the battle fleet in orbit, the technology would be the same. He'd beaten a Hind shield once; he would do so again.

Six Champions had been stuck on the outside of the shield and had spent most of the past few hours trying to figure out a way through it. Bombshell's knuckles were bloodied and burned from her attempt to simply batter through it. Johnny Go was seeing to her wounds. Particulate hadn't been able to find an opening small enough to filter himself through, but not for lack of trying. The small man had exhausted himself with the repeated efforts. Bathys reported the edge of the field went all the way to the bottom of the harbor, and it seemed to follow the contour of the seabed, so even when she dug a trench to try to get beneath it, the shield stretched to fill it. Ice-Nine's ability to solidify water didn't seem to have any useful application against an energy shield, and a single effort had proved his ineffectiveness. Only Humbug seemed to have made any dent in it at all.

Humbug was one of the rare parahumans whose bodies themselves were of inhuman appearance, such as the Chinese hero Yunbao's appearance as a humanoid leopard, or Desert Eagle's magnificent wings. She had large, insectile antennae sprouting from her forehead, which mixed with her multifaceted eyes to give her an alien, if not unattractive appearance. Harlan knew she had pincers inside her mouth, and to watch her eat was the stuff of nightmares. She had another, far more fascinating ability from his perspective, which was three sets of vocal cords. Furthermore, she had complete control over the tone of each larynx, allowing her to sing in perfect harmony with herself. She'd have been the world's biggest pop star, if not for her inhuman appearance. Instead, she used her abilities for precision sonic applications, and occasionally for karaoke in the Village on weekends.

She had experimented with using sonic frequency modulation to try to disrupt the shield itself, and had managed to make it bow inward once, and even forced some ripples across its surface, but she'd been unable to open it. Harlan felt that she would be the key to successfully doing so, and had designed his machine around utilizing and amplifying her innate powers. He made minute adjustments on his device while the others waited, some pacing back and forth, like Johnny Go, while others stood unmoving like Minerva.

Ment stood off to one side, his hands raised nearly against the shield and his face screwed up in concentration. Harlan knew the psi was struggling to reach anyone on the far side of the shield. He said he'd managed to contact Sally and she was nearby, inside Champions Headquarters just beyond the barrier. For reasons he couldn't quantify, knowing Sally was alive brought a feeling of relief to Harlan. He wouldn't go as far as admitting he cared about her, but perhaps it wasn't amiss to declare he disliked her far less than most of humanity.

"Tell her she needs to find the generator for the shield," Harlan told Ment. "I don't know how well I can open a breach or how long it will remain. Bringing down the device generating the force field is the only way we will be able to bring our forces to bear within the city."

"I'm . . . trying," Ment grumbled. "This is like . . . trying to whisper to someone across a crowded room."

"If you fail, your friends and everyone within this shield will die when the Hind realize we're not going to surrender."

Ment turned his head slightly to grimace at Harlan from behind his sunglasses, worn even in the darkness. "You suck as a motivational speaker."

Harlan shrugged. "I thought you were supposed to be an A-list psi. Maybe you'd be better off staying here with the Champions."

Ment turned back to the shield and although no physical change was apparent beyond the throbbing of veins in his neck and temples, he seemed to renew his attack upon the crackling Hind shield.

"You son of a bitch," said Hector from behind him. "I oughtta pop you one."

"It's working, isn't it?" Harlan made a final adjustment on his machine. "I've heard how you inspire the youngsters. Perhaps you and I aren't so different."

Harlan heard the muscular Puerto Rican take a step toward him but a rustle of cape and clink of metal on metal made him stop. "Hector," was all Minerva said, but it was enough.

"All right, I'm ready," Harlan said. "Minerva, I'll need you to work with Humbug to boost her abilities and sensitivity the way you do Ment."

"Of course," said Minerva.

Humbug's antennae twitched. "You think I can really open it?"

Harlan shrugged. "You'd better hope so for the sake of everyone inside of that shield."

CHAPTER EIGHT

♟

Champions Headquarters—inside of Hind shield
Battery Park, Manhattan

With the knowledge that her team was doing everything they could to breach the Hind shield, Sally turned her attention to the next problem, that of finding the shield generator. She was desperately understaffed to mount any sort of offensive against a Hind emplacement. Even if she was to scour the city for every possible parahuman asset, for every police officer and security guard and military and gangster willing to pick up a gun and fight, she would run out of time and strength long before the Hind decided they'd had enough.

It didn't matter in the end, though. Whether the rest of Just Cause managed to breach the shield with Harlan Washington's help or not, Sally's mission was clear, and she'd do her best to fulfill it with what help she had. In the meantime, she needed to do some good old-fashioned legwork.

And as a speedster, nobody did legwork better than her.

She lit out from Champions Headquarters on her own, carrying nothing extra but a granola bar and a belt flask of sports drink. Penny was already out in the city, seeking the Hind bomb with a pair of Champions. Sally wasn't putting anybody else at risk and left on her own. She needed intel. The last thing she needed was to have her makeshift army floundering around in the darkness, trying to find the shield generator. If she could find it ahead of time, they could move with a purpose.

If she happened to find Jason during her search, she thought, so much the better.

She had a flashlight with her, but she kept it in her belt. The Hind could see her heat signature, but they also seemed to be keeping within their emplacements. Digging in, she thought, in preparation for the next phase of the invasion.

As a longtime science fiction buff, she'd always imagined what it might be like to meet aliens, or what an invasion would be like. This hadn't been anything like she'd thought. The Hind were aliens in every way, from their odd six-limbed physiology to their racial psychology. The invasion was likewise a strangely familiar twist on an old trope. The Hind were gamblers at a level that would make even the strongest-willed con artists grow pale and shaky. They'd come to Earth with a display of force, advanced technology, and a threat to do far more harm. Like Sally had said to Chinook, *mighty nice planet youse got here.*

Was humanity willing to sacrifice the city of New York to keep fighting the Hind? In the movies, they might see it as a rallying point, an inspiration to rise to an even stronger resistance. In real life, too, the destruction of the World Trade Center and the loss of so many civilians and Just Cause heroes had only served to strengthen American resolve to fight terrorism.

On the other hand, so many years later, and their war against terrorist organizations had grown tiresome and forgotten by most of America. Perhaps that was the Clanmistress' plan, to play the long game, banking on humanity's unwillingness to continue a long, drawn-out conflict when an easier solution presented itself. Maybe humanity would surrender simply because it would mean they could get back to their reality TV shows and their Instagrams. "No," Sally said aloud. "I'll never surrender."

She ran to the nearest gas station and stole a souvenir bandana. It had a printed map of Manhattan upon it and that would suffice for her needs. She grabbed a permanent marker and began her search pattern of the streets, weaving back and forth across the island. She marked the location of every Hind emplacement she saw. As she reached the southern edge of Central Park, she felt sick that so many aliens were occupying *her* city, *her* world. A dozen dropships had come down between Lower Manhattan and Hell's Kitchen, leaving that area practically crawling with alien troopers.

She saw a squad of heavily armed Hind escorting one without armor, moving further north toward Central Park, and hid to watch them pass. At first she thought the one being escorted might have been a different class of Hind, like a politician or scientist instead or Warrior, but then she noted the bandaged wound on the creature's hind leg and the way it hung its head as it trotted along, surrounded by the others. A prisoner, then, but why had the Hind captured one of their own? A deserter perhaps?

Then she realized it was probably the same Hind who Penny had captured and brought to the Champions and she had to stop herself from running back to tell the others. What good would it do them to know their former prisoner was now someone else's prisoner?

The fact that the Hind had apparently done the equivalent of arresting him meant that he must have broken some rule or law of theirs. Sally grinned in the darkness. What does one do with a prisoner? They are transported to where they can be questioned, of course.

They were taking him to their leadership, and where their leadership was, Sally was willing to bet she would find their shield generator.

She followed them to Times Square, careful to keep behind solid cover as much as possible so they wouldn't see her heat signature. Times Square was lit up, but not in the way she had grown accustomed. Three dropships had landed tail to tail, their turrets facing outward to cover every possible approach. A ring of emplaced Warriors surrounded the dropships, wearing heavy armor and carrying guns that looked like they would make *giant* holes in whatever they hit. A torus-shaped shield protected the Warriors as they sat behind their portable armor walls, heads just peeking out above the edge. A large tent-like structure had been erected between two of the dropships, and Sally suspected it was the mobile headquarters for the invasion force, for that was where the imprisoned Hind was being led.

Behind the tent rose a lattice framework like a collapsible pillar. Atop it was a spinning, swirling vortex of energy from which a crackling beam shot upward to diffuse itself against the overhead shield. Sally didn't have to be a rocket scientist to know she was looking at the energy shield generator she'd been sent to find. She picked up a pizza box that had blown against a parked car and used her permanent marker to roughly sketch out a map of the defenses available. The more she marked it up, locating Warrior emplacements, the more dismayed she grew.

Taking it was going to be nearly impossible.

She considered whether to try to destroy it herself, trusting to her super-speed to get her through the assault, but immediately dismissed it as a ridiculous notion. Just Cause's strength lay in its teamwork and strategies, not impulsiveness. As easy as it was for her to make a snap decision, this was neither the time nor the place. No, her best bet would be to hurry back to the Champions, form her strike team, and plan their assault.

She had A-list heroes Chinook and Detroit Steel on her side, an experienced commander in Surfboy, and a surprisingly effective sonic attacker with Shouty Ed. Spotlight and Dolittle weren't combat-oriented by any stretch of the imagination, so they would be the ones who would have to defend Champions HQ from any surprise attacks. Besides the heroes, they had a handful of police and armed civilians up to the task as well. Sally hated calling upon them for assistance, but like she kept reminding herself, this was wartime, and certain rules had to be suspended for such dire circumstances.

She took the extra time to completely circle what she took to calling Hind HQ, ranging out far enough to locate the next closest emplacements. She didn't want to bring her people roaring in to challenge the aliens only to have a large group of reinforcements show up before her soldiers reached the shield. She didn't even know how they would destroy it.

New York Bay
Champions HQ—outside of Hind shield

Minerva had never tried to support more than one parahuman at the same time with her unique ability to boost the powers of others. She had a special connection with Ment that allowed her nearly unfettered access to his, and in return for his trust to reach inside his mind, she gave him complete control and razor-sharp focus. Their work in tandem made them one of the most powerful duos in the world. Sally had often joked how glad she was Minerva was on the side of the good guys, because she would be the most formidable enemy ever.

Sally had no idea how true a statement that was. Fortunately for Sally and the rest of the world, Minerva was firmly on the side of law and order. Currently, her emphasis was more on the *order* side than the law, for what she was doing to Humbug, Johnny Go, and Harlan could have been construed as telepathic assault by any prosecutor with half a brain.

Johnny Go was the easiest. As a speedster, he already operated on a hair trigger most of the time. Minerva just boosted his reaction speed, so that he could move with a fraction of a second's notice. He stood in a sprinter's starting stance, his hands resting upon a skateboard that held Harlan's machine upon it. If they successfully breached the shield, his mission was to push the machine into the breach and then get clear in case anything failed. The absolute worst-case scenario would be the shield snapping down upon him, freezing him in place but not harming him otherwise.

A control cable ran from the machine to a control box in Harlan's hands. The box had no switches or knobs; he controlled everything via his nanotech. If Johnny got his machine into the breach, he would fine-tune the device to replicate Humbug's abilities and keep the portal in the shield open for as long as he could. Minerva found it difficult to caress his brain the way she did others. Perhaps it was because of the microscopic devices suffusing his body to create a perfect meld of machine and man. Perhaps it was simply that he was a sociopath and his brain didn't operate the same way others' did.

He'd removed a Command Center monitor from its housing and integrated it into his machine to display waveforms. It showed three separate lines representing the combined volume, pitch, and timbre of each of Humbug's voices. Another line was overlaid upon each one, showing the current sonic target Harlan had set for her. The poor girl was hooked up to a SCUBA tank combined with a medical oxygen line—Harlan's best junkyard engineering. The line entered her nose and had carefully been fed down her throat with a slight detour around her larynxes, facilitated painlessly via Harlan's nanotech. It fed air at a constant pressure into her lungs, allowing her to maintain her tones nonstop. Minerva could tell it wasn't comfortable, and she did her best to take away the girl's discomfort even as she helped to fine-tune her voice.

At first, Harlan had thought perhaps a megaphone would provide sufficient volume, but his initial tests showed otherwise, and he ordered the others to wait for him. His nanotech armor grew around him. "Hey, where do you think you're going, *pendejo*?" Hector stepped up, fists balled up tight.

"Shopping," Harlan retorted.

"This is Just Cause, fucker. You don't *say*, you *ask*."

Harlan sighed with the weight of the world, as if he legitimately wasn't sure it was worth saving. Then he looked at Minerva. "Do you mind if I go get some equipment I need? I'll be gone no more than ten minutes and only need another ten to set it up."

"Do it," said Minerva.

He'd returned with some expensive stereo equipment that must have come out of some poor kid's car. He had Amber use her powers to create impromptu stands and sound cones with her ability and set up the speakers to have the exact same focal point with only a bare millimeter of airspace to let the sound escape. At Harlan's direction, Amber created additional braces and finally, Harlan had turned to Hector. "I'm asking now. Will you make yourself useful?"

Hector glanced at Minerva, who nodded back at him. "Yeah, whatever."

Harlan gestured toward the center of his contraption. "Brace this. The sound amplification will make it move backward. Keep it from doing so, but don't push it forward into the shield or the sound will be trapped and blow out the speakers."

Hector moved himself into position. Harlan directed Amber to build up some additional bracing around him to keep him from accidentally pushing the entire setup forward. "Hey, how do you know this pile of junk is going to work?" Hector asked.

Harlan chuckled. "Maybe you don't know my history very well. I've accomplished some fairly . . . interesting things with piles of junk."

"Assuming he gets the shield open, what do you want the rest of us to do, Boss?" Spray's dripping condensation ran into the grass at the edge of the shield, right where it intersected the Champions' building.

"Let me be clear. Nobody is to do anything if we breach the shield until Mr. Washington confirms that the hole is stable. I won't risk having any of you passing through it and it fails. We've seen it trap animals halfway through it, but we don't know that it won't cut you apart if a breach closes suddenly."

"Got it, Boss," said Jackdaw, who kept launching from an overhead perch, flying in a couple of small circles, then landing again. It was his equivalent of nervous pacing.

Harlan hissed with surprise and pleasure as the readings on his monitor reached a state he liked. "That's it," he said. "Hold it right there, Humbug. I'll bring up the amplification. From here on out, we're at microfrequency adjustments. Minerva, I'll need you to manage that, please."

Minerva nodded and glanced at Ment. "Love, I'm going to be busy for a few minutes. Mind the store."

Ment smiled at her from behind his sunglasses. He didn't reach out to touch her, knowing it would only be a distraction she didn't need. "You got it. Just Cause, stay sharp."

The rest of the team acknowledged his order as if it had come from Minerva herself.

Harlan turned back to the shield. "All right, you bastard. Let me show you why they call me *Destroyer*."

He cranked the volume on his makeshift sonic weapon to the proverbial eleven.

Time Warner Center
8th Ave. and West 59th St., Manhattan

Penny stared up at the impossibly tall, dark towers, giant black monoliths against the muted flickering of the Hind shield, and wished she'd guessed wrong.

She had to admit, grudgingly, that having someone around who could fly was a real benefit to scouting for intel. Unlike some heroes who were all fire and bluster and flapping capes and glowing energy, Toxic was noticeably silent as she wafted skyward, borne on a cloud of the worst aerial pollutants mankind had managed to pump into its own atmosphere. Penny wished they had functioning radios, and had to silently fume as she waited for Toxic to return from her reconnaissance with information about New York's rooftops. She had to trust E-Dog's sensitive dog nose and hearing, and her own sixth sense about enemies, to warn her about any approaching aliens.

The Hind seemed to have battened themselves down for the night. She didn't think it was anything more sinister than they'd achieved their initial goal and were preparing to embark upon the next phase of their invasion. With their shielded outposts full of human hostages, they'd put themselves in a powerful position for negotiations to commence, and Penny suspected they were giving humanity time to wrestle with the idea that surrender might not be such a bad outcome.

She'd suspected the bomb would be somewhere on a rooftop, which meant a building with a flat top sturdy enough to support a dropship, as the Hind couldn't have ascended through stairwells or elevator shafts. It would be centrally located within the shield, which meant Midtown, probably near Central Park, as that would be an easy landmark to spot from the air. It had been a five-mile ride on the bike, and Penny felt every bit of it in her legs. Years of police and Champion workouts, followed by Just Cause training, had her in the best shape of her life, but she'd been in a couple of tough battles already in the past several hours. She was operating on pure adrenalin and the kindness of a Greek grocery clerk, who'd recognized her and risked coming to the door of his store to press some snack bars, bottled water and coffee into her hands.

As she, Toxic, and E-Dog got closer to Central Park, it became trickier to avoid the Hind emplacements. Toxic had to do a lot of aerial scouting to find safe routes between the Hind guards, and Penny depended upon E-Dog to give her warning of anyone or anything approaching. When they stopped in the alley a block away from the Time Warner complex, Penny was certain they'd found their target. Two dropships were parked on the street before the twin towers, shields sparkling over them, with Hind Warriors crouched behind protective blocks with their axes and rifles at the ready. With something like twenty-five Hind, Penny knew she had no chance to fight her way through, and that many Warriors must have been guarding something important, and it had to be the bomb.

She looked up toward the distant rooftops and thought she saw more lights up high. She sent Toxic to investigate, "But be careful," she warned. "They look awfully alert, and I wouldn't be surprised if they have better sensors than we know."

Toxic nodded and floated upward on her stinking cloud into the darkness.

While she waited for Toxic to return, Penny examined the defensive positions below the Time Warner buildings using the scope of her sniper rifle. It would be a tough nut to crack for sure, but all she needed to do was get inside the building and she could lose any Hind who managed to pursue her inside. She needed a distraction to cross the open space to the nearest entrance. Even if it was locked, she had a limpet grenade that would open anything short of a vault door.

Toxic returned after a few minutes. She looked nervous and excited as she made her report to Penny. "It's up there. It has to be. I saw a thing the size of a beach ball on a stand. There are Hind guards around it, and a drop ship on the roof. It's not shielded." She smiled. "They must not be expecting trouble that high up."

"Good. That's my element right there," Penny said. She looked out across the open intersection with the darkness of Central Park stretching off to the north and east. "I need a distraction. Big. Bright. Noisy. Got any ideas?"

Toxic slipped her Zippo out of her pocket. "Yes, in fact, I've got just the thing. Give me time to get over to the other side and be ready to run."

"What's the signal?" Penny asked.

Toxic winked, barely visible in the darkness. "You'll know." As she flew off down a side street, a black cloud coalesced behind her and a dark, gummy fluid pulled itself from the asphalt with a sucking sound. Both stank of petroleum distillates and Penny had an idea what sort of distraction Toxic intended to create.

"We run now?" E-Dog looked up at her, his tail wagging in the darkness. Even though he was a man in dog form, his behavior was distinctly canine.

"Soon. That door over there." Penny pointed. "See it?"

"Yes."

"Get ready." She pulled the limpet grenade from her bag and armed it. "This will open the door. Make sure you're not in front of it when it goes off."

Across the plaza, the entire street erupted in a massive fireball.

The Hind gaped in astonishment at the sudden explosion. Tarry firebombs flew out of the cloud as if they were barrels of pitch from medieval catapults. The Warriors realized it was an *attack*, and they ran gleefully to engage the enemy, somewhere beyond the flames, abandoning their posts, axes and rifles at the ready.

Penny didn't wait. With the limpet in one hand and an extended-clip semiautomatic in the other, she sprinted from the shadows toward the Time Warner plaza. It only took a few seconds but it felt like an eternity of being horribly exposed. She slammed the limpet against the door, bursting the super-sticky glue bubbles on its underside. It stuck where she left it and she yanked the detonator free. A half dozen steps away and she crouched down against E-Dog. "Here we go." She thumbed the trigger and the shaped charge exploded, destroying the door latch in a jet of white-hot plasma.

Before her ears stopped ringing, Penny had her second pistol drawn and she rushed through the door with its latch still glowing red hot and into the darkened building.

Monkeyworld
Rheayara Command

Submistress Rheayara was a crafty elder with an unparalleled sense of strategy that might have been the greatest among all Clan Sharassar. Clanmistress Rhaorhir had detailed her greatest general with the task of securing Monkeyworld. Rheayara had been the one who selected the Monkey city of New York from all potential targets, the one who'd determined the size of the shield required, the one who'd spent more twelfths than anyone could count studying Monkey broadcasts to understand the psychology of the primates. Facing her under any circumstances would be at best daunting and at worst terrifying.

For Garragh, being interrogated by her was much closer to the terrifying end of the spectrum.

The first thing she had done when he arrived at her tent was to chastise the other Warriors who had delivered him to her practically naked, without so much as a stitch of armor or even a dagger. "If I wanted a concubine to entertain me, I would have requested one," Rheayara said in her soft, husky growl. "Take him from my sight and do not return him until he is accoutered properly as a Warrior should be."

Garragh's escorts had taken him to one of the drop ships and withdrawn spare armor and an axe from its stores and allowed him to dress in it. The armor itself was plain, gleaming a dull steel without a single swatch of color or pattern anywhere to mark it as his. If he wasn't disgraced, he would not only be allowed but expected to customize his armor with his own designs, whether to honor his family and ancestors, or even in a motif he found pleasing, inspirational, or one to trigger fear in opponents. Likewise, his axe was new, unblemished, without any of the character that well-used and well-loved weapons developed over many years. Carrying the untarnished weapon and wearing the untarnished armor made Garragh feel more humiliated than he had been when he'd been captured by the Monkeys.

His escorts returned him to Rheayara. She nodded her approval at the change in his appearance and ordered the rest of the Warriors to return to their duties with Laharsa. She padded over to a case that held a selection of bottles within it. She selected one filled with liquid the same orange as Hind blood and held it up to examine it. "Have you ever tasted bloodrose wine, Garragh?" she asked.

He noticed she didn't call him *Warrior*. Even though he wore the trappings of one, she spoke to him as if he were but a cub, not yet blooded in his first training. "No, Submistress."

"It is an acquired taste, to be sure. Many perceive it as overly sour and unpalatable." She decanted some of the orange liquid into a drinking bowl and raised it in both hands. "Those who persist with it, learn to appreciate the subtleties within its flavor. The tang of the shaded mountainsides where the bloodroses grow. The bitterness of harsh winters. The life force of those creatures upon whom the bloodroses feed. The acridity of death in high summer." She bent her head to the bowl and lapped up several swallows. When she raised her head, her jowls sparkled with tiny orange droplets. "A true connoisseur can identify where the roses were harvested by the flavor alone. I would offer you some, but the subtleties would be lost upon you, Garragh. It takes a lifetime of study." She took another drink of the brew. "I have spent less time studying the Monkeys than I have bloodrose wine, but that is more time than any other Hind has given to these primates. What do you think of that?"

"I . . ." Garragh didn't know what the Submistress wanted him to say. He wasn't sure how to answer such an open-ended question. He fell back upon the Warrior's Way. *"To follow orders is to be swift, efficient, and victorious. To think is to hesitate, to fail, to die dishonorably."*

Rheayara snorted. "You would quote your Catechism at me? Most of the ideas in that book were valid a thousand years ago when Hind battled Hind. We cannot apply our own philosophies to alien psychologies, no matter how much the Clanmistress would like to think we can. If we treated every world as if it were inhabited by those exactly like us, we would lose every war and never understand why. It falls to me and those like me who can take the time to understand alien psychology and form a plan that will exploit it. Have you studied the history of our Clan, Garragh? What do you know of the Kglotans? The Briese? The Ri'ar?"

Garragh knew she spoke of the other three races Clan Sharassar had found and conquered in their explorations of space. All three were primitive compared to the Hind. Indeed, they were primitive compared to the Monkeys from what he knew. "Very little, Submistress. They are Bears, Bats, and Birds."

"The Kglotans were the first. We approached them with overwhelming force, the way we would attack the Hind. They fought no matter what we did. They fought when it was hopeless. It took years and devastating half their world before we learned enough about their racial psychology that taught us they could only be bested when narrowly defeated instead of crushed. To this day, the Kglotans are still not fully subjugated, and they may never be. The Briese are masters of psychology. They nearly defeated us through making us question ourselves. What humiliation it would have been for Clan Sharassar to be beaten by stinking primitives!"

"Yes, Submistress." Garragh wasn't sure what else he was supposed to say. He had expected a brutal, torturous interrogation, and yet instead, she seemed to be more of a mood to talk than to ask questions.

"The Ri'ar presented a different challenge altogether. They are a race entirely bound by honor.

When it becomes evident they will lose a battle, they choose suicide over capture. Before we understood what it took to control the Ri'ar, fully eighty percent of their racial population was dead, mostly by their own talons. To this date, we have been forced to let them think they beat us, and only by slow, careful movements are we able to insinuate ourselves into their culture, to control and guide it as the Hind see fit." Rheayara swallowed the last of her wine and licked her lips. "So you see, Garragh, defeating a race is a matter of understanding their underlying psychology. Tell me, what did you learn about them as their prisoner?"

Garragh opened his mouth but no words immediately came forth. His thoughts were all jumbled up. How could he define the things he'd seen, experienced, felt? "They are . . . kind."

Rheayara narrowed her eyes. "Kindness is weakness. How are they kind?"

"They gave me water, food. They wrapped my wound. One Warrior-mistress protected me from others who wanted to harm me when I was bound."

"And you think reporting this information to me will somehow salvage your honor?" She stepped in close to him as if to smell his breath for a hint of cowardice. Her voice was barely a whisper. "You were captured by the enemy instead of fighting to the death as befits a Warrior. You allowed them to treat you like an animal instead of a Warrior. By all rights, I should have you put to death right now, Garragh."

He became acutely aware of her hand resting upon the hilt of her dagger as she moved directly in front of him. He stiffened but made no move to resist or pull back. *Fear not death but embrace it as the highest honor of a Warrior's life. To exist is to fight is to die for the Clan.* He would meet his fate as befit a Warrior.

Rheayara stepped back, hand still upon her dagger but making no move to unsheath it. "But we will have much to discuss after awhile. You will tell me more about the *kindness* of the Monkeys and how we may use that against them. I must think on the matter for awhile first. As much of this weakness I have seen in their entertainments, I find it strange that they would extend it to an enemy such as you."

Garragh said nothing. He felt like he had been on the verge of death at her hands, and then she had talked herself out of it. "Most Mistresses would choose to have you put to death for your cowardice. Unlike the Clanmistress, I don't spend resources lightly. Whether or not you are a coward, you are still a trained Hind Warrior who can swing an axe or fire a rifle when needed, and if nothing else, I can order you to charge the enemy to draw their fire. What will you do if I give you that order, Garragh?"

Garragh swallowed and whispered, "I will die for you, Submistress. It is my honor to do so."

Rheayara stepped back, a terrible smile creasing her leonine face. "That's more like it."

New York Bay
Champions HQ—outside of Hind shield

Harlan exulted in the sound and fury he'd created with his makeshift sonic weapon. The vibrations from Humbug's constant drone were being amplified and directed at a focal point on the Hind shield, and constant ripples flowed outward like a pool with droplets falling into it. The noise blasting against the shield was reflected back at the sound equipment and Amber had to keep repairing the cones she'd created as the vibrations cracked them. She had wrapped her head in a thick layer of amber, only leaving slits for her eyes and mouth so she could see and breathe.

"Is it working?" Spray shouted, trying to be heard over the drone.

"It better be," Hector retorted. "I can't hold this forever." His muscles bulged as he strained to keep the entire system from being flung backward.

Behind them, the windows shattered in Champions Headquarters, but Harlan paid no attention as the reading he was seeking appeared in his sensors. His fingers flew over the controls, faster than a human could see thanks to his nanotech. His device pushed a carbon fiber nanotube into a tiny breach in the shield. Before the shield closed it off, more tubes flowed inward, pushing the edges of the hole apart until they were large enough for a speaker the thickness of a finger. He fed Humbug's frequencies through his system and into the speaker and without any further fanfare, a semicircle opening appeared in the shield, the edges flowing in uneasy waves as the energy tried to reconnect itself.

In a quick blur, Johnny Go raced through the opening in the shield before anyone could react or prevent him from doing so. Fortunately for the foolish young man, Harlan was a better inventor than the Hind could have imagined and his portal held open. His next job was to make sure it stayed that way. He flipped a switch on his machine and waved at Humbug. "You can stop now."

Humbug sank to her knees, exhausted, as Minerva pulled the air tube from her throat. The sound she'd generated continued, but it emanated from Harlan's machine instead of her voiceboxes. He directed Amber to move speakers into place along the portal he'd created, using her amber as a framework to precisely position each one to maintain the sound against the shield. With her help, he built a half-ring of speakers, broadcasting Humbug's sound into the energy field, keeping it at bay. Satisfied with his work, he stood up and looked through the hole he'd created and saw Mustang Sally waiting on the other side.

Harlan had mixed feelings about the young woman. She'd personally been responsible for destroying his previous battlesuit, which had caused him no end of headaches and hardship. On the other hand, her misguided attempt to stop him had not only begun her own meteoric rise through the ranks of Just Cause, but had gotten him out of a technological rut and put him back in the frame of mind to do some real research before building the next suit. That mindset had allowed him to develop the nanotech currently flowing through his body, which in turn let him build the Preserve on the moon.

It turned out he and Sally had needed each other despite years of being at odds with each other. Despite all the death on his hands, she came to him and only him when a nanotech plague threatened to end human life on Earth. Naturally, he'd made a deal, and when he called in the favor Sally owed him, she had successfully rescued his sister, March's mother, from the coma in which she'd been stuck for two decades. It had all worked out in the end, and Harlan had found himself without any real reason to hate anyone for the first time in his life.

It had been a strange feeling.

Seeing Sally was still alive gave him another strange feeling, one he tentative identified as pleasure. It wasn't that he cared for her—he didn't care for anyone—but it would have bothered him to learn she had died, especially at the hands of these invaders.

He would make sure they wouldn't get the chance.

"Everyone through who's going through," he ordered. "I don't like the way this field is oscillating, and I don't think this gate will remain open very long."

"Harlan, I need to take Amber. She's an important part of my strike team," said Minerva. "Ment as well."

Harlan nodded. "Everyone else get moving. I don't know if we'll have another minute before this collapses."

Just Cause heroes and Champions rushed through the portal. Minerva pointed at Harlan. "Harlan, go."

"You'll need me in space," he said.

"I need you to shut down that shield," said Minerva. "I'm not sure anyone else can do it, but I believe you can."

Harlan nodded. She had him there. He wrapped his nanotech suit around himself and burst through the portal just as his system failed.

For a moment, he thought he might have to leave a leg behind.

CHAPTER NINE

U ♞ U

Champions Headquarters—inside of Hind shield
Battery Park, Manhattan

Sally watched as the majority of her team and the rest of the Champions flowed through the hole created in the Hind shield, with none other than Harlan Washington bringing up the rear in his full Destroyer getup. He cleared the gap just as it collapsed. He looked back over his shoulder once before turning his armored head back to face Sally and the others. At first she thought he might just keep his face hidden but a moment later, the nanotech that formed his helmet rolled backward into the shoulders of the suit and she saw the face of the man she didn't know whether or not to hate. He'd killed her father, the superhero known as Lionheart, as well as her mother's husband, just before she'd been born. He'd killed so many heroes, so many civilians, that it would have taken Sally a good while to list them all, even at super-speed.

And yet, somehow, she had seen the man behind the mask, and what she'd learned about him was that his damaged childhood had been responsible for much of his adult behavior. Even with his sociopathy, he still had a soft spot for his younger sister Reggie, who had spent twenty years in a coma courtesy of a brutal assault she'd suffered while still a teenager. He'd built his entire moon base as a place to keep her safe while he'd labored for many years to try to unlock the mystery of what kept her asleep. The assault upon her had left her pregnant, and Harlan had done his best to raise his nephew March.

Sally had spent some time on the moon base with Minerva, and with March, and she'd agreed to a risky procedure to try to awaken Reggie. She'd succeeded, but the woman had only lived long enough to thank her, and to thank Harlan, before she had vanished into the Dream-world she'd created with her parahuman powers. It had been a powerful turning point for Harlan, and seeing the change in him had been amazing for Sally to behold. She knew she should hate him, but yet, when she saw him standing in Champions Headquarters, her first impulse was to run over and hug him. He'd warned the world. He'd found a way through the shield. He was acting like . . .

. . . Like a hero.

Sally stepped over to him. "Harlan." She kept herself from embracing him. It wouldn't have looked good to the others, but she tried to inject a note of warmth into her voice, even though he wasn't likely to pick up upon it. She noticed the Hind axe clipped to the back of his armor. It was simultaneously anachronistic and, well, badass.

"Sally. I'm . . . pleased to see you are still alive."

She shrugged. "Long as I keep running, death can't catch me."

"What information do you have?"

Sally looked around at the others. "Normally, I'd say briefing in the conference room, but as I understand it, it's on the wrong side of the shield. So we'll just do this right here. The Hind have their shield generator in Times Square. Everybody know where that is?"

Most of the heroes nodded.

"Those who don't, stay with someone who does. They've got all approaches heavily guarded, but we have the benefit of being able to travel through hallways and corridors that they can't. Spotlight, can I have a little light on the wall here?"

Spotlight obliged by shining his eyes to illuminate Sally as she stood by the exterior wall of Champions HQ. "Stefan, I apologize. I'll help you repaint." She took a permanent marker from her belt.

Surfboy shrugged. "If we pull this off, you're about to draw me a tourist attraction. Anyone who covers it will answer to me."

Sally referenced her pizza box-map and drew it in large scale at super-speed. She was nobody's artist, but she'd spent enough years in New York that she could at least manage a rough map. "Here's where the generator is. There are three drop ships and multiple troop emplacements here, here, and here. They've got clear fields of fire down 46th, 7th, and Broadway. There's some kind of headquarters tent here, right beside the generator. What I propose is we make our approach through the subway tunnels. There's the Times Square station here, the 50th station here, and this one . . . um . . ."

"Rockefeller," said Johnny Go. "That's where all the diamond merchants are."

"Three-pronged attack," said Detroit Steel. "I like it. Good chance to get our hands dirty."

"You know it, *chica*," Hector said. He and Detroit Steel bumped fists with a sound like a ball peen hammer hitting a piece of iron.

"It's a good strategy," Harlan said as he examined the map. "Three directions of attack minimizes the chance of us getting caught in each other's crossfire, and makes Times Square into a kill box."

Sally shivered, wishing Harlan hadn't used *that* particular term. "Anyway, we take out the defensive perimeter and then capture the headquarters tent. There must be a Hind in there who can disable either the shield or the bomb or both."

"Bomb?" Harlan narrowed his eyes. "What bomb?"

"You didn't hear the message from the Clanmistress?"

"It may have happened while I was being interrogated aboard one of the Hind ships."

Sally blinked. She'd want to hear more details about that escapade once they'd driven back the invaders. "She said she'll destroy the city if we don't capitulate to her demands. Dolittle was able to read the mind of a captured soldier and learned there's a bomb that they'll set off. I sent Penny to go find it."

"You'll need my help to disarm it," Harlan said. "I'm the only one experienced enough with Hind technology."

"I was hoping you'd say that. We'll have to bring Dolittle along with us to try to interrogate whatever Hind we capture."

Dolittle looked as if she might faint.

"That won't be necessary," said Harlan. "She's clearly a liability. I, on the other hand, have a working translation of their tongue."

"You can speak it?"

"As I said, I'm the only one experienced with Hind technology."

Hector crossed his arms with a clank and Sally thought she could almost see the steam rising out of his ears. The man detested Harlan and honestly, Sally couldn't blame him for it. She knew the best thing would be to play to Harlan's ego. "Then you're indispensable for this mission. Can I ask you to lead one of the assault forces?"

Harlan nodded. "It's only logical. I'll take the Rockefeller station squad."

Sally turned to Detroit Steel. "Shawna, you'll lead the Times Square station team. I'll lead the 50th station." She held up her phone. "No signals yet, but do you all at least have enough batteries to check the time?"

Generalized agreement came from the group.

"We strike at midnight. That gives us just about an hour to set up our attack." She raised a fist in the air. "Ladies, gentlemen, it's time to change the narrative. Let's take back our city."

Fort Justice
New York Bay

The trip back to Fort Justice was quiet, and it didn't help to settle Minerva's nerves at all. She'd left for Champions Headquarters with her entire team as well as Harlan and all his equipment. They'd taken one of the motor launches because the Command Center wasn't about to authorize a flight in the *Dorothy*, Just Cause New York's VTOL transport jet, and risk splattering it and the members of the team across the Hind shield in the event of a critical accident. Minerva had found the rhythm of the boat as it traversed the wavelets to be soothing. On the way back, though, the boat was quite a bit lighter and it tended to hit the troughs a little harder, making her head ache somewhere in the vicinity of her back teeth.

Besides the boat pilot, she had Ment on one side of her and Amber on the other and nobody else. All of her other teammates, her friends, were inside the Hind shield and about to risk their lives to try to bring it down before the Hind took it upon themselves to destroy Manhattan. Meanwhile, she and her own team of operatives were about to embark upon an equally dangerous mission, to try to destroy the alien fleet—or at least, drive them away.

At an emotional level—something Minerva tried to minimize because of how easy it was for emotions to cloud one's judgment—the idea of destroying the invaders' ships was distasteful. Here were sentients who had evolved on a completely different planet, in orbit around a different star, with millions of years of biological imperatives and thousands of years of cultural experiences so different from those of Earth. Humans might never truly understand the Hind, for they were so very *alien*. On the other hand, if they didn't make an effort to comprehend the rationale of these beings who'd crossed uncounted light years just to establish a beachhead, would it cement the notion of xenophobia within the Human experience? Fear of the *Other* was what drove many people in the world to make the decisions they made, for better or for worse. The Hind had brought that to a head.

Logic dictated that they should destroy the Hind. Let those who waited behind wonder why their raiding party never returned. Minerva and her soldiers should take the alien vessels, strip the technology from them, download all the information from their computers, build warships of their own, and go bughunting. Teach the Hind that Humanity would not roll over in supplication, not now, not ever. The Hind had no idea who they were messing with, and it would be their last mistake.

"Hey, babe, you're thinking so hard you're making my head hurt," Ment said.

Minerva pulled off her helmet, set it in her lap, and leaned her head upon his shoulder. "I'm torn. We should destroy the Hind. It's the only way to keep the world safe, and that's my charge."

"I didn't think you were building an attack vessel in the basement just to go negotiate with them."

"If I chose to do that instead, do you think it would work? Would the Hind listen to us if they saw us as a threat? Or would they choose to fight more?"

"I don't know," said Ment. "They're aliens. Nobody knows how they think about things. I don't envy you the choices you've got to make."

"Permission to speak freely?" Amber asked.

Minerva smiled at her young ally. "You don't have to ask for permission, Amber. Speak your mind."

"It's just that . . . there's not going to be any right decisions in all of this. Everyone is going to analyze everything we do to death. Right or wrong, history will judge us in the end."

"So what do you think I should do?"

Amber paused. Minerva could see the tiny nodes of magic along the girl's skin, too small for anyone else to see without a powerful magnifying lens. They looked like flakes of gold nestled in her pores. The amber she generated came from those tiny wells, a magical legacy from her grandfather, the Archmage. They were beautiful to behold, and in Minerva's eyes, they made Amber sparkle like a star. At last, she spoke, her words of wisdom sounding like they came from someone far older. "We're the Native Americans. When the Europeans came to the Americas, they came as aggressors. They were convinced they were in the right. They had God on their side, or whatever. The natives welcomed them, rolled over and showed their bellies, and they kept rolling over until it was too late and they were pushed onto reservations where they're dying out. They once ruled this entire continent and now look at them. Give them a generation or two and they might all be gone." She shivered. "I don't want to be pushed onto a reservation, or massacred, or whatever horrible things the Hind will do to a race they've conquered. I'll fight. No matter what, I'll fight for my life. For my people. For all humanity."

Minerva nodded. "That's a wise observation, Amber, and I believe you are correct in your assessment. We should fight them. We *will* fight them. Whatever it takes to defeat them, we will do it." She pinched the bridge of her nose. "It's a sobering that my job is to send soldiers to their deaths. What if I'm wrong?"

"Sacrificing heroes weakens us all. But if it means the difference between losing us or losing the world, you have to let us go." She shuddered. "I don't want to die. Especially not in space. But if my death meant the world would be safe . . ." She looked up and met Minerva's gaze. "I guess there are worse ways to go."

"I swear, I will do everything possible to keep you all alive. I won't lie to you and say you'll come through it okay, but I will do my best to see you through it."

"That's fair."

The rest of the short trip to Fort Justice passed in silence. They arrived back at headquarters and found several things had come together in their absence. Davey was waiting at the dock and filled them in as they got onto the elevator. "Your team is gathered," she said. "Giant used his teleporting ability to facilitate everyone else getting here faster. They're awaiting you in the conference room."

"Good," Minerva said. "What about March?"

"He says he's nearly done. He estimates you could depart within the next two hours."

"Tell him he's only got one. We need to distract the Hind from our forces on the ground. A two-pronged attack will be the best way to save New York."

Davey nodded. "I'll tell him. Also, General Gershwin has brought you your very own flying saucer. It's on the upper deck."

"The *Daedalus*?"

"That's what he said. It's armed to the teeth from what I could see. I suspect the military has more knowledge about space combat than they've let on."

"Is the vessel's crew already in the conference room as well?"

"Yes." To someone else, Davey might have sounded brusque to the point of being rude, but to Minerva, she was the very picture of efficiency in every thing she did, whether in word, action, or thought. Minerva appreciated that about Davey perhaps more than anyone else in the entire Just Cause organization.

"I'll need five minutes to prepare and then I'll begin my briefing."

"Coffee and tea are ready and waiting, Boss."

Minerva gave Davey one of her rare smiles. "You are a rare treasure and we are fortunate to have you on our side."

Time Warner Center
8th Ave. and West 59th St., Manhattan

Penny knew there were people who ran up and down high-rise stairwells for fun and the health benefits. She cursed every single one of them who hadn't ever had to wear body armor, carry a sniper rifle and a bag full of various useful tools and *objets de lethality*. The first ten floors had gone fairly quickly. The second ten found her beginning to flag a bit in her efforts. By the time she reached the thirtieth floor, her heart was pounding and her legs felt like jelly. She'd been up for far too many hours, participated in too many battles, and had too little nourishment. She could have inhaled a Sarge's Deli Monster sandwich all by herself and then taken a ten hour nap.

Instead, she ate a granola bar, drank some water, and allowed herself a ten minute rest before climbing the stairwell again. E-Dog, typically graced with the boundless energy of a dog, sat panting in the near-darkness. Only the emergency lighting still burned within the stairwell, giving everything a washed out, blood-red look. "How you doing, Dog?"

E-Dog yawned, making a soft whine. "Bored."

Penny got to her feet. "All right, all right, you made your point. I'd like to see *you* run up these stairs lugging fifty pounds of equipment."

E-Dog sneezed and trotted up the stairs ahead of her. "Twenty floors to go," he said.

"It's twenty-five, you little shit."

He looked down at her over his shoulder. "Dogs can't count past twenty."

"That's some kind of bullshit right there." Penny's calves and thighs complained as she continued up the steps. Five more floors. Ten more. Fifteen.

E-Dog froze on a landing, his hackles raised, sniffing at the air.

Penny slipped a pistol from a holster. "What is it?"

"People. Humans."

"You feel like scouting ahead?"

"What if they have guns? Shoot me. Think I'm alien."

"You don't look anything like a Hind. Be a lost little doggie. Whiny and tail-waggy. Give me a yip if it's safe to come up."

"That's demeaning." E-Dog struggled to form the word that his lips and tongue weren't designed to recreate. Penny wasn't moved. "All right, all right. If I get shot, make sure you get me to Dolittle."

"Nobody's getting shot," said Penny. Just to be safe, though, she thumbed off the safety on her pistol. She gave E-Dog a twenty-count and then followed after him, trying to ignore the complaints in her legs.

A yip echoed down the stairwell a minute later and she lowered her gun, although she wasn't so confident as to holster it again. She did pull out a flashlight to make sure she didn't surprise anyone and continued upward until she rounded a landing on the 50th floor and found a pair of frightened young adults with complicated backpacks and haunted expressions. E-Dog sat between them, wagging his tail, looking smug and satisfied.

"You guys all right?" Penny put away her gun. The two young twenty-somethings weren't any threat to her.

"Yeah," one of them said. "You're with Just Cause? Is it over?"

"No, it's not over, and yes, I am."

"Your dog talks," said the other one. "I'm loving that."

"He's his own dog. What are you guys doing here?"

The two young men looked at each other and then one said, a little sheepishly, "We were gonna BASE jump off the tower. Right into Central Park. It was gonna be lit."

"It would have probably gotten you arrested," said Penny. "You know that's illegal, right?" She saw their hurt expressions and reminded herself that she'd once been young and dumb too. Her ex-husband was proof enough of that. "But since you didn't do it, I'm not going to arrest you. I'm a little too busy right now for that. Why did you stay up here?"

"When the, uh, aliens landed, they came down right on the roof," said one man. "We saw them. Watched them set stuff up on the roof. After that, we didn't know where to go. The people hiding in their apartments said they're down on the ground below too."

"We were thinking maybe if they left, we'd try parachuting down, but we wouldn't know if they were gone and could be parachuting down just to get captured." The other man looked like he was about to cry. "I'm a little scared."

Penny knew she couldn't tell the men why she was really there. If they knew there was a bomb to destroy the entire city just a few floors over their heads, they'd freak out. "Okay, listen, jumping off the building is a bad idea even when there isn't an alien invasion going on. You guys are a hundred percent safer inside. The Hind are too big to fit through most human-sized doors, and we haven't seen any indications of them making more than cursory efforts to enter buildings. They don't have the troop strength to clear every building and capture every human, so they're not trying to. They grabbed whoever they could off the streets or ground levels and threw them behind shields to use as hostages, and they did it in full view of the rest of us so we could see how much they weren't afraid of us." She pulled off her helmet and wiped sweat from her forehead, wishing only for the return of air conditioning.

"So what should we do?" asked the first man.

"Head lower into the building," Penny said. "E-Dog will go with you. He'll make sure you don't get surprised by anything in the lower levels."

"Why, what are you going to do?"

Penny replaced her helmet. "Evict the squatters."

Monkeyworld
Rheayara Command

Following his interrogation in Submistress Rheayara's tent, Garragh was assigned to perimeter duty. The Warrior who took him to his first post had armor painted a brilliant blue with fine filigree in gold and white, and his axe was notched and stained along the blade. His name was Ashar and he didn't even try to hide his disdain for Garragh.

"You will move from post to post to give relief to each Warrior in turn, allowing them to eat, eliminate, and rest without risk of dividing their attention between themselves and their duties." Ashar snarled. "This is not an honorable position. *There is no honor in distraction.* These Warriors have been on high alert since landing and all of them require rest to be in peak fighting shape."

Garragh didn't have to ask why his position was not honorable. He'd been on high alert as much as the rest of the Hind forces. Indeed, he might even have suffered more than most, being captured by the Monkeys. On the other hand, during his captivity, he'd had the opportunity to rest, to eat, and to heal, which was more than many of the other Warriors had. Ashar was implying that Garragh hadn't properly earned his downtime, and therefore his dishonor was to give truly honorable Warriors the time they needed.

They reached the first post, a semicircular barrier behind which a Warrior would be protected from enemy fire while guarding that particular approach toward the camp. It was still within the torus-shaped shield, but near enough to the edge that if the shield failed or was switched off, he would be the first into battle.

Or perhaps, the first to die.

The Warrior on duty glanced back at their approach. "You're relieved," Ashar said. "Recuperate."

The Warrior took note of Garragh's pristine armor, his brand-new axe, and snorted in amusement. "To obey is my honor." He loped off toward the headquarters tent.

Ashar grinned at Garragh, showing his teeth in a display of dominance. "Shiny armor makes you a bright target. I hope the Monkeys attack tonight. Let them squeal and squawk at us while we harbor the hostages. Let them bring their tiny blades and popguns to battle against our axes and lasers. They will break on us. Although, perhaps not upon you."

Garragh lowered his head. Insult upon insult had been heaped upon him, and it took every bit of his strength not to respond. He knew he might salvage his honor by attacking Ashar, but the crafty Warrior was hoping for exactly that act. With a new axe he had never trained with, and new armor in which he didn't know how to move, Garragh would only die upon Ashar's blade. He wasn't supposed to fear death, but he did, and he wouldn't be goaded into selling his life for the price of an insult.

"I have my orders," Garragh said in a low growl. "From the Submistress herself. To obey her is my honor. Would you challenge her rule?"

Ashar threw back his head and roared in laughter. "You are a coward and to call you a Warrior is an insult to all Warriors. Do your duty, Garragh. Perhaps you may yet die for the Clan."

"I'd be the first to beg for it if it meant not having to listen to you anymore."

Ashar froze. He raised his axe. "Say that once more and you die, coward."

"Ashar!" The blue-armored Hind jerked as if he'd been physically assaulted. All the Warriors looked to see Submistress Rheayara standing nearby, her forearms folded across her upper torso and her front toes tapping claws on the ground in irritation. "I forbid you to fight amongst yourselves. It may be Rhaorhir's Clan, but this is *my* city and *my* world and you are *my* Warriors."

Ashar bowed his head. "To obey is my honor."

The other Warriors echoed Ashar's sentiment, as did Garragh.

He didn't mean it as strongly as they did.

New York Subway System
Sixth Avenue Line

Harlan found himself traveling with three of the four insufferable children formerly known as the Young Guns. He knew Surfboy, Bombshell, and Johnny Go had been Sally's classmates at the Hero Academy along with Toxic. Unlike her, they hadn't been good enough to join Just Cause. They'd kicked around for awhile, starting out in San Francisco trying to make a go of it there, but eventually they'd drifted east in what Harlan imagined had been an interminably long and boring road trip and wound up having rave parties in the former Just Cause training facility. When they were duped into joining Isotope's fledgling parahumans-first organization, it might have spelled the end of them. Lucky for them, Sally had seen through the ruse and ultimately freed many of the Champions from Isotope's sway. The prevailing rumor was Sally had slain the man herself, but Harlan didn't believe it. He knew Sally was a killer—he'd seen her take lives before—but he didn't think she'd killed Isotope. Someday, he hoped to learn the truth.

He looked over his three companions, using his nanotech suit cameras as they traveled along the IND Sixth Avenue Line. Surfboy was the leader of the Champions, first by Isotope's appointment and later by the Parahuman Resources Administration. All he could do was fly, and then at fairly low altitudes. That made him in the bottom tier of power levels compared to most parahumans. Harlan had thought he was an immature goofball when they first met, and nothing the young man had done had changed that opinion. A few years of leadership had tempered his attitude somewhat, and if he survived another ten years, Harlan thought he might actually turn into something worthwhile.

Surfboy flew along with Bombshell riding on his back like, well, a surfer. Bombshell was the daughter of a San Francisco police officer and was part of the super-strong, super-tough set of parahumans commonly referred to as *bricks*. Given her background and power level, she had probably been the closest of the Young Guns to earning a position in Just Cause. Unfortunately for her—or perhaps fortunately—she had a bad temper and was psychologically unfit to represent the greatest heroes in the world. She was an exemplary hero, so long as everything was going her way, and she had her boyfriend Johnny Go to keep her on an even keel.

Johnny Go was a speedster, like Sally, and he kept pace beside Surfboy, just behind Destroyer, running along the ceiling like a spider. Although he was nowhere as quick as Sally, his ability to run along walls and ceilings gave him an unusual advantage compared to most speedsters. If Surfboy was immature and Bombshell was prone to rage, Johnny Go simply didn't take life seriously enough to be a superhero. From his flamboyant blue and red costume to his devil-may-care attitude, he didn't have the good sense to know when he was overmatched. If he wasn't best friends with Surfboy, he'd forever be in trouble. Between the two of them, Harlan thought he might wind up killing them both himself to save the Hind the trouble.

Harlan was dismayed at the three so-called heroes Sally had placed in his charge, but from a strategic standpoint he understood why she'd done so. She had two of the rookie heroes, Chinook and Spray, along with the Champion Humbug and Hector on her team. They were the weakest, most likely to suffer in a combat engagement, and Harlan would have been surprised if she'd let anyone else watch over them. Detroit Steel had her own metallic hands full of Jackdaw, Shouty Ed, and Spotlight. Harlan had wondered about the conventional wisdom of combining two sonic-powered heroes on the same squad, but perhaps their powers could play off each other to allow better results.

"Hey, you know what's best about running along the walls?" Johnny Go asked.

"No, what?" Surfboy replied.

"You have any idea what kind of shit runs out of the bottom of subway trains?"

Surfboy chuckled. "Well, they don't have bathrooms in them."

"I always assume any puddle is pee," said Bombshell.

"Probably for the best, babe," Johnny Go said. "After this is all over, we deserve a vacation away from puddles and nasty underground tubes. I'm thinking Cancún."

"Sounds nice." Bombshell smiled at Johnny.

Harlan grimaced inside of his armor. Romance was something he'd never had any desire for in his life. After his bumbling, adolescent crush on an older girl named Gretchen, he'd given up any interest in companionship. Women were more trouble than they were worth. When he'd run one of the most powerful gangs in Philadelphia, there had been numerous women, always hanging around, anxious to please, eager to be close to the money, the drugs, and the power. He'd always pushed them away.

They were a distraction, and he wouldn't let them pull him away from his own plans. Other men spent so much time and energy and effort trying to get their dicks wet. Harlan took that otherwise wasted effort and turned it back toward his own work, and in his mind, that made him more successful than most men.

He checked his inertial location app. With the Hind shield inhibiting even GPS signals, Harlan had to trust to his own technology. That was easy for him, as his technology was superior to anything built by anyone else. "Stop your babbling about vacations and human waste. We are close to Rockefeller Station. Prepare for battle." As if to illustrate his point, he pulled the Hind axe from his back and flexed it. His shoulder cannons sprouted from his suit like flowers opening and energy flowed from his reserves to the wrist blaster capacitors.

Surfboy reached down to his hip and drew a pistol with an extended clip. With no powers beyond flight, he'd be dependent upon weapons in combat. Likewise, despite his speed and clinging abilities, Johnny Go had no offensive powers. He had a police-issue side-handle baton. Harlan would have called it by its proper name, a *tonfa*, but he doubted Johnny Go had any knowledge of such things. Bombshell, as her name implied, needed no such implements to fight, trusting to her fists, her strength, and her resistance to harm.

Harlan's suit informed him they were approaching the station and multiple life signs were detected, all human. "Surfboy, Johnny, go ahead of me. You're going to be more familiar to New Yorkers. Warn them to stay below the surface until the city sounds an all-clear."

"That's awfully considerate of you, Washington," Surfboy said as he flew past Harlan. "I thought you were supposed to be a sociopath."

Harlan would have shrugged, but his suit wouldn't convey the motion effectively. "I don't care either way, but I'd rather the three of you focus on battling the Hind instead of trying to protect civilians. That's the kind of distraction that will weaken you."

"Warms my heart." Johnny Go ran past over Harlan's head, then raised his voice. "Hey, all you people up there, we're coming out of the tunnel and we're the good guys. Don't shoot us."

They burst out into the station. Dim emergency lights made for huge shadows, but Harlan could see all the people clearly thanks to his advanced sensors. A handful of people shone their cell-phone flashlights in the direction of the heroes. Cries of "We're safe!" and "What's going on?" and "Is it over?" spread throughout the station until Surfboy put his fingers to his lips and blew his best New York cab whistle.

"Everyone, settle down. No, it's not over yet, and you're not safe yet, but we're here to try to change that. We need everyone to stay down here in the station for your safety. If any aliens come down here, try to get into rooms with regular doors. They're too big to fit through most of them."

"What are you going to do?" A woman in a MTA uniform stepped forward to challenge them, apparently the de facto leader of what Harlan wryly thought of as the Rockefeller Refugees.

"Fight back," said Johnny Go. "Wish us luck, hey?"

Numerous well-wishes came their way and followed in their wake as the four heroes flew or ran up the stairs toward the surface. *Four* heroes? Harlan thought. Surely he wasn't considering himself one. He was only in it to fight the aliens who'd so rudely come into his life and interrupted his work. That didn't make him a hero.

Or perhaps it did.

CHAPTER TEN

♞

50th Station, Manhattan

Sally checked the street above the subway station and then ordered her team to join her. She'd taken charge of the youngest Just Cause members Chinook and Spray, as well as Humbug, whose faceted eyes were wide pools of nervous obsidian in the darkness. "We've only got a couple of minutes before we need to head in, and I know it's scary. I've been where you guys are right now. This isn't going to be like any training you've ever had. Chinook has a little experience with it since she came to Manhattan with me."

Chinook nodded. Her eyes were shadowed and she looked ready to drop from exhaustion. Sally wished she could have sent the girl home to rest, but the fate of New York, and even the world, might rest upon the outcome of this battle. It was time to make the hard decisions, the ones Juice had entrusted her to make years ago when he'd promoted her to command Just Cause New York.

"All I can say is that these aliens, the Hind, they're bad shots but they're very strong and love to fight hand to hand. Remember, you're not fighting for yourself, or for me. You're fighting for this city. For the civilians the aliens have captured and are holding as prisoners. You're fighting for the world.

You're fighting for humanity. You're taking a stand against these invaders and telling them we will not lay down our arms. This is our home, and we will defend it to our last breaths."

"Fucking right, *chica*," said Hector, gleaming dully in the faint light from the overhead shield.

Water ran off Spray like he had garden hoses for legs. He looked more terrified than anyone Sally had seen in a long time. She smiled at him, trying to be as encouraging as possible.

"The Hind have no idea what they're about to face. They've never seen what parahumans can do when they don't have constraints." Sally's face grew grim. "I'm authorizing you to use deadly force. Property damage. Dirty tricks and cheap shots. In this battle there are no rules. Don't be honorable. Fight to win, not to look good doing it. You leave me to worry about the aftermath. Watch each others' backs. Watch out for civilians. Anything else goes. Oh, one last thing." She smiled at Humbug. "Humbug . . . I'm sorry, I don't even know your real name."

"It's H-Hadley," the girl said.

"Hadley, a.k.a. Humbug, I am officially inducting you into Just Cause. As of this moment, you're one of us. Welcome aboard." Sally shook Humbug's hand. "It's time. Just Cause, move out!"

Chinook offered a hand to Humbug. "I can carry you. It's faster, and we can attack them from above." Humbug grasped Chinook's wrist and the two of them flew up into the darkness. Water pooled around Spray like he was standing in a fountain. It lunged forward like a wave breaking toward the shore, carrying him upon its crest as more and more water spread around him until he looked like he was riding a tidal wave down Broadway toward Times Square. Sally sprinted down the street, covering three blocks in three seconds.

Sally accelerated her perceptions until the world moved in slow motion around her, giving her more time to plan her moves. She saw Destroyer moving in to attack from the east with her former Hero Academy classmates, his shoulder cannons firing at the closest Hind Warrior. Johnny Go had his *tonfa* out and was angling across the face of a building to one side while Bombshell had leaped from Surfboy's back, aiming to crash down upon another Warrior. Surfboy had a pistol in both hands as he raced across the ground, staying low to present a smaller target.

From the south, Shawna and her team raced up 7th Avenue. She carried a taxicab as a shield while Shouty Ed and Jackdaw fired off sonic attacks around the edges. Spotlight couldn't brighten his gaze enough to be useful as a weapon, but he had a police-issue shotgun in his hands and at least looked like he knew what he was doing with it.

Then Sally was in the middle of the Hind encampment, and she turned her attention toward the most effective use of her speed. She couldn't battle the Hind hand-to-hand. The first time she'd tried to punch one at super-speed, she'd nearly broken her wrist, and even with her accelerated healing, it had taken a few hours before she'd felt able to use her hand again. Luckily, there were other ways she could fight. The first Warrior she met she took a moment to study as he tried to strike her in slow motion. His motion revealed the location of the joints and catches of his armor, and after a few fruitless attempts, she discovered the means to disengage the clasps. After that, she ran from Warrior to Warrior, stripping each one of his armor. To the others, it would have looked like the Hinds' armor simply fell off. It didn't make the alien Warriors any less dangerous, but made them much more vulnerable.

A Warrior fell to Spotlight's shotgun. Another collapsed with a skull pulped from the combined sonic attack of Jackdaw and Shouty Ed. Destroyer blasted his cannons indiscriminately, sometimes knocking fiery craters into the asphalt or nearby buildings, sometimes blasting apart Warriors. One closed upon him and he met the creature axe to axe, something gleeful in the way he battled with one of the aliens' own weapons.

Shawna swung her ruined taxicab like a power hitter in a home run derby, sending aliens flying. Hector waded into them, trusting his metallic body to protect him as he drove his fists through flesh and bone. Chinook and Humbug dropped out of the sky. Chinook used her wind to blow one Warrior across the ground like a crumpled piece of paper while Humbug emitted piercing whistles that made the small semicircle shields short out.

Spray's wave struck a trio of Warriors, sweeping them off their feet amid the dirty water. He lifted each of them inside columns of water, moving it to keep them from reaching air. They struggled for far longer than should have been possible, suggesting they had impressive lung capacity. Then he forced water into their bodies through whatever openings he could find until they stopped moving and fell, resembling overstuffed furniture.

"Spray, look out!" Sally cried as a Hind rose up behind him, axe raised to cleave the young man in half. A car whirled through the air to crash into the Warrior, sending the alien flying across the street.

"Yeah, get some!" shouted a familiar voice and Sally's heart skipped a beat. She stopped running for a moment as she realized Jason—*her husband Jason*—had joined the battle. He wore little more than ragged, battle-worn jeans. He had bloody slashes across his chest, his arms, his face, but his eyes still twinkled and his sweat-stained, filthy hair flopped in his face the way it had when she first saw him all those years ago. She started to call out to him when someone crashed into her from behind, knocking her down.

She saw Surfboy tumble across the pavement to crash into a lamppost. The side of his face was a smoking ruin. She knew he was dead before she ran over to check, and knew he might have saved her life by knocking her down. By the time she'd raced across the street to lay a finger on his throat, Bombshell had engaged the Hind who'd shot him. The powerful woman wrapped her arms around the Hind's torso and squeezed. He fought back, straining against her inexorable strength, until a sickening crackle made it clear his alien strength was no match for her fury.

"Stefan!" Johnny Go cried and ran over to slide to a halt by his longtime friend and teammate. A laser intersected his side and he fell without a sound, his heart flashburned before he even had a chance to realize it.

Sally shook herself. She had no time to mourn. The Hind had recovered from the shock of the initial assault and were regrouping, using portable shields against Destroyer's cannons and the parahumans' sonic assaults while others fired their rifles from behind cover.

She charged at them, knowing she wasn't fast enough to dodge a laser beam but hoping she was too fast for them to hit her. She thought about trying to heft one of the heavy axes and wielding it herself but she had no idea how to use one effectively. An idea occurred to her and she shoulder-checked into the barrel of a Hind's rifle, swinging it around as he pulled the trigger and dispatched one of his fellows. Before they realized what had happened, she'd gotten two more to shoot each other.

Humbug screamed as Chinook fell to the street, shot. They bounced off the top of a box truck to both crash to the ground at awkward angles.

Destroyer roared like a primal beast through his external speakers and engaged both his cannons on full automatic, their thunder drowning out everything. The sonic booms from the supersonic shells shattered glass in the towering buildings around Times Square. Hind Warriors were torn apart by his fusillade.

Even at super-speed, Sally barely got her ears covered in time as she sprinted clear of Destroyer's kill zone. She zipped across the field of battle to Jason's side just as he was lifting up a car to hurl. "Hi, babe," he grunted as he flung the car into a phalanx of troopers. "Miss me?"

"Yes, you big dope! I was about to tear the whole city apart looking for you." Sally ran over to a Warrior with his laser raised and knocked the barrel aside as he fired, targeting another Warrior instead of her husband. She zipped back beside him. "I was worried about you."

"Don't worry," he said with a grin. "I'm fine. These guys aren't so tough." He wrenched a lamp post from the cement and swung it like a golfer, knocking a Hind's helmet off and flipping the alien onto his back. He stepped forward and kicked it in the head, snapping its neck. "See?" He spotted something and frowned. "Hey, Spray's in trouble."

Sally whirled to see Spray had been cornered against a building with three Hind holding their rifles on him. Water sluiced off him like a dam had broken but he'd lost his focus and wasn't fighting back. "Be right back, babe."

She arrived at the same time Spotlight and Shouty Ed did. They made short work of two of the Hind, one using his shotgun and the other a focused sonic attack. Sally pulled the last Warrior's axe from his and with no clear idea of what she was doing, brought it down across the back of his head. The blade split the helmet and buried itself in his skull. The Warrior went down and didn't move.

A blast from one of the dropship turrets made a huge, smoldering crater in the side of the building and the instantaneous thunder blew all of them to the ground. Sally staggered against a parked car, her ears ringing, trying to regain her senses. She glanced in Jason's direction just in time to see a Hind rise up from behind a parked car and bring his axe down across Jason's shoulders with a sickening thunk. "*Jason!*" she screamed as he pitched forward, his back opened to the spine.

Fort Justice
New York Bay

Across New York Bay, beyond the Hind shield, halfway across Manhattan, Minerva could hear the distant sounds of combat and knew Sally and her team had begun their assault upon the Hind shield. She wondered if it would be a successful venture, and if so, if they could also prevent the Hind bomb from being detonated. It occurred to her that if the Hind shield was intended to contain the destructive energies of a city-destroying bomb, the loss of that shield might spread the damage much further.

Nevertheless, she had to trust that her team was doing everything it could to save New York, and that meant first of all breaking down the shield. With the nearly impenetrable dome clear, crews would be able to restore power and communications throughout Manhattan. The military, staging in Jersey City to the west, Brooklyn to the southeast, and the Bronx to the northeast, would be able to sweep into Manhattan to take down the remaining enemy soldiers. Minerva didn't doubt that without the shield, the Hind would find themselves on the losing end of the battle for New York City quickly. Her greatest fear was the Hind would trigger that bomb anyway, and it might be powerful enough to wipe Manhattan off the map. That would likely spell the end of Just Cause New York as well.

As tempting as it was to go find Penny and the bomb, the shield was still in place, and Minerva couldn't break through it herself. She had her own mission, and the heroes sitting in the Fort Justice conference room were waiting for her briefing.

She'd only met half of those in the room, and didn't really know any of them except for Amber, who sat closest to her. Javelin wore her armor, burnished gold over black, her helmet sitting on the table before her.

Her short hair stood out wildly from being matted down inside it. Her husband Blueshift sat beside her, resplendent in his own blue and black suit. Even with his heroic physique, he still had a scientist's curiosity about the Hind and had spent the time before the briefing discussing how they might be generating such a massive energy shield with General Gershwin.

Giant wore jeans and a white t-shirt, with a silver crucifix dangling from a chain around his massively muscled neck. He had kept mostly to himself since his arrival and spoke very softly, when at all. Black Ice sat across the table from him, a tough-talking upstate New Yorker whose pale skin and mass of black hair made her look almost like a caricature instead of a real person. She didn't hide her feelings about anyone or anything, and most of her ire was currently directed at the aliens who'd chosen to interrupt her birthday weekend with their invasion. Failsafe sat beside her, a heavyset bald man with jailhouse tattoos. He'd been a former teammate of Minerva's and despite his criminal history, had worked hard to overcome that and become a valued member of the Just Cause organization.

March Washington sat next to Failsafe, sipping at a cup of coffee. He looked tired from his work on the assault craft he'd built in the training center, but he'd confirmed to Minerva that it was ready and they could leave with roughly half an hour's notice. She'd given him that notice and told him they would depart as soon as their briefing was done. Likewise, she'd asked General Gershwin to have the *Daedalus* ready to depart. The stealth spacecraft's two pilots sat in a corner of the room, listening in on the briefing with the detached professionalism of the military. Finally, Gauss rounded out the group, already wrapped up in his trademark metallic skin. He had to treat his power carefully in a steel structure like Fort Justice, and his tightly controlled magnetism could have wreaked havoc on the Just Cause computers if he really let loose with it.

The group waited patiently for Minerva to speak, except for Black Ice drumming her fingers on the tabletop. Ment stood behind her, layering her own thoughts with the calming influence of his love and concern for her, and that gave her strength. She stood. "Thank you for coming," she said. "I welcome those of you who have not been here before, and wish this meeting could take place under better circumstances. You are here because the seven of you represent the best task force we could muster to take the fight to the Hind in space. We have the means to reach them, thanks to Mr. Washington's technology here, as well as a secret Air Force project called *Daedalus*. Our mission is to use the best of our stealth technology and parahuman abilities to fly into space, approach the Hind fleet, and to incapacitate it."

Javelin raised a hand. "By destroying them?"

"If necessary," Minerva said. "But you were chosen for more than just raw destructive abilities. Even the strongest of you would need time to destroy one of those vessels." She nodded at Giant. "And while that was happening, the Hind would have time to call for reinforcements, to flee and regroup, or our worst case scenario. They have a bomb in Manhattan, presumably powerful enough to destroy the city. We believe it is likely if they feel they are in real danger of losing, they will detonate the device. The only way we can prevent that is to prevent their ability to order it. We will trust to our teammates on the ground to keep it from being triggered by an alien here on Earth, but they are trusting us to keep those in space from doing the same."

"How are we supposed to do that?" Failsafe asked.

"By careful targeting of communications devices, we can limit their ability to send signals. Blueshift and Javelin will be crucial to that phase of the operation, as will the jamming devices aboard the *Daedalus* and the *Boudica*. Failsafe, Black Ice, and Amber will use their abilities to give us access to the ships' hulls, while Giant and Gauss will help us board the vessels. Once aboard, we have translation technology provided by Mr. Washington's uncle that will allow us to communicate with the Hind."

"And what are you gonna tell them?" Black Ice asked. "Pick up their balls and go home?"

"Something like that. Harlan Washington, the Destroyer, took down one of their vessels by himself. One man. And there are eight of us, plus the support of our own two warships." She allowed herself a rare smile. "Also, I can be very convincing."

Davey burst into the room, her face drawn tight with stress and emotion.

Minerva felt her heart skip a beat. "What is it, Davey?"

"The team behind the shield has engaged the enemy," she said. "The Battle of Manhattan has begun."

Time Warner Center
8th Ave. and West 59th St., Manhattan

Penny had a battery-operated SWAT-issue fiber optic camera in her bag. She fired it up and pointed the camera at the end of the lead at her own face. It barely registered anything until she switched from standard to night vision and then she saw the ghostly gray-green image of herself on the screen. She carefully fed the lead underneath the steel door at the top of the stairwell. Once it showed her the exterior of the rooftop, she twisted the lead around to try to get as clear an idea of what was in her immediate surroundings. She spotted a trio of Hind right away, standing guard over a spherical device the size of a soccer ball, mounted on a framework that looked far too slender to hold anything of significant weight. That couldn't be the bomb, could it? It was so small!

Then it occurred to her that the Hind were more technologically advanced than Humans, and humanity had already built nukes that weighed only fifty pounds.

The aliens likely had materials that would provide a higher explosive yield in a small package, and portability would be key when invading a new world. Penny knew there was a prison guard in Deep Six whose body was made from antimatter. The amount contained within her body would have blown a hole in the Earth the size of Wyoming if her shielding ever failed. Something like that could destroy a portion of a city from a small, portable package.

First things first, though. She had to take down those three Hind. As she watched, something attracted their attention, and all three of them turned away from her to look down over the edge of the building. She couldn't believe her luck. Her sniper rifle could take down an elephant were she so inclined, but at close range, it wouldn't be any more effective than her high-caliber pistols in her hands. Besides, she didn't have to assemble them. She slid one from her holster and opened the flap on the second for quick access. With her free hand, she turned the door handle as quietly as possible, keeping one eye on the scope screen.

The Hind remained interested in whatever was happening over the side of the roof, babbling to each other in their growling, hissing voices and pointing. Penny put her shoulder into the door even as she drew her second pistol.

Nine shots later and the three Hind sprawled on the rooftop, bleeding out from bullet wounds in their lengthy spines and the backs of their heads. Their orange blood pooled black on the rooftop as Penny made a quick circuit around the humongous air conditioning unit that filled the center of the space. After performing her sweep, she decided she was the only one left alive on the rooftop. They were high enough in the sky that her shots probably wouldn't have carried to ground level, and there was a rumble of distant thunder to disguise any sounds anyway.

Wait, there shouldn't have been thunder at all. Not with the Hind shield overhead. A chill ran down her spine as she peeked over the edge to see what might have interested the Hind so much.

Down below at ground level, she saw the flickering of laser light off of distant building faces and flashes that might be explosions. They were a block further to the east, along 7th Avenue, she thought. If the sound of the battle was carrying all the way up to the top of Time Warner Center, it must have been bad.

It could only mean Just Cause had engaged the enemy. Maybe they'd made it through the shield somehow, or maybe they had rounded up enough parahumans to make an attack worthwhile. There were only two Hind targets of note inside the shield, and Penny figured she had one of them within spitting distance. That meant the shield generator must have been the other. If Just Cause could get the shield down, it would be a whole different ball game. That meant armed forces could move into Manhattan to take it back. She looked back toward the bomb. If the Hind could trigger it remotely, she'd have no chance at all. At least it would be quick and she wouldn't feel it if it went off. One moment she'd be there and the next it would be like she'd never existed at all. That thought freed her from a lot of the demons of doubt. If she failed, she'd never know that she had.

But if she succeeded, she'd know that forever. As long as she could still move, she was winning. Armed with that knowledge, she pulled out her flashlight and examined the bomb. At the size of a soccer ball, she figured she could transport it, but a nudge of the frame confirmed her worst fear: the bomb was heavy, like maybe thirty or forty pounds. Trying to get away quickly with something heavier than a bowling ball in her bag would make descending fifty-odd flights of stairs even more exhausting than climbing them had been. There had to be a quicker way down. She chuckled. There was one way quicker than any other, but it would end in a rather inconvenient splatter.

She wished she'd talked the would-be BASE jumpers out of their gear, but even so, she wasn't experienced with it and would just as likely splatter herself all over the ground anyway. Then her eyes fell upon the window-washing rig and an idea came to her. Why not? She thought she could work out a way to use it to get back to ground level. Besides, she thought as she began emptying gear from her back to make room for the Hind bomb—long as she was still alive, she was winning.

Monkeyworld
Rheayara Command

A Warrior who had just returned from relief was the first to die.

The Monkeys poured out from the darkness along three of their roads, using their strange abilities. Although it was hard for him to differentiate from one Monkey to the next, Garragh thought he recognized the colors some of them wore. Monkeys didn't wear proper armor of forged metal, but many of their own Warriors dressed in outfits that were every bit as colorful and unique as Hind armor. A heavy hand fell on his shoulder and he realized he'd been standing in open-mouthed shock like a fool. Not only did he have a novice's armor strapped to him, with a novice's blade in his hand, he was acting like one as well. He should have been charging toward the Monkeys the way many of his fellows were, swinging axes and firing lasers.

Ashar's eyes were wide and a bit of froth flecked his cheeks as the controlled battle-madness of a trained Hind Warrior took hold of him. "Protect Rheayara," he shouted, his voice thick with aggression pheromones. He shoved past Garragh and charged at one of the Monkeys who was wielding a rock gun like the one that had wounded him. The Monkey fired and a gout of smoke and flame erupted into Ashar's torso. His armor soaked up most of the blast but blood splattered from several fresh wounds in his arms and face.

Garragh wanted to run and hide, but he had a duty to perform, no matter how despicable it might be. Warriors were supposed to be at the forefront of any conflict, taking on the enemy. Protecting a Submistress was a task reserved for the most junior of novices. They were not to partake of combat unless in the direct role of defending their charges.

He might not have the luxury of avoiding battle, for the Monkeys had fliers attacking from above and runners who raced through the encampment at unimaginable speeds. It would only be a matter of time before they reached Rheayara if she was their ultimate target. Winds buffeted at him as one of the flying Monkeys somehow cast gale-force winds upon another Warrior, sending him tumbling into a building face. Heavy cannons chattered from the shoulders of what he thought was a true Monkey Warrior, who wore armor and carried a Hind axe he must have stolen. More than one Hind thought to challenge him only to fall under the onslaught of the Monkey's guns or axe.

A Monkey Garragh tentatively identified as female ran screaming to where a larger Monkey had been felled by an axe. He didn't understand the way she clutched at the fallen one and tried to stanch the flow of blood from the grievous wound in his back. No Hind would have given a fallen comrade a second thought lest the distraction be a fatal one. The death of a Submistress might elicit an emotional response from her Warriors—especially those she might have chosen as concubines—but the response would be limited to an even stronger righteous fury. Perhaps the fallen Monkey was the concubine of the female in her scarlet and gold clothing. Her insistence at trying to heal him reminded Garragh of how the Monkeys had treated his own wound, given him care and sustenance when none was owed him.

Other surviving Monkeys gathered around her and she screamed at them, giving orders, perhaps. Garragh's eyes widened as he realized she was another of the

Warrior-Mistresses, like Pernhree. Did that make all the Monkeys part of her clan? Was she that powerful?

It would make her a valuable asset.

Rheayara plucked at his back. "Oh, it's you, Garragh. Come, it is time to leave. You will protect me until I am safely aboard my ship."

"To obey is my honor," Garragh said by rote. Why was the Submistress leaving?

"You Warriors," Rheayara called to a group nearby who were coughing up water after having nearly been drowned by the Monkey who sent it flowing anywhere and everywhere. "Free the Monkey prisoners. Use them as armor. The Monkeys will not attack their own."

They saluted her and trotted over to where the prisoners huddled behind their shield.

The idea of using prisoners as armor made Garragh uneasy. It smacked of dishonor, and he wasn't sure what to do when a powerful Submistress was giving that kind of order. "Submistress . . ." He stopped, not knowing how to put words to his thoughts. "We should capture one, the one in the red and gold. Monkeys understand prisoners. If the prisoner is important enough, maybe they would surrender for her return."

Rheayara paused in consideration. "Perhaps you are not a complete fool, Garragh. Yes, a powerful prisoner might be the key to our victory at last. Go fetch her for me and be quick about it." She turned her back on Garragh to call to her pilot, "Prepare to—"

A warm puff of air blasted across Garragh's face, making his fur ripple as Rheayara's head vanished in a spray of orange mist. A moment later, a thunderous roar washed over him from one of the blue-armored Warrior's cannons. He started to cry out for help, because his training as a Warrior had not prepared him for the eventuality of a Submistress being killed in his presence, but then he stopped. A cry for help was weakness, and the other Hind already thought of him as weak and pathetic, no better than a mewling cub.

The blue-armored Warrior flew past, his axe slick with Hind blood. His cannons swiveled to attack strategic points on one of the dropships. Its shield failed and the pilot ran down the ramp only to be caught in the fiery burst of the exploding fuel cell. The blast sent Garragh tumbling across the street. His armor was singed and splattered with blood and for the first time he didn't feel completely useless.

He saw the red-and-gold Monkey kneeling beside her dead companion, her head bowed to her chest. She seemed oblivious to the battles around her, and Garragh didn't understand why she was ignoring everything. A bloodied Warrior rose from behind a wrecked Monkey vehicle with his rifle leveled at the Monkeymistress. Garragh's blood ran cold as he came to a decision.

Before the Warrior could fire, Garragh brought his axe down upon the Warrior's rifle. It shattered in a flash of sparks, enough to make break the Monkeymistress' self-imposed isolation and she looked up in wide-eyed surprise. "Traitor!" the Warrior spat, and grabbed for Garragh's axe.

Garragh cleaved the Warrior's head from his shoulders and blood fountained across the wrecked vehicle as the headless corpse collapsed in the street. Garragh whirled to face the Monkeymistress, lowering his axe until the head touched the street, which was as close to surrender as a Warrior could manage. With his other hand, he pointed to the bandage upon his leg. "*Kom*," he rumbled, straining to make his mouth pronounce the unfamiliar word. "*Pernhree. Kom.*" Maybe she would recognize the sound of the Warrior Mistress' name. He pointed toward one of the two remaining dropships. "*Kom*," he said as urgently as he could, and took a step toward the vessel, his axe still against the ground.

The Monkeymistress looked from him to his axe, still dripping with the blood of his own kind. Was she understanding him? She took a hesitant step toward the dropship and his hearts pounded with new excitement.

"*Kom!*" He deliberately turned his back to her and ran past her, knowing if she chose to kill him at that moment, he would die a coward's death instead of a hero's. He'd seen how fast she could move and didn't doubt she could keep up with him. He thundered across the plaza to enter the dropship. The Monkeymistress followed right behind him.

"What is that thing doing on my ship? Kill it!" the pilot cried.

"No, take off. Quickly. The . . . the Submistress ordered it. We are to bring this Monkey back to the Clanmistress."

The pilot turned to her controls. "It better not shit all over the floor, or you're cleaning it up, Warrior."

She'd called him *Warrior*. She didn't know he'd been punished. She didn't know he was a traitor. *She was following orders he had no right to give.* Garragh wasn't sure how things would play out, because he had no idea what he was doing or what his end game was. He would bring the Monkeymistress to the Clanmistress and let her wisdom decide how to proceed. These Monkeys were unlike any race the Hind had encountered before. He couldn't say they were equals of the Hind, but he didn't see any way the Hind could subjugate an entire planet of them without turning it into so much radioactive rubble.

And that was no way to win a war.

Times Square
Manhattan

Harlan Washington, the Destroyer, was in his element. The guns on his shoulders thundered, firing particle beams that hit like explosive shells. Hind Warriors flew into flaming pieces when he hit them, and those who didn't met their ends at the blade of his stolen axe. His suit had no visor—he didn't need one when any part of it could be a camera for him—but everywhere he looked he had splatters of orange blood in the corners of his vision.

Losing half of his squad in the opening moments of the battle was both a testament to their lack of true combat abilities and to their foolish bravery. Many reasons could keep the Champions from membership in the Just Cause organization, whether it was personality issues or the inability to perform under pressure. Nevertheless, as irritating as they'd been to Harlan on a personal basis, he took the loss of Surfboy and Johnny Go as a direct affront to his leadership. He had once commanded one of the largest gangs in Philadelphia, and he'd always taken it personally when his soldiers were killed.

Sally had made the right call to have him come along on the battle. Without him, the rest of the heroes would have had no chance. Their heavy hitters were few and far between. Detroit Steel's metallic flesh seemed to be impervious to both Hind axes and lasers, and she was tearing her way through troopers left and right. Flanking her, Hector picked off stragglers. His lustrous skin was marked with numerous burns, suggesting that he was a little less impervious to lasers than was his partner.

A poor decision made by an exhausted Chinook got her killed, and possibly Humbug as well. Harlan hated seeing the odd, insect-like young woman fall because he'd taken a bit of a liking to her. Like him, she was an outsider and always would be. He could respect that.

Then Sally's oaf of a husband barreled into the fray like the proverbial bull in the china shop. Harlan hadn't even known he was in Manhattan. He must have been elsewhere in town, heard or saw the battle, and decided to join. Harlan looked upon Mastiff with the disapproval normally reserved for a father-in-law. He knew Sally was attracted to his nephew March, and that attraction was mutual. Sally certainly deserved better in her life than a big, dumb musclehead.

But when that musclehead went down, Harlan knew they were going to lose the battle unless he did something drastic. Sally was the most powerful hero of those remaining, and her super-speed had been largely ineffective against the Hind Warriors. With her kneeling beside her dead or dying husband, she'd made herself a sitting duck, and Harlan would not let harm come to her. He fired off a salvo toward a Hind who appeared to be in a command role, and smiled beneath his helmet as her head evaporated.

He continued toward the shield generator, knowing that the best hope for New York and the world would be for him to destroy it. Nobody else would be able to get through its own defenses, and his armor would protect him from Hind axes and lasers for the few precious seconds he would need to disable it. He landed beside the generator and configured his suit to duplicate Humbug's sonic attack so he could force his way into the generator.

A scream of "*Sally!*" distracted him and he focused his sensors behind him. Detroit Steel was racing toward the dropships, oblivious to the Hind trying to stop her.

Harlan realized Sally was aboard one of them as the aft hatch was closing. He whirled, guns raised, and hesitated, not knowing how to stop the ship from taking off without risking killing her. Then, just before the hatch sealed entirely, her piercing voice burst out from inside the ship. "Harlan, destroy it!"

The dropship threw itself into the sky, not with the slow, ungainly climb of a helicopter but under full power like a military jet taking off from an aircraft carrier. He could have chased it down easily, but he'd been given a task. He knew Minerva and her strike team would be launching an attack on the ships in orbit. If the Hind took Sally up there, they would be able to rescue her. And if they couldn't, Harlan could.

He reconfigured his suit and dug his fingers into the shielding around the force field generator, squeezing with the suit's muscles like he was trying to pop a soccer ball with his bare hands. Seconds ticked by. His proximity alarm warned him of something approaching from behind but his aft monitor showed the Hind Warrior get body-slammed by Detroit Steel.

The generator's shielding collapsed under Harlan's sonic onslaught and he yanked it away from its pedestal, sending nanotech tendrils inside it to learn its secrets, to find its weakness, and to shut it off. Without fanfare, the shield failed and for the first time in decades, New Yorkers could look overhead and see stars.

CHAPTER ELEVEN

U ♞ U

Hind Dropship

A whirlwind of emotions raced through Sally like she was a leaf swirling in the gale. Everything was happening so fast that she could barely begin to process it all at even at her super-speed. Arching over all of it, like a headline in the sky ten thousand feet tall, was the name of her husband.

Jason.

Every time she closed her eyes, she saw the flash of the blade descending, cutting into his muscular back that she'd always thought would be impervious to damage. She saw the transformation of his face from the joy of full-on physical combat, to the sudden wince of pain, to an expression of confusion. The blade had sparkled with reflected laser light as it cut into his back, separating muscle and sinew and bone, swung with such force and so sharp that even his parahuman toughness hadn't been able to resist the blow.

The light went out of his eyes, and he didn't have time to look at Sally before he was gone.

Jason.

What if she'd stayed by his side? Spray might have died, but Jason might still be alive. She could have seen the Warrior, warned her husband, saved his life. Could she have truly sacrificed the frightened young water-powered hero just to selfishly keep her husband alive?

She didn't know why she'd followed the Hind who saved her life by killing one of his own. His growl sounded like he was asking her to follow him, and he'd said something that sounded suspiciously like Penny. She couldn't tell one Hind from another, but she saw the bandage on his leg and figured he was the one Penny had captured. And now she was huddled in a corner of the dropship hold as it bulled its way through the sky, shaking like it was flying through a storm. She was too numb to cry, too numb to feel anything except the bumps, each one leaving a bruise. She'd heal from them in minutes, as she did most injuries, but the repeated strain on her already exhausted and grief-stricken body was taking its toll. Even as tears soaked her collar, she found her head nodding repeatedly until a jolt would shake her awake again.

The Hind Warrior who'd captured her—if that was what she was going to call it—sat on a padded pallet like a Sphinx with a single broad strap across his lower back. His axe stayed in his hands but the blade rested on the floor. He watched her from beneath the visor of his helmet, splattered with orange that had to be Hind blood. Beyond him, the ship was open all the way to the cockpit, as if they were riding in a bus. Sally could have run forward and murdered the pilot before the Warrior could have stopped her, but that wouldn't accomplish anything except getting all of them killed. She got the sense the Warrior had violated some kind of rules by capturing her and killing one of his fellows to do it. That made him a rebel.

That meant perhaps he could be turned.

Normally, Sally's thoughts whirled at super-speed during times of high stress and combat engagement. When she accelerated her perceptions, her thought processes likewise sped up, allowing her the luxury of planning ahead and thinking things through—things anathema to most speedsters. With the loss and grief piled upon her, her mind spun in stubborn circles, like a racing car burning out its engine and tires doing donut after donut.

The metaphor made a fresh bout of tears begin. Jason had talked many times about teaching her to drive and she'd always said no. She'd said no to him for so many things. Little things like duty roster assignments, training programs, and concerts. Big things, like children.

She would never again have the chance to tell him *yes*.

Maybe she *would* kill the pilot. Death in a fiery crash might be preferable to a lifetime of pain and grief. Sure, it would lessen over time. That's what people always said about it. Sally didn't believe them. She wished her friends were around to comfort her. She needed to smell the scent of Sondra's wings, with their acrid natural odor and the baby powder she used to mask it. She needed to see Jack's smile and hear his ready wit, which never failed to make her smile as well.

She needed to feel Jason's arms around her.

Stop it, she told herself. He wouldn't have wanted her to mope around. Not at a time like this when the world was at war and she'd been captured by aliens and so many of their friends had been killed. No, she needed to be strong now more than ever. She needed to take her grief and push it away, deny it. Keep it locked in a tiny, dark corner of her mind with the promise that one day, she would let it all out. Be strong, she told herself.

The Hind Warrior sat up, his fur bristling like a wolf's. She realized she'd spoken *be strong* aloud. She wiped her eyes. She had an opportunity and couldn't waste it wallowing in her self-pity. "Do you understand me?"

He blinked at her. She wished she could read his body language.

"Are you the Hind Penny captured?"

"*Pernhree.*"

"Pern . . . Yes! Yes, *Penny!*"

"*Pernhree.*" He muttered something else, a growl lost in the buffeting and rattling as the dropship climbed higher toward space.

Sally pointed at herself. "Sally."

The Hind said nothing.

Sally pointed toward the rear of the ship, where the hatch was. "Penny." Then she pointed to herself. "Sally." At last, she pointed at the Hind and said nothing.

His head tilted to one side in a manner so like a puppy's that she nearly laughed in spite of her misery. At least trying to open interspecies communication was distracting her. He tilted the haft of his axe toward the hatch, never letting go of it. "*Pernhree.*" Then he pointed at her. "*Sahree.*"

"Yes, Sally. That's me."

The haft touched his upper torso. "Garragh."

She had a sudden urge to extend her hand as if to have him shake it. She had to hold it back so it wouldn't move of its own accord. "Pleased to meet you, Garragh. I don't know what you've got in mind for me . . ." Her chipper smile faltered. "But I promise you I'm going to kill you all or die trying."

Garragh said nothing, and that suited Sally just fine.

Fort Justice
New York Bay

Upon learning the Hind shield had gone down, Minerva's first instinct was to call all the Just Cause heroes to arms. They could rush into Manhattan, bring the full force of the world's greatest superheroes to bear against the alien invaders, liberate the city. It wouldn't solve their immediate problem of the vessels in orbit or the even more immediate problem of a bomb the Hind could detonate at any moment.

General Gershwin had been on the phone nearly from the moment the shield went down, issuing orders to battalions on standby around Manhattan. He was sending in both light infantry and heavy armor, dispatching Navy jets to overfly the city, and Marine helicopters to head further inland. Minerva knew she had to trust his people, and Juice at the Parahuman Resources Administration to ensure Manhattan would be properly liberated.

If the Hind managed to set off their bomb, the city and everyone in it would be leveled. Minerva knew she could find it. She didn't need long, but she needed to isolate herself. "March, get your ship ready to fly. Everyone else, prepare to leave. I will join you in a few minutes. Ment, you'll be in command until Sally or I return."

Ment nodded. "Promise me you *are* going to return, babe."

Minerva paused, feeling an unpleasant spike of emotion amid her normal equanimity. "I will do my best."

Ment sighed. "I guess that's as much as you ever promise anything."

Minerva leaned in close to him. "I promise I will do my best to come home to you." She turned away so she wouldn't have to see the worry on his face. She didn't have to; she could smell it. She flew up the steps to the top deck of Fort Justice and kept climbing, higher and higher until she was a few hundred feet above the waves. She opened her senses to the darkness that was Manhattan and allowed data to permeate her mind.

The lights were still out. It might be a few hours yet before Con Ed could get power back to the island, and they wouldn't even try until the Army gave them the all-clear. A few sporadic lights flickered in the streets. From the slight temperature variations, Minerva thought they were most likely fires. She focused her attention in toward them and confirmed that they were burning automobiles. None of the fires looked like they had spread to buildings.

She could hear the distant sounds of Hind weapons firing and the chatter of Human guns as well, suggesting the Battle of Manhattan was far from decided. A whoosh of water where none should be and a high-pitched whine told her at least some of the Just Cause heroes were still fighting.

A star rose from amid the buildings, climbing quickly. It was a Hind dropship, leaving the island. She heard the roar of incoming jets as more dropships lifted and knew an air war was about to commence. She wanted to scrub her mission to space, to help with protecting the civilians from the dangers of falling debris and missed shots, but it would only delay the inevitable conflict. Besides, that bomb was still somewhere in Manhattan and she couldn't tell if anyone had found it yet. All the cell towers and radio repeaters were down, and no land lines were yet operational into Manhattan, so there was still no way short of moving personnel into the city to get current intelligence. The Army and Marines were already advancing along the bridges and in helicopters, preparing to establish beachheads and begin a street-by-street sweep to clear Manhattan of aliens. Minerva had to trust them.

She couldn't delay any longer.

She flew back into headquarters and descended to the Tank where the *Boudica* was preparing for launch. March was already sitting inside in the pilot's chair, his arms and legs inserted into control sleeves that would allow him to maneuver the ship as if it were an extension of his own body. The others were standing upon pads outside the ship, looking distinctly uncomfortable as nanites wove spacesuits around them.

"How are these supposed to keep us alive? Real spacesuits are bulky as shit," said Javelin, who'd been forced to remove her armor to accommodate the nanotech suit.

"Don't think of them as suits," said Blueshift, who seemed remarkably composed and fascinated as the protective covering grew up the contours of his body. "Think of them like a second skin, except this one will protect you from vacuum and temperature extremes. You'll be able to wear your armor over it."

"That still doesn't tell me how we're going to breathe," said Failsafe. "Where's the air tank?"

"Tanks, plural," March said over the ship's external speaker. "There are m-microscopic pockets all over the s-skin. When you seal them, you'll huh . . . have ten minutes of air."

"Ten minutes isn't much time," said Amber. "We'll have air inside the *Boudica*, right?"

"Yes."

"The suit air is only in case of emergencies," said Minerva. "Or if we need to expose ourselves to vacuum while boarding a Hind ship."

"What is the plan?" Black Ice asked. "Are we destroying or boarding?"

"Boarding," Minerva said. "We will ask them to leave our solar system alone."

"What if they say no?" asked Javelin.

"We will convince them."

"What if they set off their bomb?" Gauss asked.

Minerva sighed. That was the least appealing scenario in her mind. Losing a major city like that would not only wreck the world's economy, but it would cause the kind of psychological harm that could eventually become mankind's undoing. She'd seen the way America had faltered after terrorists had destroyed the World Trade Center. Losing New York City would create scars that might never heal.

"Then we retaliate."

Time Warner Center
8th Ave. and West 59th St., Manhattan

Penny could have filled a book with what she didn't know about window-washing rigs, and she had very little in the way of tools to work with as she struggled to turn what was supposed to be an electrically operated winch into one she could lower manually. She'd managed to remove what she was pretty sure was the emergency brake that was designed to keep the rig from falling. With that brake removed, she knew if she released the catches keeping the rig atop the building, it would fall over the side and continue until it ran out of cable or hit the ground, whichever came first. If it ran out of cable, the force of its sudden stop might pull the framework over the side as well, leaving her still on the roof with nothing to show for it.

On the other hand, if the rig made it safely to the ground—*safely* being purely subjective in this case—Penny had a gizmo in her bag that would allow her to ride the cable down like she was her own elevator. It was a spring-loaded contraption that would lock around the cable and use friction-braked wheels to control her descent speed. It was purely mechanical and operated via a simple twist-and-squeeze motion that required very little effort to brake or stop. It would get her back to the ground in less than a minute at a safe, steady speed.

If it failed, though, she supposed it wouldn't matter. Either she'd die in the impact or she'd die when the Hind detonated the bomb she'd sequestered in her backpack. She considered whether she might be better served to just go down the stairs instead, but that would take her time she didn't felt she had, and she would be exhausted at the bottom.

No, she would ride the cable down. It would leave her with enough stamina to fight her way out of the area if she had to.

The shield overhead winked out and she gasped as she saw the stars overhead, as well as the distant lights of New Jersey across the Hudson. She immediately checked her phone but was dismayed to see it still had no connectivity. "You're still on your own, Penny Lane," she muttered.

There was no use waiting any longer. Either her teammates had managed to shut down the Hind shield or else the Hind had done it themselves. Either way, it meant Humans were on their way to retaking Manhattan, and that meant the Hind might decide to go ahead and detonate their bomb.

She released the catches at the edge of the roof, her heart pounding in nervous excitement at the thought of dumping a heavy window-washing rig off the top of a skyscraper. "This would be the best viral video," she grumbled. "Nobody's ever going to see this crazy shit I'm about to pull off." She kicked at the last catch and jumped clear as the rig slid off its tracks and banged down the side of the building, cracking panes of glass as it bounced. Smoke rose from the winch as the cable drum spun faster than it was designed to, friction-burning the grease. The whine set Penny's teeth on edge and she scooted further and further away from the winch, fearful it might shatter when the rig reached the end of its range.

With a distant crash that Penny felt in her boots, the rig crashed into something that stopped its fall. She waited to see if the winch would go after it. It remained bolted to the tower's structure and once she played her light across the winch, she saw it still had perhaps another dozen turns of cable left. She crawled to the edge of the roof and peeked over the side. She couldn't see where the rig had stopped in the darkness below, even with her flashlight. It was too far.

"Well, what are you going to do?" she asked aloud. She didn't know if the rig had reached ground level or a terraced part of the building. She didn't remember the exact layout of the Time Warner tower. She would have to go as far as she could and then improvise, which was fine, because she'd been doing that all damn day.

She had to leave most of her gear on the rooftop so she could carry the heavy bomb in her backpack. Her cherished sniper rifle would have to remain, as would most of her munitions and what she called her *rainy day toys*, which were various items that she might only ever use once in her life but would need them above all else. Her descender was one of those toys, and she was glad she had it.

She clamped the descender around the cable. Its default state was locked tight and she would have to squeeze the manual release to allow the friction wheels to turn. If she let go of the clamp, she would stop. There was a folding seat that straddled the cable below the descender that would keep her from having to stand during the descent. She snapped carabiners above and below the descender, and attached them to her integral harness. In the event that she slipped off the seat or completely lost hold of the release, they would keep her from falling away from the cable.

Once she was thoroughly strapped onto the cable, she wormed her way to the edge. She was actually glad the power was still off in Manhattan, for she didn't have to see how far it really was to the street below. "Last chance," she said. "You want to fuck off this rig and take the stairs, you still can." She knew once she went over the edge, she was committed to the descender. She'd never be able to climb back up a braided steel cable.

"Congratulations, Penny," she muttered. "We're promoting you to Just Cause. You get to play in the big leagues now." She wanted to shut her eyes, but instead she kept them focused on the black glass of the building's face and began her steady descent down the cable into darkness.

Monkeyworld

The pilot said her name was Loasrah. She was an ambitious young Submistress, whose aptitude for piloting had skill fast-tracked her as a ranking officer in Rheayara's command. She was much smarter than Garragh—that much was obvious, for she immediately understood that he was violating orders by bringing the Monkey onboard. Garragh struggled to make himself understood why it was so important to bring her to the Clanmistress when he himself didn't have the vocabulary to explain it.

Once the dropship was high enough not to be at risk from the armaments of the Monkey airjets, Loasrah locked the controls and disengaged her pallet harness so she could better look at the Monkey huddling against the bulkhead. "Is it hurt?" she asked. "I've seen animals act like that when they're hurt."

"I don't know, Submistress," Garragh admitted. "They're fragile compared to us. They break easily. Their skin is thin." The Monkey raised her head a little and looked at him. In her eyes, he saw the stare of a Warrior. "They have strength though. She may be hurt, but she isn't beaten."

"Then you should teach her a lesson, Warrior. Subjugate your enemies."

"Yes, of course." He took a step toward the Monkey and she was on her feet faster than he'd seen her move. Her fists were clenched and she vibrated like an engine about to explode. Hurt or not, she was going to try to kill him, and he believed she might just manage it.

"What is it? Why do you hesitate?"

"It's just that . . . I think she is important. A Mistress of her own people."

Loasrah snickered. "Monkeys don't have Mistresses. They're primitives. Barely better than animals. They need the guidance of the Hind to achieve meaning in their wretched lives."

"They're more than just primitives. They . . ." Garragh stopped, not knowing how to explain the brand-new notion of compassion. "They help each other."

"Lots of animals work in groups. That's biology. It doesn't mean anything."

Garragh backed away from the Monkey, trying to make it clear he wasn't going to attack her. She seemed to relax and huddled against the bulkhead. "Aren't we here to defeat them?"

"Of course that's why we're here. To conquer the primitives. To enlighten them. To add them to our empire, to the glory of our Clanmistress . . . Or whomever leads Clan Sharassar."

"Maybe she has the ability to surrender on behalf of all Monkeys. Maybe she can bring this struggle to an end."

Loasrah snorted in disdain. "A Warrior, looking for the end of war? You must be wounded in the head." She turned back to the controls. "You are likely right, though. Even Rheayara said we must treat the Monkeys differently than other races we have beaten. She studied them. She probably understood them better than they understand themselves." She returned to her pallet and took the controls again.

Garragh moved forward to stand closer to the pilot. He spoke in low tones, even though there was nobody else aboard to hear him but the Monkey, and she likely didn't speak Hind. "There's something more. Something I'm trying to understand. Something about these Monkeys. They are . . . tied to each other. They fight like Warriors but they . . . they *think* like Mistresses. I think they may be very dangerous, and . . ."

Loasrah burst out laughing. "You're afraid of them! You, a Hind Warrior, are afraid of a Monkey. You should open your own throat for that. There's no place for weakness in a Warrior."

Garragh didn't dare confirm Loasrah's interpretation of his mindset, even though it was accurate. He *was* afraid of the Monkeys. He didn't think they would ever stop fighting. What would it gain for Clan Sharassar to destroy Monkeyworld? What would it gain them to keep fighting a war they could not win? And on the tail of that thought, what could it gain them to reach an arrangement with the Monkeys? He didn't know the word *alliance*, but he understood how the Accord of the Fist was an arrangement between Clans. What if Sharassar could make an arrangement with the Monkeys? It would create something in its place almost unheard of among the Hind. It would mean an end to war, which Garragh felt deep down was what he really wanted. "I need the Clanmistress to see for herself. Perhaps in her wisdom, she can understand what I do not."

Loasrah stamped one of her hind legs, indicating her indifference. "The Clanmistress is a fool, and this is a fool's errand you have me on. Whatever makes you happy, Warrior. My job—for the moment—is to fly. I have higher aspirations, and that is where my thoughts lie, not with your ridiculous fantasies. Do you understand, Warrior? Unless I see the Monkey is of use to me, I do not care."

"I understand, Submistress."

"Good. Promise me one thing."

"What is that?"

"The instant we land, you get this damn Monkey off my boat. It smells."

Times Square
Manhattan

"H-hello? Is anyone reading me?" The voice, crackling and heavy with signal interference, came over the Just Cause-exclusive frequency that Harlan had his suit monitoring. He ordered his onboard CPU to scrub the message of its distortion and run a voiceprint analysis. A few seconds later, his system reported it was Penny Lane, the young woman they'd recruited to replace a far better tactical genius in Crackerjack.

His first inclination was to ignore the call. He was thinking about the best way to pursue Sally and retrieve her safely from the Hind. It bothered him that she'd been captured in a way he couldn't clearly define. Penny was transmitting on an open channel when the repeaters and signal boosters throughout Manhattan were still inoperative. She must have known it was hopeless but still she tried. He wondered what had inspired her to do so.

"Anyone who's listening, please notify Just Cause that Penny Lane has found the package. Repeat, I have the package in my possession."

Harlan stopped cold in his mop-up of the remaining few Hind Warriors who were stubbornly fighting to the very last despite losing both their commander and their reason to fight. An axe blade bounced off his armor and he spun his shoulder cannon around to blow apart the Warrior who'd thought he could sneak up to deliver a lethal blow. Lane must have found the Hind city-destroying bomb. The Hind could choose to set it off at any moment. For a moment, Harlan's sense of self-preservation urged him to flee, to get as far away from Manhattan as he could before it was turned into a smoking radioactive crater.

Instead, he activated his own radio. "Lane, this is Destroyer. I am reading you, over." He turned his suit's head to face in the direction of Detroit Steel, who he believed to be the ranking survivor in the field. "Your ally Penny has found something we need. I'm going to find her."

Without waiting for her reply, he fired his boot jets and catapulted into the starry sky.

Lane's voice came over his radio, crackling with interference. "Destroyer? Shit, of course it would have to be you. You can fly, can't you?"

"Affirmative. What is your location?"

"Time Warner Center. West side of the building. Somewhere between the roof and the ground, and I don't know how much longer this goddamn rig is going to hold."

Harlan didn't know what she meant by that last statement, but suspected he would find out soon. A map of Manhattan overlaid his viewscreen and at his command, marked both his and Lane's suspected positions. He angled his flight and poured on the speed. She had sounded like she was in danger, and he would need her alive to tell him where the bomb was. He had spent enough time rummaging through the systems of the fleet ship that he felt confident he could disarm a Hind explosive device. All he needed was to get hold of it and let his nanotech do the rest.

His infrared systems found her before visual reckoning. She was a single hot spot against the darkness of the building face, some hundred feet above the ground. As he approached, she broadcast a single, curt word.

"Hurry."

He didn't know how she'd managed to descend the face of the building, or even why she'd attempted such a dangerous maneuver. With no power to the building elevators, she must have ascended the stairs on foot. Climbing to the top would be exhausting for someone without parahuman strength or endurance. Returning down the same way would have taken a long time, and if she had the bomb in her possession, time was of the essence.

Whatever was holding her failed high up on the roof and as Harlan approached, he saw her tumble, trailing a long cable. He opened his jets to full power, knowing her life was measured in less than three seconds. He couldn't simply catch her—the impact against him would be only slightly less damaging than impacting the ground. Instead, he collided with her and applied as much lateral speed as he could, turning her headlong tumble into a parabolic arc like she was coming down the initial drop of a roller coaster. Almost as an afterthought, he extended a cutting tool from his hip and sliced through the braided steel cable. His control surfaces whined as he fought against her momentum and the Earth's gravity, and then finally braked to a halt. Smoke rose from the pavement as his red-hot boots sank an inch deep into the asphalt.

He rolled back his helmet so Lane could see his face, lit from within the suit. He brought his own lights to bear upon her. She had thick, black grease staining her clothing and face, looking like someone who actually worked for a living. "Are you all right?"

Lane started to say something, but a great crash behind them made Harlan whirl, his shoulder cannons sweeping the area, searching for something at which to shoot. "It's all right," said Lane. "It's probably the window-washing rig winch. I was afraid I'd fucked it up too much." She wiped sweat from her forehead, smearing grease across it. "Nice catch, Washington."

"Do you have it? Where is it?"

She snorted. "Guess I should have figured you weren't one for niceties." She slipped off her backpack and held it out to him. "Here. If anyone can shut it down before they set it off, it's you."

CHAPTER TWELVE

♙

Hind Fleet
Axeship Blood Afire

Sally jerked awake at the sudden absence of sound. She realized she'd dozed off in the back of the dropship and immediately felt guilty about it. She should have been doing something. Fighting to take control of the vessel. Using her powers to defeat one Hind and bullying the other into taking her home. Crashing the damn thing into one of the fleet vessels in a glorious, heroic sacrifice.

Instead, she felt nothing at all except a gigantic hole in her soul where Jason had been torn away from her. People talked about how people who you loved stayed with you after they died. That was supposed to be a salve, something people said to make themselves feel better. The truth was when Jason had died, a part of Sally had gone with him and left behind a cold numbness. She could have embraced that emptiness, made it her driving force. It would have transformed her into a fearless Warrior, the kind of whom stories were whispered in the darkness. In the end, it would have consumed her. She hadn't personally seen darkness overwhelm any heroes she knew, but that didn't mean it didn't happen. Her father's former teammate Tommy had let the darkness take him, and in the end his death had led to the death of her father as well.

The sense of motion had ceased and Sally was certain they had landed. She couldn't see stars or the Earth through the front windows of the dropship. Instead, a wall of metal filled her vision. The gravity was funny. It was strong at the level of the floor, keeping her from drifting into the air. The further away from the floor, the weaker the gravity. She could have set something in the air beside her head and it would have stayed there instead of falling.

All that was fascinating to the science fiction fan in her, but her tactical mind was struggling with ways to turn the Hind's technology against them. Harlan must have managed it. Surely she could as well. She might not have been in the same league as him when it came to sheer intelligence, but she was crafty, and they hadn't put her in charge of the world's greatest superhero team because of her good looks.

The Warrior who'd sort of captured her indicated she should stand. The dropship ramp lowered to reveal a full dozen Hind Warriors, decked out in full armor with weapons of some kind leveled at her. She doubted they were the same kind of lasers they'd used back on Earth. With their lousy aim, the Hind would have saved her the trouble of killing them all by shooting holes in their hull. She was sure they'd considered that shortcoming when constructing their vessels.

Nevertheless, it was clear to her the Hind respected the threat she represented to them by the sheer number of Warriors they'd brought to greet her. This was no honor guard for an important guest, but a group of hardened fighters prepared to take on a dangerous opponent. Harlan must have impressed them during his brief incarceration in the fleet. The thought warmed Sally's hardened heart for a moment. *Good.*

The Warrior who had ostensibly captured her nudged her from behind with his axe and even though she could have flashed out amid the Warriors before any of them could set claw to trigger, she stepped down the ramp into the alien hangar bay. Two other dropships were snug in their berths, ready to be launched by whatever means the Hind used. Several other berths were empty, and Sally knew those ships must still be on Earth, unless they'd been destroyed at some point.

Her mind was turning over and over, focusing on details to keep from dwelling upon the pain of Jason's death. It had taken the better part of an hour for the dropship to reach the fleet. She wasn't sure about the realities of velocities in space, despite being a longtime science fiction fan, but she knew that unless other dropships were already returning to their home berths, it would be at least an hour before any backup troops could arrive. Whatever Warriors were aboard the fleet vessels were all she would have to face when she decided it was time to bring the war to them.

The Hind formed a phalanx around her, those behind keeping their weapons pointed at her back. Her captor stayed beside her instead of disappearing elsewhere. Whatever his mission was, it seemed he intended to follow it through to the end. She still didn't know what to make of him. He'd killed one of his own to save her. His motivation was a mystery, but she didn't think he had brought her all the way to his fleet just to kill her.

"Any of you assholes speak English?" she asked aloud. The Warriors bristled and for a moment she wondered if she'd violated some kind of rule and was about to be shot in the back for her trouble. After a moment, she decided she'd just startled them. Despite their ferocious appearances, massive axes, and armor, they were a skittish bunch of pussycats. A thought occurred to her and made her smile. These Warriors had been assigned to stay behind while the others got to land on Earth and fight a glorious battle. These were the losers, the weak, the dishonored. No wonder they were afraid of her.

She'd see to it they found good reason to continue fearing her.

As they escorted her through the corridors of the ship, she tried to memorize the path. There didn't seem to be many turns or twists, and intersections were few and far between. The vessel seemed to be one long straight line. She didn't know if they were traveling in a main corridor or an auxiliary corridor, but she was put in mind of an aircraft carrier. The corridor walls were decorated with murals and paintings that showed Hind Warriors in battle, fighting each other, or different alien races. They aggrandized their exploits in the way of some martial cultures on Earth. Sally was beginning to understand a little about their racial psychology by looking at their art. With it filling their walls, it was a constant reminder to them that they were the greatest race, the apex predators at the top of the interstellar pyramid. If they knew defeat, they kept it well hidden.

Learning it firsthand would be a difficult proposition for them to swallow, and Sally intended to show it to them. They had to be taking her to their leader. It was the only logical solution. Their Clanmistress, whatever her name was, had spoken in English in her broadcast. She was probably going to offer Sally an ultimatum: surrender the Earth and the Hind would be merciful and spare them. Sally wasn't about to be a traitor to her planet. She'd die first.

And she'd take as many of them with them as she could in the process.

The Boudica

"What's our ETA to the Hind fleet?" Minerva asked March. She had unhooked her safety straps and moved forward to stand behind the young man. She could feel the unnatural thrum of the *Boudica*'s pulse engines through her feet. The energies within them violated physics, as did those in the *Daedalus*. Minerva wasn't sure if it was stolen alien technology or something developed by earthly scientists. "Six minutes to orbital space. After that maybe f-forty-five minutes."

"*Boudica*, come in. This is *Daedalus*. We have a message for you from Rhapsody. Repeat, we have a message from Rhapsody."

Rhapsody was the code name for General Gershwin and the operations staff at Fort Justice, after George Gershwin's "Rhapsody in Blue," which Minerva thought was an excellent reference.

Minerva leaned forward to touch the radio control. "Go ahead, *Daedalus*."

The pilot, who Minerva recalled was a small brunette with a perpetual wry grin, read off the message in her nervous soprano. "Um, Rhapsody says the package has been secured, repeat, the package has been secured."

Minerva smiled. It was a rare event for her, but it was about time something had gone right for them. She could infer from that message that forces on the ground had found and disabled the Hind bomb. If the Hind didn't know that, it gave her team an advantage because they didn't have to try to keep a signal from being transmitted to detonate the bomb. She relayed that information to her strike team.

Despite the nervous tensions amongst her team, the news was welcomed with grins and high-fives. "So we don't have to be as careful?" Javelin asked.

"We don't know that yet, but it appears if the Hind want to blow up an earthly city, they'll have to deliver a new bomb. There are enough eyes watching them all over the world that if any ship launches toward a new target, it will get shot out of the sky almost before it enters the atmosphere."

March cleared his throat. "Everyone? We're officially above the d-demarcation line. Congratulations. You are all ast . . . astronauts."

More cheers erupted from the team. Minerva let them have their celebration. She was afraid it would all come crashing down any moment as the Hind realized they were on an intercept course. *Daedalus* was a stealth vessel, impossible to detect by earthly radar, and *Boudica* had that technology built into her own hull. It wouldn't surprise Minerva in the least if they were detectable by the Hind.

"*Boudica*, this is *Daedalus*. Come in, *Boudica*."

Minerva felt like slapping her own face. If the damn *Daedalus* pilots kept transmitting, even on a tight beam, sooner or later a Hind receiver was going to detect it, and then it wouldn't matter if they were stealthed or not. "Go ahead, *Daedalus*."

"New information from Rhapsody. He, uh, they say the, uh, the wild pony has been corralled and taken to the biggest barn. Repeat. The wild pony is in the biggest barn."

An icy chill came over Minerva's heart. The message was as clear as day to her.

"What is it?" March asked, seeing her dismay on her normally reserved face.

"The Hind have Mustang Sally." Minerva felt lost in a way that was unfamiliar to her. It was rare for her to experience any kind of strong emotion—that was a side effect of her extreme sensory perception. She was terrified for the safety of her friend. She was afraid for the team she'd assembled, like they were ants about to attack a human. And more than anything, she was . . . angry. The Hind had come to her world. They had attacked her city. They had killed her people. They had taken her friend. It was like defeat piled upon defeat until the crushing weight was almost more than anyone could bear.

Minerva would bear it, and she would thrive despite its pressure.

She wiped her eyes before the errant tears could escape, before anyone might perceive her as weak in the face of insurmountable odds. "March, I need an image of the Hind fleet so I can identify targets for the team."

March touched a few controls. "Done."

Minerva turned back to the others, who stared in open-mouthed shock back at her. All of them had heard her quiet pronouncement about Sally. "What do we do, boss?" Amber asked.

Minerva studied the image of the four ships of the Hind fleet. It had moved away from the remains of the fifth ship that Harlan Washington had destroyed in his initial assault. "March, give me vector information on the fleet's movement as well as our inbound path."

Colored lines overlaid the image, showing how everything was moving relative to each other. Minerva walked around the image, studying it from every angle. At last, she reached the conclusion she needed to find. "We're going to give them something to worry about. While they are distracted, we will rescue our teammate. Destroyer took out one of those vessels on his own, without any help. There are eight of us."

"Nine," said March from up front.

"And the *Daedalus*," Blueshift added.

"March, I'm designating these vessels as Targets Alpha through Delta. Send this image to the *Daedalus*. Tell them to fire all ordnance at Target Delta only and then withdraw. They will be unable to assist us after their initial strike and will only serve to add risk and complication." Minerva crossed her arms.

"What if they refuse?"

"Tell them to go reload if they must do something." Minerva turned to look at her team, focusing her gaze upon Amber and Black Ice. "You two. It's time to give the Hind something to think about. March, what's our closing velocity with the fleet?"

"Four k-kilometers per second right now."

Minerva nodded. "Gauss, Amber, Black Ice, make me a couple of projectiles outside the *Boudica*. Something in the four to five hundred pound range. Failsafe, we'll use your force field to aim them. At this speed, they should hit with roughly four times the force of a naval gun."

Giant whistled. "That's almost as hard as I can hit."

Minerva looked at him. "You'll get your chance too."

Time Warner Center
8th Ave. and West 59th St., Manhattan

Washington leaned back from the bomb. His helmet visor rolled back and he reached up to mop his brow. Penny looked at him and didn't know what to think. Destroyer had been a thorn in the side of Just Cause for more than thirty years, and hadn't ever stopped to think about what that actually meant about the man inside the suit. His short, tight curls had gone gray at the temples and the rest of his hair was that dusky gray that was unique to black men. He was thin, either by nature or by dietary choices. He had the hard lines around his eyes and forehead that Penny's mom had always called *scowl lines*, common to people who were generally unhappy with the world.

Despite his serious demeanor, he had a certain peacefulness about him that seemed incongruous with his reputation, like a man who had achieved his goals in life and was satisfied with the results. "So, uh, you shut it down then?" Penny asked, hating how she felt like a green rookie in front of this supervillain. *Was* he a supervillain? He seemed to be on the side of Just Cause. Maybe it was a case of *the enemy of my enemy is my friend*. She didn't think she could be friends with someone like him, given the number of heroes who had died at his hands over the years. They would just have to agree on a temporary truce.

"Yes, it's disarmed. This is an antimatter bomb. It explains a lot about how the Hind power their fleet. The amount of antimatter inside this casing would have obliterated Manhattan."

"Then I'm glad you stopped it."

"I've only disabled the trigger. It's still an antimatter bomb."

"But it's not going to go off?"

Washington looked at her. "Not at the moment."

"Good. Also, uh, thanks again for the save. If you hadn't showed up when you did, I'd be . . ."

"Dead," Washington said. "Coming down the outside of the building the way you did was an amateur mistake."

"Yeah, well, fuck you. We can't all fly. I'm trying to thank you for saving my life. That means you're at least supposed to acknowledge it."

Washington looked at her with eyes that seemed dead. "I acknowledge that I saved your life."

Penny snorted. "Well I guess that's as good as I'll get from you. How's the Battle of Manhattan going?"

"I believe our forces will be victorious. The primary Hind emplacements have been destroyed and with the shield down, the Army will be moving in. I suspect Manhattan shall be liberated within a few hours if the Hind do not make any new moves."

"That's good. Everybody come out all right?"

"No." He paused, as if perhaps trying to come up with a way to deliver the bad news with less of a punch. It didn't matter. It still felt like someone had stabbed Penny in the guts as he listed those who had fallen in the line of duty. "Mastiff, Chinook, Surfboy, and Johnny Go are dead. Humbug is severely wounded and I do not know if she will survive. Mustang Sally . . ." He hesitated, as if he actually felt some real pangs of remorse. "She is a captive of the Hind and they took her in a dropship."

"Dead? So many . . ." Penny felt her knees turn to water. She clutched at Washington for support. "God . . ."

"It is a war, Penny. Soldiers die."

"They were my friends!"

"If you would not form emotional bonds, their deaths would not bother you."

Penny's mouth dropped open, her tears forgotten. "You callous son of a bitch!"

Washington's faceplate closed, shutting him out from her. She found herself beating against his chest plate. "You asshole! Don't you dare just up and leave now! You saved my life. Why couldn't you save them?

Why couldn't you save any of them?" She sank to the ground, no longer caring if he took off or not.

His faceplate withdrew and he bent down to put his face near hers. "Because I'm not a hero."

She looked up at him. "You're wrong, Washington. They always said you were the smart one, but you're dead ass wrong about not being a hero. A hero warns the world of an attack. A hero goes out to fight against impossible odds. A hero leads others into battle without losing sight of the goal." Her voice hardened. "But taking revenge on those who wronged you, that's not heroic. And right now, I'm not feeling so goddamned heroic. I want to kill those bastards, Washington. I want them to die. All of them. You feel me here?" She wiped an angry tear from her cheek.

He nodded. "That is the first thing you've said that makes sense to me."

"So what are we going to do about it?" She nudged his armored hand that was wrapped around the straps of her bag. "We've got an antimatter bomb right there. You can fly into space. Maybe we give them a taste of their own medicine."

He said nothing, just stared down at her with those emotionless eyes.

"Dammit, Washington. I'm saying I'll help you kill them. I want to see them die. I want them to know we beat them in the end."

He sighed. "I . . . agree. I will need more than just this bomb."

"What do you need? I'm in fucking Just Cause. I'll get it for you." Penny's laugh was bitter.

"More antimatter. "

"I know where there's more."

"Deep Six." It wasn't a question; Washington already knew about the Antimatter Woman who worked as a guard in the underground prison for parahuman criminals. "Even at my best flight speed, it would take me a couple of hours to get there, and I'd be foolish to walk into the most secure prison in the world. I'm a wanted man."

"Leave that to me," said Penny. "Actually, leave both of those things to me. I can get us there in a few minutes if someone at the PRA is awake, and I can ensure your safe passage in and out of the facility."

Washington closed his faceplate. "Perhaps I was incorrect in my assessment of you. You have more of Crackerjack in you than you know. He didn't follow the rules when it suited him not to."

"I'll take that as a compliment."

"It was meant as such."

Penny snorted as she pulled out her phone. "Careful, Washington. My heart's all aflutter now."

Hind Fleet
Axeship Blood Afire

The guards outside Clanmistress Rhaorhir's Clanroom were unhappy about the Monkey.

"It smells," said one.

"And it's filthy," said the other. "You can't take it into the Clanroom like that. We'd have our guts sliced out."

"The Clanmistress will want to speak to her," Garragh said. "This Monkey is a Warrior and a leader to her people."

"Her? It's female? And a Warrior? What kind of mixed-up world is this?" The guard laughed.

The other slapped his axe haft against his hand. "I don't care if it's the Clanmistress of Monkeyworld. It stinks. Go hose it off, or there will be trouble."

Garragh knew he had no choice. The guards outside the Clanroom outranked all other Warriors. They were the Clanmistress' Chosen, and they had final say over her security. "Fine, we will clean her." He motioned for the Monkey to follow him. The phalanx of guards stayed arrayed around her, ready to take her down if she made a move. Garragh didn't tell them she was probably fast enough that they couldn't stop her if she made a serious effort. He suspected she was biding her time, waiting for an opportunity to do . . . what?

He actually didn't mind taking the extra time to clean her up. It would give him time to think over what he was going to tell the Clanmistress. The Warrior Monkey was a leader of her people. She seemed much more powerful than others of her race. It only stood to reason that she was at least a Submistress equivalent if not a full Clanmistress of some kind. Their limited lessons about Monkeyworld suggested there were hundreds if not thousands of Clans spread across the chaotic planet. It wasn't unrealistic to think she might in fact be a Clan leader. That made her someone to deal with, someone the Clanmistress might be able to speak to—not as an equal, for a Monkey could never be the equal to a Hind, but as one would speak to a subordinate leader.

It might mean the Monkey could speak for her people, for her planet. If she could surrender on their behalf, it would mean the end of the war. It would mean a great victory for Clan Sharassar, and much prestige upon the battle fleet's return to Hind space. To take an entire world with such a small expeditionary force meant Sharassar was unrivaled in the art of warfare, and they would all become legend.

In Garragh's mind, it was vital that she didn't realize how powerful she and her people were in comparison to the Hind. Only two or three sixes of them had managed to take down Submistress Rheayara's well-defended compound and destroyed the shield into the bargain. As the dropship had approached the fleet, Garragh had seen one of the Axeships had suffered grievous harm, enough to split it apart. He was a well-trained Warrior, and he could tell it had been in a firefight. It was possible the captain had somehow managed to offend one of the other Axeship commanders and had suffered a final, horrible correction for it, but none of the other fleet ships bore any notable damage. Something had attacked and destroyed twenty percent of the Clan's forces, and Garragh was suspicious a Monkey had been behind it.

The guards brought the Monkey Warrior to a wash bay where they hosed off equipment that had become contaminated with waste or dust or even interstellar residue. They threw her against the wall and turned the hose on her. She shrieked and squalled as the high-pressure spray blasted against her, knocking her from her feet and spinning her around. The guards laughed at her struggles and her misery as she took the spray in her face, leaving her coughing and choking. "We'll get you clean yet, Monkey," one of them called. "Fit to meet the Clanmistress in no time."

Garragh turned away, not wanting to watch as his brethren tormented the Monkey. He'd seen her fight in a blur of motion, and knew she could have decimated all of them where they stood had she chosen to. For some reason, she was *letting* them torture her, and that frightened him more than he could explain. He was a Hind Warrior; he wasn't supposed to fear anything.

"You." He looked up and saw Submistress Loasrah, standing in the doorway to the maintenance bay. "Come here, Warrior."

He obliged. Following orders was something he understood, something he didn't have to decipher.

Loasrah checked to make sure the other guards were occupied teasing the Monkey, then pulled Garragh around the corner into the corridor. "You know something about that Monkey. Something important. I want to know what it is."

"It's not just her. It's all of them. All of those like her."

"What do you mean? She's just a tiny little Monkey."

"You were in the dropship. You didn't see the battle around Rheayara's compound. The Monkeys . . . routed us. They beat us."

Loasrah snorted. "Your Monkey Warrior, yes?"

"More than just her. At least a dozen, but not much more than that. They knocked the shield down. They killed the Submistress. And they did all that with only a couple sixes of their own Warriors." Garragh lowered his voice. "There could be six hundred of them. Or six thousand. Or six million. We can't beat them. Maybe if we had the full force of Clan Sharassar to drop a hundred twenty thousand Warriors, we might secure a few cities, but they could turn right around and destroy us and then we would have nothing at all."

Loasrah dropped her voice to a low growl. "You're speaking treasonous words, Warrior. Tread carefully."

"You saw the fifth Axeship. It's destroyed. How do you think that happened?"

"Not by a Monkey. They live on the ground."

"I wouldn't be so sure." He shivered. "I've seen them fly."

"So why bring one here then? Aren't you putting the Clanmistress in great danger? They'll flay your fur off for it."

"We need to convince her to surrender Monkeyworld to us."

"The Monkey? Surely it couldn't be that hard."

"If the Clanmistress can't convince her that we can destroy her world . . ." Garragh bowed his head. "I do not think we can defeat them."

Loasrah snorted. "A thinking Warrior."

"I only know what I have seen."

Loasrah looked past his shoulder. The guards emerged from the maintenance bay, one of them dragging the Monkey by a wrist. "What happened?"

The guard raised the Monkey. Her eyes were shut behind bedraggled hair. "It's delicate. All tired out from playing too hard. We're to lock it up. Submistress Hsharra's orders."

Garragh and Loasrah watched them leave. "I should follow them. The Monkey knows me. At least, she trusted me enough to board the dropship. Maybe I can convince her to surrender her world so we don't have to fight them and lose."

Loasrah scratched her chin. "All this seems like the kind of thing that could get a Clanmistress replaced. I will have to think on this further."

"You?"

"Yes, why not? I'm young and I'm smart." Loasrah showed her fangs in a smile. "And I'm very ambitious."

Time Warner Center
8ᵗʰ Ave. and West 59ᵗʰ St., Manhattan

Penny lowered her phone and grinned triumphantly at Harlan. "You're gonna love this, Washington." She held the phone out to him.

He shrugged and took it. "What am I supposed to do with it?"

"Answer it when it rings. That's what you do with phones."

He snorted. "This is your big plan? A phone call?"

"Not just any call."

"It takes a lot to impress me." The phone rang. He touched the *answer* button.

A cloud of blue and gold energy swirled from the speaker to resolve into a man in an old-school one-piece bodysuit. It was a bright sky blue that shone even in the darkness, with golden lines running down from the shoulders and then turning right angles toward the center of his chest but stopping part way, ending in dots with an arch over the top. Most people wouldn't have any idea what the insignia meant, but Harlan immediately understood he was looking at an electrical schematic of a circuit breaker. He handed the phone back to Penny. "I'm impressed," he said softly.

"Hey there," said the man. Despite his heroic costume, he didn't have a particularly heroic build about him. His arms and legs were skinny and the costume didn't fit him well, bunching in the crotch and under the arms and stretching too tightly across an incipient paunch. "Names Benjie, but you can call me Circuit Breaker." He looked Harlan up and down. "Huh. I thought you'd be taller."

"Did you actually just . . . transmit yourself via a cellular network?" Harlan asked. He knew of another parahuman who could travel through live electrical circuitry, but she was constrained by her inability to cross an air gap, whereas this Benjie character didn't seem to have any such limitation.

"Something like that." Benjie showed his teeth. "The exact nature of my abilities is classified. I wouldn't even be here if the Director hadn't called in a favor with my boss."

"Who's your boss?" Penny asked.

"Just someone at an organization I'm not at liberty to discuss. That said, I'm here, and the Director said I'm to place myself at your disposal to assist in whatever way I can." He looked back at Harlan. "We're going after the aliens, right? Because I'm totally down for that."

"Can you transmit all the way to their ships?" Harlan asked, thinking of Sally.

Benjie looked away and Harlan knew the man was about to lie to him. "I don't know."

Harlan nodded. He would uncover Benjie's secret eventually. He couldn't let an ability like that go without exploring the possibility of recreating it through his technological innovation.

"But you can transport us here on Earth though, right?" Penny asked. "The Director said you could."

"Yeah, I can bring along passengers. It's only safe to do that here on Earth because you won't be digital for more than a fraction of a second. I can maintain a protective quantum field for that long. You must have a lot of pull with the Director to get me pulled off of . . . well, off of what I was doing."

"There's an attempted alien invasion of the Earth," Harlan said. "I'd like to know what you considered more important than the defense of your homeworld."

Benjie shrugged. "Look, it's a big planet, and you guys seem to have New York well in hand, and everyone's got problems. Now where do you need to go?"

"Deep Six," Penny said. "Quick as you can get us there."

Benjie touched a device strapped to his forearm. It looked like a modified tablet with some extra, unfamiliar controls upon it. Harlan's fingers itched to get hold of it. He wanted to know if Benjie's powers were technological in origin or strictly parahuman. If they were the former, Harlan could figure out how to duplicate them. If he could do that, he could cast off the irritation of his physical body forever and live eternally as a creature of pure energy. *That* would be real power. Benjie swiped his fingers across the tablet screen until he achieved a result that made him smile. "Got it. You guys need to do anything before we go or can I let my fingers do the walking?"

"What do we do?" Penny asked.

"Take hands," Benjie said. "I need a single point of contact."

Harlan hesitated, but Penny reached out and seized his gauntlet. He looked over at her, almost in shock. He was unused to physical contact. Since his armor was generated by the nanites within his body, he could feel her hand against his as if his skin was bare against hers, and it felt strange. He'd touched her before, when he'd rescued her, but that wasn't the same thing as willful contact.

She must have mistaken his stunned shock for interest and gave him a tight smile.

Benjie touched Harlan's and Penny's joined hands. With his free hand, he tapped out a sequence of numbers on the device upon his wrist. "Okay, hold onto your potatoes. This may feel a little strange."

"Command Center," said a voice from his wrist.

"Hi, stand back, please," Benjie said.

"Who is this? This is an official line. What are you—"

As fast as blinking his eyes, Harlan found himself standing in a high-tech control room for what he presumed was Deep Six. "—doing on it?" finished the jumpsuited man speaking into the phone. He jumped back from the three intruders in fear. Harlan noticed his feet didn't actually touch the floor, which was an odd ability. "Holy shit!" he yelled.

Penny flashed her Just Cause badge. "Stand down, everyone. We're from Just Cause."

A woman with her hair caught up in a sloppy bun stepped forward. "I'm Warden Cassandra Haig. I recognize you, Penny Lane. What are you doing here, and why are you traveling with a known felon?" She looked at Harlan, who did his best not to provoke her.

"You're aware of the emergency in New York, Warden?" Penny asked.

Haig nodded. "Yes, we've been told to prepare for the possibility of alien prisoners."

Large, floor-to-ceiling panes of reinforced glass gave an unimpeded, semicircular view of a large cavern with a cement floor. Out on the floor below, Harlan saw several guards who had come into the lobby, presumably at the warning about intruders. One of them was the Antimatter Woman, a Guatemalan native who had been created within a parapower-generating reactor of Harlan's design. That had been fifteen years ago, but it felt like it had been someone else's life entirely. Harlan was a different person now. He didn't hate the entire world. He didn't even hate people.

It was a waste of his effort to do so, because now he had the Hind to which he could devote his full attention.

CHAPTER THIRTEEN

♘

Hind Fleet
Axeship Blood Afire

They brought Sally before their queen, or whatever she was called.

After she'd been hosed off like an animal, the Hind had thrown her into an empty room, unadorned with furnishings and not even any art upon the walls. She ached from head to toe, and even her rapid healing couldn't fix the hole in her heart.

The part that hurt the worst was that their last real conversation before the battle had been full of words spoken out of irritation and anger, as had been more often the case in recent months. She could tell him she loved him now, but she would never again hear it from him. She remembered all the hurtful things she'd said to him, but she couldn't remember the last thing he'd said to her, or she to him. The only thing that stayed in her mind was the vision of that axe blade falling and the look of confusion on Jason's face as his life ended.

She would never forget that moment.

The Hind who'd taken her-she refused to say he'd captured her because of course she'd gone of her own accord-stayed on guard outside the room where they kept her. He paced back and forth, staring often at her as if her were the one in a cage, until another Hind had arrived to collect them both.

She was escorted under heavy guard. Her Hind walked right behind her, his heavy footsteps thudding on the deck. It seemed they had artificial gravity along with their interstellar drive and energy shields and lasers. And yet, they didn't seem like they were thousands of years more advanced than humans. Maybe only a couple hundred, she thought. Maybe they had more to offer each other than more warfare.

Then she hardened. They'd killed Jason. She would make them pay for that, and as they brought her before their queen, she decided the queen would be the first to die.

A Hind wearing a harness covered with pouches and devices approached her, holding a round device that reminded her of one of those air fresheners that people stuck on walls. Sally shrank back as the Hind growled at her but a voice speaking English came from the device. It was a translator, obviously, but for some reason the Hind had perfectly copied the old Microsoft Anna voice and Sally had to keep from laughing at the incongruity of it all. "This is a translation device. You will wear this translation device. Do you understand this translation device?"

"Yes." Sally wiped her eyes to contain her frantic amusement. She knew it was because she was in shock and struggled to maintain her dignity when a Hindish growl emerged from the device.

The Hind pressed the translation disc onto Sally's chest beneath her throat. The alien's claws poked painfully against her skin through the fabric of her uniform but she said nothing, making herself sober and studying her potential opponent. The Hind was not a soldier but a technician or scientist of some kind. At least they weren't an entire race of axe-swinging barbarians. Perhaps they could be reasoned with, Sally thought. Or at least properly threatened.

The scientist Hind turned to the Clanmistress and said, "The Human is ready, Clanmistress."

For the first time, Sally noticed the Hind at the far end of the chamber. She'd been so wrapped up in her misery that she'd barely even bothered to look at her surroundings. A Human Clanroom might have steps leading up to a platform, but the Hind apparently preferred gently sloping ramps instead. A large shapeless pillow took the place of a throne and the Clanmistress lay upon it, her four feet tucked beneath her. She wore nothing but some accouterments Sally thought were probably jewelry. No armor marred her shining fur, no straps crisscrossed over her. Cosmetic paint had been applied to her in a delicate, decorative abstract pattern. Of course she wouldn't be armored, Sally thought. What better way to show how much power one had among all the Warriors than to go unarmed and unarmored, unafraid of harm?

Clanmistress Rhaorhir yawned, licked her chops with a long pink tongue, and regarded Sally through contemptuous, half-lidded eyes. She toyed with a silver dual-blade dagger in one six-fingered hand while beckoning to Sally with the other. "Approach, Human."

Her clothing torn and bedraggled, her damp hair stringy from the firehose the Hind had sprayed at her, and her bruises and scratches from combat not yet healed, Sally felt less prepared to speak to royalty than she ever had been for anything in her life. Nevertheless, she dragged her tired, numb feet forward until she reached the base of the ramp to look up at the Clanmistress.

"What do you want?" Sally asked, unwilling to play court games.

A sharp intake of breath from around the room suggested she had just uttered the most devastating insult, and that thought warmed her just a little.

A guard stepped forward, his axe raised. "You address the Clanmistress, Monkey. Speak with respect!"

"The next Warrior who speaks out of turn will be slain," Clanmistress Rhaorhir's growl was soft and menacing.

The guard who'd spoken bowed until his nose was nearly touching his forelegs, exposing his entire back and neck to the Clanmistress in a clear gesture of supplication, but he said nothing.

The Clanmistress appeared to have been appeased by his humility and returned her attention to Sally. "Speak, Human."

"What do you want?" Sally repeated.

"Your world. Give it to me"

Sally realized the Hind had interpreted her question literally. Perhaps the translation into the Hind tongue was equally bland and devoid of character as was the Microsoft Anna voice translating into English. "It isn't mine to give."

The Clanmistress made a waving gesture in front of her nose, as if she were brushing aside an annoying insect. "Give it to me. You are Mustang Sally. You lead New York. New York leads the world. I want your world. Give it to me."

Sally tried not to laugh. Somehow with all their watching Earth television signals, the Hind had managed to completely misinterpret her role. The Clanmistress had it exactly wrong. "You should get better researchers. I don't rule the world. I don't rule New York. Most days, I'm not even sure I'm still in charge of Fort Justice. You're wrong, Clanmistress. Wrong about everything."

The onlookers gasped at Sally's effrontery but she didn't care. Let them get angry with her. It would just add fuel to her righteous fire.

"Oh?" The clipped syllable from the translator was so brief Sally might have missed it if not for her slightly accelerated perceptions. "Tell me how I'm wrong, Human."

"You came here and immediately attacked us. We're not an unreasonable people. We might have welcomed you at least as guests, but instead you came down and attacked people. K-killed them."

"You would welcome invaders? You are weak, Human, like prey."

"Why invade us at all? We've been sending messages out to the stars for, like fifty or sixty years now. Maybe even longer. We *want* to meet you! We've *dreamed* of meeting you—or at least, I have." She shuddered. "And instead you come in here to kick over our sand castles."

The translation disc spent some time providing the Clanmistress with the best version of Sally's words, as if struggling to find the right tone.

"Being conquered is an honor. You will be ... elevated within the Clan, to show the other clans our power."

Sally snorted. "That's your best argument? Join you so we can make you look better to your peers? *Look at my pet Earthling. She does tricks. She's well-trained and housebroken.* Well, we're not your pets, and we're not going to join your fucking Clan."

Tension ran through the room like someone had turned on the showers. Sally felt the electric current of nascent combat.

"Enough of this. Give me your world, Human, or I will slay you and find someone who can do so."

Sally laughed with bitter, mocking amusement. "You know what I think, Clanmistress? You came all the way out here to Earth from whatever shit little empire you call home, thinking you'd get an easy win. But you know what? *You already lost.* You lost New York. My friends took that shield down and you've already tried to blow up your bomb but you can't do it, because they stopped that too. You've got *nothing.* You think you can bluff your way to victory, but we can see through it. My people will come for you, and they'll destroy you, because you Hind might think you're hot shit with your axes and lasers, but Humans? We're better at war than we are at anything else, and you've just given us somebody new to fight that we don't have to feel bad about beating." She took a step forward, feeling her strength returning for one single burst of super-speed. "You killed my husband, and I don't much care if I live or die right now, and I swear the last thing you see will be me standing over you as you bleed out on the floor!"

The room dropped into a frozen tableau as her accelerated perceptions kicked in. Sally delivered a half dozen super-speed punches to the face of the nearest Hind guard, shattering his nose in a splash of orange blood under her onslaught. She felt her knuckles bruising but that didn't matter; either they'd heal when she rested or she wouldn't live long enough to feel the discomfort. She twisted the heavy axe from the guard's hands, using her speed as a substitute for strength. Armed at last, she raced up the ramp, swinging the axe around in an arc to bring her prophecy to fruition and split the Clanmistress' skull like a virtual ninja cutting apart virtual fruit.

She crashed into an invisible barrier and the darkness took her.

The Boudica

The *Boudica* and *Daedalus* raced in toward the Hind fleet, using a combination of military stealth technology and nanotech dampening to stay as invisible as possible. Outside the *Boudica*, a pair of missiles floated, apparently motionless. Both had metallic cores and tips with amber packed around them and wrapped in layers of dark ice to make them nearly invisible. They were using ancient technology against the Hind. As Minerva said, they were essentially throwing spears in the darkness. At four kilometers per second, they would concentrate a tremendous amount of kinetic energy, and when they impacted at that speed, it wouldn't matter that they were largely brittle materials.

Minerva spent a lot of time studying angles, studying the imaging of the Hind ships. She had the telemetry information from the vessels' initial arrival as provided by the data in March's nanotech as well as the data pulled by the communication satellites that had carried the Clanmistress' signal around the world. Sally would be on the fleet's flagship; of that she had no doubt. They would fling their spears at the other vessels, as would the *Daedalus* with her missiles, while the *Boudica* would land upon the flagship and fight their way inside to find Sally.

It was selfish, and foolish, and Minerva knew it. She knew if she lost a single soldier, or in any way failed in the mission to protect the Earth, it would likely mean her career. She also knew Sally wouldn't hesitate to come after her were their positions reversed. As good as a leader as Sally was, she still allowed emotions to guide her decision-making, and sometimes that meant making choices that were strategically wrong but morally correct. Minerva had always taken the logical choice given the opportunity, but she was trying to learn to open her emotions more and to trust her human instincts.

She helped Failsafe form complex energy field structure around each missile, redirecting it superficially by fractions of a degree until each one was aimed at the vessels designated Target Beta and Target Gamma. At last, satisfied with their courses, she had him release his fields and they continued on their ballistic course with impacts targeted midships on each of the Hind vessels. "March, give me a tight-beam comm to *Daedalus*."

"Go ahead, Minerva."

"*Daedalus*, deliver your payload to Target Delta and then bug out. You can't do any more good once you're running empty."

"Roger, *Boudica*. We'll stay in the area, just in case somebody misses the bus."

Minerva sighed. It was the best she would get from the two dutiful Air Force pilots flying the stealthy saucer craft. "Roger, *Daedalus*. Clear skies."

"Good hunting, *Boudica*. The check is in the mail."

That meant *Daedalus* had dropped its missiles on a dumb, ballistic course to make them harder to target. When they reached a predefined distance, their engines would activate and they would close upon their target.

"D-deceleration," March warned from the cockpit. "Setting inertial dampeners t-to full."

The air inside the *Boudica* seemed to solidify as fields suffused its interior, holding everyone in place as if they'd been cast in concrete. It was possible to move within the dampening field, but only with slow, deliberate motions. The fields resisted sudden movements, like those stemming from hard deceleration that would have pulped the crew.

Minerva moved through the inertial dampening field so she could see through the front window of the *Boudica*. Her vision telescoped out toward the Hind fleet until she could see it clearly. Her silent missiles penetrated the energy shields of Targets Beta and Gamma and she saw the flash of impact followed by an escaping cloud of atmosphere and expanding debris from the points where the missiles struck. A moment later and the flare of missile engines firing lit the cosmos as *Daedalus*'s ordnance went live and raced in toward Target Delta. Unfortunately, the missiles were slow enough that Delta's shields went up in time to catch all but one of the missiles. The one that got through struck near the aft and must have hit something important enough to cause several chain-reaction explosions across the hull. Whatever it was that blew up didn't seem to affect Delta's performance in the least, for its engines glowed bright as it swung around to face the direction from where the missiles had launched.

"Take us in, March. Get us onto Alpha's hull and we'll make our way inside." Minerva saw motion on the hulls of all four vessels and realized turrets were swinging in their direction. "Hurry. They've seen us."

Space lit up with a barrage of particle beams from the Hind fleet, stuttered bolts instead of unbroken beams. They were poorly aimed, but that didn't mean they wouldn't get a lucky shot. March juked the *Boudica* back and forth, looping her around in a wild corkscrew that the passengers barely felt due to the dampening field.

"Everyone seal your suits," Minerva said. "We could take a shot at any moment."

"Won't we hit their shields?" Failsafe asked. "They got those, right? Like mine?"

"Harlan Washington reported that they cannot fire through their own shields. As long as they are shooting at us, we don't have to worry about colliding with their shields."

Giant laughed. "Then we are all grateful they keep shooting."

Brilliant, devastating light filled the cabin for a moment followed by the rush of air evacuating into the void. A hole the size of her fist had appeared in the front windows, outlined by a white-hot glowing ring. Minerva felt through her feet the stammer of the engines as they took on a stutter like March's. She turned to look back but she already knew from the placement of her people before she saw. Black Ice was gone. The particle beam had passed through her like a bullet through paper, leaving a smoldering crater through her torso.

Her ears filled with screams and shouts of dismay from the other heroes as their suit radios came online. She knew how they felt. She wished she could join in their anger and fear and grieve the loss of a hero she barely knew, but this was war and Minerva had always known there would be losses. She modulated her voice, utilizing combinations of harmonics and pitches that she rarely except in circumstances like these. "Be still," she commanded, and everyone's comm babble ceased. "She's gone, and there's nothing we can do about it right now. We're not out of danger yet, and our comrade is still a prisoner of the Hind. We continue the mission."

The rest of the heroes mutter their agreement. She knew she'd played their emotions with her vocal control, and she knew that might come back to haunt her in the future, but this was a difficult mission with a low forecasted percentage of success. She needed her team to stay focused.

"March, can you get us down to the flagship?"

"We're g-going to get there no matter what at th-this point. Impact in ninety seconds. Lateral control is gone."

Minerva nodded. She'd suspected *Boudica* might only be a one-way trip. "All right, Failsafe, you're up. Amber, Gauss, Giant, March, inside his shield with me. Javelin, Blueshift, give us some covering fire."

A shimmering energy sphere formed around Failsafe and the others, filling the *Boudica*'s cabin. Failsafe would be able to slow their approach toward the Hind flagship using his field control so they wouldn't splatter across the hull. The *Boudica* wouldn't be so lucky. Gauss used his power to split the vessel in half so they could float free. The broken vessel drifted ahead of them, keeping the momentum of its approach as they slowed. Minerva focused the totality of her attention on the guns of the distant Hind vessels, filling in targeting lines in her mind and directing Failsafe which way to nudge his energy sphere to keep the particle beams from striking it. His field might have been proof against a Hind beam, but Minerva wasn't keen to find out.

Beside the sphere, Blueshift and Javelin zigged and zagged, waiting until the Hind fleet was within their firing range. Their target profiles were too small for the Hind to hit with their generally inaccurate weapons except via blind luck. Blueshift surrounded himself with an electromagnetic shield that would dissipate any beams harmlessly around him, while Javelin had a force field similar to Failsafe's. As they closed in on the fleet, they opened up with their own offensive weapons, targeting Hind turrets. Blueshift's electromagnetic blasts were functionally similar to the Hind particle beams, while Javelin used high-powered lasers; one was a blunt club, the other a scalpel. Their attacks flashed against the black of space.

The *Boudica* impacted against the Hind flagship, silently breaking apart against the hull and causing no visible damage to the gigantic vessel. It amazed Minerva that they'd managed to make it into space in a vehicle so flimsy. Explosions flared around the flagship where Javelin and Blueshift attacked turrets. Minerva's perspective shifted as Failsafe's energy bubble descended toward the vessel. It felt more like they were attacking a skyscraper. It occurred to her she didn't know the layout of the interior and she might be completely correct in her assessment. It could very well have followed a skyscraper deck layout instead of a cruise ship layout.

They'd know soon enough, she thought as the bubble touched the ship's hull. "Blueshift, Javelin, regroup."

The two fliers approached the shield and Failsafe reshaped his field to envelop them along with the others. Both heroes' masks and helmets kept their facial expressions hidden, but there was no mistaking the grim pleasure in either of their voices. "The only way they can hit us now is by firing on this ship from the others," said Blueshift. "And we've seen how well they aim."

Javelin pointed at the cloud of debris that had been *Boudica.* "Pretty sure they heard us knock. Should we wait for them to answer the door?"

Minerva gave one of her rare, treasured smiles. "No, I think we'll let ourselves in."

Deep Six, Montana

Penny watched Harlan Washington, the Destroyer, pace back and forth in the conference room like a caged animal. He'd reabsorbed his nanotech armor for the moment, and wore a basic black body suit that showed off the physique of a middle-aged man who didn't eat well or frequently enough. He'd asked for the impromptu meeting with Warden Haig and the Antimatter Woman, whose real name was Lania. Now that he'd achieved that goal, he seemed ill at ease.

"Washington," Penny said in a low voice. "Settle yourself down. Nobody's going to arrest you."

He snorted. "You couldn't contain me if you tried."

Warden Haig cleared her throat. "Mr. Washington, I assure you that I am under strict orders from the PRA

IAN THOMAS HEALY

to allow you to leave here without any strings attached. I'm going to follow those orders, because this is bigger than you or me or this prison. We're on the same side, at least for the moment."

"The enemy of my enemy is my friend, Warden?"

Haig smiled. "Let's just call it a temporary suspension of hostilities and leave it at that. Agreed?"

"Agreed," said Harlan. "I need—"

"Harlan," Penny interrupted. "You have to say it. You promised you would." She'd had it out with him for a few minutes before the meeting commenced. She'd made him promise to make amends with the Antimatter Woman for his role in her creation. He'd flatly refused, but Penny wouldn't accept *no* for an answer. She'd gotten right in his face, which was easier than she'd thought once his armor disappeared, because he was a lot shorter in person.

"We don't have time for this bullshit, Lane," he said.

"Make time. It's the right thing to do."

Harlan sighed and turned to Lania. "I built the reactor that turned you into what you are today." He glanced over at Penny, who gave him an encouraging nod. "For my role in the difficulty of your life, I . . . apologize."

The Antimatter Woman crossed her arms. Her containment suit had shrunk over the years thanks to technological improvements. Once it had been bulky, heavy, and awkward, like a suit of plate armor wrapped in layers of foam six inches thick. Now it was more like a full-body wetsuit with a helmet, allowing her the full range of motion without letting her antimatter flesh come into contact with the matter of the world. If it did in totality, it might be an extinction-level event.

"It was a shitty thing you did," Lania said at last. "You killed many of my people, my countrymen. You come here now to apologize, to face me. That takes *cojones.*" She nodded. "I'm not forgiving you, but I accept your apology."

"All right, now that's out of the way, why are you here?" Haig asked. "I got the call from Director

258

Forsythe himself. I'm to assist you in any way I can. I presume it has something to do with Officer Batrez."

Penny leaned forward, her hands clasped on the table. "The Hind were going to use an antimatter bomb to destroy New York City, Warden. We stopped them. We have their bomb, and we're going to use it against them."

"It's not enough," Harlan said. "I need three more bombs to destroy their fleet. Nukes might not be powerful enough, and I don't have time to go steal them anyway. Not when there's a readily available and portable source of pure antimatter right here."

The Warden narrowed her eyes. "You're talking about a person, Washington, and she's right here."

"Cassie," Lania said. "I *am* right here. Let's hear them out."

Harlan chewed on his knuckles for a moment, then stepped over to the white board at one end of the conference table. The first marker he grabbed was dry but the second had enough ink. He drew four small boxes. "Here's the fleet." He drew a triangle beneath the boxes then connected each corner to a point above with a dotted line, then circled each of the four corners.

Penny saw what he was doing right away. Four vertices, with the fleet at the focal point between them.

"Bombs at each of these points. Shaped charges focusing the blast inward. The Hind bomb has about eighty grams of antimatter in it. That makes about a three point five megaton blast. Put four of those together and you're approaching the Castle Bravo test blast."

"What's Castle Bravo?" Penny asked. It sounded familiar. She thought she should know what it was.

"March 1, 1954," Harlan said. "My birthday. The United States performed its largest ever bomb test in the Bikini Atoll. This is how we destroy the invading fleet. I've seen their technology up close. Their force field could contain one blast, but not four."

Warden Haig stood, disbelief spread plain across her face. She turned to Penny. "Is he for real?"

Penny nodded. "I have no reason to think otherwise."

"So you need, like, a pound of antimatter? That seems like a lot. I don't think I could shed that much safely without risking it getting past my containment." Lania shook her head. "Even here in the middle of nowhere, I can't risk that. Too much could go wrong."

"Only a half a pound," Harlan said. "And we can't do it here. I need my lab to extract it properly and still maintain containment."

"And where's that? You have your own private island somewhere, Washington? Someplace with no other humans, no ecology to risk?" Warden Haig crossed her arms. Penny could see she had already made up her mind to say no.

"As a matter of fact," Harlan said, "It's on the Moon."

Haig burst out laughing. "Of course it is."

Penny cleared her throat. "He's not lying, Warden."

Haig laughed. "The Moon. All right, fair enough. Do you have a rocket in your pocket too?"

"We can get there the same way we came here' Harlan said. "Via transmission."

Haig's humor evaporated. "Yes, I'm a little concerned about that. It's a security breach we simply haven't ever had to address before. I see that we'll have to from now on."

"You have my word it won't be a problem, now or in the future' said Penny. "Warden, please. This is the best chance we have to destroy the aliens."

"Why destroy them at all?" asked Lania. "Is a defeat not enough?"

"No." Penny spoke with more vehemence than might have been necessary to convey her point. "They're fighters and Warriors. You beat them and leave them alive, they'll regroup and come back with a bigger and more powerful army. They came this time with five ships. What if they come back with fifty? Or five hundred? If we defeat them here and now and take away their ability to return to their people, it becomes a mystery to the Hind back home. Maybe they don't send another expeditionary force."

Haig sighed. "Ultimately, this is Lania's decision. I won't order her to go, or not to, but I will abide by and defend her decision."

Lania nodded at Penny, and for the first time time, Penny noticed just how beautiful the woman was. The magnetic fields her body generated to contain the antimatter played across her skin, giving her a bluish-white glow like moonlight in snow. When she'd first come to America, it had been at the hands of a powerful psi working with Harlan, and she'd been more of a creature than a person, thanks to her recent transformation. She required electricity in massive doses to keep her fields intact and would stop at nothing to obtain it.

Now, many years later, she'd regained much of her humanity and that was what Penny saw when the guard spoke. "Of course I'll go. There's no choice here. *Do I save the world or not?* I'm happy to be someone who can say *yes, I will.*"

Hind Fleet
Axeship Blood Afire

For a moment, nobody moved out of sheer shock. One moment the Monkey had been making threats against the Clanmistress, and the next she lay unmoving on the dais, apparently knocked unconscious by the Clanmistress' personal shield. Then the Clanroom exploded into chaos. "How did it get past us?" one of the guards shouted.

"It took my axe! *My axe!*" another cried.

"Kill it!" the chief of the guards roared.

Blood Afire shook with a sudden impact, making Hind hiss like frightened cats. "What is the meaning of this?" shouted the Clanmistress.

"We're under attack, Clanmistress!" cried a Submistress from her computer station.

"What? Here? Another Clan?"

"N-no, Clanmistress. The bridge is saying . . . They're saying it's the Monkeys."

Another Submistress laughed, her growl scornful. "They're just filthy animals."

The Clanmistress grabbed an axe from one of her guards and buried it in the Submistress' skull. "One of those filthy animals destroyed *Wind Roar*. They may be animals, but they are crafty, and anyone who dismisses them because they don't have enough legs or fur only begs for a coward's death. Am I understood?"

"Yes, Clanmistress," chorused all those present in the Clanroom.

Up until that moment, Garragh had only thought of the Clanmistress as a distant, disinterested leader. Now he'd seen her in action, he understood how such a female could have risen to the heights of leadership within the Clan. She was fearless, inventive, and unhesitating when it came to decision-making. She spat orders like a laser firing. "You guards, escort me to the bridge. I will command this engagement personally. You there, get this traitorous body out of my sight, but leave her blood as a warning to others who might question me." Her gaze fell in Garragh. "You, Warrior. Take this Monkey back to a cell. See that no harm comes to her. She is valuable."

"I obey, Clanmistress." Garragh leaped forward to fulfill her bidding. He knew she had seen the same importance of the Warrior Mistress he had, and somehow that had elevated him to a position of importance. He hefted the Monkey over his back like a blanket. She barely weighed anything, and he marveled that someone so slight could carry so much weight of personality.

As he galloped through the corridors of *Blood Afire*, the cruiser shook and shivered as whatever weapons the Monkeys had brought to bear struck it. As he reached the cellblock, the ship listed hard enough to one side to overcome the artificial gravity and he bounced off a bulkhead, losing his grip on the Monkey. She ricocheted off the corridor wall and tumbled into a boneless heap.

Garragh crouched down beside her, sniffing to see if she still smelled of hot blood and breath. What if he'd accidentally killed her? Killing an unarmed foe, especially one who was no threat due to injury or unconsciousness, was a dishonorable act and the sort of thing that could get a Warrior permanently assigned to mucking the ship's sewers or worse. "Monkey," he whispered, wondering if her translator would still work without Submistress Hsharra's presence. "Do you live?"

"What are you doing?"

Garragh whirled to see Submistress Loasrah regarding him, her eyes narrowed in suspicion. His hackles rose in an unconscious admission of guilt, even though he hadn't actually done anything prohibited by either law or culture. "I . . . dropped the Monkey when the ship tilted. They're fragile. I was checking to see if she was still alive."

"Is it?"

"*She.* It's a female and a Mistress of some kind."

"So you said. Is *she* still alive?"

"I think so."

"Can you wake her?"

"I don't know," he admitted. He reached down to nudge her. "Arise, Warrior Mistress."

The Monkey made a tiny sound, the moan of a hurt animal. It made the fur on Garragh's haunches stand on end. He would be punished if the Monkey was to perish while on his watch. It wouldn't matter that the injury occurred when *Blood Afire* suffered a grievous blow of its own. The Clanmistress had charged him with looking after the Monkey, and he would suffer if she died.

"I heard it. It's alive," said Loasrah. "Does it speak?"

Garragh pointed at the device Submistress Hsharra had given to the Monkey. "This makes it so she can understand us, and we can understand her. Although . . ." He rubbed his chin. "She speaks with an odd accent."

"Make it talk to me, Warrior."

"I—I'll try, Submistress." Feeling foolish, Garragh knelt before the Monkey again, trying to remember the sounds of her name. "Warrior Mistress . . ." he began, feeling Loasrah's eyes upon him. "Warrior Mistress, wake."

The Monkey moaned again at the translated Hind speech coming from the device stuck to her torso but didn't open her eyes or move.

Garragh tried again. Having Loasrah behind him made him nervous in a way he couldn't define. He wasn't afraid of being attacked from behind, but the Submistress was smart and clearly ambitious, and she was working some kind of angle with the Monkey playing a key role. Likewise, Garragh knew he played a key role in her plan, and feared perhaps it would cost him his life. "Sssahrr . . . rrhee." It was a close approximation of the Monkey's name and the best he could manage with a mouth not designed to pronounce Monkeyspeech.

The Monkey opened her eyes at last. She saw the massive Hind Warrior kneeling over her and gasped. Garragh raised his hands, showing open palms in a gesture of supplication. "I won't hurt you."

"You . . . You're the one who brought me here." The Hind voice coming from the Monkey's translator sounded tinny, almost like a cub's. "What do you want?"

"It's not me," Garragh said. He looked back over his shoulder and saw Loasrah waiting for her chance. "It's her, the Submistress."

Loasrah pushed him out of the way. "Stand guard at the door, Warrior. The Monkey and I have things to discuss." She closed the door in Garragh's face.

He turned his back to the door and wondered what troubles he had unleashed by bringing the Monkey aboard. A storm was coming, he feared, and he wasn't smart enough to make sure he wasn't swept up in its twists and turns.

The Preserve
Luna

Benjie was both nervous and excited at the prospect of transmitting himself to the Moon. He said it would be much further than he'd ever gone before, ever even thought about going.

"Can you do it or not?" Harlan asked.

Benjie snorted. "Relax, Destroyer. I'll get you there in one piece. And your companions too."

"Companions?" He'd planned to bring Lania, as he would need equipment in the Preserve to safely withdraw the antimatter he needed from her, but beyond her . . .

"You're goddamn right, companions. You think I'm letting you run off unsupervised now?" Penny stepped up and pointed at him. "Like it or not, we're on the same side, Washington. Humans against aliens. Us against them. You can't win this war by yourself."

"You don't know that." He turned away from her. He didn't need the distraction she posed. He felt a hand on his arm, and it made nervous shivers run down his back. He didn't like to be touched, and it had been years since anyone had.

"I know that you don't have to. You have allies. Friends, Harlan. People you can trust." She held out a hand to him. "Me. I owe you my life. The least I can do to repay it is to help you with these bombs."

"You're no scientist, no engineer." He wanted to snarl at her, to spit the words in anger, but they came out far softer than he intended.

"No, but I'm a Warrior. I'm a sniper. I've got steady hands. What if the Hind have found your base? What if you need a third hand to do something? What if you just need someone to watch your back?" She moved her hand toward him, encouraging him to take it. "Let it be me."

"God, will you two just get a room already?" Benjie chuckled behind his mask. "Okay, I've got a secure connection to a receiver on the Moon. It's where you said it is, Destroyer. I don't know if there's air on the other end, though."

"There is. It is awaiting my return. Let us depart."

Instead of the instantaneous transfer, the trip to the Preserve lasted more than a second. That second was the closest to non-existence Harlan had ever experienced, and he suspected that was what death would be in its final moments.

They emerged into the darkened control room of Harlan's moon base, with a fine sheen of frost coating all surfaces. After confirming no aliens awaited them either in the same room or anywhere else in the base, Harlan ordered life support to come back to full power, and hot air blew from the heat vents as the power plant spun back up to operating levels.

"Oh, shit, I'm on the Moon," said Penny as she bounced in the lighter gravity.

Harlan smiled despite himself. "Sally said that, too."

"What was she doing here?"

"That's a long story for another time."

"Can you bring the heat up faster? I c-can't feel my toes. I'm not d-dressed for this."

Harlan paused. He knew a regular person would apologize for the discomfort, but he had no idea how to actually do such a thing. "It will take a few minutes. Go stand by a vent. It will be warmer there."

Penny did so, slapping at her arms and shivering. "Aren't you c-cold?"

"No. My nanotech self-regulates my body temperature."

"Lucky."

Benjie was likewise shivering in his ill-fitting costume that clearly didn't insulate him in the least. "Hey, Destroyer, if you don't need me anymore, I'm gonna phone home. The Moon is cool and all, but I'd rather be somewhere warm. No offense."

"Do what you want," Harlan said. "I've got what I need."

Without additional fanfare, Benjie said, "Good luck and give 'em hell." He vanished into the radio transmitter.

"So what happens now?" Penny asked, jumping up and down to try to warm herself.

"Now I strip enough antimatter from the source to create three more Hind bombs."

"The source has a name, and it's Lania . . . Destroyer," the Deep Six guard said. "How are you going to do that? Do you have magnetic bottles already?"

"They are being manufactured by my nanites even as we speak. By the time we reach the lab, I will have a method to contain your antimatter. I will require you to disperse it. I understand that is in your capability."

"Yeah, I can shoot off bits of it. As much as you said you need might take awhile."

"I believe I can expedite the process."

"That sounds suspiciously dangerous," said Penny.

Harlan knew he would need to distract the Just Cause hero. If she knew that Lania might not survive the process, she'd veto it, and then he'd have to kill her, which he was surprised to discover he didn't want to do. "It should be quite safe," he said. "In the meantime, I believe it will make the bomb delivery process easier if you are nanotech enhanced as I am."

"What exactly do you mean by that?" Penny folded her arms.

"I have four bombs to deliver. I can deliver three of them between me and my . . . assistants. If I can count on you to deliver the fourth, it will be that much easier to bring this to an end."

"You want to give me armor and lasers and stuff, like what you have? The stuff that comes out of your skin?"

"Yes."

Penny paused. "Will it hurt?"

"Yes, but only for a moment. Then you won't ever feel pain again unless you want to."

Penny moved over beside him, invading his personal space in a way he hadn't expected. Likewise, instead of his response being to sweep her aside, he only turned to look down at her. She was short, like Sally and Minerva, but somehow her personality made her seem larger. "Why would anyone want to feel pain? Do you feel pain?" Her voice was quieter.

He nodded. "Every day."

"But you don't have to. Why would you choose to?"

"I have . . . caused tremendous pain to others throughout my life. Over the past few years, I've . . . learned something about that." When his sister passed onto the Dream-world after he'd spent two decades fighting to keep her alive, it had left a hollowness inside him. He'd filled it with his new hobbies, with his science, and with pain; pain to remind him he was still alive, to remind him his sister wouldn't want him to shut himself off from humanity entirely.

She reached up to touch his face gently. He should have recoiled, and he felt himself tense from the contact, but he didn't move. "I can see it in you," she said. "I'm sorry you hurt."

Lania clumped across the room in her suit, and the spell was broken. "We gonna do this today or what?"

"Yes, yes of course," Harlan said. "Let's get you down to the lab so I can begin extracting antimatter, and then, Penny, we can prepare you."

"What's this preparation entail?"

"It is simple. You will just receive a series of injections. The nanites will do all the work after that."

She snorted. "What, you're not going to make me get naked?"

He blinked. "No. Why would I do that?"

She smiled. "You show a girl a good time, bring her back to your place, talk about an injection. It's a hell of a first date, Washington."

Harlan knew she was teasing him, but it wasn't the kind of teasing that he'd grown up facing every day. No, there was no ill will, no cruelty behind her words. She was being casual, flippant. She was treating him like a person instead of a suit of armor.

He realized he kind of liked it.

CHAPTER FOURTEEN

Hind Fleet
Axeship Blood Afire

The Hind paced back and forth in front of Sally, keeping her upper torso twisted so she was always facing her Human captive. Sally could tell the Hind wanted something from her but as of yet hadn't said anything specific. Instead, she paced, and studied the captive. For herself, Sally knew she was probably suffering from yet another concussion. The team doctor had repeatedly warned her about head injuries. After multiple concussions over the years, she knew she was living on borrowed time every time she ran headlong into combat. But then, she was a speedster; running headlong into combat was what she did best.

Between her exhaustion, her entire body aching like she'd gone through a hard training session against her team's heavy hitters, and the yawning emptiness that had been Jason's place in her heart, she felt like curling up into a ball and surrendering to it. The pacing Hind stopped her endless back and forth and faced Sally at last. "My Warrior tells me you are a great Warrior yourself."

Sally said nothing. She didn't owe the Hind a response.

The Hind placed her forearms on her forehips. For the first time, Sally noticed the complexities of six-limbed musculature. It made her wonder a little about the creature's internal organs. They must have been equally complicated. Perhaps she'd open one up and find out. "Would you fight to save your own life?"

Again, Sally didn't respond. There was an old Mafia saying her friend Jack had quoted to her once. *Let your enemy talk. When he is finished, let him talk some more.* This Hind wanted to talk. Fine. Sally would let her.

"Would you fight to save the life of a loved one?"

That one stung. Sally knew her face betrayed the pain of Jason's loss, but she composed herself at super-speed. The Hind wouldn't know what her facial expressions meant.

"What about the planet below? Would you fight to save that?"

Sally raised her eyes to meet the Hind's gaze. The female watched her from beneath her deep-set eyes, overshadowed by a heavy brow ridge. "I'm listening."

The corners of the Hind's mouth twitched in an expression that seemed as much of a smile as if it had come from a human. "I can guarantee an end to this war. One where you walk away and the Hind leave Monkeyworld further untouched. So I ask you again. How great a Warrior are you?"

"I could kill you before you drew breath to ask why," Sally growled. "The only reason I haven't is that I'm listening to what you have to say first."

The Hind twitched her head in a peculiar fashion that Sally took to be an alien nod. "I want you to kill a Hind."

"That makes two of us."

The Hind sneezed in amusement. "There is a catch. You will have to fight for your world. All of it. The Clanmistress believes you have authority to do that. Will you fight with your world on the line? Lose, and the Hind will take it."

Sally laughed. "You can't. We already established that. I bet there isn't a living Hind left on the Earth."

The Hind before her remained in an impassive stance. "If you lose, it will be recorded, and sent back to the Clans. It will be evidence that Clan Sharrasar has legal authority to claim your world. They will return with a full battlefleet in force. Just because we did not bring one to Monkeyworld does not mean we do not have one available. We landed in one city. We could do so to a thousand. We can darken your skies with our dropships and erase your cities one by one until you surrender to us, and we will have all the authority we need to do so by your loss."

Sally shook her head. "You sound just like your Clanmistress. I promise you humanity will fight to the last living soul. You'll have to sterilize the Earth to claim victory. Somehow I don't think that figures to be in the wins column for your Clan."

"That is only if you lose."

"So what if I win?" A tiny flicker of hope sprung up in Sally's heart.

"It will leave a power void. I will take command. I will order the fleet to withdraw."

"Just like that? I presume you want me to kill the Clanmistress. So I do your dirty work and you become the new boss?"

"It appears you understand." The Hind crossed her forearms. "You will clear the way for me and I will become the new Clanmistress. The Clan will follow my lead."

"Pretty ambitious plan if you ask me. You think it's going to be that easy? Everyone will just roll over and show off their bellies and the backs of their necks to you? How do you have a claim on the title more than anyone else does? Are you the Clanmistress's sister or daughter or something? Is the title hereditary?"

"The title belongs to she who can hold it against all challengers. My Warrior has seen your abilities. I have seen them in the Clanroom. You will fight for me as any Warrior under my command would. The difference is you will be securing my position as Clanmistress."

"And once you're secure, as you say, you'll order your fleet to leave the system? To go back to where you came from and never return?"

"Yes, Monkey. Those are my terms. They are not negotiable. Do you accept them?"

"Not yet. I want to talk to Garragh."

The Hind snorted. "Why would you speak to a mere Warrior? They exist solely to fight for us. We Mistresses are the ones who plan, who make decisions, who speak to captives. Anything you have to say, you will say to me, Monkey."

"Call me *monkey* again and you'll see just how good of a Warrior I am. Now go get Garragh so I can talk to him and then you can fuck right off until I make my decision." Sally took on the tone of command she used when she had to keep Hector from bludgeoning her younger teammates into dust. It was what she secretly referred to as her *Doublecharge voice.*

For a long moment, the Hind stared at her, and Sally wondered what thoughts were passing through the alien's mind. Then she backed out of the room and another Hind—*her* Hind—entered.

"Garragh," Sally said.

"*Sahree.*" The Warrior sat back on his haunches. "I am here."

"Let's talk."

Hind Fleet
Axeship Blood Afire

Giant tore a hole in the hull of the Hind flagship. Blueshift and Javelin rushed inside to secure the entrance. The others followed and then Amber and Gauss filled the hole with an airtight plug of steel-reinforced amber. They found themselves in a long, wide corridor with low ceilings but plenty of room for the large Hind to pass each other. Orange lights flashed in time with a wailing alarm and Minerva knew they would only have moments before they'd have to begin a fight that might not end until every Hind or every human on the vessel was dead.

"Blueshift, Failsafe, Giant, cover left. Javelin, Amber, Gauss cover right. March, stay here beside me. I need a minute or two." Minerva shut her eyes and knelt on the deck, noting the Hind maintained Earth-normal artificial gravity on board. She presumed it was so the Warriors would have had time to acclimate before their arrival. She spread her fingers upon the deck, barely brushing it so she could better feel the vibrations transmitted through the ship's structure. She broadened her aural and olfactory senses as much as she could until she could pick out individual scent molecules from the melange of the ship's atmosphere and inhabitants, and the sounds and vibrations of footsteps and heartbeats. If Sally was somewhere aboard the ship, she would find out.

She forced herself to tune out the sounds of combat —the high-pitched whine of Blueshift's electromagnetic blasts and the sizzle of Javelin's lasers, as well as the roars of the approaching Hind Warriors. The stink of burnt fur and flesh seemed to fill all of her senses as casualties began to pile up on either side.

Then she caught it. A stray molecule of human sweat, tinged with the deodorant Sally preferred, the soap she bathed with, her last couple of meals, the Kevlar fabric of her outfit, and fear. Once she knew that her friend had at least been on board the vessel at some point, she focused upon the vibrations through her fingertips. Heavy Hind footsteps rattled the floor. Their dual hearts thudded in stereo, but there were human heartbeats aboard the ship as well, and once she filtered out those of her strike team, only one remained and if it wasn't Sally's, it was someone the same size and build as her.

Minerva opened her eyes to the fire and blood of a dual-sided battle in the corridor. Failsafe had made a semicircular shield across the hall and Blueshift fired just past the edge of it, picking off Hind Warriors with his blasts. Giant tore off pieces of the interior bulkheads like he was peeling off fruit leather. Then he crumpled them up into baseball-sized pieces and hurled them into the attacking crowd. Many Hind went down, wincing at broken legs, wrists, or ribs. Behind her, Javelin crouched behind a shield of amber that Amber kept replenishing as Hind lasers burned into it. Javelin's own lasers were far more accurate and several Hind had fallen at that end of the corridor. Gauss used his powers to draw blade-shaped extrusions from the bulkheads to hamper the Warriors.

"I've got her," Minerva called over the din of combat. She still wasn't sure about a direction but they were stuck in between two opposing forces and she had to make a decision before the sheer number of Hind overwhelmed their ability to fight back. If the Warriors managed to close to melee combat, she was going to lose someone else, and Black Ice's sudden death still weighed on her conscience. She chose to push toward the flagship's bow, figuring they would either find the bridge or a way to get to it. "Amber, Gauss, fill the corridor behind us, thick and deep as you can. Let's go."

Gauss drew pieces of metal across the corridor, floor-to-ceiling and side-to-side, creating a lattice like a chain-link fence. Amber created a massive plug of the golden material. The sounds of axes hammering against the metal and lasers burning into it. "I thought amber was flammable," said the man wrapped in metal.

"Mine isn't," Amber said without going into detail.

"Gauss, seal any side doors. Javelin, you're on rear guard. Squad, move out," Minerva said.

They began their push down the corridor. The Hind, clearly not used to retreating, struggled with giving ground as the party moved ahead. Nevertheless, they fell back after their commanders roared orders at them. "March, can you understand any of it?"

March opened his mouth to reply when Failsafe's shield faltered for a moment and several poorly aimed lasers flashed past them all. Gauss yelped as one clipped his metallic armor. "I'm okay. It didn't get me," he said.

"*Lo siento*," Failsafe said. "Never held my shield for so long before . . . I'm really tired."

It flickered back into existence as Minerva propped him up. She could hear the change in the reflection of sound off the walls. "There is a large chamber thirty meters ahead," she called. "They won't be able to box us in there. Fight hard!"

They battled down the hall. Giant tore up a huge piece of flooring to act as a combination shield and bulldozer blade to give Failsafe a rest. Gauss reshaped it to give it a smooth, flat bottom and convenient handles for the muscleman. Giant shoved it a foot at a time, digging his feet into the floor as Hind Warriors put their shoulders against it, trying to push back and finding they weren't quite the immovable object to his unstoppable force. Javelin and Blueshift took point-defense shots at any Hind foolish enough to peek or stick a rifle around the edge of the blade. Orange streaks appeared on the walls and floors where Hind had gotten themselves caught and scraped raw by Giant's blade.

Up ahead, Minerva sensed they were nearly to the large chamber. From the acoustics and airflow, she could tell it probably encompassed two or even three decks, with room enough for her and the others to fly, and numerous corridors branching off it like arteries. She couldn't tell its purpose except that it was open space, which put her team at a defensive disadvantage but would improve their offensive abilities. "When we reach the room, everyone scatter. Failsafe, keep March with you. Amber, you stay by my side. You'll need to use your ramping ability. I'll find our destination route and we'll converge upon it. Giant, if anyone gets seriously hurt, take that person and teleport back home." She paused. "Is everyone ready to fight?"

March's basic black bodysuit took on a reflective sheen like liquid metal. It rolled up and over his face to fully envelop him. "Ready," he said from beneath the armor.

Minerva reached into the place—she'd never named it, but a quantum physicist would have called it an extra-dimensional pocket in normal space-time—where she kept her spear when she wasn't using it. She kept other things there too, such as her grandmother's sword and helmet, and mementos from her journey as a superhero. Someday, perhaps, she'd enter it herself to see what it was like. For the moment, she was satisfied keeping things there, like a closet. When she withdrew her hand, her spear was in it, honed to a molecule-thick edge and made of unbreakable material. As Giant reached the edge of the doorway, she whispered into his ear, "Go left."

She raised her spear, took to the air with an ululating battle cry, and went right.

The Preserve
Luna

Penny gasped in sheer delight as she saw the two humanoids in Harlan's nanotech lab. "You have robots! I feel like Princess Leia. She always had robots hanging around her."

Harlan chuckled and Penny smiled, knowing she must have found one of his buttons. The guy didn't seem like a supervillain most of the time. He reminded her more than anything of one of her neighbors back when she'd still been married. Bob was an older gentleman who lived alone without any family or pets or anything. He had always been stiffly polite to her until one day, when she'd managed to thaw him out with a box of Christmas cookies she and Avery had decorated, him with the sticky fingers of a delighted two-year-old and her with all the intent of being the next Cookie Picasso. Bob had opened the box when she and Avery had delivered them and his eyes had crinkled up when he said he loved Christmas cookies and nobody had ever made them for him before. After that, he'd always been ready with a cheerful smile and fist bumps for Avery. That had been the last year of Penny's marriage, but she still remembered Bob fondly and made sure to stop by and say hello on the days she picked up Avery from his father.

Maybe *Star Wars* was Harlan's Christmas cookies.

Penny walked over to admire the two robots, standing quietly in alcoves and plugged into power couplings. "Hey, these look familiar to me. Why do I recognize them?"

Harlan stepped up beside her. "These are my hobbies."

"Supervillains have hobbies? Like knitting and stamp-collecting?"

"And building robots. This is a recreation of the Steel Soldier. I . . . destroyed it. Twice, actually. Each time, I felt good about what I'd done. Later, not so much. I always told myself if I ever had the time, I would try to rebuild it."

"Like a penance?" Penny ran her eyes over the robot's blocky lines, with armor designed to deflect shots away from it, and let her gaze linger lovingly upon the large shoulder-mounted cannon.

"If you like."

"What's the other one?"

"Carousel was a member of the Lucky Seven for many years until they disbanded, I fought them once, years ago, when I was working on the reactor that created the Antimatter Woman. I thought Carousel's fluid motions and liquid metal flesh was fascinating in its very . . . nonrobotic appearance. I wanted to try to recreate it myself, but it wasn't until I'd developed this nanotechnology that I managed it."

"I thought she looked familiar. I remember when the Seven disbanded. Where's the real Carousel now?"

"I do not know."

"I could try to find her for you, if you wanted."

"Perhaps some other time. Right now I need you to sit here and prepare to receive the injections." He indicated what looked unsettlingly like a dentist's chair in the middle of the room with many-armed torture rack behind it.

"I hope you're kidding."

"I'm not."

Penny stared at the rack with its hinged armatures and syringes and tubes and felt like maybe she would be happier just being plain old Penny with her super-sniper power and a chip on her shoulder about it. "Maybe you should go check on Lania first?"

"She's fine. I've got her in another lab with devices peeling away antimatter a few thousand molecules at a time. I'll check on her once the process for you has begun."

"How long will it take?"

"Not long. You'll have time to learn about your new capabilities before you have to put them into use."

"Wouldn't be the first time I've been dumped in the field with incomplete intel." She steeled herself for the worst and eased herself into the chair. "Okay, Dr. Feelgood, do your worst."

"I'll have to restrain you for your own safety. Moving during the nanite influx could be harmful."

"What do you mean, *harmful*? How harmful are we talking, here?"

Harlan tightened a leather strap over her wrist. "I don't know. My nephew consented to the restraints."

"Did you give him a choice?" Penny watched as he strapped down her other wrist. The straps seemed so old-fashioned compared to everything else in the lab. Why didn't he have automatic clasps that slid out of the chair? At least the straps weren't so tight she couldn't have gotten herself free. She felt secure but not imprisoned. Maybe it wasn't going to be so bad after all.

Then she saw the needles as the armatures adjusted around her, taking positions at her forearms, upper arms, calves and thighs, shoulders, and probably others she couldn't see. She felt cold sweat break out all over her. "Washington? I d-don't know about this."

"It will be fine. The pain will only last a moment."

"Does it hurt as much as being shot? I've *been* shot. That's my benchmark for hurting like a sonofabitch."

"I don't know. I've never been shot."

"All these years as a supervillain and nobody ever shot you?"

"That's why I wear armor." His forearm control panel grew out of his bodysuit and he made some kind of adjustment to it. "I've maximized the pain control measures. I promise you it won't hurt as much as you're afraid it will."

Penny felt herself on the verge of panic. Her heart was pounding like she was back in battle and she couldn't look away from the needle hovering over her left shoulder. She knew there were others, but that was the one she couldn't deal with for whatever reason. "H-Harlan? Please . . ." She made grasping motions with her hand. "Don't leave me."

He looked down at her hand, confusion on his face.

"Take it. Please. Oh God, please. I hate needles. Please."

Harlan took her hand with all the lack of confidence of a man who had no idea what he was doing.

She clasped her fingers around his, tight enough to make him blink. "Okay. Okay. Do it. Do it now, before I change my mind. Do it. Do—"

"Penny."

Penny gasped at the sound of her name on his lips. He'd said it before but just in the middle of a sentence, as if differentiating her from someone else. This was the first time he'd said it directly to her. It made her feel dizzy.

Or wait, something else was making her feel that way.

Harlan's face swam in and out of focus as he said, "I injected you while you were panicking about it. You didn't feel a thing."

"I'mma kill you . . ." The world became a bright blur, then a dark blur, and then nothing at all.

Hind Fleet
Axeship Blood Afire

"So, she seems . . . nice," Sahree said. "Your Submistress Loasrah. Pleasant. Thoughtful. Ambitious. Everything one wants in a despot."

Even with the translation device, Garragh didn't understand most of what she said. The Monkey—no, Human; they were called Humans. He would try to remember—paced back and forth like a caged animal, her arms clasped tightly around herself. Garragh felt equal parts afraid and ashamed. He was afraid because he'd had the rare idea to try to end the war before it began, with a shortcut to a Hind victory, and it was all falling apart around him. He was ashamed because he was afraid, and Warriors should be fearless or die. Even the Way of the Warrior said as much: *I will not fear my wounds; I will not fear my defeat; I will not fear my death; I will not fear.*

"Why did you bring me here, Garragh? What did you hope to accomplish?" Sahree gave up her nervous pacing and sat suddenly, her back against the bulkhead and her legs crossed in a way that made Garragh's hips ache just looking at them.

Garragh hunched over in the position of shame. It was a reflex from the time when Hind weren't yet sentient. Eighteen thousand years had done little to change the ingrained reactions from millions of years of evolutionary behavior. "To end the war."

"But you're a soldier. I can see that much. You Hind seem to love to fight. Why would you want to end a war?"

Garragh couldn't answer for a moment. He couldn't bring himself to admit his fear, even to an alien for whom honor might only be a word. "I want . . . *not war.*"

"Not war? That's what you want?"

Garragh bowed his head and said nothing.

Sahree took a deep breath and winced, as if she'd experienced a sudden twinge of pain. Blood Afire shuddered and Garragh felt his hearts pounding on his chest. Over the usual sounds of the ship—the hiss of the air recirculation, the thumping of fluid and solid transfers in pipes behind the bulkheads, the hum of the gravity generators—he could hear the distant singing of lasers, the percussion of impacts, and the chorus of dying Warriors.

In trying to escape the war, it seemed the war had followed him aboard. He didn't know if it was more Humans or if another Clan had discovered them and Hind were warring against Hind. He only knew the battle would sweep across him like a spinstorm over the plains of Hindraa.

"You're afraid," said Sahree. "That's it, isn't it? You don't want to die."

Garragh looked up at her in shock. His muscles tensed as his fight reflex took hold.

Sahree took a deep breath and blew it out. "Garragh, stop it. I don't want to fight you. But if I have to, I will, and I will kill you. All this is your fault. Your people. You came here to fight and conquer, when we could have welcomed you as guests. We could have been friends. You, and me. Do you even have friends? Do you understand what it means?"

Garragh lowered his head again and said nothing.

The Human sniffed, sounding congested when she did. "Goddamn, you don't know. What kind of fucked-up culture do you have where you don't understand friendship? A friend is someone you care about. Someone whose company you enjoy. Someone you love." Her eyes leaked water. "Someone you can spend your life with." She wiped the water away with a quick swipe. "A Hind killed my husband. My mate. Do you understand that much, at least?"

Garragh looked up for a moment. "We mate. If we are chosen."

Sahree shook her head. "When Jason died, a part of me died with him. It hurt worse than anything. It still hurts. It's like being stabbed over and over in the heart and I can't dodge no matter how fast I am." She held up her hand and looked at it. For a moment, it moved so fast it was only a blur, but it stopped as quickly as it had begun. "I'm tired, Garragh. I'm tired and I'm hurt and I think I have a concussion and I don't know whether I want to go to sleep forever or die tearing every Hind on this ship to pieces." She lowered her voice. "I could do it. It wouldn't make the pain of losing Jason stop, but it might help."

Garragh didn't know what he should do. Common sense would be for him to jump upon her, to close his teeth over her throat, and to rip it out. Somehow, though, he would have found it easier to turn upon another Hind than this Human. She had so much wisdom in her words that he couldn't believe she wasn't a powerful Clanmistress.

Her next words chilled him to his core. "Loasrah wants me to kill just one Hind. Rhaorhir. She says if I kill the Clanmistress, she can take command and stop the attack on the Earth."

Garragh gasped. He hadn't realized the depth of Loasrah's ambition. If the Clanmistress died, especially at the hands of a Human, the entire battle group would dissolve into chaos until a new leader, a powerful Hind who could secure her position against all challengers, would take command and force any resistors to submit to her authority by force.

"You think she can do it," Sahree said. "But you're her right hand man, aren't you? You'd do whatever she said." She lowered her voice until Garragh had to lean in to listen. "You don't have to do that. You've been among us. You saw what kind of people we are. We . . . care for each other. We don't leave our wounded to fend for themselves. We even care for our enemies. It's what humans do. You have your clans, but our entire race is one clan. We may argue and fight amongst ourselves, but in the end, we're a clan seven billion strong. You've got no chance against us."

"I know . . . Mistress." Garragh's voice was barely a whisper. The words he had just spoken were pure treason, and if anyone beside the Human had heard them, his life was forfeit. "I believe the Clanmistress will destroy your world if she sees she will lose."

Sahree made a sound Garragh interpreted as laughter. Was she truly amused in the face of so much death? When her own mate had been killed before her eyes? When her entire planet was facing sterilization from the missiles packed into the Axeships? Garragh came to a sick realization that the Humans were better than the Hind. The Hind only faced death without fear; the Humans thought so little of it that they laughed at it. "And what about Loasrah? What will she do in the Clanmistress' place? Pack up the kids and get back on the interstellar freeway for home?"

The ship shuddered again and Garragh thought the battle was likely getting closer. He needed to me a decision before he lost his chance to.

"What is that? That's the second time I felt it," Sahree asked.

"Battle," Garragh said.

"Against who? More Hind? Humans?"

"I do not know."

"It's probably my people, coming after me. Those stupid assholes. They should have stayed home to help defend it."

"You are their Mistress. They fight for you." Garragh took a deep breath, feeling his pulse racing. He'd already spoken treason, and treasonous thoughts filled his mind. He had to give them voice. "I will fight for you, Mistress Sahree."

Sahree laughed again. "Oh, goddammit. That's all I need. I just wanted to get a fucking dog." She sniffed and wiped her eyes again. Then she froze, staring at Garragh.

"Mistress?"

"Loasrah said whoever defeats the Clanmistress becomes the next Clanmistress. That's like your law, right?"

"Yes," said Garragh, who wasn't quite certain.

Sahree stood and tugged at her bunched up clothing. "Tell Loasrah I'll do it, and then take me to your leader." She showed her teeth. "I always wanted to say that."

The Preserve
Luna

Harlan checked Penny's vitals as the nanotech insinuated itself throughout her body and smiled, pleased at the results. Once again, his technology had triumphed over nature. Then he realized he wasn't looking at the datastream any longer, but at the woman behind it. Her eyes were shut and her face looked serene, the way his sister's face had when she was in her coma.

Penny's face wasn't unpleasant to look at, and Harlan could have stayed to watch longer, even though the nanotech process was automated and self-monitoring. His presence wouldn't do anything except delay the inevitable, and Lania really did need his attention. He sighed and left the lab, pausing at the door long enough to look back toward Penny. When she awoke, with his nanotech infusing her body, she would be a living weapon the way he was. It was the greatest gift he'd ever given someone. Even his nephew March hadn't gotten the complete package. The young man carried a much more peaceful mindset, and no matter what tech he had at his disposal, he would never be a true Warrior. Penny would be every bit as lethal as Harlan, and he thought that was magnificent. She awoke something in him, thoughts and feelings he'd shoved aside as unimportant and distracting many years prior.

Better he should keep them buried. Nobody ever won a war when all they could think about was romance.

What he had reconfigured into an antimatter lab was suffused with so many electromagnetic fields it was difficult for him to move through it. He needed the multiple levels of failsafes, for the amount of antimatter in Lania's body could possibly crack the Moon in half were all containment to fail at once. As it was, he had her suspended in multiple fields, stripped of her protective suit and floating in the middle of the lab. Angled shear fields with molecule-width edges carefully peeled away thin layers of Lania's flesh, and then other fields directed those cuttings into nanotech-built bomb casings. Lania's body glowed with brilliant blue-white energy, bathing the entire lab in its radiance, while the places on her arms and legs that had been sliced away showed angry red.

"Are you in pain?" Harlan asked, more because he was curious than he cared.

"No," the prison guard replied, sounding weary. "I don't feel it except that parts of my body are no longer connected to me. It doesn't hurt. It's just . . . exhausting."

"I . . . am sorry for your discomfort." Harlan stammered through the apology. It felt odd coming from his mouth, like he was speaking a foreign language.

Lania's laugh was acidic. "Don't be. If you hadn't built your damn reactor in Guatemala all those years ago, I wouldn't be here, about to save the world." She paused. "We are going to save the world, aren't we?"

"Yes. The four antimatter bombs, aligned at strategic points around the fleet, should easily destroy them. Anything caught within the focus of the four wavefronts from the antimatter explosions should be utterly destroyed."

"Did you tell Penny?"

"Tell her what?"

"That this is going to kill me."

Harlan asked, "How do you know it will?"

"I've spent years keeping myself from blowing up half the planet. My body is a fragile creation. Any major upset to its energy patterns will cause a cascading failure. I've come close before and nearly died from it. The amount of my body you need . . . Well, it might not seem like that much, but it will be enough to cross the threshold. You didn't tell Penny, did you?"

Harlan coughed to cover his sudden unexpected twinge of embarrassment. "I, uh, did not."

"That's probably for the best, Washington. She's got enough to worry about without trying to figure out how to save me."

"Do you think she would?"

"Yes, of course. She's a superhero. She would do whatever she could to keep me safe and alive." Lania said nothing for several seconds as the energy shears continued to do their work. "I'm not afraid to die. Why should I be? I've spent half my life not truly being alive. Maybe death will be like a journey to another place. Or maybe it'll just be like nothing at all. Either way, I'm ready for it."

Harlan checked his equipment. The natural fields holding Lania's body in permanent suspension, keeping her antimatter from contacting the atoms of the positive-matter universe, were failing. She was right; the extraction process was going to kill her. He'd suspected it would, but bringing it up was something he hadn't considered. Death and sacrifice were a part of life, and sacrificing one's own life for the survival of billions was a no-brainer. At least, it was for Lania. Harlan hadn't quite wrapped his own mind around the idea of true altruism, since it was as foreign to him as being polite to strangers or letting anyone get close enough to him to truly call him *friend*. "You are sure you don't feel any discomfort?"

"No, not really. Listen, can you record something for me? I'd like to say goodbye to my friends. I don't have any family but the folks back at Deep Six will feel cheated if I don't wish them well."

"Everything in this lab is being recorded. I will ensure your message gets to your people." Harlan stood back and folded his arms. "Do you wish me to leave while you speak your piece?"

"No, please stay. I don't mind dying, like I said, but I don't want to be alone here at the end. When I'm finished, take whatever quantity of me you need to complete your work and let the rest of me pass on to the next life."

"That sounds like something my sister might have said before she died."

"I'm sorry about your sister, Washington."

Harlan clasped his hands behind his back. "She went peacefully. I was grateful for that."

Lania proceeded to say her goodbyes. Harlan listened with a scientist's curiosity. He didn't have anyone in his life close enough for him to record a goodbye message of his own, and even if he did, he wouldn't have known what to say. She thanked the people of Deep Six for giving her the opportunity to survive, to feel included, to have a purpose. She thanked the people of Just Cause for backing her and helping her when she could easily have been locked away as a supervillain forever.

"And last, I have a message for you all about the man Harlan Washington, who is called Destroyer."

Harlan blinked. What was she doing?

"I want you to know that the man before me is not just another bogeyman out to terrify and kill you. He may have been so once, but people can change. I believe he has. I know he warned you all about the attack on the Earth. Someone who hated humanity would not have done that. He went to fight the aliens on his own. He went to Earth to destroy the aliens in New York. He fought like a true hero, and you should see him as such. He came to me and said I could help save the world, but it would mean my death. How could I say no to that? What is one half-life against billions? I accept my death gladly, and I hope Mr. Washington's plan is successful. Whether it is or not, please know that I am doing this of my own free will, and you should not condemn him in any way for his honest attempt to defend the Earth the best way he knows how."

"You didn't have to say that." Harlan's voice quivered, and he didn't understand why.

"I know I didn't. I chose to." She paused. "I am ready, Mr. Washington. Take what you need from me. Go destroy the Hind. Save the world."

Harlan touched the controls for his energy shears. They lopped off several large chunks of her body in quick succession, pulling them away before her failing containment fields could intercept and collapse them.

"Oh God," Lania whispered. "It's beautiful! It's—"

The remainder of her form collapsed into a cloud of sparkling blue-white pinpoints of energy as her containment fields failed entirely. Her individual atoms of antimatter, too small to retain their energy without anything to bind them to their neighbors, flared and died like firework sparks burning out in the sky.

The antimatter bombs sealed themselves and Harlan's instruments reported they each contained the requisite amount of explosive. He had in his possession four bombs the size of basketballs, each with an approximate yield of roughly four megatons.

No fleet of spaceships, no matter how powerful their shields might be, was going to resist that force of nature.

Harlan smiled.

CHAPTER FIFTEEN

Hind Fleet
Axeship Blood Afire

The ship shook repeatedly, often making Sally stagger into bulkheads or tumble to the floor. There must have been an astonishing battle going on somewhere aboard the vessel. She thought it was probably her people, coming to get her. She knew everyone on the Just Cause New York team would have thrown caution to the winds for a chance to come rescue her. It made her proud, like a mother watching her children grow into successful people. On the other hand, she feared learning of their deaths, for nobody passed through a battle unscathed, and before all was done, she was certain the Hind would claim more of her loved ones than Jason.

Jason.

He had loved her so much, and she had truly loved him more deeply than anyone. Even over the past year, when the stresses of his long-term injury, her struggles with leadership, and the ongoing conflict about children, the love had always persisted. She didn't think she could ever feel that again.

She suspected Loasrah was leading her to her death. The ambitious Hind must have been working hard behind the scenes to build enough support behind her to be able to take charge and hold her position of power against any other challengers to the throne should Sally be successful in slaying the Clanmistress. Why would Loasrah risk someone doing the same to her with Sally's hands? No, the devious pilot would already have thought of that eventuality and come up with a simple solution to prevent it from happening again. The only way to ensure it would be to kill Sally.

Sally didn't know if she could stop her. The events of the day had taken a tremendous toll on her, physically and emotionally. She knew she had a concussion, and her rapid healing ability didn't seem to be doing anything about it. Doctors had warned her repeatedly about further head traumas after the number she'd suffered over the years, and this latest one might have been the one that caused injuries she couldn't heal. A side effect was her inability to see clearly, and she could tell her super-speed just wasn't what it should have been. She tried to accelerate her perceptions, but it only lasted a second before she snapped back into the same reality as everyone else's. She might be able to move with super-speed still, but her brain didn't want to operate any faster than else's, and that would make it very difficult for her to use her parahuman ability.

There was a very real chance that she might not defeat the Clanmistress, and even if she did, she might not have the strength to fight against Loasrah and her Warriors, should the choose to turn on her. Her only hope lay in the mysterious forces fighting aboard the Hind ship. If they were indeed her friends, they might just turn the tide. Garragh's heavy footsteps sounded on the deck behind her, and more than once he held out a hand to steady her when she staggered. He was the wild card in the equation. He'd claimed to want to stop the war, but he seemed to be in Loasrah's corner, and his allegiance to her might be stronger than any he claimed to hold toward Sally.

A wide-eyed Warrior raced around the corner, leaking orange from multiple stab wounds. "Monkeys!"

he cried. "They've overrun the Parade Deck!" He saw Sally and raised his axe.

Loasrah shot him where he stood. "Interloper," she grumbled as the Warrior collapsed with a smoking hole where his face had been. Hind as a rule tended to be terrible shots, but Loasrah was clearly comfortable with a laser. Perhaps being a pilot meant she had an innately superior sense of spatial relationships compared to most of her kind. She turned to Garragh. "We have to cross the Parade Deck to reach the Bridge. Tell your Monkey friend to make the others stop or else her life is forfeit."

Sally didn't wait for Garragh to speak to her. "I need to see what's happening. *Would somebody get this big walking carpet out of my way?*" If she'd had any booze with her, she'd have poured out a dollop for Jack. He wasn't dead, but he'd have appreciated the *Star Wars* quote more than any of her other friends. She shoved past Loasrah and as she did so, she felt the tip of a knife against her back.

"One wrong move," the Submistress whispered in her ear. "And I will cut out your spine to decorate my quarters."

"I'll behave myself," Sally growled. She looked out into a room that seemed far too large to belong inside an alien battleship. It must have been close to the size of a football field, nearly twice as long as it was wide, and arching to a high overhead point. Loasrah had called it the Parade Deck. It made sense that a militaristic society would have a large area in which to drill and train. At the moment, it was being used for a running and flying battle between several superheroes and a couple companies of Hind Warriors. As she watched, a hero she recognized as Giant swung a huge piece of steel girder at several advancing Hind, scattering them like bowling pins. He fought his way to where her former teammate Failsafe had fallen and was trying to layer his force field strong enough to keep himself alive under the onslaught of multiple Hind.

Nearby, Amber flung glob after glob of her amber at Hind, cementing their arms to their heads, or their feet to each other. Once they were immobilized, she wrapped their heads in a thick layer of amber and moved on to the next opponent. Warriors lay dying or dead, suffocating when they'd been unable to shatter the amber encasing their heads.

Blueshift and Javelin, whom she had known for many years, flew back to back and spun in a circle, trying to fire in every direction at once. Javelin stopped firing and shouted, "I'm empty!" over the din of combat. Blueshift did his best to extend his personal force screen to protect his partner, but both of them sported ugly laser-burns.

A hero she didn't recognize reshaped the metal of the bulkheads and melted axes. More than one Warrior fell, screaming as razor-sharp spikes grew from the inside of his armor, like being pierced by a dozen swords simultaneously.

Beyond them all, Minerva darted like a hummingbird, her spear flashing in the bright overhead lighting. Every time she lunged, a Hind died upon it. Beneath her, Sally saw a figure wrapped in silver, reflecting away lasers that struck him. She realized it was March and her heart stung. She'd been considering an affair with him ever since their Dream-world adventure together on the Moon. The guilt of it nearly overwhelmed her now that Jason was dead. It felt like Jason's death had been her fault for considering the infidelity.

"Minerva," Sally said in a soft voice, knowing her friend and teammate would hear it. "Stand down. That's an order."

Minerva whirled and shouted something at Giant over the combat noise, projecting her voice in such a way so he would hear it clearly above all else. He reached one hand out to Projector and stretched the other up to snag Javelin's heel. With a roar of displaced air, the three heroes vanished. The Hind who had been fighting them picked themselves up where the sudden blast of wind had knocked them. For a moment, an unnatural silence filled the Parade Deck.

Minerva planted her spear in the deck point first, making it ring like she'd struck a bell. "Stand down, Strike Team."

Loasrah shoved past Sally. "All Warriors are to cease this battle immediately."

The Warriors picked up their fallen weapons and shuffled their feet with unease, but nobody took a shot at any of the Humans.

"Loasrah," Sally said.

The Submistress turned.

"Go find your Clanmistress. Tell her . . . I'm ready to deal."

Hind Fleet
Axeship Blood Afire

Minerva gathered the remainder of her squad around her, warning them to take no offensive action. Hind Warriors arranged themselves in a semicircle around the Humans, eschewing their axes for long broad-bladed spears with energy crackling around the tips. Minerva smiled at those. She approved of spears. She had begun her superhero career wielding her grandmother's sword, but Lady Athena's weapon of choice had never felt quite right in her hands. She still recalled the day she'd reached into her storage space and came out not with the sword, but a spear in her hand instead. Since then, she'd made a point to only remove the spear. It felt more natural to her, like it was a part of her. The Hind seemed far less comfortable with spears than they did with axes. Minerva noted the way the tips wavered and approved of that as well. The Warriors' discomfort with their weapons would be their downfall when the time came to do battle. In the meantime, they kept those tips proximal to the squad, making Amber's hair stand on end until she made a cap of amber to hold it down.

Sally trudged across the Parade Deck until she stood before Minerva and her team. She looked more beaten down than Minerva had seen anyone in a long time. Minerva wasn't given to expressions of emotion or affection, but at that moment she felt like Sally could use a hug. Unfortunately, the best person to give it to her was back on Earth, dead. She knew March harbored strong feelings for Sally but he kept them tightly wound out of respect. Perhaps, in time, those feelings might unwind some. Although she excelled at observations, Minerva was no fortune-teller, and only time would tell what might become of Sally and March in the future.

"You look terrible," Minerva said, knowing it would bring out the wry humor of Sally's personality. She was not disappointed.

"Really? I must be improving, then. Where's Giant and the others?"

"Back on Earth, I presume." Minerva nodded toward the Hind shadowing Sally. "Who's that?"

"My . . . guard." Sally had made a lightning-quick motion of her mouth in the brief pause between words, mouthing something else only Minerva could have seen. *An ally.*

"I see. What is your plan?"

"My plan? . . . Don't die." *Kill the Clanmistress.*

Minerva blinked to see such a bloodthirsty statement come from the lips of her friend.

Sally sighed, clearly fed up with trying to lip-sync her thoughts in the middle of her phrases. She dropped her voice to the barest of whispers, but it was as clear as if she'd been standing beside Minerva in a quiet room. "There's a power struggle brewing. This place is a powder keg. I'm going to light a match. Do you have a way off this ship?"

"Not presently." Minerva focused the sound of her speech into a narrow tube, like a tight-beam radio transmission. "Our ship didn't survive the journey. I was hoping to steal a dropship."

"Can you fly one?"

"March can." Minerva said it with a confidence she didn't feel. "Maybe your . . . guard can help."

"I don't think so. He's just a Warrior, not a pilot." Sally glared toward a female Hind who was roaring down another. "She's a pilot. And no, we can't trust her."

"March," Minerva said. "Translate for me. I need to speak to Sally's Warrior."

"His name is Garragh," Sally said.

"Garragh," Minerva repeated. The Warrior's head rose. "Do you serve Mistress Sally?"

March listened to the translation his nanotech provided and then repeated Minerva's world in the growl of the Hind tongue.

Garragh made a quick motion, like a salute, fast enough so nobody would notice it.

Minerva nodded, satisfied. "Go find us a ship. Fastest one you can."

Garragh ran. Minerva hoped it was to fulfill her bidding and not to report on their intentions.

Clanmistress Rhaorhir descended a ramp from an upper level, flanked by muscular Warriors who eschewed armor in favor of having their fur dyed. Minerva took it as a status symbol, showing all who saw that they feared no attack and would die in the service of their leader. She frowned. Such unquestioned loyalty would be tremendously difficult to sway. Perhaps Sally was right and a system such as that of the Hind was ripe for exploitation. The pilot Sally had indicated paced back and forth, growling at anyone who dared question her. Minerva didn't need to speak the language to see the female's dangerous mix of aggression and ambition. Despite evolving on different soil, the Hind maintained some behaviors that seemed to be common to Earthly predators.

March plucked at her elbow. "Uh . . . Uncle Harlan cr-cracked their translator. I can understand w-what they're saying."

Minerva nodded. "I think I get the gist, but fill in the blanks if I need help."

Servants brought forth a large pad with a cover of some sort of woven fibrous material. Rhaorhir took her time arranging herself upon it before deigning to look in Sally's direction. She growled and snarled and the disc on Sally's chest uttered the translation. "I understand you have changed your hearts," Rhaorhir said. She selected a strip of sharp-smelling smoked meat from a servant's tray and took a slow, deliberate bite before finishing her thought. "You wish to surrender your world to me now?"

Sally's laugh was as slow and deliberate as Minerva had ever heard. It also carried an unpleasant streak of venom that felt like spiders crawling down her spine. "Not even close, Clanmistress. You have to earn a victory. You've gotten fat eating your jerky and laying around on pillows and you think everyone's just going to give you what you want."

The tension level among the Hind on the Parade Deck rose a thousandfold.

"You should be cautious, Monkey. You are completely outnumbered. I can have you killed like the beast you are."

"If you could have, you would have. You're afraid, Clanmistress. Afraid of me, a mere monkey. You're afraid of what I can do, of what I represent, of what I can inspire. You're a coward."

A Warrior leaped forward, brandishing his axe. "Let me kill her, Clanmistress!" he shouted. "In your honor, let me stain the deck with this Monkey's innards!"

Minerva tensed, ready to fly into battle, but the Clanmistress roared at him and he dropped his axe and scuttled back into formation.

Before the Clanmistress could address Sally's accusations, Sally shouted at her. "You are weak. You are a coward. You are unfit to lead these Warriors, and I challenge you." Her voice echoed across the silent Parade Deck.

Minerva frowned. This was turning into a spectacle and it felt like things were about to get far more chaotic than they had been only minutes earlier.

"You are a Monkey—" Rhaorhir began.

"—Who can defeat you," Sally finished. "I bet my world I can beat you."

"You said you don't speak for your world."

"I lied. I'm a better Warrior than you, Clanmistress, and I put my world up as the stakes. You win, you get the Earth, just like you want. But if I win? I put my own Mistress in charge and she will see this fleet leave the Solar System and forget it ever existed."

"Your planet will abide by this?" Rhaorhir snarled.

"They'd better." Sally turned to look at Minerva. "Make sure they know."

Minerva understood. "I will convey the message."

"So how about it, Rhaorhir? You willing to put up or shut up? Or are you too chickenshit to fight me in your own arena?"

Whatever the translator turned *chickenshit* into must have been exceptionally foul, for rumbling growls swept through the onlookers.

Rhaorhir stood. She shoved away the servant holding her food tray and shoved her way past one of her unarmored guards. She picked up the fallen axe, left behind by the exuberant Warrior, and raised it. "To the death, Monkey."

Sally slipped her horseshoes off her belt. To Minerva's surprise, the Hind hadn't bothered to disarm her friend when they captured her. Sally preferred to fight with the antique iron horseshoes clutched in her fists, letting them add more *oomph* to her 300-mph punches. They'd been a gift from her grandmother. She raised the horseshoes in a mocking salute. "To the death. Yours."

The Preserve
Luna

Penny opened her eyes and felt like she'd just run a marathon after a half-day training session with Hector beating the snot out of her. The only reason she didn't collapse on the floor crying in pain was the lunar gravity made it much more tolerable. Right away, she could tell the difference in her own body. It felt heavier, denser, like someone had replaced her skeleton with depleted-uranium. For all she knew, that was what Washington had done to her. She noticed a flickering in the corner of her vision, like the blank cursor of a computer awaiting input. It was irritating and she wished it would go away.

It quietly winked out of existence.

Could she bring it back just by thinking about it?

It returned to the corner of her vision, blinking patiently like it had all the time in the world.

"What the hell?" she said aloud, and a voice inside her own head responded to her.

::I am the collective artificial intelligence network that controls your nanites.::

"Collective . . . what?"

::Collective artificial intelligence network. The brain of your nanotechnology. If it makes you more comfortable, perhaps you might think of me as a smartphone.::

"So you're like, uh, Siri?"

::If you wish.::

"What do I call you?"

::You may call me anything you like, or nothing at all. You do not need to speak to me aloud, for my network is aligned with the communication centers in your brain. You may think to me, or speak, or even text if it makes you more comfortable. Simply glance toward the cursor if you want to text me a command and I will respond.::

"Okay, uh, I'm going to call you Cain. You know, an acronym for that network thing you said you are."

The voice became deeper, like a more resonant version of her own voice. It reminded her uncomfortably of her ex-husband's voice. *::Do you wish me to identify as male? Cain is traditionally a male name.::*

"Absolutely not!"

Cain responded with a professional-sounding feminine voice that was like a more mature version of Just Cause New York's administrator, a highly competent woman named Davey. ::Is this more suitable?::

The confidence in the voice did wonders to help Penny get used to the idea of a *very* personal assistant. "Okay, so what do we do now? Why do I hurt all over? Why am I exhausted?"

::You have absorbed approximately two hundred and forty pounds of nanites into your body. They are established in network beneath your skin as your armor, ready to call forth at a moment's notice. They have formed support lattices around your skeleton and musculature, making you far stronger and tougher than an ordinary human. With their assistance, you should notice very little difference in the way you move and should acclimate quickly. They have also formed support systems for your organs as well as built several new, entirely artificial organs to assist you in various ways. The discomfort from this process should alleviate within a few hours.::

Penny was still hung up on the *two hundred and forty pounds* part, but she tried to push past that. It was so much to take in and she wasn't sure where to begin. "Is there, like, a manual or something for how to operate you?"

"You're thinking about it all wrong," said a new voice. Penny turned to see Washington standing in the doorway, his hands clasped behind his back. She started, feeling guilty about being caught off-guard, even though she knew she hadn't been doing anything she shouldn't have. "The nanotech operates instinctively. You think about what you want it to do and it will either perform the action or its best reasonable facsimile. There are certain . . . preprogrammed commands that facilitate the most common uses, but you can re-engineer those as you see fit."

Something about Washington's demeanor belied his neutral, helpful demeanor. "What is it? Something's happened. I can see it in your face." To Penny's surprise, a quick display appeared over his face in her vision, highlighting indicators of suppressed emotional responses. She flicked her gaze toward the cursor in the corner of her eye and the display went away.

Washington's voice was soft and had an unexpected tremor in it. "Lania is dead."

"What? How did it happen? Did you kill her?" Penny leaped to her feet and her body seemed to rearrange itself. Blue armor plating burst painlessly out of her skin to form interlocking plates like those that formed the Destroyer suit. Her vision became a Heads-Up Display showing such indicators as armor integrity, suit power, blaster power, thruster power, and an intriguing menu entitled *Heavy Weapons*.

Washington made no move to respond to her sudden aggressive stance. "I suspect I did kill her, but because the amount of antimatter she gave me reduced her beyond a minimum safety level. I did not murder her. She did not suffer."

"You're lying. You're a goddamn supervillain! Of course you're lying!"

He shook his head. "I may be a great many things, but I'm not a liar. People lie because of shame. They are ashamed of who they are, what they think, or what they have done. I am not ashamed of myself or my actions. I have no reason to lie."

The display over his face popped up again, indicating no temperature gradients, perspiration, or muscle tics to indicate dishonesty. As quickly as it came up, giving Penny time to take it in, it vanished to keep her field of vision clear. Cain, it seemed, was already learning her preferences. "All right, I believe you. For now. At least Cain doesn't think you're lying."

"Cain?"

"It's what I named my, uh, passenger." She felt the armor and was astonished that she could touch through it, like it was an extension of her skin. "What do you call yours?"

"It does not have a name."

"You should name it. You'd name a dog, and your AI is a lot better than a dog."

"I've never had a dog," Washington said.

Penny really looked at him again. "Are you sure you're all right? You look a little upset. I imagine for you, that means you're probably devastated."

He looked at the floor. "I'm fine."

::Lie:: said Cain.

Penny thought about reabsorbing her armor and wrapping herself in a plain bodysuit, like what Washington wore. The sight of the plating melting into her flesh was fascinating and more than a little horrifying. She decided it would be better not to think about it. "I guess Lania's death maybe bothered you more than you thought."

"I said I'm fine."

"Suit yourself, Washington. Did you at least get enough antimatter for your bombs?"

He nodded. "They are ready to deploy."

"So what happens now?"

"We—wait."

"We wait? For what?"

::I have detected a transmission on an ultrahigh frequency, facilitated by a parahuman ability, from your teammate Minerva. It is directed toward Destroyer. Shall I play it for you?::

"Yes, please!" Penny forgot herself and spoke out loud, but then figured it didn't matter when she heard Minerva's message. "We've got to hurry," she said to Washington. "They don't have much time."

He nodded even as his armor flowed out through his skin to form around him. "I'll prepare the Soldier and Carousel. Do you understand the space capabilities of your armor?"

Penny shrugged. "No, but I trust you do, and I'll figure out the rest as I go along."

Hind Fleet
Axeship Blood Afire

The Submistress' command echoed in Garragh's head like a refrain, like it was part of his Catechism. *Find a ship. Find a ship.* He didn't have to think, to make plans. All he had to do was follow an order, and that was what he'd been trained to do since he was a cub.

As he fled the Parade Deck, he heard the roars and cheers of the rest of the Warriors as the battle began in earnest between Mistress Sahree and Rhaorhir. He knew his Mistress was tired and upset about losing her mate, but Rhaorhir wasn't a Warrior by any stretch of the imagination.

He honestly didn't know who would win.

He hoped Sahree would prevail. Then Loasrah could take charge and end the war for Monkeyworld. She would gather the remaining fleet around her and they would return home. There would be a great many questions to answer when they returned to Hindraa with the losses they'd suffered and no victory to show for it, but at least they would be alive. Garragh was beginning to think that dishonor might not be so bad, because he very much wanted to stay alive.

He would never know the true level of dishonor to which a Hind could be subjected, for he was certain he would never again set foot on the great savannahs of his homeworld. After the traitorous acts he had fomented, and was continuing to perform, he could never again face his own people as anything but someone whose life was forfeit.

Find a ship. Find a ship. Find a—

He stopped short in the corridor. He'd started to head in the general direction of the dropship launch bays, but something in the back of his mind had surfaced. There was a ship much closer to the Parade Deck than the bays, which were at the *Blood Afire*'s aft, near the engines. The Clanmistress had a personal vessel assigned to her, docked near her quarters. It was a high-performance runabout that she used whenever she wanted to visit another vessel in her fleet, or even take an excursion. He'd never been aboard it, but given Rhaorhir's expensive tastes, he imagined it was comfortable, roomy, and powerful.

He reversed his direction in the corridor and skirted around the Parade Deck using a service tunnel normally reserved for maintenance workers but known to every Warrior and Mistress looking for a quick way around the Parade Deck when events were taking place upon it. He found the ramp leading to the upper deck and trotted up it. The sounds of Warriors roaring cheers echoed through the corridor and he wondered if Mistress Sahree was holding her own against the much larger Clanmistress.

The corridor was empty of other Hind. They must have all rushed to the Parade Deck to witness the challenge or else gathered around viewscreens where they could watch the live feed of it. He reached the corridor crossing that led to the bridge and he heard the growls and snarls of the crew watching the combat unfold. He padded past to the access tube which led to the Clanmistress' private vessel, which was called *Dagger*.

A Warrior stood guard at the entrance to the access tube, a dark visor shielding his eyes and his Armor decorated in the Clanmistress' favorite colors. He was one of her elite guardsmen. Garragh felt his bowels turn to water and wished he could go find a latrine. Instead, he took a deep breath and marched up until he was facing the guardsman. "You're relieved," he said with enough authority as he could muster.

The guardsman said nothing.

Garragh tried again. "I said, you're relieved. The Clanmistress is fighting a Monkey and you're to be present in case things go . . . badly."

"Relieved?" The guardsman lowered his head a fraction of a degree as if noticing Garragh for the first time. "By you?"

Garragh folded his forearms, making sure that the head of his axe stayed lowered to show he was not threatening. "Yes. Those . . . are her orders."

"I do not answer to you. I only answer to the Clanmistress." The guardsman's head raised and Garragh had the sense that the Warrior was done speaking to him.

"Would you answer to the Monkey who defeats the Clanmistress? Because that's exactly what's going on down on the Parade Deck. The Clanmistress is in deep mud and the Monkey's going to beat her."

"Ridiculous." The guardsman's voice suggested it was a preposterous notion, but Garragh saw his rear legs shift, an unconscious indicator of uncertainty.

Three Hind ran down the crossing corridor and skidded around the corner, two Warriors and a Submistress, pelting for the access to the Parade Deck.

"You see?" Garragh whispered. "The Clanmistress will lose and then whose orders will you follow?"

The guardsman took a step, then halted. "Whose orders are *you* following?"

"I'm . . . uh . . ." Garragh felt the spell he'd woven begin to disintegrate.

The guardsman raised his axe. "Answer me, you mewling cub. What traitorous bitch sent you?" He charged.

Garragh raised his own axe and met the charge. The guardsman was larger and stronger and bore him backward, his claws scraping along the deck as they sought traction. The hafts of their axes crossed as each Warrior sought to overpower the other through sheer muscular strength. Twelve hundred generations had taught that the winner of such a bout normally triumphed in subsequent combat, as exhaustion quickly took its toll on the loser in a contest of strength.

The guardsman hadn't been trained to fight upon Monkeyworld, and therefore he hadn't been subjected to the lower levels of oxygen that the invading forces had. Garragh found he could hold his own against a stronger fighter just because his body had been trained to operate more efficiently on less air. With that hope in mind, he released his grip on the axe with his lower hand. Deprived of a resisting force, the guardsman lunged forward off-balance and the head of his axe buried itself in the bulkhead beside Garragh's hindquarters.

Too close to use his own axe, Garragh drove his empty fist upward in an uppercut to the guardsman's chin. The Warrior's head snapped back and Garragh continued his upward thrust with an elbow to the guardsman's throat. Bone cracked against bone and the guardsman staggered back, coughing. He was still a well-trained fighter, and as he stepped back, he swung his axe low, angling it to sever Garragh's forelegs.

Garragh wheeled back on his hindlegs to let the whistling blade pass under him. As he brought his own axe up and over his head for a downward blow that would cleave the guardsman's head in half, his axe struck an overhead conduit and the handle shook itself right out of Garragh's fists. The axe spun away and Garragh realized he was unarmed. The guardsman took a moment to laugh at Garragh's plight.

Garragh was already backed against the bulkhead. He braced his back legs against it and sprang forward to tackle the guardsman. The two Warriors rolled over and over, raking at each others' bellies with all four legs while they wrestled for control of the guardsman's axe. Their yowls and hisses echoed off the corridor walls Garragh felt a claw gouge deep into his skin and yelped.

As the guardsman tried to press his advantage, Garragh's hands found purchase on his throat, beneath the strap of his helmet. He locked his hands around it and began to squeeze. The guardsman's throat had already been weakened and bruised by Garragh's elbow-strike, and he grimaced as he struggled to tear Garragh's hands away.

Sweat dampened Garragh's fur as he squeezed. Seconds ticked by and the muscles in his arms threatened to cramp. The guardsman grew limp in his hands and Garragh felt relief.

A hard first crashed into the side of his head as the guardsman took a sudden swing at him. The Warrior had played him for a fool! The blow knocked him off balance and he tumbled to his side. The guardsman leaped at him, finger-claws extended to rend Garragh from throat to belly. Garragh's hand closed on the haft of the guardsman's axe and he swung it around in a fast arc.

The blade whistled through the guardsman's neck, meeting only the slight resistance of the Warrior's spine before passing out the other side. The heavy guardsman's body crashed onto Garragh. He shoved the dead weight aside and rolled onto his feet. Blood dripped from the scratches in his abdomen, and he could feel a torn muscle that twinged with every step from his right hindleg. Perhaps the Humans would treat it for him.

He looked down at the dead guardsman in satisfaction. "That *traitorous bitch* is Mistress Sahree, and she's better than your Clanmistress."

Garragh ran off to inform the Human Submistress he'd found a ship.

The Preserve
Luna

Harlan made last minute checks on the devices he'd attached to the Steel Soldier and Carousel, who would be carrying the third and fourth bombs. It would require precise spatial geometry to deliver the bombs to the correct locations. Without a surface to redirect and focus the explosions, they should be spherical, and it was imperative that the shockwave from each detonation reached the fleet at the same time.

"Why's it so important it happens that way?" Penny asked. She was busy trying to learn more about her own armor and how it would protect and convey her in the process of delivering the bomb.

"Why can't you just set off the bombs wherever and be done with them?"

"Antimatter is funny stuff," Harlan replied. "If a bomb goes off early, or late, it changes the forces at work at the focus. It could actually throw the fleet clear instead of destroying it."

"Well, wouldn't that, you know, turn the crews into paste? That could be just as lethal."

"They have inertial dampening systems and shields. The combination of the two could conceivably protect them, and then we'd be fucked. The entirety of stored antimatter on Earth is in these four bombs."

"You can't make more?"

"I probably could, given enough time, but not in this quantity. You've got to understand how rare this stuff is. The fact the Hind have harnessed it is magnificent and I fully intend to explore that technology once we've destroyed their fleet."

"What about nukes, then? We have one or two down on the Earth, you know."

"You mean large, easy-to-detect and target nukes that would have to be delivered conventionally?"

"They might not be *that* easy to target," Penny grumbled. "I've seen the Hind shoot. So you're saying this is our only shot to take them out all at once?"

"Probably not the only shot, but the most likely to succeed."

"*We're Just Cause. We make the impossible ordinary.* Crackerjack said that."

"Are your systems nominal?" Harlan had already checked Penny's armor and confirmed it, but he wanted her to feel comfortable."

"Sure, everything's coming up roses here. I'm only about to fly into deep space to deliver an antimatter bomb. What could go wrong?"

Harlan took her arms. Through the haptic sensors in his suit, it felt as if he were touching her with his bare fingers. "Nothing will go wrong. We'll deliver the bombs, get to safety, and as soon as your friends are clear, we'll set them off. I have distances calculated down to the millimeter, and everything is tied to the ultrahigh frequency tight beam communication between our suits, the robots, and March."

"You're making it sound easy."

"It is easy, Penny."

"What if something goes wrong?"

"Then I'll figure it out. This is what I do, what I've done for almost thirty years. Destroy things."

Penny smiled at him through her visor. "I'm glad you're on our side this time around, Harlan."

"I don't take sides, Penny. I just don't like bullies."

"You keep on telling yourself that. Now are we going to fly or am I going to have enough time to talk myself out of it?"

"We fly."

Harlan led her to the airlock. Like the robots, his bomb and hers were attached to their back by nanotech clamps. Their suits would coordinate distances and angles precisely and then kill their momentum relative to the fleet, release, and arm the bombs. They stepped out onto the platform and he gave Penny a moment to stare out at the lunar landscape around them. They couldn't see the Earth as it lay below the horizon. They'd see it soon enough once they took to flight.

"Oh, wow," Penny breathed over the radio. "It's beautiful out here."

"Now you know why I moved here. It will be awhile yet before gentrification sets in."

Penny snorted. "Let's go."

Their boot jets fired, as did those of the two robots, and the quartet blasted into the vacuum away from the Moon. The preprogrammed courses set in and the four fliers began to drift apart. Penny and the two robots would drop their bombs in an equilateral triangle roughly flat to the lunar plain below, while Harlan would travel to the furthest point to complete the tetrahedron.

He didn't tell Penny about the numerous concerns plaguing his own thoughts. He was normally a confident man, but in spite of his extensive research into theoretical high-energy physics over the past several hours, he was still unsure of what might happen when they detonated the quartet of antimatter bombs. He figured the worst-case scenario would be the bombs didn't detonate in synchronicity and the Hind fleet was blasted into the Earth, which might not be an extinction-level event, but would be catastrophic however one defined it.

If the bombs were somehow far more energetic than anticipated, the Earth or the Moon might be bathed in some extreme or unusual radiation, which could have all kinds of consequences. He'd compared his bombs to the Castle Bravo detonation, but even that had been three times more powerful than expected. It was unlikely that his bombs would do that, but as he said, antimatter was tricky stuff. He'd read a theory that instead of destroying what was at the focus, the bombs could conceivably tear a hole through the fabric of time and space, and nobody could say what would happen in that kind of eventuality. Maybe he was about to create a wormhole.

Ultimately, he didn't know what would happen, and that was both terrifying and exhilarating.

He contacted March, aboard the Hind flagship, using text only because the power level of the transmission would be barely detectable above background cosmic noise, and someone would have to be listening in on the precise frequency to detect it at all. *March, situation report.*

::Hi Uncle. Sally is going to fight the Clanmistress for control of the fleet.::

What if she wins? Is the war over?

::I don't think so. We're caught up in a political struggle between at least two factions.::

More likely that we will not be discovered. Do you have a way off the ship?

::Yes, I think so.::

Harlan sent his nephew coordinates. *Notify me when you pass that point. I have calculated it to be the minimum safe distance.*

::Safe distance for what?::

I'm going to destroy the fleet. See that you are get past that point. You should be safe there.

::I hope you're right.::

So do I.

CHAPTER SIXTEEN

Hind Fleet
Axeship Blood Afire

The battle was inherently unfair from the beginning. Sally was exhausted and suffering from a lingering head injury, the Clanmistress was rested, and the gravity grid where they fought had been adjusted to more closely match Hind-normal than Earth-normal gravity. There were no walls, no cage where they would battle, but they were surrounded on all sides by a tight press of Hind Warriors, making it feel like an arena to Sally.

Even though she wasn't built like a Warrior, the Clanmistress was still much larger and heavier than Sally, by a factor of perhaps five to one. Although the Hind eschewed armor—fighting a duel wearing armor would have been seen as weakness by her subjects—she still bore an axe. Sally had only her horseshoes. She could have taken a cub-sized axe—that much was permitted, at any rate—but what she didn't know about fighting with axes could have filled a couple of notebooks.

On the other hand, the Clanmistress was only fighting for her honor and the right to retain her position as Clanmistress, whereas Sally was fighting for the entire Earth. She didn't believe for a moment that anyone on the Earth would recognize her arrangement with the Hind as valid, but the aliens believed it, and that was what mattered most. Via March and Minerva, Sally knew Harlan Washington was out there in space, preparing to work his most destructive techno-magic, and it was imperative the Hind didn't discover him.

That meant Sally needed to make it a good fight.

Loasrah waited in the wings to seize power, and she seemed to have amassed several other Mistresses and a few dozen Warriors to her cause. The fleet's government was on the cusp of a civil war, and Sally was going to do what she could to drive the factions to battle, because it could only benefit Earth by delaying any further Hind action and giving Harlan time to work.

Fighting in Hind gravity was so difficult that she might not have done any better if she'd been fully rested and healed. Every step was murder, like she was fighting with another person strapped to her back. Rhaorhir swung her axe and it came down so much faster than Sally expected in the higher gravity that if she hadn't been able to trigger her super-speed for a moment, she'd have been split from forehead to navel.

She'd been in brutal fights before, against the Archmage's minions, against the creatures of the Dream-world. Fighting Rhaorhir was like nothing Sally had ever experienced. The Hind crouched low, using her splayed legs for balance, spinning herself around faster than should have been possible for a creature so large. Her upper torso bent forward at the waist to keep herself low and present less of a target from the front. Overhead chops were infrequent and most of her blows were lateral, necessitating Sally constantly back away. She couldn't find any opening to engage the Clanmistress. Every time she tried to flank Rhaorhir, she scuttled around like a crab and swung that vicious axe in a wide, sweeping arc.

A near miss split Sally's costume at her belly and drew a thin line of fire across her skin as the blade sliced her flesh. Blood beaded along the wound before her accelerated healing shut it off. Her natural healing ability had kicked in as the adrenalin from the combat flooded her system, and it was helping her head more than anything else. "First blood, Monkey," said the Clanmistress.

Sally saw an opening and dropped to her knees, leaning back like she was doing the limbo as the axe blade whistled over her head. Every muscle protested as she forced herself back up. As Rhaorhir slowed her swing, about to reverse into a backswing, Sally ducked in close to the Clanmistress and delivered a series of rapid-fire straight jabs into Rhaorhir's nose, boxing-style like Hector had taught her. The horseshoes clutched in her hands added mass to her otherwise lightweight fists, and her super-speed meant blows struck like machine-gun bullets.

Rhaorhir staggered back, her ruined nose a mass of ragged tissue and orange blood. "It's not first blood that matters," Sally gasped. "It's last."

The heavy gravity was taking its toll, and Sally's heart pounded the way it rarely did except when she'd been running flat-out for too long. The overhead lights seemed far too bright and the edges of her vision tinged with black and she wondered if she was close to fainting. If she did, it would mean her death. Hours ago, she might have welcomed it. Now, she was furious with the invaders who had upended her entire life, and she wouldn't give them the satisfaction of seeing her die.

She forced herself to accelerate her perceptions, even if she couldn't do the same with her muscles. Where were the Hind's weak spots? Eyes were always good targets, but with them protected by a heavy brow ridge, she'd have to hit them precisely to do any real damage. She'd already savaged Rhaorhir's nose. Like her nose, her ears were protected by a bony ridge to prevent them being torn apart. What she really needed was the Hind equivalent of pressure points, something like the legendary Five Point Palm Exploding Heart Technique. She hadn't ever studied anything resembling real martial arts. Her long-dead father

Lionheart might have known such a secret technique. Even her half-sister Yunbao might know it, but she couldn't exactly put her fight on *Pause* and make a quick long-distance call to Hong Kong.

She put her tactics aside as a bloody-faced Rhaorhir charged in at her, sweeping the axe in yet another flat, scything motion. Sally ducked beneath it. She spun her horseshoes in her hands so the ends pointed upward and beat the inside and outside of the Clanmistress' elbow, trying to find a weak point.

Rhaorhir squalled like a cougar and the axe slipped from her fingers to clatter upon the Parade Deck. Okay, Sally thought, work the joints some more. She twisted to go after Rhaorhir's other hand but it grabbed hold of her wrist before she could move. The Clanmistress twisted it and Sally's wrist snapped like a pretzel. She screamed, for it hurt worse than any other injury she'd suffered over the years. She'd cracked ribs, been beaten down, collided with solid objects at high speed, but the broken wrist hurt so bad she wanted to cry and throw up and pass out all at the same time.

"So fragile," Rhaorhir crowed. "I will break all your bones, Monkey, and then use your remains to stuff my cushions. You have not the hearts to beat me."

Tears streamed down Sally's face and she held her injured arm close to her body. Something about Rhaorhir's gloat stuck in her mind, but she couldn't focus on it enough through the pain. She could still manage a taunt, though, and if she angered the Clanmistress enough, she might make a mistake. "Yeah . . . well . . . I'll only be dead, b-but you'll always be ugly."

Somewhere behind her, Blueshift snorted in amusement.

Rhaorhir roared, splattering Sally with orange blood droplets from her shattered nose. "Foul Monkey! I will tear your hearts out and eat them in front of you!" She lunged for Sally, but Sally was no longer there.

She'd figured it out.

The pain in her arm sharpened her focus and she stepped into the space between seconds, moving around the sudden statue that was the Clanmistress. The Hind kept saying *hearts* and Sally remembered the Hind had two of them. She didn't know precisely how their circulatory systems functioned, but a heart was like any other muscle; it could be induced to cramp. She slipped beneath Rhaorhir's belly and pummeled the space between her forelegs for all she was worth, as fast as she could.

When Sally had first joined Just Cause as an intern, Juice was defending a low-level supervillain named Anchor who'd been accused of murder after she punched an equally low-level would-be hero in the chest. He'd gone into an immediate cardiac arrest and died before paramedics could reach him. She'd managed to strike him in the exact moment between heartbeats that caused a fibrillation of his heart. With Juice's help, she'd bargained down to a lesser charge and had since reformed and gone into sports medicine.

Sally hoped she might accomplish the same thing with Rhaorhir, but on purpose. The shattered bones in her wrist sandpapered together and she nearly fainted from the pain. She rolled out from beneath the Clanmistress as her perceptions and bodily speed finally dropped back to normal range. She nearly didn't have the strength to stand in the heavy gravity.

The Clanmistress stood still, making no move to charge or otherwise attack. Her sides quivered and her eyes bulged out as she made weak, frantic motions at her torso. Nobody moved to help her; Hind didn't care for their sick or wounded the way Humans did. With a boneless thud, Rhaorhir collapsed to the Parade Deck. Her sides didn't move. Her body didn't twitch in the least. If she wasn't dead, she was close enough for Sally's purpose.

Sally staggered forward, put one foot on Rhaorhir, and raised her undamaged hand in the air. "I win, you assholes."

Hind Fleet
Axeship Blood Afire

Sally wavered in her stance, showing the depth of her exhaustion. Blood stained the front of her suit where the axe slice hadn't healed the way it should have. Minerva knew her friend was in a bad way and they had to all get off the flagship as soon as possible. Nevertheless, Sally shouted above the murmurs of the surrounding Hind. "By your law, I am now your Clanmistress. I order you to stand down and prepare to leave this star system forever!"

A Submistress stepped into the circle where Sally's battle with Rhaorhir had taken place, flanked by a pair of truly gigantic musclebound Warriors. "We reject you, Monkey. Clan Sharassar will rise under my leadership, and your world will fall before our onslaught."

Another Hind jumped into the ring. "Your claim on the title is weak, Hsharra. You were bested by a single Monkey who didn't even consider you important enough to kill. I assert myself as Clanmistress, and I have more than a couple of thickheaded dimwits to back me up. I, Korashas, shall lead the Clan!"

A roar of support echoed from a dozen Warriors and Submistresses around the Parade Deck.

"Kittens, all of you!" screamed another Submistress, and she charged into the ring, her claws spread wide, and attacked Korashas.

Minerva whirled to face the remainder of her strike team. "Gauss, Amber, clear us a path. I see our Warrior has returned. Blueshift, you'll need to carry Sally. She won't be able to keep up with us in her state. March, I need you to translate what I'm about to say into Hindish and give it to me phonetically so I can shout it, unless you feel up to the task."

March shook his head. "I p-probably stutter in Hindish too."

"Go!" Minerva ordered, and Blueshift zipped through the air to land beside Sally and gather her in his arms before she could either faint or be cut down by the increasing hostilities between the Submistresses. Gauss reshaped floor panels into barricades while Amber flung up spiky walls of amber around them to force the Warriors away.

Minerva got the translation from March's program and used her voice like a weapon, projecting over the rising sounds of battle and growling and snarling in Hindish like a native speaker. Her words touched off a dozen separate battles among the surrounding Warriors and Submistresses and in seconds, the entire Parade Deck seemed to be awash in blood as Hind fought Hind.

"What the hell did you tell them?" Gauss shouted over the din as the party began pushing their way through the fray toward the exit where the Hind Garragh awaited them.

"I told them the Monkey showed her strength by defeating the Clanmistress and all Warriors should dispatch the pretenders to the leadership." Minerva offered a rare smile. "It appears I've thrown quite a bit of gasoline on the fire." She took her spear in hand. "This is taking too long. Amber, surf us out of here."

"I don't know how to do that!" cried the girl.

Minerva touched Amber's hand, letting her voice carry through the girl's bones like they were speaker wires, and shared knowledge of Amber's powers that the girl had yet to discover.

Amber pointed her hand toward the deck and a stream of amber shot forth to puddle into a solid base.

"Behind her," Minerva told March and Gauss. "I'll cover you."

The two men stepped onto the material behind Amber and she accelerated the stream to make a river before them and a rising wave behind them. They slid along the stream exactly like surfers.

Ahead, Blueshift landed at the corridor entrance where Garragh waited. The Warrior was bloodied and his axe was dripping. Amber's surfing-stream pulled the trio closer and closer, climbing up and over much of the combat while Minerva darted back and forth, using her spear for pinpoint defense by stabbing Warriors' hands as they raised laser rifles.

Hind died all around them as the factions battled for supremacy. Minerva had no clear understanding of who might ultimately win out, but she suspected no matter the victor, Earth would suffer unless Harlan succeeded in his plan. Amber's surfing wave arrived at the ramp to the bridge level, depositing her, March, and Gauss at the foot of the ramp. Garragh stood with his back to the Parade Deck, facing the ramp to guard them from a surprise attack from the rear. Sally huddled against a bulkhead, pale-faced and shivering, clearly in shock. Blueshift stood his ground at the base of the ramp, firing off energy blasts at any Hind who came too close to them.

Minerva touched down, made a quick survey of her team's preparedness for the next phase of their escape, and issued her orders. "Gauss, block this corridor off from the rest of the Parade Deck, then secure our passage through the ship. Garragh, take the lead. Blueshift and I will be on point defense. Amber, make a mobile chair or stretcher for Sally. March . . ."

March was already kneeling beside Sally, rubbing one of her hands between two of his.

Minerva nodded. Given their history, his presence might be more healing for her than any amount of medical care. She knew Destroyer had left some nanotech inside Sally after their last visit to the Moon— she could smell it inside her friend. Perhaps March's own nanotech would help Sally's to help her recover.

Bars shot from the walls, floor, and ceiling to make a crisscross lattice of bulkhead metal across the entrance to the Parade Deck. Gauss followed up his basic construction by making a forest of spikes grow outward from the lattice to make it uncomfortable and awkward for anyone attempting to rush the barricade.

No other Hind challenged them as they ascended first to the bridge, and then past it to the hatch for the *Dagger*. Apparently the battle to rule over the Clan had pulled in so many Mistresses and Warriors that the *Blood Afire* was at least temporarily uncontrolled. "It's now or never," Minerva said. "Garragh, can you fly?"

Sally's translation disc, remarkably undamaged after her bout with Rhaorhir, growled. Garragh snarled back and the disc replied, "No, Mistress."

"March, you're the closest thing we have to an expert on Hind computer systems. You are now our pilot. I will assist you the best I can. Amber, Gauss, do what you can to keep Sally comfortable. Blueshift, as our resident nuclear physicist, you get to be Chief Engineer. Keep us running at top speed however you can. Garragh, you need to point out anything important we miss. I'm going to lean on you heavily, because if we don't all work together here, we're not going to survive the next hour."

On Approach to the Hind Fleet

Penny had long dreamed of being able to fly. So many parahumans had the ability to leave the ground behind without so much as a second thought. Even Surfboy, with his extreme altitude limit of about fifteen feet, could travel without his feet ever touching the ground. But no, fate had seen fit to grant Penny the ability to make world-record sniper shots, throw coins into vending machines from across a room, and other generally useless parlor tricks.

Now she flew through the emptiness of space with the Moon a basketball-sized orb behind her and the brilliance of Earth below her and not a goddamn thing else around for perhaps thousands of miles. She wasn't space-sick, so at least that was something. Perhaps her nanotech was keeping her symptoms to a minimum.

She didn't like not having a visible horizon or ground somewhere she could actually see it instead of the undefined blue-white of her homeworld's clouds. "Cain, can you overlay my visor with something so I'm not looking at emptiness?"

The AI didn't reply, but a set of crosshairs appeared in her vision, along with a range finder, a targeting scope that looked like it had come right out of a videogame, and a slowly scrolling feed of data pertaining to her armor. Some of the surprising information jumped out at her and she began to understand what a potent weapon Washington had bestowed upon her. She was traveling at the unimaginable speed of nearly eighteen kilometers per second but the only indication she had of her velocity was the rapidity with which she approached the target drop point for the bomb.

Still, she felt more alone than she ever had in her life. Her son was thousands of miles away, somewhere below her in the northeast of North America, just brightening into dawn as the planet turned to bring the west into sunlight. "Cain, talk to me. Please. It's so damn quiet up here."

::It's space, Penny. It's supposed to be quiet.::

"Is that supposed to be a joke?"

::Humor is a difficult trait for humans to master. My programmer is notoriously underdeveloped in that area. It is unlikely I would ever intentionally make a joke.::

"Now I know you're making fun of me."

::About what would you like to converse?::

"I don't know. What do I talk to a computer about? Any juicy gossip happening in the virtual world?"

::I can connect you to the internet if you would like. Perhaps you would enjoy watching some cat videos.::

"That's the biggest load of . . . wait, can I make a phone call?"

::Who would you like to call? I am tapped into worldwide cellular networks.::

"Well, I'd like to call my son, but I don't know what time it is back home in New York."

::It is five seventeen in the morning.::

"No, no calls. He won't be up yet and the last thing I need today is to get a lecture from my goddamn ex husband about how terrible of a parent I am."

::Would you like to call someone else?::

Penny sighed. "No, it's probably best to keep radio silence. Besides, I don't know anybody but goddamn superheroes anyway." She flew onward, watching the range to her destination point shrink. In the distance, against the blackness of space, she could see the blocky, unnatural shapes of the Hind fleet, huddled together like LEGO creations of her son Avery. When the fleet arrived, there had been five ships, but Washington had destroyed one all on his own. She wondered if she contained that kind of firepower within her own armor. He was a tinkerer and constantly engineered bleeding edge technology. Had he given her better than he had himself?

"Cain," Penny said.

::Yes?::

"Give me a rundown on my offensive capabilities. Where do I rank on the Devereaux Distribution now that I've got Harlan Washington's Magical Snake Oil Elixir running through my veins?" The Devereaux Distribution was a table developed by Dr. Grace Devereaux of the Parahuman Medical Institute in Paris as a way of categorizing parahuman power levels. It had a great many layers of complexity, but there was a quick, simple method on a scale of zero to nine. Unpowered humans rated a zero on the scale. Low power parahumans, like Penny, rated from one to three. Penny had been a *one*. Someone like Mustang Sally rated an *eight*, as one of the elite high-powered heroes.

::Your current abilities place you as a nine on the Devereaux Distribution.::

Nine meant a force to be feared, the kind of hero who could take an entire platoon of lesser villains . . . or an enemy battleship. Destroyer ranked nine on the Distribution. She was every bit as powerful as him. That gave her pause. He had given her that kind of power without the slightest thought as to consequences. He could do that to anyone, given enough resources.

Her biggest question was what to do once the Hind had been defeated and the Earth saved from the interstellar threat. She had to operate on the assumption they would be successful. Otherwise, why even bother with the bomb on her back? Being given the power she had meant she had to accept a much greater responsibility than she ever had been asked to. She could already feel the weight of it upon her shoulders, like she had been tasked with supporting the entire world.

::Stand by for deceleration. We have nearly reached the target point.::

"Can the Hind detect us? Should we be ready for evasive maneuvering?" Penny felt the force of deceleration only distantly, as the nanotech within her body provided the necessary support to protect her from its effects.

::Data suggests that we may be too small for them to detect, and certainly too small to target, given their rudimentary weapons aiming systems.::

The indicator on Penny's visor turned from red to green, meaning it was time for her to drop her bomb. She had only just formed the thought to tell Cain to release it when the catches on her armor withdrew back into her suit and the bomb floated free. She turned to look at it. It seemed so innocuous, just a beach ball-sized metallic sphere surrounded by the majesty of space with the brightness of the Earth reflecting off its surface.

::Penny, I am receiving a broadband transmission from the Hind. I can translate it for you.::

"Please do."

Cain pitched its voice in an admirable impression of a Hind speaking English. "This is Clanmistress Loasrah. I have assumed command of Clan Sharassar. The Monkeys who killed Rhaorhir have fled *Blood Afire* in the *Dagger*. The captain whose ship successfully destroys the *Dagger* will earn a spot on my council, and the gunner who takes the fatal shot will become that vessel's new captain."

Penny's eyes widened as she interpreted what had happened. The four ships of the fleet began to sparkle as laser turrets opened fire on a bright spark that must have been the fleeing *Dagger*. "Can you reach Minerva? Or Washington?"

::I cannot reach Minerva, but I can open a tight beam to Destroyer.::

"Harlan, it's Penny."

"Go ahead."

"I'm assuming you heard that transmission. We've got to go help that ship!"

"No. That is impossible. We've already placed our bombs. The only important thing now is to reach safe distance. You must return to the Preserve, Penny."

"No, I'm not leaving my friends behind! I've got to help. I'm a goddamn sniper, Washington. I can take out those turrets."

"I believe you, but I need you at the Preserve. You're the closest to it, and you have the key to unlock its full operating potential within your armor. If that Hind ship approaches without the base being unlocked, the Eggbreakers will destroy it. They are automatic. You have to go disarm them."

"Goddammit, Washington! Those are my friends! My teammates! I'm not going to just stand by and let them die without trying to help them!"

"That's exactly what you will do. *Override code Reggie Washington one nine eight five.* Return to the Preserve."

Penny's armor spun around and the engines opened wide with her pointed at the Moon. "Washington, you son of a bitch!"

"You got that right, Penny. I have to fly past the fleet to reach the Preserve. I will call Carousel and the Steel Soldier in to help. We will defend the *Dagger* until it is clear."

Impotent tears floated away from Penny's eyes, blurring her vision in the lack of gravity until, she assumed, nanobots pulled them away. "Harlan Washington, when you get back to the Moon, I'm going to beat the shit out of you."

"I'll take that under advisement."

Hind ship Dagger

The Human Mistress who could create odd-smelling yellow material out of thin air had to use her ability to create a makeshift pilot's seat for the one garbed in the shiny armor. Garragh was pretty sure the one piloting was actually a male since his scent was markedly different from the Mistresses. At least the Pilot understood proper Hindish and could converse in it, which meant Garragh wasn't kept completely in the dark.

With Garragh's help in identifying controls, the dark-haired male had somehow made tentacles grow out of his arms and was using them to operate controls that a Hind would normally be able to reach but a Human could not. The Mistress with the red cloak stood behind them both, resting one hand on the Pilot's back and one hand on Garragh's flank. It was an odd sensation to be touched by an alien hand, and yet somehow he found her presence soothing in a way he couldn't understand. She had taken the translation disc from Mistress Sahree and installed it on his breastplate. The device gave him nearly real-time translation of the Human tongue and helped the Humans to understand him.

The other Humans huddled around Mistress Sahree, who had suffered wounds in her battle with Rhaorhir and seemed to be in grave condition. Garragh hoped they would bandage her the way they had bandaged him. The Humans cared for their injured, which he wasn't sure he would ever truly understand.

Loasrah's voice came over the ship's communicator and Garragh's blood went cold. The ambitious Pilot had made her move and apparently secured her position with enough strength to lay claim to the Clanmistress role, and her first proclamation had been to offer a reward to the captain and crew who would successfully destroy the *Dagger*. So much for her glowing promises of an end to the conflict. She would end it in a proper Hind way: by stabbing a blade through it.

Suddenly space filled with crisscrossing laser beams and questing tractors seeking to lock onto the fleeing *Dagger*.

"Well I'll say this for the new Clanmistress," said the Human Garragh thought of as Mistress Crimson, after the color of her cloak. "She certainly knows how to motivate her people."

The Pilot sent the *Dagger* twisting through space. "They're n-not very accurate," he said.

"Are our shields activated?" Mistress Crimson asked.

"Yes."

"Garragh, how powerful are the weapons of your capital ships? Powerful enough to overwhelm our shields?"

Garragh bowed his head forward, then realized the Human might not understand the significance of the gesture. "I do not know, Mistress. I am just a Warrior."

"No worry. March, the safest thing is to avoid us getting hit and having to find out."

"I'm t-trying. The tractor beams are broad and sweep q-quickly. If one of those catches us, they m-might be able to hit us with a turret gun." New lights appeared on the scanner and Pilot March reached out to tap it. "Missiles?"

"They are most certainly dropships," Garragh said. "They will box us in like a hunting pack."

Mistress Crimson crossed her arms. "And of course, we can't fire through our own shields." She turned to look back at the other Humans. "Blueshift, can you do something about that? Change the oscillation of the shields or the lasers or something so we can fire back without losing our protection?"

The Mistress in the blue and black stood from where she—no, not a Mistress, but a male. Garragh kept trying to remember the Humans did not break into such specific gender castes as Warriors and Mistresses. One could be both or neither. Blueshift was a Warrior, certainly, for Garragh had seen him fight, but Mistress Crimson spoke to him as to another Mistress. Blueshift said, "I'll see what I can do, but I'm basically a caveman banging rocks together to try to fix a '75 Chevy." He raised his hands and they glowed with a purplish energy, spreading outward to suffuse the *Dagger*'s hull.

The dropships closed in on the *Dagger*, orange-lining their engines well past safety tolerances. Two of them exploded as the fields containing the reactions within their engines failed. Three more perished due to what Mistress Crimson termed *infighting*. Garragh tried to explain that the crews of the dropships that attacked other ships were only trying to be the first to take down the *Dagger*, but he didn't have the vocabulary to break it down cleanly.

"Can't . . . can't this bucket of bolts go any faster?" Garragh turned and his hearts jumped to see Mistress Sahree standing on her own feet, albeit supported by her companions. He rushed forward and genuflected, presenting her with the back of his neck.

"Mistress Sahree," he whispered. "I am pleased to see you are well."

"Garragh," she replied. "I'm not well yet, but I'm getting better. Minerva, how are we doing?"

"Not well," said Mistress Crimson. "The fleet is attacking us. They've sent dropships in pursuit. They may reach us before we reach Harlan's minimum safe distance coordinates. The fleet has a new Clanmistress who appears to be every bit as aggressive as Rhaorhir."

"Loasrah?" Mistress Sahree asked. "I met her. Lovely woman. Really forward-thinking. I was hoping she might die in the free-for-all, but I guess she planned better than that."

The *Dagger* shook hard with an impact, staggering everyone despite the vessel's inertial dampening and artificial gravity systems.

"Tractor beam!" March shouted. "I'm trying to b-break us free!"

"Those dropships are coming in fast," Mistress Crimson said. "Blueshift?"

Blueshift lowered his hands, the energy dying upon his fingertips. "It's no good. I can't re-tune anything on this jalopy."

Garragh wondered if the Humans' strange abilities would allow them to battle in deep space. He wouldn't have been surprised if they did, but they made no move to open the airlock or even to put on protective gear.

"Sally, any orders?" Mistress Crimson turned to face Mistress Sahree.

Sahree waved her off. "No, I'm not up to making decisions yet."

The Pilot gasped. "Sally! It's Uncle Harlan. He's g-going to free us."

"How's he going to do that?" asked Sahree.

The Pilot left his station and went to a bulkhead. "He's going to destroy the tractor beam." He pulled open an access panel to expose the power leads beneath it. He pointed out a specific spot to Blueshift. "Right there. St-steady feed of power. Between two-point-nine and three-point-two j-joules."

Blueshift reached into the access panel and energy shone across his face as he fed it into the leads. "Sure, let me just activate the joule meter I don't actually have in my suit."

Mistress Crimson moved beside him. "I will help you."

The Pilot returned to his seat. Garragh stayed where he was, out of the way of the others. He watched as the indicators of the approaching dropships drew closer and closer to the *Dagger* and wondered if they were going to die.

Hind Fleet

Harlan sent tightbeam transmissions to Carousel and the Steel Soldier to converge upon the fleet after they placed their bombs. He dropped his at the appropriate coordinates and opened his jets wide to head into the fray. His only surviving family member, March, was on board the stolen *Dagger* ship, and Harlan would see to it that he survived the day. Likewise, he was certain Mustang Sally was on board, and that provided him a sense of . . . happiness.

Penny would hate him for a long time for taking control of her armor the way he had, but it was imperative to have someone he could trust take charge of the Preserve until he could return. In the eventuality that he couldn't, only March and Penny would be able to safely disarm the defense mechanisms. Learning to protect what was his was one of the first lessons Harlan had learned as a child, and some lessons one never forgot.

His display showed the *Dagger* was being held by a beam from one of the smaller fleet vessels instead of the *Blood Afire* where he'd been briefly detained. While held in place, a half dozen dropships raced toward it, and from the transmission he'd heard from the new Clanmistress, the intent was not to capture prisoners but to kill fugitives.

He would not allow that.

He ordered the Steel Soldier and Carousel to attack the tractor beam emitters on the target vessel and subsequently those on the rest of the fleet. If he denied the Hind the chance to hold the *Dagger* in place, that would allow the stolen vessel to reach safety.

That was only half the equation. The *Dagger* was still outnumbered and outgunned by the approaching dropships. The only way to tilt those odds was to give the Hind a more compelling reason to return to the fleet than to continue to pursue the fugitives.

To that end, Harlan launched his attack upon the flagship itself.

While the Steel Soldier and Carousel raced across the surfaces of the capital ships, tearing apart the tractor beam emitters with cannon rounds, living metal blades, or brute force, Harlan flew across the superstructure of the *Blood Afire*. He went after what he considered to be soft points instead of strategic targets. He didn't want to take away *Blood Afire*'s ability to fight back; he wanted to show that it was useless. He fired energy blasts into the rotation mechanisms of turrets until they could no longer swivel. No porthole, no window was safe from his wrath. Every hull breach he created shot out a cloud of air until the flagship's emergency systems sealed off the damaged sections.

An indicator on his screen turned from red to green as the last of the tractor beam emitters went down, sliced apart by Carousel's liquid metal blades. "March, you should be clear to flee. Get to safe distance and make for the Preserve. Penny Lane will be there to disengage the security features."

"What about you, Uncle?" March's transmission was heavy with static from the frequency bleed of the energy weapons firing.

"I've got the Soldier and Carousel running interference. As soon as those dropships peel off and come back to fight me, I'll leave them to fight, go to stealth mode, and get myself clear."

"G-good luck." March didn't sound convinced, but Harlan didn't need him to be. He just needed his nephew to keep heading away from the bomb blast area and not get any foolish ideas about coming back to rescue his uncle. Harlan wouldn't need rescuing; he'd been getting himself out of predicaments long before March had been alive.

He changed his tactics to go from strategic targeting to full-scale destruction, specifically targeting the sublight engines, and ordered the Soldier and Carousel to do the same. From what he'd learned in his subtle hacking into the Hind systems, their sublight engines functioned more or less the way any engine would, pushing energy out of the rear and using that to propel the ship forward. They were much more efficient in design than the best non-experimental Human engines, and a step or two up in technological wizardry since they only required power to operate, not fuel. If he and his robotic allies damaged the sublight drives of the fleet sufficiently, the only option they would have would be to activate their stardrives and warp out of the Solar system.

And if that didn't work, well, he still had his bombs sitting quietly at their designated anchor points, waiting his command to unleash their antimatter-fueled destructive power.

He cruised past the flagship's main thrusters, blasting the energy-guidance vanes apart with cannon rounds. Only a few turrets remained active on the *Blood Afire*, and they couldn't target him in his current location, so he continued his destruction undisturbed and undeterred until his armor informed him the dropships had reversed course and were racing back to intercept him at flank speed. He notified his robots. "Bogies incoming. Converge upon the flagship. Target inbound vessels."

The dropships rushed in upon Harlan and the two robots with unbelievable, even reckless speed. Without their inertial dampening systems, the rapid deceleration and sharp maneuvering would turn their crews to pulp. Harlan knew where those systems were located in the vessels, and he shared the targeting information with his team. "March, status update." He forced extra power into his transmitter, pushing the signal past the morass of electromagnetic interference from all the energy weapons firing in the vicinity.

"Thirty seconds t-to minimum safe distance. You have to g-get out of there, Uncle."

"Don't worry about me. We're holding our own."

The truth was that Harlan was a little concerned for his safety. The Hind's accuracy with their lasers hadn't improved in the past several hours, but with the sheer volume of energy blasting back and forth, one of them might get in a lucky shot. Two dropships had already spun out of control, holed by friendly fire, and impacted explosively along the hull of one of the smaller capital ships. It drifted in a slow twist, atmosphere and debris leaking from the impact site.

He checked his own flight time to reach safe distance. He could do so in sixty-five seconds. The *Dagger* should have been nearly to safety. It was time for his own departure. He'd have the robots defend and cover his escape. He didn't mind losing them in the explosion. They were robots; he could rebuild them easily enough. As he started to issue the orders, a heavy, energetic impact shook him and sent him spinning wildly through the fleet. The status board on his visor went red as nearly every system in his armor failed.

He knew what had happened. A laser blast had struck him and although his armor had protected him, his nanotech had paid the price. Hundreds of thousands of his nanites had perished shielding the fragile human within their lattice. They dissipated the energy around him instead of into him. A cloud of dead nanites drifted away from him, pushed out of his body by the microscopic robots that still functioned within him. His armor was intact but nearly all his other systems had failed or were failing. *Propulsion. Weapons. Shielding. Damage Control. Nanotech Transformation. Life Support. Memory Backup. Communications . . .*

The icon showing his Communications system status flickered from red to yellow, showing partial system function had been restored. Unable to do anything else in his spinning tumble, he focused upon that system. He could transmit, but not receive. "Goddamn," he said aloud. "This is how it all ends." There was no time left. Even if he called the Soldier and Carousel to come to his aid, he'd likely be dead before they could follow through, and he couldn't risk any of the Hind ships escaping.

He had no idea if March had followed his last order and taken the *Dagger* beyond the safe point. All he could do was hope, and send a couple of brief messages.

His spin came to a sudden, undignified halt and he found himself facing a dropship with a still-functioning tractor beam emitter. He could see the pilot staring at him through the cockpit window, her face twisted into a gleeful snarl. A movie hero might have had some kind of witty parting statement, but Harlan was no hero. He didn't shut his eyes; it wouldn't have made a difference. He sent his final message, a simple activation code for four innocuous objects placed at specific locations in nearby space.

And nothing more.

CHAPTER SEVENTEEN

♘

The Preserve
Luna

The bombs that Harlan had detonated did not function at all the way anyone could have foreseen. Instead of directing their force outward in all directions, as might have been expected, their energies largely went inward, toward the focus between all four bombs. The implosion forces had been so strong that the *Dagger* had nearly been pulled back into the zone of destruction. Minerva had said something about tearing open the Universe. March had said it had been the equivalent of a catastrophic blowout inside a pressurized vessel, except in this case, the pressurized vessel was the Universe and the hole led to . . . somewhere else.

All Sally knew was that the Hind fleet was gone, although whether it had been completely atomized or thrown into another Universe or otherwise cast through space-time, nobody could say, but she had her suspicions.

There had been a Steel Soldier android in the Seventies and early Eighties before Harlan had destroyed it in 1985. The Soldier had first been discovered within a destroyed building, and prevailing theories were that it had been an unintentional time traveler. Sally's former teammate on the Lucky Seven, Carousel, was likewise an artificial being whose origins were enshrouded in mystery. She believed they must have been cast backward in time from the force of the antimatter implosion, although they had wound up in completely different times and locations. It stood to reason, then, that the Hind fleet might have been sent elsewhere, or else*when*, as had Harlan Washington.

Wherever or whenever they had gone was moot. History didn't have any record of a man like Harlan Washington or his armor-suited alter ego Destroyer existing outside of his normal timeline, so if he was still alive, nobody could say when or where he was. He certainly hadn't believed he would travel anywhere except to the Great Beyond, based upon the brief messages he'd managed to transmit just prior to the detonations. Three messages: one for his nephew March, one for Penny Lane, and one for Sally.

When March had landed the *Dagger* on the Preserve's platform and the dome had closed overhead, Penny had been the one to meet them. She looked different to Sally, scarred in a way that tended to come from extended contact with Harlan Washington. "Welcome to the Preserve," she told them, "Although I understand several of you have been here before."

She went on to explain how Harlan had loaded her up with nanotech and sent her back to the Moon so she could disable the security devices that would otherwise have destroyed the *Dagger* on approach.

"We're glad you managed it," Minerva said.

Penny shrugged. "I have no idea what I'm doing. It's like I got plugged into a supercomputer but I'm not much more than a monkey with a gun." She bowed her head. "Anyway, Harlan sent some messages before he . . . before the bombs went off. March, one is for you, and one is for Sally. If you want to listen to them privately first, there are rooms you can use."

March said he would take his in his quarters. Sally said she'd listen to hers in the lounge facing the lunar surface. She'd spent hours in there when she'd first been brought to the Preserve to help Harlan's sister, and she wanted to be in familiar surroundings. Minerva had taken Blueshift, Amber, and Gauss to the galley for refreshments, while Penny had taken Garragh with her, leaving Sally alone to stare out at the stark contrast of the white lunar dust and the black shadows. Just at the edge of the horizon, out against the darkness, she could see the multicolored, swirling space storm that was the remnant of the antimatter implosion. It had shrunk in size and intensity steadily and she figured it would be gone soon.

Harlan's final words haunted her.

"Sally . . . it is not in my nature to apologize for my actions. Everything I have done in my life has led me to this point, and that includes killing your father. You helped me in my time of need and for that, I am grateful. Perhaps . . . in different circumstances, we might even have been friends."

She wished there had been more. More time for him to say what he wanted to. More time for her to perhaps find some sort of closure with this supervillain who, despite his protestations to the contrary, had saved the world not once but twice. Harlan Washington, the Destroyer, had been a major guiding force in the woman she had become. His attack on Tornado's funeral in 1985 had killed both the man she'd thought was her father and her actual father before she ever had a chance to be born. His attack in Chicago in 2003 had been her first true parahuman battle, even before she'd become a member of Just Cause. Then in 2007, with nowhere else to turn, Sally had come to him when a nanotech plague threatened to make humans extinct. Then in 2009, he had come to her to help save his sister, which had introduced her to March as well as ended Destroyer's war on Just Cause.

And now he was gone.

"*Ave atque vale*," she whispered into the silence. "I salute you, Harlan Washington."

With those words, she finally allowed grief to take hold of her and cried for him, for Chinook and Surfboy and Johnny Go, and for Jason.

The Preserve
Luna

Minerva was every bit as exhausted as the remaining members of her strike team. Amber had fallen asleep at the table in between bites of a sandwich, and Blueshift had removed his face mask to show the rings of exhaustion around his eyes, making him look like a raccoon. He'd asked if there was a radio or something that he could use to call his wife Javelin to let her know he was still alive. She told him there was, but she estimated it would be a couple more hours before the local interference from the antimatter implosion cleared up enough that they could transmit to the Earth.

"How will we get home? I mean, can we take that Hind ship with us?" Gauss asked.

"I don't think so. It is unfamiliar technology and potentially dangerous," Minerva said.

"All technology is potentially dangerous," said Blueshift. "That's the point of it." He yawned.

"By keeping it here, less of that potentially dangerous technology is likely to fall into the hands of people who would use it against other people." Minerva sipped at her tea, letting the heat warm her even though it wasn't cold in the galley. "There are private individuals and governments, including our own, who would weaponize whatever tech they could derive from the Hind."

"Maybe that's not the worst thing that could happen," said Gauss. "If they come back, we'll be ready to fight them on their own terms."

"I don't think that will be an issue," Minerva said. "A handful of parahumans defeated their fleet and their invasion force. If they come back to investigate why nobody returned, they'll meet the same fate. If they return in force, well . . ." She gave in to a rare smile. "Just Cause will be ready to meet them." Her brief moment of good humor subsided as she considered the toll the incident had taken upon her friends, her city, her world. "We all will be."

The Preserve
Luna

Penny got Garragh established in a room where he could at least be comfortable while she determined what to do with him. Somehow, she didn't think returning him to Earth would be a good idea. He was an enemy combatant, a prisoner of war. He would be tried for war crimes and probably executed for them. If any other Hind Warriors remained alive on the Earth, she suspected the same would happen to them. Given what she knew about them, it was unlikely any of them had survived to be captured. They would all have gone down fighting in a blaze of honor and glory, because that was their way. Garragh was unique among the Hind in that he didn't *want* to throw himself upon the weapons of his enemies.

No, she would keep him there, in the Preserve. He would have the chance to learn, to cultivate that seed of peace that had taken root within him and let it grow.

Washington's final message to her had taken her by surprise. She didn't think she'd been that important a part of his life in their all-too-brief time together to warrant him targeting a few words to her, and yet he had. "Penny . . . I'm entrusting you with the Preserve. It was my hideaway from the Earth, but it needs to become something different. You have within you the ability to make it something greater. Something for the good of all the world. I wish I'd had more time with you."

That last sentence had haunted her. He'd *liked* her. She'd sensed it during the time they'd spent together. Likewise, she had found herself attracted to him, even though he was quite a bit older and, well, a supervillain. He was honest with her, which was more than she could have said about her piece-of-shit ex-husband. He'd treated her like an equal. He'd given her the best gift he could: the same nanotech he himself had possessed. It was as if he'd given himself to her.

And now, he'd given her his moon base and asked her to use it for the benefit of the world. How was she supposed to even begin to do something like that? She'd spent her life dealing with small problems as a mother and a cop, and later as a superhero—although to be fair, she still didn't consider herself anywhere in league with the rest of Just Cause even though she knew now she surpassed them all. How was she supposed to take that kind of small-problem mindset and apply it to the entire world? It was as if someone had given her the keys to the kingdom but she had no idea what to do once she opened the door.

Then it came to her. She could take the Preserve and make it into its true namesake. There were already doomsday seed banks on the Earth. She could build one in the Preserve, using the nanotech for the labor. She could retrieve genetic information from animals as well. Even people. She could make the Preserve into the ultimate emergency backup for the Earth in the event of a global disaster. On the heels of that thought, it occurred to her that she could backup all the world's data as well. It would give new meaning to the phrase *cloud storage*. She could capture all the electronic data as it passed through the networks around the world and store it. It would be a database of the whole of human history, culture, and creativity. If the world ended in a catastrophe, she would have a record. *Look, this is who we were. This is what we did.*

The thought of it was enough to weaken her even in the lunar gravity. She collapsed into a chair, feeling the weight of the world, of humanity on her shoulders. "How am I supposed to do that?" she asked aloud. "Where do I even begin?"

::*Engage the Sentinel Protocol*,:: said Cain in her mind.

"What's the Sentinel Protocol?"

::*Activating it unlocks the whole of your nanotech and puts the Preserve fully at your disposal. You may do anything you wish after that, and those nanites in your body and the Preserve's pool will do their best to follow your wishes.*:: Cain paused. ::*Do you wish to activate it? You need only give the word.*::

In Penny's vision field, an icon appeared in one corner, labeled *Sentinel Protocol*. The name gave her one more idea, and she realized that was the most important thing of all. Storing the seeds, the genetic information, and the data of the world wouldn't do anyone any good if she couldn't protect it. There were hostile aliens out there in the Universe. They'd already come calling once. They might come again. If not the Hind, someone else would eventually arrive. The world would need a protector, a watchtower, a Sentinel.

"From now on, our mission here is to guard the Earth," Penny said softly. "That's what Washington meant. *Something for the good of all the world.*" She smiled. "Cain, engage the Sentinel Protocol."

The Preserve
Luna

Garragh knew he was alone. Not alone without any companions at all, but alone without any other Hind. He knew any of those left behind on Monkeyworld—no, *Earth*. He had to call it Earth now. Every Warrior would —or should—have gone down fighting, leaving nothing but corpses for the Humans to sift through. Humans might have devised a way to take down Hind without killing them, and given their cunning nature, Garragh wouldn't have been surprised. He hoped if any Hind had been captured alive, that the Humans would treat them as well as he had been treated. He would ask Pernhree or Sahree about it when he had the chance. They'd given him some time to be alone, to lick his metaphorical wounds as he considered his place in this new world.

He didn't think he'd be allowed to return to Earth anytime soon, which meant a life spent living in a hermetically sealed bottle, like his life had been aboard the *Blood Afire*. He hoped someday he would feel the breeze and smell the scents of a real world once again. He would understand if the Humans never allowed him back on their world. After all, he'd come there as part of an invading army.

He regretted his role in it. If he could change it, he would.

There was a reflective surface in the room where they'd placed him, and he regarded himself in it. His borrowed armor was dented and splattered with the blood of his own kind. His axe was notched and had another Warrior's sweat and scent on the cloth wrapped around the handle. The axe was the symbol of his people. From the earliest days upon Hindraa, when they were barely better than the animals that surrounded them on the veldt, the axe had been the first tool to differentiate them from the beasts. For twelve thousand generations, the axe had been the constant companion of the Hind.

He felt it might be time for that to change.

There was no Catechism he could repeat that would encompass the feelings in his hearts. Nothing in his training had prepared him for the possibility of a life without conflict, without war at its very core.

With slow deliberation, he started to remove his armor. Piece by piece, he undid the clasps, loosened the straps, and tossed the parts into a corner. They drifted and spun in strange, slow motion in the low gravity of the moon before clattering to a rest in a pile. At last, he took up the axe. He'd set it beside him, as all Warriors did when they needed their hands for other work. It was the weapon of a stranger, not his. He wasn't even sure where his had gone. It was surely back on Earth with Pernhree's people.

It could stay there.

He loped over to the pile of armor and set the axe down atop it. It felt as if he'd released a great weight when he did so. Naked to the world at last, he turned his back upon the tools of his caste and went to the great window where he could stare out at the swirling maelstrom that had taken the rest of his people into darkness. He tucked his fore and hindlegs beneath him as he sat upon the floor, clasped his hands before him, and let his mind begin the unfamiliar process of contemplation.

Location Unknown

Harlan opened his eyes. He was adrift in space, twisting and turning slowly. He could barely move with his suit power levels down to bare minimums. The vastness of the cosmos stretched out before him in all directions, with no nearby stars, planets, or moons anywhere he could see. He was alone in the silence, surrounded by the beauty of the Universe.

Well, if he had to die, there were worse places to do so. He configured a portion of his remaining power to keep him in a suspended animation state. It would last a specified amount of time, and then he would simply die, lost and alone. The rest of his power would go toward a beacon. It would be dim compared to the brightness of the firmament, quiet compared to the background hiss of trillions of stars, but it would at least serve as a tombstone for him, a marker to show that in the end, he had mattered.

He shivered as the armor plunged his body temperature and his last thought before his eyes froze over was of Penny.

ABOUT THE AUTHOR

Ian Thomas Healy dabbles in many different genres. He's a thirteen-time participant and winner of National Novel Writing Month and is also the creator of the *Writing Better Action Through Cinematic Techniques* workshop, which helps writers to improve their action scenes.

When not writing, which is rare, he enjoys watching hockey, reading comic books (and serious books, too), and living in the great state of Colorado, which he shares with his wife, children, house-pets, and approximately five million other people.

Visit *www.ianthealy.com* for more information.